STANDING AGAINST THE WIND

A DYING TRUTH EXPOSED,
BOOK TWO

HER FIGHT AND LEGACY CONTINUES...

MARCUS ABSTON

CHAPTER 1
Healing Through Salvation

SUNLIGHT BEAMED THROUGH THE SUNROOF of Albert Brooks's living room, illuminating the space. Surrounded by his family, Albert picked up a thick old photo album from the large wooden chest and placed it on his lap.

"All of the information in this photo album has helped us hold onto the truth," he said. He wiped the dust off the album, opened it, and then reached into the wooden chest again and pulled out several old letters encased in plastic film. "John and Samuel rescued Annabelle from Mercy, Missouri. Her story had only begun, even though she didn't know it," he said. "God never promised life would be fair. Annabelle knew this. She was on her way to Indian Territory, a land of uncertainty."

Albert's daughter, Liz, shook her head. "Daddy, you never told us Benjamin was murdered. Why was that?"

Albert sighed. "I made the mistake of believing it wasn't important. Even painful history should be told. Annabelle remained almost in denial of Benjamin's death. But Benita's death was her breaking point."

Liz held her six-year-old daughter, Elisa, closer to her. "I couldn't imagine burying a child, especially a baby."

"When Elisa brought up the differences between her hair and Christina's, I thought of it as a simple comparison to her sister. But when Christina questioned our Cherokee heritage, it hurt. I thought you had abandoned the truth. I'm a hypocrite. I got on your case because Christina and Elisa didn't know who they are, but looking back, I failed all of you."

"That's not true, Daddy. I'm proud of my heritage because of you and Mom."

Albert lifted an old letter encased in plastic film. "As written in one of Annabelle's letters, the ride to Indian Territory was hard for her. Since she was a child, she'd lived as a house slave, befriended her slave master's daughters, and had even become best friends with Judy Mays, the youngest daughter. She'd sacrificed a lot giving up her friendships to free herself from Master Brown's grip. She'd fallen in love in Mercy, Missouri. It was proof she'd tried to leave her past behind. It's sad that all her efforts were destroyed.

"Following Annabelle's tragedy, two days passed as John and Samuel took turns guiding them to Indian Territory. Their attempts to be cheerful and the jokes they told distracted Annabelle, though her broken spirit caused the days to be spent in a blur. She kept her Bible and *The Three Musketeers* in her lap. Those two books were the only things she owned. As they traveled, Annabelle saw prairie grasses taller than her, few trees, and beautiful wildflowers.

"Continuing their ride to Cherokee territory, the group also came across a herd of pronghorn. Annabelle had never seen the animals before. John and Samuel gladly talked about the animals to Annabelle in an attempt to cheer her up. However, she felt drained of the ability to express happiness.

"On the third day, the group arrived in Indian Territory with a few people greeting the men as the carriage went through the town. Annabelle watched the people. The town seemed calmer than Mercy. They continued to travel through, passing a few farms and buildings until John stopped the carriage in a more rural, empty side of the town. Neighboring farms with people working the land could be seen in the distance, surrounded by tall grass and forests. Samuel helped Annabelle down in front of a small house made of logs. She had never seen a house like it before. Chickens roamed inside a small, fenced area partially lined by flowers. On the left of the small house was an even larger log cabin. The larger house looked older, and a sizeable barn stood farther back alongside a crop field Annabelle barely saw."

John and Samuel walked ahead of Annabelle toward the small log cabin.

She followed them for a few steps, but John stopped and turned to her. "Welcome to Tahlequah, Annabelle. Please wait here while I get my sister," he said.

Annabelle nodded and went back to wait by the carriage while she petted the horse. The two men breathed heavily as they approached the small house, looking at each other with wide eyes. Before going inside the house, they waved to a young woman. Annabelle heard the cheerful voice of the woman but couldn't make out what she was saying. The woman had two long braids and wore a green dress with several small embroidered white squares near the hemline going in two horizontal loops. The white trim on the bottom of the skirt bounced in time with her steps as she walked toward the larger house.

The men knocked on the door of the small house as Annabelle waited, lightly tapping her finger on the horse's shoulder. *I can't believe Hildebrand murdered my baby Benita and Benjamin,* she thought. *Jesus, I hope he burns in hell. Ruthanne, Elizabeth, Rebecca...y'all tried to help me. What can the Cherokee do any different?* Annabelle watched the men enter the house and lightly kicked at the grass.

"Grace, it is good to see you. These past couple of days have been interesting," John said.

"Oh, you always have some kind of story to tell me dealing with the white people," Grace said. "How is old Mr. Boston?"

John smiled. "He's doing well."

Samuel sat down at the dinner table and bit into an apple as Grace turned, her brown high-necked cotton dress swirling as she stared at him.

"I swear, Samuel, if you weren't my cousin, I'd beat you," she said.

"Calm down, Grace. You get angry over the smallest things," Samuel whined.

Grace replied, "No, I don't. It's called manners, fool, and you don't have them."

John glared at Samuel, signaling him not to aggravate Grace.

"What is wrong with you anyway? You normally have a lot to say before eating my food."

John replied, "Grace, please take a seat. We need to talk about what happened to me and Samuel."

A crease formed between Grace's eyebrows while she sat down, and John placed himself next to her at the dinner table. John explained Annabelle's situation as Samuel sat quietly, watching Grace cross her arms and an intimidating, unsympathetic expression cover her face.

"Well," John said, "I guess the next step is getting her a home. I was hoping you would take her in until we can figure out the next step for her."

Grace gave a deep sigh. "You really didn't think this through, John. I expect something this crazy or stupid from Samuel." The moment Samuel reached for another apple, Grace slapped his hand. "You don't eat another thing in my house." She grunted as she stood before walking in a circle in her living room. "You want me to take in a Negro I don't even know?"

John shrugged. "Well, you've always been against our people having slaves. Even as children, you always hated the idea."

Grace's voice rose. "That don't mean I would house one I don't know."

John calmly lifted his hands, exposing his palms. "I'm asking you to trust me, not trust her."

She put a hand on her hip. "What if she decides to make a run for it? If she gets caught, that could put her back into chains. Did you think about that?"

"She had plenty of chances to run away from me and Samuel but didn't."

Grace scoffed. "You fool. She lost her entire family within a day. She is probably still grieving. I know I would be. To lose your husband and unborn child in less than a day. I'm surprised she didn't try and take her own life."

John's lips turned down. "You think she might be that hurt?"

Grace gave a lopsided smirk. "I don't know, John. I don't know her. You barely know her. Stopping by Mr. Boston's store once or twice a month isn't enough time to know someone."

"Take a look at her. It's not like she's an animal."

Grace reluctantly went to her door. Slightly opening it, she peeked outside and observed Annabelle petting the horse.

"Well, I think she is too tired in her feelings to run anymore."

Intrigued with Grace's observation, Samuel asked, "What makes you say that?"

Grace stared back at Samuel with narrowed eyes. "Because you two idiots left her out there with two horses and an empty carriage! I would've left the two of you!" she yelled.

"Why are you always angry when important things come up?" John asked.

Grace stuck her finger out at John, "Because you didn't think all this out, and Samuel is useless in these things. Our story of where she came from must be believable."

John shook his head. "Well, I did have some idea of a plan."

Grace's face relaxed. "What did you think of?"

"I can say I bought her and set her free."

Grace snarled. "You fool! The council keeps records of that type of purchase."

John scowled. "Look, don't call me a fool. I did think of something."

Grace placed her hands on her hips as she glared at her brother.

"White travelers do come through our towns," Samuel said.

"Quiet, Samuel. I'm thinking," Grace said. "Well, I guess that can work without much question. Our family is respected. We'll get her on record as a slave sold to us and set her free without anyone opposing it."

Samuel smiled. "See, Grace, I can give good ideas."

"Shut up, Samuel. Your plan is a part of mine. It would be too suspicious if she appeared out of nowhere, especially with these Indian agents," Grace bickered. "Well, I guess I can go introduce myself. She is probably worried because we've been talking for so long."

———◆———

A woman opened the front door and approached Annabelle. Her long, unbraided hair blew in the mild breeze as she marched ahead, and her light brown, almond-shaped eyes locked onto Annabelle. In her dirty blue plaid dress, Annabelle felt intimidated by the caramel-skinned, high-cheekboned woman. They stood eye to eye as Annabelle continued to rub the horse's black mane.

"Hello, Annabelle. My name is Grace Lightning. I'm John's older sister."

"It's a pleasure to meet you, Grace," Annabelle said.

Grace's eyes widened, and she tilted her head. "Your speech... It is impressive for a Negro woman. I can see how you were able to hide so well."

"I learned from an old friend, Judy Mays. She did a lot for me when we were children."

Grace continued to examine Annabelle. "So, I'm guessing you lived a rare life of having masters that treated you and the other slaves well, or you were the favorite."

Annabelle exhaled, and her eyes shifted to the grass.

"I'm sorry, but your response means one of those is right," Grace commented.

Annabelle pursed her lips and continued to avoid eye contact with the other woman.

"Well, I guess that's enough questions for now. Please follow me." Grace whirled and walked toward the cabin.

Annabelle followed Grace, feeling herself moving in a sluggish manner. The women entered the well-lit house, finding John and Samuel sitting down at Grace's table. In the small, wooden-floored house, there were three rocking chairs next to a fireplace. A silver-colored Castrol stove sat across from the dinner table, and three windows allowed sunshine through. Annabelle also noticed a short hallway off the kitchen and living room leading back to two rooms.

"Please take a seat here, Annabelle," Grace said, her voice calm and smooth.

Annabelle sat down in a rocking chair, and Grace grabbed another seat, moving it so she was facing Annabelle.

John stood up and approached the women. "Annabelle, would you like an apple?" he asked.

Annabelle replied, "Yes, please. That would be nice."

John moved toward the table and grabbed an apple before bringing it to Annabelle.

Grace leaned toward Annabelle, her eyes filled with sympathy. "Annabelle, you will be living with me," Grace said. "I know you don't know me, but my brother told me everything Mr. Boston told him. To say that I'm sorry for the loss of your daughter and husband, in my thoughts, will bring you no comfort. I have a hard time imagining what you must feel...losing a child."

Annabelle took a bite of the apple and stared emotionlessly at Grace. "I don't need you reminding me that I lost the most important things in my life. I also lost four women I considered family. Who could imagine white women loving a Negro woman? So please don't remind me again. I've already lost my soul."

Grace frowned. "I will leave you to mourn in your own way, but don't let the sadness take over you. I've seen real misery. Don't believe I don't know what it means to lose a lot of people you love in a short time."

Annabelle noticed the pain in Grace's eyes, but she took another bite into her apple, hoping it would help her fight the sadness.

"Now that I know how you feel, let's get to a problem that must be talked about now," Grace said.

John stood next to Grace and folded his arms.

Annabelle looked at them both as nervousness overcame her. "Before you say anything, please tell me this," she said. "How do you speak English so well?"

Grace looked at John with lifted eyebrows, seeming slightly insulted by the question. "Okay, I guess that's a fair question. Though many of my people don't speak English, we have had to deal with white people for generations. My family learned the importance of reading and speaking in their language. The government of the United States has never kept their word, and to fight against this, we learned what we could. My family is a little different than many. We're made of warriors and educated people. So that's how I speak English so well. If my English was poor, the white men would respect me less. It's bad enough I'm a woman. Their disrespect toward me angers me. I hope that satisfies you because now, a real problem must be fixed." Grace sighed. "Our nation, the Cherokee nation, is a slave-holding nation. I really have no idea how many slaves we have, but the number is in the thousands for sure. Some of us hate slavery, some see slavery as a way of pleasing white folks so they'll stop trying to control us, and the rest see slavery as a way to make money. I personally hate the idea of slavery. It poisons my people and makes us slaves to something we have never needed before."

Annabelle's eyes stayed focused on Grace while she listened to her Southern accent. Grace's stance on slavery was similar to Ruthanne's, but Annabelle felt like Grace had a more powerful reason.

"We can't protect you well if you appear from nowhere," Grace explained. "I don't fear our council, but it's the Indian agents that regularly come through our towns that bother me, so we need a real plan."

Annabelle folded her hands while she held the apple. "What ideas have you come up with?"

"The best plan is to fake your slave records and set you free."

Annabelle felt her throat tighten as she gulped and looked over at John. She rubbed her hands together as she tried to think of something else that would allow her to stay.

"Annabelle, we're talking about two days," Grace reassured her. "Two days of having the title of a slave and then not being a slave. I know you have been through a lot, and nothing can change that. I'm asking you to take this one risk and trust me a little so this works."

Annabelle took a deep breath and exhaled while looking at Grace. "I will go with your plan. I don't have much choice. Is there something I can do here to earn money?"

"Well, I think I have a great idea that you'll like. It's similar to what you did in Mercy. We actually own one of the local supply stores, and I think you'll fit in nicely there with me. Normally, I would be there today, but I needed a day to myself."

Samuel quickly stood up. "We own that store, Grace. You can't tell her that we will pay her when the store is in my father's name!" he yelled.

Grace stood up, her blazing brown eyes narrowing on her cousin.

John took a step back, and Samuel froze in place.

"What did you say?" Grace asked, her tone noticeably deeper.

Samuel cleared his throat. "Um, you know, I'm sure if you talk to Tsula and Lisa, they would be glad to have her there."

"I will talk with my cousins, and I'm sure they will agree

with me. I think you should stay concerned with the crops, Samuel."

Samuel sat down and avoided eye contact with her.

"Thank you, Grace," Annabelle replied. "I will do a good job. How much do I have to pay you for rent?"

"Do you snore or make noises when you sleep?" Grace asked.

Annabelle tilted her head, confusion filling her. "Why no, I sleep deeply."

"Good, you owe me no form of rent. The supply store always opens at 7:30 a.m. So don't be late to the supply store in the morning."

Annabelle leaned forward. "Why are you being so nice to me?"

"I was honest when I said I have a problem with slavery being a part of my people's lives. My brother seems to have a lot of favor toward you, and you don't snore at night. I could live with someone like you."

Annabelle looked at John, and he looked back at her with a convincing smile. "You and Samuel fought to get me out of town. I don't think there is anything I could do to ever repay you."

"There is nothing to repay, Annabelle," John said. "When I lost my wife, you gave me so much encouragement every time we saw each other. Such a good heart deserves to live in peace. Well, I think it's time I got my son. I'm sure he is ready to see me."

"I'll leave with John. I'd like to see my little cousin while he's good," Samuel said.

"Don't say that about my son."

"Look how serious he got now." Samuel chuckled as he walked to the door and stopped to look at Annabelle with a smile. "Welcome to Cherokee land, Annabelle."

"Thank you, Samuel," Annabelle said.

Samuel walked out of the door with John following.

"I will see the two of you later," John said.

Annabelle nodded. "Bye, John. Wait, you said you had a son."

John nodded. "I do. I know I never told you, but bringing him up would've brought me more pain, so I didn't."

Annabelle's left cheek pinched, her eyes a little wider and sympathetic. "I see. Thank you again."

"See you later, John, and feed my chickens while you're out there," Grace said.

"I said I need to see my son," John replied.

"The chicken feed is right there by the fence," Grace responded. "Feed the birds."

John scowled at his sister and closed the door.

Samuel reopened the door with a grin. "Annabelle, you should ask her why nobody lives with her," he suggested.

Grace rushed toward the door, but Samuel quickly closed it. "I can't stand that little boy. He's always testing my patience." Grace grunted.

Annabelle giggled a little, relating to Grace's frustration.

"Do you have brothers or sisters?"

Annabelle nodded. "I have one younger brother, but I'm not sure what has become of him."

"He's still a slave?"

"Yes. Not much I can do about that."

"Be careful not to let things that are out of our control take over your thoughts," Grace warned.

Annabelle nodded.

Grace smiled. "You don't have to be so shy with me. You're probably confused as to why I speak to them so boldly."

"Well, yes. I didn't want to say something and cause problems. I'm so tired of conflict."

"I understand. I'm a Cherokee woman. I'm not like these white women who sit when they're told to sit and stand when they're told to stand. In the old days, the women actually owned the land, not the men. We even helped determine if the tribe was to go to war or not. I'm very much traditional Cherokee in speaking my mind, though my uncle is the head of the family.

My culture is far more important to me than pleasing white people. We already dress like them, but I'll say no to my voice being silenced because I'm a woman."

"It must be different here."

"It is. Even though we have laws like the white men, many of us are still Cherokee. Well, there is some stew here that I made, and of course, you can have another apple if you want. I have to make a trip to the courthouse to get some important papers."

Annabelle's eyes widened. "How long will you be gone?"

Grace shrugged. "Not long. Hopefully less than an hour. I will be back."

"Okay, I will sit here and wait for you."

"Oh no, go and settle into your room. Walk down the hallway, and the room on your right is yours. The bed already has sheets on it. This is your home now."

Annabelle half-smiled at Grace.

"I will see you soon."

"Okay, Grace," Annabelle said, a feeling of calm settling over her.

Grace grabbed her handbag and rushed out of the house.

Annabelle explored the house, entering a bedroom with a short wooden dresser and one bed. The sunshine through the window gave her a strange sense of peace. She sat down on the bed and fell asleep, exhausted from her traumatic experience.

CHAPTER 2
Identity

G RACE MARCHED THROUGH TOWN, GREETING others she passed. After arriving at the courthouse, she entered the building, and her eyes lit up when she saw a slightly taller, middle-aged man holding a briefcase. "Ah, Mr. Gross, how are you doing today?"

"Grace Lightning, I'm surprised to see you. Do you need help with anything?" Mr. Gross asked.

Grace grinned. "I was on my way to your house to see Lillian but decided to see if you were in the courthouse. I couldn't help but wonder how you are doing."

Dimples appeared when Mr. Gross beamed. "Why, thank you, Grace. I was just on my way home. Walk with me. I'm anxious to see what Mrs. Gross is making today."

Grace tilted her head as her smile grew. "Sounds exciting."

As the two traveled to Mr. Gross's home, Grace asked, "I was curious, Mr. Gross, how it is to own a slave?"

"Why, it's not bad. There are good days and bad days, but I have good Negroes. I treat them well and make sure they're fed and have good clothes. They work like they're supposed to."

"That sounds fair to me. I believe that's a good way to make things work."

Mr. Gross nodded. "I like your thinking. I wish these white men would agree."

Grace's eyes narrowed as she sneered. "Why would you say that?"

"Those Indian agents always try to tell us how to handle our own slaves. They want us to be harder on the slaves, but many of us refuse to do so. Our slaves are happy, they cooperate, and runaway slaves are uncommon. But these white men keep trying to turn us into them."

As Grace listened, the corners of her mouth turned down, and her eyes shifted away from Mr. Gross.

"Where does this sudden interest in the slaves come from? Since you were a child, you hated the thought of keeping slaves. Your opinions would even wear out your father."

Grace's face went blank. "Things do change, and our supply store is doing well, but having one or two slaves would make life easier. Lisa does a good job of managing our finances, but more hands on the labor would benefit us."

"I understand what you mean. I suggest maybe asking one of our own for a slave rather than traveling to one of the states to purchase."

"Thank you for the suggestion. I do have another question. What did you do with old property papers for slaves that died or you freed?"

"In most cases, I've kept records of my dead slaves in my study, but I have never freed any of them. I don't want to send the wrong message to the rest of them. As long as I keep my authority, treat them well so they do their chores, and give favor to none of them, they know their place. We have balance, and in my opinion, it keeps us separate from the white men so eager to tell us how to live."

Grace forced a smile. "I understand."

They arrived at Mr. Gross's home and were greeted by two house slaves. "Good afternoon, Master Gross," one slave woman said.

"Good afternoon, Marion," he replied. "Go get Lillian for Miss Grace here. She has come to visit her."

"Yes, sir. I go now," Marion said, entering the house.

"I'm going to the kitchen to see what's for supper. You can join me, Grace."

Grace dismissively waved her hand and smiled. "Why, no, Mr. Gross. I will wait here by the staircase. It's always a pleasure to be in your home."

Mr. Gross nodded and walked down the hallway to the kitchen.

From what Grace observed, most of the house slaves were upstairs or in the kitchen. She quickly moved through the house toward Mr. Gross's study. After checking to make sure no one was around, she entered the room and searched quickly through the drawers. Her senses were heightened as she focused while keeping track of everyone's movements.

Grace opened a drawer with several forms of slave property papers. She recognized slave names of those who were alive, but she suddenly came across the record of a slave she knew had died about five years ago. The paperwork was in good condition, and she stuffed it into her handbag. She was about to rush out of the room when a slave walked past the entryway, forcing her to hide on the side of the door. After hearing the slave go upstairs, she quickly walked to the front door.

Grace waited patiently as Lillian came out of the living room.

"There you are, Grace," Lillian said. "I had begun to think that you had left."

Grace turned and noticed the brown-skinned young woman who had an inch over her and black shoulder-length hair. "Without saying goodbye? I wouldn't, Lillian."

Lillian scoffed as she licked her lips, her hands brushing over the checkered skirt of her yellow short-sleeved plaid dress. "It would not be the first time."

Grace chuckled and forced a smile. "I always enjoy your sense of humor. You know I care about you."

Lillian pouted and then sighed, her round brown eyes looking at the wooden floor. "You always seem to have something else on your mind, Grace."

"I'm twenty-one years old, Lillian. I should have many things on my mind."

Lillian moved closer to her. "I wish I thought like you sometimes."

There's a reason you will never think like me, Grace thought, but she continued to entertain Lillian until Mrs. Gross walked out of the kitchen.

The brown-skinned woman had her dark brown hair put into two buns. "Grace, how are you doing?" she asked.

"I'm doing well, Mrs. Gross," Grace replied. "I was about to leave. I need to prepare supper for John and the others."

Mrs. Gross's almond-shaped eyes widened. "How is your little sister? I haven't seen her in a few days."

Grace forced a smile. "She is fine. She's staying at home more to help John with David."

The other woman's expression turned sad. "Oh yes, it does take a while for a young child to heal from losing their mother."

Grace squinted, forcing herself to continue smiling. "Well, I must leave. It was good seeing the two of you."

"Until we see you again, Grace," Mrs. Gross said.

"Bye." Grace left the Grosses' house. While she went through the town, she tried to avoid any conversations because she feared Annabelle might try to run away. *There's no way Annabelle knows the bounties on runaway slaves are taken seriously here.*

—◆—

Grace arrived at her home but didn't see Annabelle. In a panic, she charged down the hallway and looked into the bedrooms. Much to her relief, Annabelle slept on the bed, seeming comfortable. *She must be worn out.*

After tending to her garden outside, Grace walked inside her home to a groggy Annabelle coming down the hallway.

"I must've fallen asleep a long time for you to be back already," Annabelle said.

"You were sleeping for some time, but you did look peace-ful," Grace said.

Annabelle pressed her lips together. "I wish I felt that way about all of this."

"Change is never an easy thing to go through. That's some-thing I learned as a young child. I guess in a way, it made me into who I am today."

"You remind me of two people I had in my life. You don't seem scared of anything, you speak your mind, but there's kindness to it."

Grace giggled while she sat down. "The only person to ever say I'm nice is my nephew, David, and that kid is three years old. I guess part of that is my fault...always feeling like I'm the one who has to lead."

Annabelle sat down at the table. "I don't think I have much of what it takes to be a leader. I have always felt like I have a voice, but it seems like someone is always there to guide."

"I do see something different in you," Grace commented.

Annabelle smiled as she received Grace's words.

"So, I want to know, were your masters actually good to you and your people, or were you seen as a favorite?"

Annabelle took a deep breath. "I was more of a favorite with Master Brown's daughters ever since I could walk. For reasons I don't know, they took a liking to me, and one of his daughters was the same age as me. We became close friends. I stayed a favorite with the other daughters. When Judy Mays got mar-ried, I lost a great friend. The rest of my story you know."

"That's a tough thing to go through. I bet Judy Mays was hurt when you ran away."

"I never thought of it that way." Annabelle scratched the back of her head while she bit her lip. "I wish I'd been able to give Judy Mays a clue I would disappear."

"Well, there's nothing you can do about it now. Keep moving forward."

Annabelle nodded.

"I have something to show you," Grace said. "Come here."

Annabelle moved toward Grace and sat in one of the rocking chairs next to the other woman. Grace opened up her handbag and pulled out the slave record she had stolen.

Annabelle gasped as her eyes widened. "How did you get those?"

"Don't worry about it. Soon these will be your records."

Suddenly, the front door opened. A young, beautiful high-cheekboned woman boldly marched in and stared at Annabelle and Grace. She wore a dusty and red cotton printed summer dress, and her long hair formed a long braid down her back. The young woman was shorter than Annabelle and Grace, with deep brown almond-shaped eyes, sharing the same caramel tone as Grace.

"Who is this?" the young woman curiously said in a high-pitched Southern accent.

"What are you doing here, Lizzie?" Grace asked.

"I wanted to come over. Is that a problem?" Lizzie asked, her voice condescending.

"Well, no, but you opened my door too fast. You scared me."

Lizzie rolled her eyes, ignoring Grace. "Who is the Negro?"

"Lizzie, this is Annabelle."

"So, you are Annabelle. Well, John had already told me about the runaway slave. I never expected her to look like this. She's pretty. I already guessed you were the runaway, but my sister is very social. She brings home anything, but I can see why John recused you. Seems to run in the family now."

"Lizzie!" Grace snarled. "That isn't necessary."

"What? I'm just saying. First, it's John, and now you come to the rescue," Lizzie grumbled.

Annabelle rubbed her fingers together, and Lizzie appeared agitated.

"What do you mean?" Annabelle asked, her voice quiet.

Grace replied, "Don't worry about it. My sister has a terrible sense of humor."

Lizzie answered, "I spoke the truth. Never said I didn't like

Negroes. Know your place here, or the next time you need rescuing, it might not happen."

Grace scowled. "That was not right of you. Don't act like that. I'm sorry, Annabelle. She likes to hide her real feelings."

Annabelle turned her eyes to Lizzie, who re-braided her hair. "What have I done to you that you tell me to know my place?"

Lizzie raised an eyebrow. "I don't agree with this slavery my people have accepted, but you need to know you'll never be Cherokee. You're not one of us."

Grace gripped the armrest of her rocking chair. "She will be working with us, so I suggest you get over it!" she bellowed.

Lizzie continued to re-braid her hair. She sneered and held her tongue.

Annabelle leaned forward with a skewed frown. "I don't understand what her problem is with me."

"Her real problem isn't with you. Her problem is that it bothers her that she does care. Two months ago, she and a family friend had an argument. What makes it harder is he is a mixed-blood."

"I don't understand. Is it wrong being a mixed-blood?"

"Those of our people who are mixed with Negro blood are not recognized as citizens of the tribe. It's been like that for a while. It doesn't matter what family you come from. The council won't recognize them as citizens. Very few have been able to get their Negro relatives recognized."

Annabelle's eyes widened as her eyes quickly shifted away and back onto Grace. "Why would your people agree to make a law like that? We're not your enemies."

Lizzie giggled sarcastically. "The law wasn't made to declare your people enemies. The law was made to make white people happy and hide the members of our tribe who already had Negro blood. It was done as a political move to make us full-bloods better than you. The truth is, it's done nothing but bring us grief. How stupid we look now adopting their ways. It didn't stop them from forcing us here. I'm going to see Victoria."

Annabelle's mouth dropped open in shock at Lizzie's answer. She turned to Grace, who felt her face burn with shame.

Lizzie left the log cabin, the door clicking behind her as it closed.

"I'm sorry, Annabelle. She could have said that a different way," Grace said in the silence that followed.

"No, it's okay. I can see it bothers her," Annabelle said. "It feels like she has a good heart, but she wants nothing to do with me."

"Well, I think we need to get started on this." Grace showed Annabelle the certificate of sales again. "It has a seal on it from Georgia, and I know who to write down as a witness. This will be a big help overall."

"How will it help? It has been written on."

"I know how to deal with that problem." Grace brought the paper over to the table and took a knife. She patiently scraped every section of the paper requiring dates and signatures.

Annabelle watched as Grace showed great patience, humming in beautiful tones as she worked. When she finished removing the names on the document, she quickly walked into her room and came back with a quill pen and ink.

"Well, now the fun begins," Grace said.

Annabelle smiled. "You're making me feel excited!"

Grace beamed and picked up the document, crunching it up to make the document appear poorly kept. "Well, now that's complete, here comes the real fun part. What do you want your name to be?"

Annabelle sat back in the chair, gazing at the ceiling. After several moments, she looked back at Grace with her lips tightened and mouth pinched. "Please write Annabelle Mays. Sasha is dead."

Grace wrote down her new name.

"So your slave master's name should be... Oh, I know. Lawrence Mays."

Annabelle raised an eyebrow. "Why that name?"

Grace bit her lip. "I knew a white man by that name. I hated that name. I've always thought it belonged to a girl."

Annabelle chuckled. "It'll be believable."

Grace laughed. "I'll be able to make it believable. White people can't leave us alone, and there are always a few that pass through our land. We should go to the supply store so you can meet Lisa and Tsula. I know they'll both be there at this time."

"Okay, I'm ready to go when you are, Grace. I hope they are not like Lizzie."

"Oh no, they're different than Lizzie. Especially Lisa."

"Well, I look forward to meeting them."

Grace stood and took the slave record into her room, placing the forgery into an old oak dresser. She then went through the hallway, excited as she regarded Annabelle drumming her fingers on the table.

"Well, now is the time to see my cousins. This was supposed to be my day away from that store, but who can predict what happens? After we go to the store, I'll show you the rest of our land."

"Do you mean that bigger house?" Annabelle asked.

"Yes, I do. But these houses are called log cabins. It's all we really had to use to build."

"Well, that's a different name."

"My uncle and the rest of the family lives there. It's all we have," Grace said.

"John went there?"

"Yeah, he and my nephew sleep there. We also do a lot of family suppers there and spend time with each other."

"That sounds like such a good time. It makes me remember the Keyses' home," Annabelle said. "Your family sounds like they're very close."

"We are, but that isn't always a good thing. We don't always have the same opinions on protecting our people." Grace forced herself to smile.

CHAPTER 3
Strongman

THE WOMEN LEFT THE HOUSE and went down the dirt roads of Tahlequah to the supply store. Annabelle noticed the Cherokee people didn't stare at her as she walked with Grace. It was very different from moving through a mostly white town. A few Cherokee even greeted her while they greeted Grace. It gave Annabelle a feeling of culture shock. She forced herself to smile as people showed kindness toward her.

The two women arrived at the supply store. Annabelle rubbed her hands together as Grace reached for the door.

"Hello, my lovely cousins!" Grace said.

Annabelle stood behind Grace and saw two women behind a counter. The woman she saw waving to John earlier that day had high cheekbones currently framing a welcoming grin and round brown eyes as she approached Grace. Her two long braids trailed down each side of her head. Medium height with a lighter complexion, she was shorter than Grace but taller than Lizzie. The other woman wore a polka-dotted blue dress and was about the same height as Grace and Annabelle. Her hair formed two buns on either side of her head, further exposing her own high cheekbones, which were complemented by almond-shaped brown eyes and a dimpled smile.

"Annabelle, this is Tsula and Lisa Strongman. Annabelle will be helping us with the store from now on," Grace said.

"This must be the Negro Lizzie spoke so much about," the woman in the green dress said with a chipper Southern accent. "I see no reason for this to be a problem. I think she's a runaway slave though. That's a reason for us to be worried, Grace. These white men hunt them down like they hunt gold mines. She clearly isn't one of the mixed-bloods of our people, though she is cute for a Negro."

"Tsula!" Grace snarled. "She can hear you. She isn't deaf. Show some respect. What makes you think she is a runaway slave?"

Tsula smirked. "Honestly, she looks frightened."

"You beautiful Negro woman," the woman in the polka-dotted blue dress said. The other woman spoke with a slight Southern accent with broken English but well pronounced.

"Thank you," Annabelle said.

"See, that's better. Thank you for saying that, Lisa," Grace said. "I wish Tsula would show she has manners. It is clear my sister has done her damage here."

"Well, what is her story? I think Daddy will have a problem with her," Tsula said. "Lizzie really didn't say much but that she seemed different. I think you seem nice."

"Thank you," Annabelle said.

"This is exciting. There are not very many free Negroes around," Lisa said.

"Okay, calm down. I need to tell you both the whole story," Grace said. "I feel if I don't, everything will fall apart. Is there anyone else in here looking around?"

Lisa said something in a language Annabelle didn't understand.

Grace smiled. "Okay, let's lock these doors for a little while."

"What did she say? What was that language?" Annabelle asked.

"Nobody has been here for a while," Grace explained. "And that was Tsalagi, or Cherokee."

The women moved to the store's counter, and Grace shared Annabelle's origin with the two young women as they listened attentively. Tsula cocked her head and narrowed her eyes as Grace spoke. Lisa gazed at Annabelle sympathetically. Annabelle could see Tsula was a little hesitant, but Tsula's expression saddened when Grace finished explaining.

"I don't see much of a problem with her working here, but this is still dangerous for us," Tsula said. "This puts our family in danger, Grace. You know there are those of our own people who would send her back to Mississippi."

Annabelle could see the fear in Tsula's round brown eyes.

"But maybe this is my challenge to trust the Creator more and do what's right," Tsula admitted. "I won't stand against her working here."

"I also see no reason to say no to her," Lisa said. "I think it is...inspiring, or perhaps 'encouraging' is the right word?"

"They mean the same, Lisa," Grace said.

"Ah, good. I welcome you, Annabelle. Annabelle is such a beautiful name. Maybe one day, I will have a daughter and use your name."

Annabelle was flattered by the young woman's remark. "Thank you, Lisa," she said.

"Well, now that she's set to work here, I will show her around," Grace said.

"I would like to show her the horses," Lisa said.

Grace put a hand on her hip and smiled. "Let me show her the rest of the store. Then you can show her the barn."

Lisa grinned. "Okay."

Annabelle followed Grace as she showed her where things went in the store. It was similar to Mr. Boston's store back in Mercy. The back door led to three large green chicken coops where almost a hundred chickens were housed.

Annabelle shook her head as she looked at all the birds. "How do you have so many chickens here?" she asked.

"We sell a lot of our chickens to others in town, but we also need them to feed ourselves. It helps us not suffer as bad as the others. Having little is normal here. It's become a way of life for many of us, especially those of us who won't get slaves to work fields. We have our soybean, squash, and corn crop and sell enough that we have a little left."

Annabelle looked at Grace with sympathetic eyes. "Y'all live like this but are still willing to let me live here?"

"It's not as bad as it seems. We're better off than some other families. So don't worry about it. If we do good this year, we'll have little to worry about with food."

Annabelle felt guilty even though Grace assured her it was okay. The two women entered back into the store while Lisa stood and smiled by the door.

"Are you done showing her around, Grace?" Lisa asked.

"Yes, you can go show her the horses in the barn," Grace said.

Lisa grinned and signaled for Annabelle to follow her. The pure happiness Lisa showed caused Annabelle to question her age, and she glanced at Lisa while they traveled back to the log cabins.

"How old are you?" Annabelle asked.

Lisa's eyebrow lifted, and she smirked. "I have nineteen years. I mean, I'm nineteen years old now."

"You're as old as me!" Annabelle said.

Annabelle couldn't understand why Lisa spoke broken English. Lisa's poise assured Annabelle she was actually an intelligent woman, but she wondered if maybe she had speech problems the others were used to.

Lisa giggled the moment they approached the large green barn. "I older than Tsula but not Grace. Grace is more my sister than my cousin. We grow up together and in same clan." Lisa's dimpled smile was full of love and happiness. It made Annabelle smile, though she was reluctant to open herself up.

"I know how that feels to be so close to someone. Even if they're not your blood in your heart, they're like a sister." Lisa continued as they walked.

When they arrived at the large green barn, Lisa opened one of the massive barn doors. The women entered, and Anna-belle looked around, reminded of the barn she had once been whipped in front of as a child. The large two-story barn held six stables and housed four horses, all in their own stable. All the horses neighed, excited to see Lisa.

"I never have seen horses so happy. As soon as they see you, they get excited."

"They are my babies. I grow them all up." Lisa approached a reddish-brown horse with a white patch on its back and petted it. "This is Ray here."

"He's one of the horses that pulled the carriage."

Lisa went over to a black horse with white heels as Annabelle followed. She petted the horse when it rubbed her face. "This Cari. She prettiest one. Hi, Big Boy!" She waved to a large white horse with small brown patches on his hindquarters.

Big Boy neighed with excitement when she came up and petted him. The horse sniffed at Lisa and affectionately rubbed her. The horse tried to smell Annabelle, but she was startled by the boldness of the horse and stepped behind Lisa.

"Oh no, he good horse. Don't be scared," Lisa reassured her.

"Okay, I guess. He's a big horse, but I'll trust what you say."

Lisa continued to pet Big Boy and skipped over to the last horse. "Queen, my queen, look how pretty you are."

The brown speckled horse with a black mane stepped toward the stable door.

"She most obedient horse. She sweet. Works well in the fields," Lisa explained.

"And she was the other horse that pulled the carriage. She let me pet her."

Lisa grinned at Annabelle and looked back at Queen. Annabelle noticed the love Lisa showed toward the horses. The feeling was mutual from them to her. However, Annabelle had no strong interest in becoming too close with the horses, especially Big Boy. The horses made her think of Benjamin. Her husband had worked hard with the horses in Mercy and loved his job. She had never imagined he would be murdered while doing a job he loved.

As the women left the barn, a man walked out of the large

log cabin. The tall man strode toward the women, invisible waves of authority pouring from him. He wore a dirty brown high-collared shirt, a beige vest, and beige trousers. The man said something in the Cherokee language that Annabelle had never heard before. Lisa immediately approached the tall man and greeted him with a hug.

The man with short, grayish-brown hair chatted with Lisa while Annabelle stood alone, unsure of the man. He pointed to Annabelle as he talked to Lisa, who folded her arms. The two approached Annabelle as she stood humbly, hoping to avoid a confrontation.

"My daughter here tells me that my niece has bought you," the man said with a Southern accent.

Annabelle's eyes widened as she looked at Lisa, and the woman signaled back with her hands, silently telling her to go with it.

"Yes, sir. I was bought by Miss Grace," Annabelle said.

"You look real young and strong. I never thought my niece would ever do something like this. My niece is strong-willed. Always has been. My name is George Strongman. You call me Mr. Strongman. I see no reason to have you call me Master. I doubt Grace would allow it since she bought you. My niece has her mother's temper. They could have been twins."

"Papa, I take her back to the store to learn what to do," Lisa said.

Mr. Strongman replied, "Okay. Tell Grace I think this woman will fit in nicely, but I want to know how much she paid to get her."

Lisa nodded. "Yes, Papa. I will tell her." She approached Annabelle and wrapped her arm around her shoulder, leading her away. They walked back to the supply store with their arms intertwined. "I sorry about that telling my Papa you a slave. I hope I didn't mess up Grace's idea," Lisa said. "She can get angry easily sometimes, but she forgives easily."

"I hope everything is okay. Your papa seems like a nice man," Annabelle said.

"He can be a nice man, but he does not like Negroes that much. He is weird like that treat the ones that mixed with white really nice, but not with others."

Annabelle scoffed. "He sounds almost like a white man."

During their walk through Tahlequah, Lisa frowned. "We learned much from white people, but I think Grace is right. We too much like them now. We learn a lot of evil things from them. Not all Cherokee equal now. I think Jesus and our ancestors cry."

Annabelle was surprised by the sudden maturity Lisa displayed. The childlike nature Lisa showed was quickly overshadowed by a concerned and intelligent woman. She became more curious, wanting to learn what Lisa meant by not all Cherokee being equal, but before she could ask, they had returned to the supply store.

Grace suddenly walked out, seeming aggravated. "What took the two of you so long to return? You had me worried, Lisa," she said.

"I'm sorry, but as we leave, Papa saw us and speak with us," Lisa said.

Grace's eyes widened. "What did you tell him, and what did he say?"

"He seem happy. I got scared and tell him Annabelle was your slave. I hope I did not mess up, but he liked Annabelle and wanted to know how much she cost."

"Okay, I'm a little surprised he was nice to Annabelle. Maybe it was because Annabelle was with you."

Lisa shrugged. "Papa say she look strong and young. It probably make him happy."

"Yeah, that's probably why he was welcoming. It'll be interesting to see how he responds when I release Annabelle. Well, we can't worry about it now. Lisa, take Annabelle inside, and you show her where we put our extra supplies. I rather you start working now than for my uncle to come here and see you doing nothing, Annabelle."

"I understand," Annabelle said.

"Come, let's go inside now," Lisa said.

"Can I follow you inside, Lisa? I wanted to ask Grace something."

Lisa cheerfully replied, "Okay."

After Lisa anxiously went inside, leaving the door open, Grace asked, "What is it, Annabelle?"

"There's something weird about Lisa's speech. I don't mean to be rude. I want to know what it is," Annabelle said. "I can see that she is a smart woman."

Grace looked at Annabelle as a crease shaped between her eyebrows, but her face cleared as she cackled. "You mean her accent and why sometimes her English is bad."

Annabelle's gaze went downward. "Well, yes. I've never heard someone speak like her."

"Lisa speaks that way because Cherokee is her real language, not English. English was not the first words I learned either, but it was spoken to me earlier than Lisa. A lot of us speak with the accent, but many speak worse English than Lisa. We'll have to teach you Cherokee, so you seem more like the people here."

Annabelle squinted. "Why does it feel like a Southern accent?"

"It is. Lisa was born in Georgia, like most of us in my family."

"Wait, you were born in Georgia?"

"Yes, I was, but we can talk about that later."

"I thought the Indians were kicked out of the South a long time ago, not within my life. Yes, we need to continue this," Annabelle replied, entering the store.

Grace stood outside, watching the other townspeople pass. As the day ended, she quietly watched Annabelle's interaction with Tsula and Lisa. The sisters were talkative with the young slave woman, but she kept her distance. It had been a long time since the two women had encountered a new free Negro in Tahlequah. Most of the free Negroes were either born in Indian

Territory or had survived the Trail of Tears. Annabelle held their attention, especially Lisa's.

As the evening arrived, Lizzie arrived at the store. Lizzie stood in front of Grace while she swept the floor, and Tsula carried soybean bags to the storage room. "Are y'all ready to close the store now? It's getting close to supper time," Lizzie said.

"We're closing everything up. Be patient," Grace said. "Annabelle and Lisa should be almost done putting all the chickens in their coops by now."

Lizzie put her hands on her hips. "You have the Negro working already? That must've been hard for you."

Grace stopped sweeping and glared at Lizzie. Tsula seemed to notice the abrupt tension and watched attentively.

"I'm still trying to understand your attitude lately, but don't play with me," Grace said, her voice low. "I will whip you with this broom. I know how you really feel about Negroes. Stop acting like you don't care."

Lizzie stared at her sister, breathing heavily. She snatched off her white bonnet to brush her hair back and noticed Tsula staring at them. "What are you looking at, Tsula!"

"Don't take your anger out on me because you know Grace will smack you," Tsula replied.

Lizzie threw down her white bonnet, stomped on it, and stormed out of the store. Grace turned to Tsula as she huffed. The cousins cackled as they continued to close down the store.

"I love her, but that's your sister," Tsula said.

"I love her too, but there are those days," Grace said, shaking her head. "I wish she would stop being so bitter."

"I don't know why she'd let herself fall for Jacob. She's a beautiful girl. Why bring trouble into the family we both know my daddy wouldn't approve? We need to stay together, not make selfish choices."

"But was it selfish of her, Tsula?" Grace asked. "She grew up with Jacob. We all did, and she felt their friendship change into something more. I respect him for telling her he has stronger feelings for someone else."

"Lizzie was still in the wrong. We're here surviving. The last thing we need is another person making half-bloods."

Grace frowned. "Would it matter if he wasn't part Negro, Tsula?"

Tsula stared at Grace, and her jaw dropped. She placed a bag of soybeans she held on the counter. "You know I don't have anything against mixed-bloods. I'm not my daddy."

"But would you have anything to say if Jacob was Cherokee and white?"

"Yes, I would have a problem with it," Tsula snarled before yanking up the bag of soybeans and entering the storage room.

Annabelle and Lisa came through the back door with feather-covered dresses and brushed the feathers off their clothes. Grace stared at the two women, her brown eyes narrowing as she thought about her freshly swept floor. Lisa chuckled and continued to pull feathers from her garment, which added to Grace's agitation.

"The chickens didn't want to go inside today. They kept jumping around," Lisa said in Cherokee. "But we got them all, so let's go home."

Grace held back her anger out of mercy for Annabelle. "Next time, clean your dresses off outside, Lisa," she replied. "Well, I'll sweep this, then we can leave."

——◆——

After Grace swept again, Tsula double-checked to make sure she put up all the soybean bags. The women left the store and traveled through Tahlequah's dirt road as other townspeople passed them. During their walk, Annabelle realized that most of the buildings were made of wood. Few of them were made of brick or stone. It was quite different than Mercy. The difference saddened her because she realized how much poorer the town was than Mercy.

The women arrived home and were greeted by a little boy wearing an off-shoulder neckline gown. Grace knelt down as the long-haired boy anxiously ran up to Grace, and she gave the boy a hug. The little boy's speed surprised Annabelle.

"Auntie Grace, I been waiting for you," the little boy said.

"Aw, little David. Auntie Grace loves you so much," Grace said.

"Auntie Lizzie go inside."

"She did. Did she give you a hug and a kiss?"

David happily nodded while she beamed. Grace suddenly grabbed him and cuddled the toddler, and he laughed as she gave him kisses.

Tsula knelt down, grinning at the toddler. "It's Auntie Tsula's turn," she said, grabbing David from Grace and kissing him as he giggled. Tsula then turned and gave David to Lisa.

Lisa held him, rubbing her nose against David's. "Do you want your special hug?" she asked.

David anxiously nodded while Lisa gave him a hug and three kisses on his cheek. Annabelle felt her heart swell as she watched the affection they showed the toddler, but it also reminded her of what she was missing.

"Hi," David said.

Annabelle smiled at the toddler. "Hi there."

David nestled up to Lisa shyly and waved back at Annabelle, grinning.

"Annabelle, I would like you to meet my nephew, David. This is John's son," Grace said.

"How old is he?" Annabelle asked.

Tsula replied, "He's three years old and a handful."

Annabelle chuckled. "He's adorable."

"Don't let that fool you. He won't stop asking questions," Grace said. "Annabelle, for now, I need you to go back to the other log cabin. We need to make it believable that you're a slave, and when I can arrange it, you can eat with the rest of the family. I wish we could have you inside, but my uncle would get upset."

"I understand. I'm grateful for your kindness."

Grace nodded.

Annabelle went to the smaller house while the others went inside to greet the rest of the family. The women cooked supper in the large kitchen and talked among themselves. By the time they finished cooking, a whole chicken, soybeans, and corn-bread had also been made. Before the family sat down to eat, Grace took a plate over to Annabelle.

Grace arrived at the smaller house and opened the old wooden door. To her surprise, she saw Annabelle sitting in a rocking chair and reading a slightly burnt book. "Oh my, you can read!"

Annabelle's eyes widened. "Is something wrong with that here?"

"Well, not really. I didn't mean it like that. I'm surprised. We'll talk when I return from eating with the others. Here is your food."

Grace approached Annabelle and handed her the plate as Annabelle put down the book.

"Thank you, Grace. It means a lot."

"Don't worry about it. I will be back soon."

Annabelle nodded, and Grace left the log cabin with a lop-sided grin. "So, you can read," she murmured.

Grace quickly opened the door to the large old cabin and almost knocked John down as she rushed inside. "Why are you running inside?" John asked.

Grace answered, "I was trying to hurry back so Uncle George wouldn't notice I had left."

John cocked his head. "Where are you coming from?"

"I'm coming from my log cabin. I needed to give Annabelle her food. It would be stupid to have her eat at the table with us."

"Does Uncle George know about her yet?"

"Yes, he does, and we are in play. So for the next two days, she is my slave, and you were there when I bought her."

"I understand, but how much of a plan did you make?"

"The white man that sold her to us is named Lawrence Mays. I paid him four hundred dollars for Annabelle. He was a rough-looking white man that was a wanderer. That's the plan for now. I also plan to take Annabelle to an elder later on."

"Four hundred dollars isn't much for a slave. I think we need to rethink this."

Grace lightly bit her lip as her mouth pinched. "It will surprise him, but I can make it work. All this does is support how badly the man wanted the money. Make sure you don't forget the name I came up with."

John sighed. "I won't forget. Did you tell Lisa and Tsula?"

Grace put a hand on her hip as her eyes narrowed. "They know what they need to know."

John gulped before reluctantly entering the lamplit dining room and sitting down at the old oak table. Lizzie brought in the plates as Grace walked past her sister to bring the food in with the other women. The women placed the chicken on the table, having cut it up to hide that some of it was missing.

The smell of the well-done bird filled the dining room and attracted George's attention, who sat at the head of the table next to John. He smiled as the women brought in two trays of beans and a tray of cornbread slices to further hide that some had been given to Annabelle. The women stood around the table, followed by David.

"Michael and Samuel, we will eat without you. Hurry in here," Tsula said.

Samuel rushed into the dining room, followed by a teenage Michael, believing Tsula's threat. Michael was a skinny teenager, shorter than everyone but David. He had round brown eyes and a darker complexion than Samuel. His hair was cut short like John's, and a diagonal scar marred his right hand.

George and John stood up, and everyone held hands.

"Every day we gather, I see it as a blessing from Jesus that we are here as a family," George said.

George prayed over the food, and the men sat down. Uncle George was served first by Grace, then Tsula served John and

Samuel as Lisa served Michael. The women fixed their plates and sat down, enjoying each other's company. David sat in Grace's lap while she fed him off her plate. The family talked in the Cherokee language as they continued to eat their meals.

"That's a strong-looking Negro you got, Grace. You surprise me," George said. "What made you change your mind? You and your mother always argued against our people keeping slaves."

"I feel that it has been difficult for me and the others to handle the store alone while dealing with the chickens and keeping our soybeans healthy," Grace replied. "She is respectful. I see no problems to come from her."

Uncle George nodded while he continued to eat. "Where did you get her from, and how much did she cost us?"

"I got her from a wandering white man. At first, he wanted seven hundred dollars for her, but I told him I would only pay four hundred. He appeared desperate. He was a dirty-looking white man. John was with me when the man approached. The man agreed. He showed me her slave papers, and it showed they were from Georgia."

George huffed, and his gaze went to his plate and back to Grace. "I'm confused. Why so low of a price for a young and healthy slave? She spoke well and looks healthy. I think she has all her teeth too. The man must've been desperate to return to Georgia and let go of a slave like that."

The others at the table remained quiet. Michael was familiar with Annabelle because of Samuel telling him. He was the only one besides Uncle George that was clueless about the plot Grace had developed.

"I think he really wanted to leave our territory and saw Annabelle as a burden," Grace said.

George raised his eyebrows. "Annabelle... To be given such a nice name, she must've been valued."

Grace gave a skewed frown. "Is that a problem, Uncle George?"

"No, I have no problem with it. I also know that arguing with you about buying her without calling for me would be useless.

You have your mother's spirit. May she continue to be blessed in heaven. At least John was there to protect you."

"You need to trust me more, Uncle George. I made a good choice."

"I do trust you mostly, but you need to continue to let the men of this family lead. Where will she sleep, and what was the white man's name? Those will be the last questions I will ask."

"She will sleep in the empty room in the other house. Lawrence Mays was his name."

The others continued to eat their food while they watched George's expressions.

Uncle George stopped eating his chicken, listening to Grace's answer. "Lawrence!"

"Yes, Laurence was his name," Grace said, her voice sharp.

"Like the white man that threw horse crap at you when you were a teenager? It must've taken a lot for you to smile at that man when he told you his name. I know what it was. He saw a good-looking Cherokee woman and became weak." George laughed, and the others laughed with him. "I would've enjoyed seeing you weaken a man with your beauty. It's not your way, but there's nothing wrong with using a little bit."

Grace bit her lip while she shook her head a little, and her grip tightened on her fork. However, she relaxed while she watched her uncle laugh and not ask questions. George continued laughing as he returned to eating his chicken. The family continued to eat and talk. After the family supper ended, Grace returned to the house as Lisa followed.

"Lisa, what are you doing?" Grace asked.

Lisa replied in Cherokee, "I'm following you because I want to learn more about Annabelle."

"There is nothing more for you to learn today. Go play with David."

"I have plenty of reason to learn more about her, and you made up a good story. Papa wouldn't be happy if he learned she came from Mercy."

Grace stopped walking and turned around, staring at a persistent Lisa. "Go play with the horses like you normally do."

"It's too dark. You know that." Lisa grinned at Grace while she wrapped a blade of grass around her finger. "Maybe you do need a man in your life to remove all that anger you hide so well."

"I'm not angry. I would like some peace...and not to be asked about my love life."

Lisa quickly replied, "What love life would that be?"

A smiling Lisa sprinted to the house door as Grace pursued her. The moment Lisa reached for the door and opened it, Grace smacked her hand. Outside the door, the women childishly slapped each other's hands.

Annabelle appeared alarmed as she looked at the opened door and heard the two women arguing in Cherokee. She saw their shadows in the sunset while she slowly approached the door entrance with a book in her hand. Annabelle took a step back. The two women turned their heads, hearing her footsteps.

"Annabelle?" Grace said.

"Annabelle, how did you like the food?" Lisa asked.

Annabelle slowly walked back up to the door entrance with big eyes. The women standing next to each other noticed they had frightened Annabelle and grinned to lighten the mood.

Lisa noticed what she held. "Annabelle, is that a book?"

"Yes, it is an old book," Annabelle said.

Lisa seemed enthralled, but she remained silent. "So you can read?"

Annabelle's glance went down a little. "Well, yes, I can read some."

Lisa beamed. "You should teach me to read English! Will you help me?"

"Lisa, I said I will teach you how to read better. Don't pressure Annabelle," Grace snapped.

Lisa replied, "I think she'll be more fun than you. So she can help me start, and you help me with hard words."

Grace sneered. "Leave Annabelle alone."

"It's okay. I don't mind helping her," Annabelle said.

"Thank you, Annabelle," Lisa said.

Grace gave Lisa an annoyed glare as Lisa entered the cabin. Annabelle sat down in one of the rocking chairs as Lisa sat next to her. Grace followed, taking in a deep breath and relaxing her shoulders. Lisa took down her hair. It was odd for Annabelle, but Lisa's persistent happy nature appeared to comfort her.

"So, what was it like being a slave?"

"Did you really have to ask that?" Grace asked, anger coloring her voice.

"I really want to know. I want to know what slaves think," Lisa said, pouting. "We have many here. I curious. Maybe they think like Annabelle."

"I guess that's a fair question," Annabelle said. "I grew up on a cotton plantation in Mississippi and worked as a house slave. I've only worked two days in the cotton fields as a child, and it was hard. I didn't keep my mouth shut, so I got whipped badly. Now I have seven scars on my back. The masters were surprised by how I healed because my scars look more like stripes than real scars. My best friend was the master's youngest daughter, and she protected me a lot." Annabelle took a deep breath and continued. "Her daddy forced himself on me when I turned sixteen years old. I couldn't tell her my pain. Almost two years, he would make me his toy. Made me feel like I had no life. It near killed me when Judy Mays got married and left me. I obeyed my master, scared of his anger and of his wife. Cooking food, eating leftover food, cleaning everything, taking care of white children, always feeling angry... There's not a lot of moments of happiness. Most of my happiness came from spending time with Judy Mays and her sisters.

"I didn't see my parents often. They worked the fields. My brother was too young to work when I escaped the plantation. I got no time to say bye to my papa or my brother. My momma helped me escape. She was a wise woman that didn't believe in her own wisdom. That sounds crazy. I know a wise person that don't think they're wise. That was what it was like for me to be a slave, Lisa. It was torture."

Tears shimmered in Lisa's eyes while she listened to Annabelle's experiences. Grace noticed sadness clouding Lisa's face as she frowned.

"What do you mean 'forced himself' on you?" Lisa asked.

Grace inhaled and pressed her lips together while she looked at Lisa's expression.

Annabelle's face saddened, and she leaned forward in the rocking chair. "He kept me on a bed and put himself in me, even though I didn't want to be touched."

Lisa lifted her hand to her mouth and glanced at Grace. "Grace, what does she mean?" she asked in Cherokee.

In the Cherokee tongue, Grace replied, "Annabelle is saying he raped her the same day she turned sixteen years."

Lisa's mouth dropped open, her eyes filling with sympathy that fell on Annabelle. She replied in Cherokee, "Are you sure that's what she is saying?"

"Yes, she was raped for two years as a slave."

Lisa turned to Annabelle, her wavy hair tumbling down her shoulders, and clutched her dress. "I'm very sorry I didn't understand you," she said. "You a strong woman to keep living after he hurt you. I hope my people are not doing the same. No woman should feel that pain, to be with someone you don't love. It would bring shame to the Creator and our ancestors to be so evil. Maybe tomorrow, you show me how to start reading?"

"I would like to do that," Annabelle said. "You'll be the second person I've taught how to read."

Lisa smiled, knowing Annabelle was serious about teaching her. Grace noticed a real moment of happiness Annabelle showed with a real smile.

"I noticed your dresses don't have a hoop. Why is that?"

"We do a lot of work like men, unlike white women," Lisa said. "Lizzie is stronger than she look."

"Well, I think we need to call this a night. The sun is gone, and the moon is looking beautiful tonight," Grace said.

"Okay, I see you tomorrow," Lisa said. She stood, her thick hair falling down her back.

Annabelle shook her head and blinked, looking at Lisa's long hair.

Lisa joyfully left the house when Grace stood up to stretch. "So you learned from your friend, the white girl," Grace said.

Annabelle replied, "You mean to read?"

"Yes, thank you for wanting to help Lisa read. It might help her speech too. Keep this from my uncle. Some of the same rules from the South are in control here too."

Annabelle stood up, holding the slightly burnt book. "I understand how to say nothing now. Thank you for letting me stay here."

Grace beamed at Annabelle. "It is a pleasure."

"I guess I'll go to bed too. I know there is still more I need to know."

"Yes, tomorrow should be a good day." Grace went to the kitchen table and turned off the lamp as the moonlight highlighted the interior of the cabin.

The women walked down the wooden hallway to their rooms and lit the lamps, both exhausted from the day.

━━━◆━━━

Annabelle noticed a white nightgown had been placed on her bed. Annabelle struggled to hold back her smile to avoid getting her hopes up. Annabelle took off the top part of her dress and sat down on the bed, looking at the stars.

Suddenly, Grace opened the door. "Annabelle, I wanted to— Oh, I'm sorry." Grace gasped while she stared at Annabelle's back. "They really do look like stripes! Incredible how all seven of them look that way."

Annabelle faced Grace with her back still turned toward Grace. "I'm sorry if it bothers you. I'll put my dress back quickly."

"No, hearing someone tell you about their pain is different than seeing it right in front of you. I wanted to say I'm glad John did the right thing saving you from those people. I hope you'll find happiness again."

"Maybe I will."

"Good night, Annabelle Mays." Grace nodded and closed the door.

Annabelle put on the nightgown. She placed her right hand on one of her back scars and exhaled. She lifted up the wool cover and lay in the bed, staring at the moon through the dirty glass window.

This is a strange town for me to stay in—a town full of slave holding Indians. I must want to die.

Annabelle fell asleep, exhausted from meeting so many new people.

———◆———

Grace combed her long dark brown hair, humming to herself. She stared at herself in a small mirror hanging on the wall. "Maybe showing Annabelle love is what my people need as an example of how we should treat these Negroes," Grace mumbled. "I'm so tired, Jesus. I don't know what to do with Lizzie. She's become cold since Jacob told her he doesn't have feeling as strong as she does; it's bad enough he's half Negro."

She took off her brown high-necked cotton dress and stared at herself in the small mirror, her undergarments the only things covering her. She put her hands on her hips, smiled at herself, and put on her white nightgown. She lay on her bed, hoping the unexpected arrival of Annabelle would be the beginning of something beneficial to her family.

CHAPTER 4
Sought Guidance

THE SUN ROSE HIGH, GREETED by songbirds flying past the small house. Annabelle was determined to ignore the birds, but the sudden crowing of a rooster made it difficult. She stumbled out of bed when she smelled something. She left her room, hearing Grace in the kitchen. She went down the hallway and saw Grace cooking at the old silver-colored Castrol stove.

"Good morning, Annabelle," Grace said. "I didn't think I would have to wake you. I'm making grits. It will be done soon. There are two outhouses right behind us if you need to use them."

"Thank you, Grace. I don't know how to thank you for being nice to me," Annabelle said.

"Don't worry about it. You're welcomed here."

Annabelle smiled and went back down the hallway of the log cabin. She put on her dress, trying not to become too excited that Grace had cooked for her. She left the log cabin, marching toward the red-painted outhouses. While she walked, a thought came to her.

I could run away from all of this right now.

But the more she thought about it, the more she realized there could be a chance of her getting caught and re-enslaved.

I can at least try it here. Maybe there's more to the Indians, and I can always learn them.

She returned to the house only to see two bowls of hot grits on the table with Grace patiently sitting down, waiting for her.

Grace cocked her head. "I hope you like them. I know you're probably not used to this."

"I had it a long time ago as a child. A slave named Ruth knew how to make it. I guess it all makes sense now. Ruth was half Indian. I shouldn't be surprised if y'all cook the same."

Grace grinned while Annabelle sat down at the wooden table across from her. "I'll say a prayer." Grace prayed over their food, and the women ate their breakfast. "I think you're going to do fine here. Maybe over time, we can take you to one of the northern states to help you more and put you around more Negroes.

"I think someone will still be after me."

"Who would that be?" Grace asked.

"Judy Mays. I think out of the kindness of her heart, she'll look for me. The bad thing is her daddy is also looking."

"I think there comes a time when the Father takes us away from people so we can heal. Sometimes, people return to us at the right time, and other times, it is good that they're gone. Poison is poison, no matter how sweet it may taste."

Annabelle nodded deeply, thinking about what Grace had said. The women finished their meal. Grace went to her room to change and braid her hair. Annabelle waited for her by the front door.

"Okay, I know you're ready to go," Grace said.

"I'm not ready to go. This will be different than being around white people all the time."

"Well, we still have white people always coming into our territory. Many of them work for the US government, others are travelers, and others are missionaries, so there is no reason for you to be nervous."

"Okay."

Grace huffed. "And you still have to meet my cousin, Michael. He's Samuel and Tsula's little brother."

"Why didn't I see him yesterday?"

"He's very shy...a kid only in his teens. I'll make sure he sees you later today."

Annabelle beamed. "Okay."

The women traveled through the town to the supply store, and Annabelle noticed that the town seemed to struggle with happiness. Two young boys played in the street, both wearing beige cotton shirts and brown trousers. The boys ran in front of a passing one-horse carriage, startling the white-maned brown horse. The horse's owner yelled at the two boys as they ran off. The older man stared at Annabelle and Grace and nodded at the two women before continuing on his way.

It was still an awkward moment for Annabelle, seeing so many Indians and being either acknowledged or ignored by them. No feeling of fear was present. It tempted her to drop her guard, but the fear of being alone was strong. The women arrived at the supply store before Tsula and Lisa.

"Well, it's time to get everything prepared," Grace said. "The first thing I need you to do is to open up the chicken coop doors. The chickens will walk out by themselves. Then come back inside, and Tsula can teach you how we feed them."

"Okay, that should not take me long."

Annabelle walked outside through the back door and opened up the chicken coops. It amused Annabelle how confident the chickens were as they marched out of their pens. During this time, Tsula and Lisa arrived at the store. Tsula had her hair put into two buns while Lisa had her hair put into one bun.

"Good, you're on time today," Grace said.

"We're always on time," Tsula retorted.

Grace rolled her eyes. "Don't lie, Tsula. You look ugly when you lie."

Lisa chuckled while Tsula glared at Grace with pursed lips. "It's funny 'cause it true," Lisa said.

"Nobody asked you, Lisa," Tsula bickered. "At least my English is so good. People say that I'm smart."

Lisa stared at her sister. She folded her arms as her face fell. Tsula smiled.

"Enough, it is too early for the two of you to start arguing," Grace said. "Annabelle is outside letting out the chickens, and when she comes back in, I need you to show her how we feed them, Tsula."

"Why me? I would rather pull out the grain and cornmeal bags."

"Because Lisa is better at organizing the money, and I can get those things ready first."

"Well, okay," Tsula said. "But what do you want me to show her next?"

"Show her the small soybean field and start gathering the beans. The seasons are changing. We need to start storing up what we can."

Annabelle suddenly entered the store with the sounds of chickens behind her. "Good morning, Tsula and Lisa. Those are pretty dresses you're wearing." The young women beamed at Annabelle.

"Good morning, Annabelle. I hope you sleep good," Lisa said.

"I did. Seeing the moon shine so bright helps."

Tsula grinned and moved closer to Annabelle. "Well, I guess now is the time I show you how to feed the chickens and work the soybean field in the back."

"Yes, don't get lost in the field," Lisa joked.

Tsula stuck out her tongue. "At least I can read."

Lisa gasped while Tsula coaxed Annabelle into going back outside, and she gave Lisa a leer.

"This will be interesting," Annabelle said.

The women walked around in the yard fenced by large sticks and wooden planks. Tsula showed Annabelle how to feed the chickens with grains and old cornmeal.

"I hope you don't find this boring, but it is important we keep them fed," Tsula said.

"No, I don't find it boring. I think they're funny little animals. We had a few of them on the plantation I used to live on. I didn't take care of chickens until I started working for Mr. Boston."

"How was Mr. Boston? I met the man a long time ago. John and Samuel like him."

"He is a kind old man, like a father to me. He always asked how I was doing and always welcomed me, even the first day I met him. He always gave me extra food when I was pregnant, and he never let me leave without fresh bread or fruit to eat on my way home. I will miss him and that spoiled cat of his." Annabelle giggled at the sweet memories going through her mind.

"It's sad thinking how different things would be if there were more like him."

Annabelle sighed. "I think they would rather kill themselves before changing for the better."

Tsula put a hand on her hip. "You think they struggle that hard to treat us better?"

"I have never met a white man from the Deep South that ever saw me as something more than a slave. I think they would rather kill us all if they can't control us. There's nothing Christian about that."

"I, too, find that funny, these missionaries coming here to try to tell us how to live. But they really don't understand how to love people different than them. They talk about Jesus but do little or nothing He did."

"Are you a Christian, Tsula?"

"I believe in the Jesus the white people talk about, like most of my people, but I believe few have fully read that Bible themselves. These white people argue with me as to what I should call the Creator. They tell me my whole life I'm going to hell because I don't call him God. I will never call my father in the heavens God. Not after these white people destroy the name with how they treat us. He was the Creator, and the beginning, and my father. That's what I will always call him. Not God. What do you believe in, Annabelle?"

"I believe in God, and I believe Jesus is his son that died for my sins. I wonder about God right now. It would be foolishness for me to doubt his presence, but after losing my family, I want little to do with him right now. Sometimes, I wish every white man was killed from this world so we can live free. To hold my daughter in my arms and watch her die... I saw evil again, and not even the life of a baby could change their hearts."

Tsula was saddened while she watched Annabelle walk off and continue to feed the chickens. Tsula spoke under her breath. "I guess I would be a liar if I said I would never wish to see them die too. She is in her right to be angry with these people." Tsula stretched her arms. "Alright, let's go out to these soybeans. It's September. We can start collecting them."

"This will be new for me. Do they stab you like cotton?"

"No, they're easy to pick, but it takes a lot of work. Be happy you're not John and the other men since we don't have slaves. Could also be why my papa was so happy to hear Grace had bought a slave."

Annabelle's eyebrows lowered when she followed Tsula. Tsula noticed the quick change in nature of Annabelle and quickly turned around. Annabelle stopped.

"There isn't nothing for you to be scared of. My papa is a lot of talk. I'm sure he won't be happy when Grace frees you, but don't worry."

Annabelle thought, *She knows nothing of what it means to be a slave, but I can see that she hasn't had a great time living either.*

The women arrived at the small field. Tsula explained to Annabelle what pods were ready to be picked and which ones needed to mature. As the women went through the field, Annabelle suddenly saw a Cherokee man with a stocky build walking down the small dirt path. The bronze-skinned man wore a green turban, a white cotton shirt with a green cravat around it, and brown trousers. His dark brown-silver hair was cut short like a white man, and he seemed cheerful.

"Tsula, what blessing to see you today," the man said.

"Ah, Mr. Tate, it looks like you're enjoying this morning," Tsula said.

"Why yes, I'm on my way back to the farms. I will be sending some corn to the store soon."

"Well, you know we will have room for it."

Mr. Tate chuckled as he stopped in front of Tsula. "Who is this Negro woman?"

"This is Annabelle. She is Grace's new slave."

Mr. Tate's eyes widened. "A slave? Your cousin paid for a slave? Why that sounds nothing like her. Is she feeling well?"

"She is feeling fine, Mr. Tate. She bought Annabelle from a traveling white man because she felt we needed help after all."

"Hello, Annabelle. My name is Mr. Tate."

"Hello, Mr. Tate," Annabelle said shyly.

Mr. Tate smiled. "No need to be scared of me, young lady. I myself have ten slaves. Grace is a good woman. You should be happy she bought you."

"I am grateful to Miss Grace."

"She speaks English very good, Tsula! I'm surprised. No wonder Grace took the chance to buy her. What a smart choice."

"Grace has always thought strongly, Mr. Tate," Tsula said.

"That's the truth," Mr. Tate said. "Well, I must get to Jacob. I know he is waiting for me. Annabelle, it has been nice to meet you."

"It was nice to meet you too, Mr. Tate," Annabelle replied.

Mr. Tate waved. "Enjoy the day, Tsula."

"Thank you, Mr. Tate. The same to you," Tsula said.

Mr. Tate smiled and left while Tsula and Annabelle watched him continue down the dirt path.

"He owns slaves?" Annabelle asked.

"Yes, he does," Tsula said. "We grew up with his four children and played with them all the time. My papa didn't like it too much, but the Tate family is like another part of our family."

"I never really heard a slave master speak so nice," Annabelle said. "He was not pretending when he was being nice to me, was he?"

"No, he wasn't. Mr. Tate has always been happy. I have always wondered how he stayed that way even after we were forced to move here."

Annabelle was fascinated with Mr. Tate. His genuine kindness baffled her because he was a slave owner. However, she still kept up her guard as she fought her curiosity to not see his slaves.

———◆———

As the women continued to search the small field for mature soybeans, George arrived at the store with a big smile on his face. While giving a woman a bag of soybeans, Grace watched him as he brushed off his faded blue vest.

The woman walked by with her beans and grinned at George.

He nodded at her. "It looks like you're having a good day, Grace," he said.

Grace beamed at her uncle while he stood in front of the old oak counter. "Uncle George, you know I always have a good day."

"That's because you make everyone else miserable."

Grace felt her smile fade as George and Lisa chuckled. Lisa carried a small bag of wheat to an aisle.

"Don't give me that look, Grace," George said. "It reminds me too much of your momma and your auntie."

Grace smirked at her uncle the second he shook his head. "Like I said, I always have good days, Uncle George."

"Ah, enough of that. I do have something for you."

Grace tilted her head. "What would that be?"

George plopped down a whip on the old oak counter he had been holding in his right hand. "This is for you just in case you need something strong to keep Annabelle in her place. I think you have surprised me more than I ever thought you could. Maybe this is the way we need to go so our family can continue to do good."

Lisa gasped as she dropped the bag of wheat she carried. George turned to Lisa while she quickly picked up the bag and placed it with the other wheat bags. George looked back at his niece, seeming to take notice of her scowl and crossed arms.

"I have no reason to lower myself in order to control my slave," Grace said.

"It isn't lowering yourself!" George shouted. "It is about creating an understanding that you're the master, and she must follow. What are you showing David if you were to allow Annabelle to do as she chooses?"

"We have plenty of slave owners around not using things to keep things in order. I won't be one to do such harm to Annabelle," Grace argued.

George grunted as he brushed back his grayish-brown hair and walked toward the exit of the supply store. "I'm not taking that whip back. I'm going back out into the fields with your brother and my sons. For once, you need to listen to me, Grace."

Grace stared at her uncle with her brow furrowed and mouth curving downward. She took the whip and placed it in a drawer. "Don't tell Tsula or Annabelle about this," she said. "And especially not Lizzie. We don't need her adding to the problem."

Lisa nodded, speaking in Cherokee. "I won't say nothing, and I'm sad papa made an effort to get a whip. I think if Annabelle sees the whip, she'll become frightened."

"I think it will cause us more problems," Grace replied in Cherokee. "She'll be a slave for one more day. All I need is for your father not to scare her away. If she's captured in the wilderness by the Chickasaw or Creek, that will be the end of her freedom."

"I will pray to God for more answers. I now believe papa won't take it well when you free Annabelle."

"I think you're right, but at the same time, the council may not like my choice either. I need more power and support. I prayed to Jesus for more wisdom, and I was given an answer. After we close the store, I will take Annabelle to Elder Joyce. I know her kindnesses to the Negroes. It is time we do what the white people won't do. We're Christians. We should show it."

Lisa replied, "I think Tsula will agree. She is stronger against papa than me."

Grace shook her head. "Don't worry about it. Pray to Jesus and support my stance. I will be the one to catch most of his anger, if not all of it. Time is short."

Lisa moaned. "Tomorrow will come quickly, and the next day will be a great storm. Will John be ready to support us? I know Samuel is more scared of you than papa, and Michael has little authority on anything big."

Grace's voice became stern. "I will keep John aware of the plan. It was all his last-minute planning that got us involved this, even though I like Annabelle."

Tsula opened the back door with a small bag filled with soybeans. "We have a couple of beans ready to be picked," Tsula said. "Why do both of you look so serious?"

Annabelle entered the store right behind Tsula, gently shooing away a chicken.

"There isn't anything wrong," Grace replied. "We were talking. I thought maybe you had more beans. You took longer than normal out there."

Tsula rolled her eyes. "Mr. Tate was walking on the dirt trail, so we talked for a little while."

"Was Jacob with him?" Lisa asked.

Tsula shook her head. "No, he wasn't. Were you looking for him to help you with the horses again?"

Lisa replied, "Well, no. I was just asking."

"That Mr. Tate was nice for a slave owner. I have never met someone like that before," Annabelle said.

"Most Cherokee slave owners have white blood, but Mr. Tate is the rare class, being full-blood and having slaves," Grace said. "He is actually a good man. We grew up with his children, Jacob and his three siblings."

Annabelle fixed her eyes on Grace. "Y'all talk about them like they're family."

"In a way, they are like family to us," Grace said. "The family has always lived near us even before all of us were born."

———————◆———————

Annabelle felt jealous of the women, but she understood what Grace meant. It did nothing but remind her of Mercy. The women continued to work at the supply store as the day continued, giving Annabelle a different experience than what she gained at Mr. Boston's store. She was either greeted or received a nod of acknowledgment. She was confused because she knew at least some of the Cherokee saw themselves as better than her.

Lizzie arrived at the store carrying a sack of soybeans. "It looks like all of you are having a fun day," she commented.

"It makes the day go faster," Lisa said.

"I know it does," Lizzie said. "Since I'm outside half of the time helping John and the others, I'm just glad the weather isn't so hot anymore. I'm tired of soybeans and chickens. Anyway, I have these new beans to be sold. It looks like we did a good job this year."

Tsula approached Lizzie and took the sack.

Lizzie glared at Annabelle but quickly shifted her gaze off her when she walked to the counter, tugging her long braid. "We have two hens that have laid a new clutch of eggs, but I can't tell who the mothers are, so I'm taking a chicken from the back."

"Take one of the roosters, Lizzie. We have ten of them now," Lisa said softly.

"Okay, I'll do this quickly so I can get back to David. Those men have no idea how to deal with a toddler."

Lizzie went to the chicken coops as the other women continued to do tasks in the store. Annabelle swept the floor while the other women checked supplies and counted the money in preparation for closing. Annabelle continued to sweep when Lizzie opened the back door, covered in feathers and carrying a rooster in a sack.

"Lizzie, would you please brush off the feathers where you stand so I can clean them up?" Annabelle asked.

Lizzie glared at Annabelle and snarled, "I will do as I please. I've cleaned this store more times than you can count."

"Lizzie!" Grace shouted.

Lizzie quickly moved past Annabelle, brushing feathers all over the place as she left the store. Annabelle's grip tightened on the broom the moment Lizzie exited the store, but she took a deep inhale and swept again.

"Annabelle," Grace said, "I will clean the rest of this up. Lisa needs help getting the chickens into their coops for the day."

Annabelle handed Grace the broom, and the other woman gave an apologetic expression at Lizzie's actions.

"Let's go!" Lisa excitedly said. "You're good at telling the birds to go inside."

Lisa opened the back door, and Annabelle followed Lisa outside. Grace continued to sweep up the mess Lizzie made as the others finished their tasks.

When the women returned inside, Grace locked the raggedy door.

"I ready for some sleep. I don't care about supper today," Lisa said.

"I feel almost the same way," Grace said.

"Both of you are crazy. I need to eat before I can go to sleep," Tsula said. "What about you, Annabelle?"

Annabelle replied, "I agree with you, Tsula. I can't say no to food."

The women giggled as they closed the store and strolled down the dirt road of Tahlequah.

"Before I forget, Annabelle, me and you have a special trip to make," Grace said.

"What is so special about this trip?" Annabelle asked.

"We are going to see someone very special. She is the oldest person in our tribe. I'm sure she'll be pleased to meet someone like you. To be honest, we need all the favor we can get."

Annabelle gave a concerned look. "Okay, I'll go with you."

"Well, then we will see the two of you for supper," Tsula said.

"Without a doubt," Grace said.

The women went opposite ways. Annabelle looked back, noticing a cheerful Tsula and Lisa speaking to each other in Cherokee. It was a slight reassurance for her, who still struggled to form any trust. While Annabelle and Grace went through the town, Annabelle noticed even more how different it was than Mercy. Most buildings were built out of wood, and others were built out of brick or stone. Some houses lined the town, and some of them were built out of old wood. Crop fields large and small appeared to be their life source while cattle roamed free in a few fields.

The two women walked past a few log cabins, greeting the residents living there, when the women stopped in front of a house roughly the same size as Grace's. The house was made of old wood and had a small area housing a few chickens fenced in by sticks and planks. An outhouse was directly behind the fenced-in chickens.

Annabelle felt her throat tighten. It was clear neighbors from a distance were watching the two women. She believed people only paid attention when something serious was about to happen. Grace knocked on the old wooden door, and sweat went down Annabelle's back as her eyes widened. The door suddenly opened, and an old woman with long silver hair stood in the doorway. The copper-toned woman stood eye to eye with Annabelle and Grace and wore a polka-dotted, dark green cotton dress.

"My, my, look what the wind carried this way," the old woman said.

"Elder Joyce, it's good to see you today," Grace said.

"Don't try to talk sweet to me, Little Grace. You and your kin haven't come by to see me in over a month," Joyce complained. "The courage to come to my home, with no gifts for an old woman after not even coming by just to say hi. Shameful, just shameful."

Grace pouted as Joyce stood in the doorway scowling at her.

"I don't know what to say," Grace said. "I really have been busy with David and the store. At least we've seen you at church. I'm sorry. I will make sure this doesn't happen again, and—"

"Oh, hush, child." Joyce cackled. "I love that look on your face. It almost makes you look ugly."

Grace's face cleared up, and she exhaled.

"But I'm disappointed I haven't seen any of your family for a month outside of church."

"I'm sorry for that, Elder Joyce."

Joyce dismissively waved her hand. "Enough of your apologies. Now, who is this young woman?"

"This is Annabelle."

Joyce smiled, saying, "My, you're a pretty young thing. Where are you from?"

Annabelle answered, "I was originally from Mississippi, ma'am."

"Hmm, I think it best you two young ladies come inside." The women entered the old log cabin, and Joyce closed the door once they all had entered.

The old house smelled like pine as sunshine lightened up the cabin and created a peaceful presence. An old rocking chair with white chipped paint sat in a corner, and an old oak table with four chairs was set next to an old iron stove.

"Please take a seat."

The women sat down at the oak table, and Joyce followed them. Annabelle's heart raced as she lightly patted her thigh.

Joyce sat down next to Grace and huffed. "How does a Negro woman make it this far from Mississippi of all places?"

Grace replied, "Well she—"

"No, Grace, I'm asking her," Joyce said. "I want the whole story. I can tell if you're lying now. I've been around for a lot of years."

Annabelle looked at the old woman with her slightly wrinkled face and almond-shaped eyes, and she felt her throat tighten again. "I guess I need to start back at the plantations then," Annabelle said.

She told the entire story of how she ended up in Indian Territory. Joyce kept her eyes fixed on her. Grace tried to take side glances to see if there was any sympathy being expressed, but Joyce remained expressionless. Annabelle finished the story, and a small frown was on Elder Joyce's face.

"You're a runaway slave that managed to run into some white women that liked you, and all of that was ruined. Grace, who's idea was it to make her your slave?"

"It was the only thing I could think of so nobody would look for her," Grace said.

"This is a dangerous plan. Where did you get the slave papers from?"

"I got them from Mr. Gross's home. It was the papers of a dead slave."

"This is a serious risk. I don't like this. Did you pray on this child?"

Grace shook her head. "No, there was no time."

"There is always time to pray, especially on something this big. The council has done things like the white man for a long time now. We do things now out of greed, not what's good for us Cherokee. Freeing Annabelle will scare them that more of us will continue to free their slaves, mostly those who have kin with Negro blood. That's who they fear the most, sadly."

Grace looked at Joyce with a frown. "Will you please come with me to the council to support me freeing Annabelle?"

Joyce lifted her head as she squinted. "Why do you want

their approval? Child, they'll give you a hard time even with me there. It would be easier to manumit her. Much of what we did in the South came with us. You're too young to remember, but we changed much to please the white people. Prepare yourself for a lot of pain, Grace. You may not get the support you want."

Annabelle felt her heart drop while she looked at the table. "If I stay a slave longer, will it make it easier for them to accept my freedom?" Annabelle asked.

"It might, child, but they'll certainly question why Grace bought you and decided so quickly to free you instead of selling you to someone who has slaves. I will show up at the courthouse tomorrow, but I must pray on this. This problem divides our people. I honestly wish you'd free the girl and be done with it."

Grace replied, "Yes, I know."

"And you should know that as passionate as your momma was about slavery, she tried hard to be peaceful, rest her spirit," Joyce continued. "Well now, you young ladies go home. I would like to enjoy this beef stew alone while I read. Ignorant Indians get cheated in life."

"Thank you, Elder Joyce."

"It was nice to meet you, Elder Joyce," Annabelle said.

"Hmm, two young women in so much trouble, they're able to smile," Joyce said. "It is nice to meet you too, young Annabelle. Grace, tell your troublesome family to visit me, especially Lisa. I need some young spirits around me."

Grace replied, "I will, Elder Joyce."

The women left the log cabin as Joyce sat in her chair and said, "Lord, what have you brought me now?"

———◆———

Annabelle and Grace arrived at the Strongman cabin as the sun began to set. Lisa was outside playing with David before she kissed him on the cheek and put him inside the house. She then quickly left the cabin, going toward the two women.

"What did Elder Joyce say?" Lisa asked. "Will she help?"

"She said she'd help, but she thinks we may have a hard time," Grace said. "Elder Joyce also believes the council will be really angry with me for freeing Annabelle because it could cause others to do the same."

Lisa inhaled and bit her lip. "What will you do?"

"I'm freeing Annabelle tomorrow. We'll go to the council to see if I'll get support for my decision. But the real fight, I think, will begin when I bring Annabelle back as a free woman. She wouldn't be the first Negro freed on Cherokee land."

"I don't know how I can thank any of you for what you're doing for me," Annabelle said.

"Don't worry. We like you," Lisa said.

Grace grinned at hearing Lisa's bluntness. "Well, we need to finish this day normally," Grace said. "I will bring you food, Annabelle, and then tomorrow is a new beginning for all of us."

Grace and Lisa joined the rest of the family for supper, and Annabelle stayed in the smaller log cabin. After supper, Lizzie took David to one of the bedrooms while Tsula and Lisa cleaned the dishes. Grace approached John as Samuel and Michael walked to their room.

"John, come with me," Grace said.

"What do you want?" John asked.

"We must talk while uncle is asleep."

John's eyebrows lowered as he stared. "Is this about Annabelle?"

"Yes."

John followed Grace outside to the side of the large house.

"I'm going to free her tomorrow," Grace explained, "and I will need you to come to the courthouse with me. I also talked to Elder Joyce."

"What did she say?"

Grace grunted. "She isn't pleased that you haven't visited her, and she said she'll support my decision. But the council won't be happy."

As the moonlight shined down on them, John could see the worry on his sister's face. John placed his hand on his sister's shoulder. "We're strong, Grace, and as long as we stay together, we can help Annabelle."

"You surprise me. For so long, you looked down on the Negroes. Momma tried so hard to teach you to love them, but you followed Daddy's ways. I was afraid to ask you when you first brought her home because I didn't want to see the old you. Why now? Do you care if Annabelle stays a slave or not?" Grace stared into John's eyes and put her hands on her hips.

John brushed back his short hair and sighed. "Papa pushed it so hard on me, even when we was children, not to like them. He treated me different than you or Lizzie, and he talked mean to me if he saw me play with Mr. Tate's children. But when Camille died, I felt nothing but pain. You know this, but soon after, I really left home to get away from all of you.

"Seeing David killed my spirit. He has her laugh. When I went to Mr. Boston's store, it was healing for me. Annabelle was so nice to me. Every time, she was always smiling. She told me how she lost a baby and how much it hurt, and she knew how I was feeling.

"We lost momma and then papa, but Camille was my heart. She left me. I felt Camille give up to that sickness, and I couldn't forgive her, but it was loving words from a Negro that helped me see I was wrong. Camille loved me and David. She tried to stay. I had no reason to be angry at her. Annabelle showed me that, and she also showed me I need to forgive myself."

John cleared his throat. "Annabelle said something I can't forget. We all have a purpose that God gives, us and all things happen for a reason. When she told me how she lost her first baby, she said she didn't even get a chance to birth the child, but she still had the strength to tell me a smile can go a long way. I saw right there that papa was wrong about the Negroes. We've been following the white man's ways for too long now. I see now. We're hurting our own people, lying to ourselves that those with Negro blood are lesser. Uncle George won't like this, but I stand with you."

"You have a big heart, John. That's a gift from the Father that you're able to learn in such a way."

John looked up to the sky, groaning. "Please don't push the talk of Jesus on me now. I agree the Negroes should not be slaves, so be happy with that."

Grace playfully pushed John. "I'm happy with that. I wish you would have listened to more of what momma and Auntie Shay were trying to teach us. Why is it so hard for you to see the truth?"

John raised his voice as he said, "Look at us, our people! I won't worship the white man's God when they don't act like this man they speak about."

"Jesus was not a man, John. And no, there were no good reasons for what they have done to our people, but what they did does not represent the Father."

"I'm happy now as I am. The Creator can judge me as a man and not based on these rules made by white men."

Grace frowned and looked away from John. "Well, enough of this. I will take Annabelle to the courthouse in the morning. We may bring a lot of attention to our family that we don't want."

"We can't agree to any unfair agreements. That will be the real burden on us if we let it happen."

Grace nodded and turned to walk next door to the small cabin. "I will see you in the morning, brother."

John smiled and went back into the old log cabin.

Grace entered the house and looked at Annabelle as she sat in one of the rocking chairs. She read her Bible while her finger tapped on it.

"There are many answers in that book, and as I remember, it says to give your cares to the Lord," Grace said.

Annabelle looked up at Grace with a half-smile. "When did you accept Jesus?" she asked.

Grace replied, "I was eight years old when I chose that path. My momma tried to teach me and the others what she could, even though my papa was against it. When did you?"

"I was six or seven years old. Master Brown would read

scriptures to us. Sometimes, he read what really was in the Bible, and other times, he lied to us. I knew that because of Judy Mays. He was a terrible example of Christian men."

"I could see that being a weapon against your faith. It looks like you were able to hold on to it."

Annabelle closed the Bible. "Do you know how your momma was taught?"

Grace walked to the wooden rocking chair and sat down, yawning. "My momma was taught by white women who came with missionaries. One of them was called Liz. So Lizzie is named after a white woman my momma really liked.

"She had her doubts about this Jesus. It was confusing for her. They talked so much about him but acted little like him. She believed love was the hardest thing for them to show to our people. White people are so quick to call our ways wicked or savage, but they took no time to understand our ways. It bothered my momma, and it bothers me still. So she always prayed for the Creator to show her what those white people can't.

When she was sixteen years old, she was in the forest getting berries alone when she heard a branch snap. She was scared because normally, she would've been with my two aunts, but she was angry at them for taking too long to follow her. She dropped the berries and backed up, trying to see what made the noise. When she turned around, a cougar jumped at her. My momma said she screamed as that big cat grabbed her shoulder with those big paws and tore the top part of her dress, and she punched him. She ran and tripped over a log, then rolled down a hill.

She thought maybe she came too close to a dead deer, but the cat chased her while she fell down the hill. My momma said she thought he wanted to kill her and not let her go. She got her footing and ran, crossing through trees. She kept looking back and seeing the angry cat. She believed she was too close to his home or something. She tried running in different paths to be harder to catch, but when she looked back again, she hit her head on a branch."

Grace stretched her arms and yawned. "She quickly got up, but the cat was right there and letting out that scary roar. She was gonna try to run away, but it stopped in front of her. Then she noticed how much she was bleeding. She thought he was gonna end her life. Said she was shaking with her arms up, trying to protect her neck and face. The cat stared at her, and she was so scared, she couldn't move.

"It looked over her shoulder, and she heard a soft voice tell her not to fear and that her Father is here. It was so clear that she looked back, ignoring the cat, but nobody was there. My momma said she felt warmness and peace around her. That cat looked right into her eyes with his big green-yellow eyes. The cat sat down and licked the cuts on my momma's shoulder, cleaning it. He turned around and walked away.

"She then noticed the cuts on her shoulder were healed, so she went back to the village in shock, following the river when she noticed a book on the ground. She walked over to it, picked it up, and opened it. Can you believe her name was written in that book all fancy and pretty? The pages were a little wet, but the book was fine. It was impossible, and she knew it was a sign. She picked up the book, then looked behind her. That oversized cat was standing right there. But then he lay down, and my momma slowly left, never taking her eyes off that cat.

"After that, she told the others in our town, and it drove my momma to learn how to read because she could only read a few words and her name. Not long after, she accepted Jesus not because of these white people but because of the mercy and love she was shown. She was close to Jesus, and she prayed a lot. That's what guided her. Hearing the Holy Spirit speak to her... She would always say it's different than the inner you.

"I never understood until I started to pray a lot and ask for guidance, so when I do hear the spirit speak to me, it's joyful for me. That's why I know Jesus can make a way to reach anyone. The Creator used a big cat to get my momma to run down a path she would never take, and it led to her believing the whole truth. It gives me hope for John."

Annabelle's eyebrows slightly rose. "John doesn't believe in Jesus?"

Grace shook her head. "No, he doesn't believe in Jesus like that. He thinks Jesus was a great healer, but that's it. He is a lot like our papa, unfortunately."

"I will pray for him. Like you said, your momma got saved in a crazy way, but I think her heart was opened to listen and try."

"My momma showed me her scars on her left shoulder. My momma named me after that day. Grace. Not everything is meant to last forever, but I think she wanted that memory to last forever."

Annabelle scoffed. "How could anybody forget about a cat like that?"

"It's easy to forget what you're blessed with, Annabelle. I think that scared my momma. She was proud of her scars. She really was our rock, and my family doesn't like many of the white people's ways. That's why they don't like to call him God."

"I understand. What was your momma's name?"

"Her name was Sarah. Maybe when I have a daughter, I'll name her that. But what's more exciting for me is tomorrow. It is a big day."

Annabelle beamed at Grace. "Yeah, tomorrow is the day."

<hr>

Grace smiled back and went to her room. Annabelle sighed deeply as she stood up and carried a lamp with her to her room. She was encouraged in having learned about Grace's mother, but she was still worried about what may change tomorrow. She dressed into her nightgown and lay in her bed.

God, she thought, *please spare me more pain. I don't know how much more I can take.*

<hr>

That night, John rolled over in his bed and stared at David. "What kind of a man would I be if I taught you to hate?" John whispered. "There's no reason for you to do things the wrong way like me, copying these white men and letting their ways corrupt you."

John suddenly fell asleep and dreamed. He noticed he was playing with three tree stumps. One tree stump was old, the other was rotten, and the third was new with a green leaf growing out of a branch.

"What is this?" John asked in Cherokee.

"It is choice. Two lies and the truth," said the soft echoing voice of a man in the Cherokee tongue. "Many have a hard time accepting there is one truth. Is it better to serve a man and love him as a brother than to live alone with treasures?"

"Depends on what the treasure is."

"No treasure in the land can replace the life of a brother or sister. No great stone, no amount of land, no valley, or Great River can replace the life of a brother or sister."

"That isn't how people think, and that's more truthful than what you say."

"Your mother would say differently. She is a loving woman willing to give her life for those she loves, over gaining profit. She would even risk her life for someone not of her blood."

"My mother has passed on. Her spirit guides me."

"Your mother's role was to bring you into this world and guide you and your family. It isn't her place to guide you now."

"What is this? This is no normal dream. Who are you to say my mother can't guide me now?"

"You already think you know me, but you've allowed the sins of your brothers to hold onto so much hate, you closed your heart to listen to anything that isn't Cherokee. Culture and tradition can never silence the truth. The truth is always eventually shown to the people, and they must choose to believe individually."

"My people have always done right by others," John said. "We've been the ones that were betrayed for many years, and we've suffered for it."

"Just as others, your people haven't been blameless. Revenge has been one of the greatest weaknesses of the Cherokee. Unwilling to forgive, unwilling to move forward and heal from the pain, and many have allowed greed to be the deciding reason."

John balled his hand into a fist and looked down at the three different tree stumps. John felt his heart pounding. Sweat trickled down his forehead. "Do these stumps have meaning?"

The man said, "The old stump was an old tree. It held to the old ways, refusing to drink from the living water. It was arrogant, believing its ways were better because that's what it learned from other trees. It produces bad spirit fruit. This fruit is unforgiving, holds to self-pity, believes it does not need to change, and is ungrateful. This blocks the love it could produce.

"The rotten stump is from a poisoned tree. It only speaks enough truth to benefit itself but poisons all creatures trying to live off its rotten fruit. The poisoned tree thinks it is better than the other trees not like it. Spreading its poison unaware, the poison is killing it too. The tree knows of the living water but lies to other trees about it to have power over them, making it hard for other trees to accept the truth the tree actually tells. The tree produces evil spirit fruit of deceit, hate, prejudice, pride, and self-destruction.

"The stump that has a branch with the green leaf growing out of it comes from a tree that has drunk from the living water. It will never thirst again. It spreads love to the other trees. It isn't perfect, and it understands it isn't perfect. The tree remains grateful, forgives the fault of other trees, and works to improve. It produces powerful fruit of the spirit, love, wisdom, peace, joy, patience, kindness, faithfulness, gentleness, and self-control. Each fruit grows at a different pace on each tree that has drunk from the living water because each tree has its own purpose."

John scratched the back of his head as he continued to look at the stumps. "I don't understand all of it, but are you saying I can only be one of these trees?"

"You've already chosen what tree you want to be, but there is enough time for you to change. Be honest with yourself to see what kind of stump you would produce. The truth can be painful, but it will set you free."

John scoffed. "I can't forgive those that have caused my family and my people so much pain. They go unpunished and free. What do we have left to us but poor dirt?"

"When I was a child, I spake as a child, I understood as a child, I thought as a child: but when I became a man, I put away childish things. Open your heart to be the man you desperately want to be, John."

John bit his lip as he squeezed his hand into a fist. Suddenly, John awoke from the dream, taking deep breaths and looking over at David. John looked over to Michael and Samuel, seeing both of them sleeping deeply. A tear of anger went down John's face.

"Why ask me to forgive?" John whispered. "The white people deserve no such thing for what they did to my people."

John spent the rest of the night tossing and turning while he gripped his sheets.

CHAPTER 5
No More Chains

THE MORNING SUNRAYS WERE STRONG the next day. Annabelle and Grace ate breakfast together, but Annabelle barely had an appetite.

"Well, today might be a hard day for you, Annabelle," Grace said. "Remember, no matter what happens, God has control."

Annabelle nodded at Grace, accepting the other woman's attempt to keep her hopeful. However, she thought, *Leaving it to God is what scares me. Haven't I been through enough?*

The women left the house. Grace wore her hair styled into two buns while Annabelle made sure her coarse, curly hair was nicely brushed. The warm summer breeze of September was eerily calming as they went to the larger house and waited for John to come outside. Grace tapped her foot.

John eventually exited, wearing a black frock coat, a white high-collared shirt with a blue cravat, a green vest, and black trousers. In his right hand, he held a walking cane. Annabelle's eyes widened when she saw John's handsome appearance. She almost forgot why she was standing there.

"Well, it took you long enough," Grace bickered. "I guess it has been a long time since you dressed like that." Grace giggled as John huffed and approached the women.

Annabelle gave a half-smile. "You do look nice, John."

"Thank you, Annabelle," John said. "At least someone can take me seriously sometimes."

Grace smirked at her brother and mumbled, "Someone still doesn't like being teased." Louder, she said, "Well, it's time for us to go."

The three traveled to the courthouse, all anxious.

Grace kept reciting to herself, "Do not show anger and be polite."

John mumbled any questions the council might ask so he could be ready to give an answer. Annabelle felt sweat running down her back and struggled to push out any negative thoughts. They arrived at the courthouse, staring at the large brick building while other townspeople went past them.

"I was hoping Elder Joyce would be here by now," Grace commented.

"Maybe she is still on her way," John said.

"Either way," Grace replied, "we need to go inside while all of the council is here. John, go inside and see if she is there. If she isn't, we wait for a while."

John went inside and greeted those in the courthouse, but Joyce was not present. The two waited outside for Joyce, but noon was soon approaching. Grace paced around while Annabelle feared Joyce might have changed her mind. John opened the courthouse door and stood in the doorway, signaling Annabelle and Grace. Grace entered the courthouse first, then John and Annabelle fell into step behind her.

An olive-toned woman with ringlets stood at a counter, organizing papers. "Grace, how are you doing?" the woman asked.

"I'm doing well, Jane," Grace replied. "John and I are actually here to show an important document to the council. I've decided to free my slave."

Jane's mouth slightly dropped. "I can give the affidavit to the council announcing you're giving her freedom," Jane said. "Do you have her slave records?"

"Yes, I do. John was with me when I bought her."

"I will go and let them know. There's nothing else going on today, so you'll be heard in a few minutes."

Jane went into the council's room with the fake slave records for Annabelle. Several minutes went by as Grace rubbed Annabelle's shoulder in reassurance.

Jane eventually came out and held the door open. "They are ready for you."

Annabelle, Grace, and John entered the council room. All four men sat at their desks.

"Good morning, Grace. Please come forward," Mr. Gross said. He seemed imposing in his red turban and vest, which held a golden pocket watch that covered his high-collared white shirt and red cravat.

Grace walked forward as all the men looked at her, their faces solemn. They all had their black frock coats resting on their chairs and dressed much alike in their usual vests, high-collared shirts, and cravats.

"Good morning, Mr. Gross," Grace said.

"I must say it is surprising to see you here, Grace. It is rare we have a case like this appear. This is also worrying for us. You spoke to me about owning a slave, and I gave you advice. You seemed to listen well and were willing to take on a newer way of life, but now, literally after two days of owning a slave, you're setting her free."

"Yes, Mr. Gross, that's my legal plan today. I know it is surprising to you and the others, but I think it is the right thing to do in this case."

"In what way do you see this as the right thing to do?" a councilman asked.

Grace answered, "Mr. Whitetail, I believe her to be too smart and respectful for me to even look at her as a slave anymore. She has given me no trouble and has shown great respect to my family."

Mr. Whitetail sat forward with folded hands, listening to Grace's answer.

"This is dangerous behavior. As an intelligent Cherokee

woman, you're doing something foolish," said another councilman. "I don't think your mother would've done a thing like this so randomly."

"I haven't done this randomly," Grace replied. "I mean what I say, and I believe a woman of this level deserves her freedom. I bought her with my money, and my mother has nothing to do with this."

"I believe if you truly think she deserves her freedom, where should she go?" Mr. Gross asked.

"She is welcomed to still stay at my house with me. I see nothing wrong with it," Grace answered. "If she chooses to move further north, I will give her what she needs to make it."

"Nothing wrong with it!" a councilman shouted. "If you're thinking of giving her land, you've overstepped our laws, Grace."

Grace held up a hand. "I have no plans of giving her anything, Mr. Ridge. If anything was to happen to me, my family would be the ones to get my things."

"I still see the bitter young girl that lost her father shortly after her mother," the other councilman said.

Grace's eyes narrowed. "Why do you continuously treat me like a child, Mr. Smith? I have come here for your approval! I could have freed her—let her go into the wilderness and said nothing."

"I think the only reason you haven't done such a thing is because of the Chickasaw," Mr. Whitetail said. "You've always been a clever girl. I think your feelings are too heavily involved in this."

"I agree. I hate to say this, but I think you were unfit to be a slave owner from the beginning," Mr. Gross said. "I'm assuming that you also bought her alone from this white man, Laurence Mays."

"That isn't true," Grace replied. "John was with me when I bought her."

Mr. Gross lifted his head from reading the slave records and looked at John. "John, please come forward. You've been quiet. I want to hear what you have to say."

"My sister is strong-hearted," John said. "She does have a hard time letting me and our uncle lead our family. I see a lot of our mother in her. She is her own person. She felt strongly about this choice to free Annabelle. I have no reason to go against her because all she has spoken is true. I was there when she bought Annabelle from the white man, so I ask you to take her plea respectfully."

Mr. Gross sat back in his chair, rubbing his forehead. "I still see no good enough reason for you to give her manumission," Mr. Ridge said. "I see this as putting another burden on our people."

"I agree with Mr. Ridge," Mr. Whitetail said. "You could give her to someone else who is more fitted to be a slave owner. Why not give her to Mr. Gross? We all know he treats his slaves fairly."

"I could take her in, Grace," Mr. Gross said. "I even have two young slave men. I'm sure she would hold their attention. At least let this be the solution so this doesn't encourage other slave owners to do the same. We have enough free Negroes out here. Stability is what our people need right now."

"No!" Grace boldly said. "I don't accept the offer. I'm sorry, Mr. Gross. I'm keeping my word to Annabelle in these poor times. She is skilled enough to help me and my family in our supply store, and I believe that's best for her. Besides, the affidavit given to you already shows that as of now, I declare her free."

Mr. Whitetail sat forward in his chair, scowling. "She won't be welcomed well among our people," Mr. Whitetail said. "She will be nothing but another mouth for your family to feed, and there are few free Negro men to place her with. I see this as a waste of time."

"I agree with Mr. Whitetail," Mr. Ridge said. "Such a decision will continue to send the wrong message to the people. I would have strongly recommended that Annabelle be held as a slave for another year, then maybe you should have considered such a serious decision."

Grace clenched her hand into a fist as her eyes shimmered with tears. "I came here hoping to show Annabelle she is welcomed here and to have your support!"

John placed his hand on his sister's shoulder, reassuring her.

The council room's door opened. In the doorway stood Joyce. Everyone went silent due to the abrupt appearance of the authoritative old woman.

"Elder Joyce, you made it," John said.

"I apologize for being late," Joyce said. "We have no laws that could stop you from freeing Annabelle, but I did need to pray for guidance on your choice, Grace."

"Elder Joyce, it's a surprise to see you," Mr. Gross said.

"I suppose it would surprise you for me to suddenly come," Joyce replied, "but this child wanted me to come here to show my approval. She has it."

The men looked at Joyce with scowling faces.

"Well, this was a waste of time," Mr. Ridge said.

"This was not a waste of time, Harry," Joyce snarled. "What a shame. This child made the effort to look for your approval when she could have freed Annabelle without saying a word to any of you. All four of you should be ashamed."

"I've heard enough of this! All of you are free to go!" Mr. Smith shouted.

"Don't get bold against me, little boy!" Joyce shouted. "I wiped your grandma's hind end, your momma's hind end, and your hind end too. So keep your mouth shut, blue eyes, and you need some sun to get some color back in that pale skin."

Mr. Smith sat back, avoiding eye contact with Joyce while the others said nothing.

"As for the rest of you, shame on you for not seeing that Grace really looked for your acceptance of her decision," Joyce continued. "Maybe this is the end of our people. We've accepted so much of the white man's way that only two of you sitting there can speak Cherokee easily."

All the men now avoided eye contact with Joyce as they took deep breaths.

"Well, now that this matter is over, we're leaving," Joyce said.

Grace and John walked to the door as Annabelle followed them.

Joyce reached for the door and turned. "You boys better behave yourselves, or I'll have a word with John Ross myself."

The men watched Joyce leave the council room, seemingly exhausted from the brief confrontation.

"Thank you so much for coming to support us, Elder Joyce," Grace said.

"It was my pleasure, child. Now, I want you and Annabelle to come to my cabin. We have more to talk about. John, I'm sure your uncle will be looking for you to help in the fields. You should go home now."

John replied, "Yeah, I'm sure he will be looking for me soon. Annabelle, this is your first day as a free woman. I'm sure you'll never forget this day."

Annabelle grinned at him. "Yes, it is, and it feels great."

John left, and the women went the opposite way to Joyce's home. The feeling of freedom was surreal for Annabelle while she strolled down the dirt road of Tahlequah with the other two women. Grace had a big smile as they walked, but the left side of Joyce's mouth curved downward, and her lips were clamped tightly shut. The women arrived at Elder Joyce's home and sat down at the old oak table.

"My goodness, Grace. I was hoping you would change your mind and free Annabelle without going through any pain," Joyce said. "I guess the next step is telling George what you have decided. It will certainly upset him that he has no power over your choice."

"I've been preparing for what he may say or how he might behave," Grace replied. "Still, I don't know how badly he'll act when I tell him at supper. Lizzie, I'm sure, will have something bad to say, but all of that is an act."

"What is the matter with that child? She has never been one to hide her feelings before, but it sounds like something happened to her."

"She told Jacob she liked him and wanted to know how he felt. He told her he only has feelings for her as a friend, and he didn't want to change it. She's been bitter ever since, having a strong attitude against anyone with Negro blood."

"Then you need to send her to me. Lizzie needs to know how to let go and how to love people that don't feel the same. The world does not give us everything we want. Now, young Annabelle, it is time you start to learn how to be Cherokee."

"I'm willing to learn," Annabelle said.

Joyce nodded. "There's something you need to do first before I teach you what you need to know to truly learn."

A slight crease appeared between Annabelle's brows, in sync with one of her eyebrows lifting. "What do you mean?"

"I saw it yesterday, baby. You are hurting. You are holding onto so much pain, it's killing you, and you know it."

Annabelle frowned, avoiding eye contact with Joyce.

"Annabelle, you've done so good so far, but you need to forgive them," Joyce said. "Will you let an old woman pray for you to help you heal?"

Annabelle looked up at Joyce and Grace, emotionless. "I don't want no prayer. I'm not sure what I want now. I'm grateful to y'all, but I don't want no prayer. That's not going to give my daughter or Benjamin back to me." Annabelle sighed as she tilted her head. "I can forgive that evil man, but right now, I don't know how."

Grace looked from Annabelle to Joyce. "Forgiving him won't kill the memories or love you have for them. Instead, it will set you free to move on and heal."

Annabelle slapped her hand on the table. "I don't want to heal! I want nothing to do with God right now!" Annabelle's eyes flooded with tears. "He failed me! He failed my family!"

Joyce frowned. "Calm yourself, dear. I understand your pain, and so does Grace."

Annabelle shook her head. "I'm sorry, but what do you know about my feelings? I watched them both die in front of me, and I couldn't even say goodbye to the people that tried to save me. And I'm tired of hearing I'm pretty for a Negro. Why can't I just be told I'm pretty?" She broke down in tears, her body trembling.

"There's a lot you need to learn about my people. The suffering we've gone through has changed us. We've lost thousands." Joyce stood up and went to the other side of the table, and she sat down next to a sobbing Annabelle. "It is good to grieve, but it poisons you to hold onto the hate."

Annabelle stopped sobbing as Joyce rubbed her back.

"Nunna daul Tsuny, or the trail where they cried, is what will forever be known as the journey that nearly killed my people," Joyce explained. "Gold was discovered in Georgia by white men. Andrew Jackson, that evil man, did everything in his power to hurt my people and every single Indian. The white people got guns and came to our homes with no real warning, pointed those guns at our faces, and forced us from our homes. Several of my people were killed as soon as they opened their doors. The rest of us were taken to prisons to suffer. It was cold, they gave us almost no food, and many became sick and died. We couldn't even bury our dead."

Joyce took a deep breath. "The white men burned down our homes and properties. My home—the house I was born in—was burned to the ground. I was reminded we were still seen as the lesser of the Creator's children. We started in Red Clay, Tennessee and continued on from there through the winter of 1838. I lost three of my children coming here, and I lost two of my grandchildren to sickness once we settled here. Grace lost her grandparents, her cousin, and her mother to sickness shortly after we settled here. The forced removal happened over years."

Annabelle looked at an emotionless Grace and thought, *She was a child when this happened.*

Joyce huffed. "Sarah became sick in Missouri. She got a coughing sickness and never recovered from it. It was the fault of several fools, including Major Ridge, his foolish son, John, Elias Boudinot, and Stand Watie, who signed a treaty. Those men signed that treaty when most of us didn't agree to it. The government used it against us to force us here. I was angry at the Creator for allowing such horror to happen. I didn't understand it, and there are still some questions. So much pain, but we still remained for a purpose.

"During that terrible winter, a soldier broke my wrist by hitting it with a rifle when I held my dead daughter. I wanted to die right there and move on to the next world with my daughter, but the others needed me. I didn't get movement back into my wrist until six months later. It was unfair in every way, and these people called themselves Christians. There was a time when I cursed them. I hoped they would suffer as my people did, but I felt the Creator speak to me so strongly to love and forgive them for what they did. It took me a while, but I did it. But forgiving also doesn't mean forgetting.

"Much has changed. There was a time when the women stayed with their birth families, and the men left their families to live with their wife's family. It was how we did things then, but now it's mixed. When John married Camille, John should have gone with Camille's family, but only three of her family members lived at the time. David is now almost the last of them. Camille almost lost all of her family coming here, and I raised her for four years before giving her to her Auntie, who became old enough to raise her. Our world is broken, and that's why bad things happen to good people."

Joyce folded her hands on the table. "People that love the Father and their families... It's hard to see them suffer, but fifty years ago, I accepted Jesus. A young woman named Olivia, who was very different than the missionaries, would speak with me and helped me learn English. I wanted to read the scriptures for myself. She was willing to let me. One day, I felt the Father speak to me, and the experience touched my spirit. I learned this was the right path to follow and to help others see the truth.

"There are always different views on the truth, but the truth can't be changed. People either accept the whole truth, or they live in rebellion of it, prideful. Don't fall into that path. It leads to loneliness and death. I've survived the smallpox when I was young, and I remembered the fear of being turned into a slave myself. Before they brought over the Negroes, the white men went after Indians. Even now, my people have kin in the South with chains on them. How can we get them back? I don't have an answer. We've made the mistake of forgetting that not too long ago, it was common practice to enslave us.

"The Shawnee once attacked us and sold some of my people as slaves, and we were never able to trust the Creeks. I've fought in several battles and a major one against the Creeks, and I fought in that Revolutionary War the white people are so proud of. I was a war woman but a mother before anything else. I have seen 123 harvest seasons. It seems I'm meant to continue to live on to remind the people where we came from. I've seen a lot of sad things over these many years, but many great things that stand above it."

Annabelle's eyes widened, and her head lowered in thought. *Only in the Bible have I read of people living such long lives.*

Joyce could see the surprise in Annabelle's attentive brown eyes. "I was born into our Deer Clan in 1724 around this time of the year." Joyce chuckled. "Those prideful white people have no idea and refused to accept the truth of when I was born. The census they took of me shows me at ninety-five years old. It's nice. I imagine looking a hundred years old or older in most people's minds isn't a good thing." Joyce placed her hand on Annabelle's shoulder. "If you don't want prayer, that's fine, but remember it's impossible to love again with hate in your heart, and lust can never replace love. Your old master was a lustful, power-driven man. I'm sorry you experienced it, but now it's time to move on."

Annabelle's eyebrows lowered. "What do you mean?"

"It's one thing when people hurt you, but it's another when people hurt the people you love. That creates a different feeling of pain, and you need to take control before it takes control of you."

Annabelle sat back in the chair in deep thought, not wanting to turn into someone the people she loved wouldn't recognize.

"You can't control life, Annabelle, but you can control how you respond to it."

Annabelle pouted. "It's not fair. None of it is fair."

Joyce nodded. "This life was never promised to be fair. We can only attempt to live and love each other in this harsh world. Well, I think that is enough for now. You can come by now when you're not working at the supply store. I will teach you our language, and you can practice it with the girls. Grace is a member of the Wolf Clan. They're protectors and good at it."

"Thank you, Elder Joyce, for putting time into us," Grace said.

Joyce reached across the table and placed her hand on top of Grace's hand reassuringly. "This is what I'm here for, baby," Joyce said.

"Thank you, Elder Joyce. I have a lot to think about," Annabelle said.

"Focus on one thing at a time, baby. You will make it through this test."

Grace stood up and moved around the table to give Joyce a hug, and Annabelle did the same. The young women exited the welcoming log cabin and stepped into the sunlight as its rays blazed down on Oklahoma.

"I feel so tired," Annabelle said.

Grace giggled, saying, "Yes, she can do that to you, but did you understand it?"

"Yes, I understood it. I wish it was easy to do what I need to do. So, you're from the Wolf Clan? What is that?"

"We have seven different clans in our tribe. A clan is a family group of the tribe, and we see each other as brothers and sisters in a way, so things like marriage between two people of the same clan are seen as disgusting. That would be like me marrying John. As the Wolf Clan, we are known as the protectors of the tribe. We're the largest clan."

"So, is it just you and John or the whole family?"

"Well, no, you belong to the clan of your mother. My Uncle George isn't from the Wolf Clan. He is from the Paint Clan. He married my Auntie Shay, who was my momma's sister. All of us in the family but Uncle George and David are members of the Wolf Clan. David belongs to the Panther, also called the Blue Clan."

Annabelle was intrigued by the family structure of the Cherokee. The women arrived at the supply store and walked into an overzealous Lisa and smiling Tsula.

"She's free!" Lisa shouted.

The strong welcome forced a smile out of Annabelle. The sisters gave Annabelle a hug when they walked her behind the counter and hounded her with questions.

———◆———

"How does it feel to be free?" Tsula asked. "Did Elder Joyce show up?"

"What did the council say?" Lisa asked. "You look tired. Are you tired?"

"She can't be tired. It's the afternoon," Tsula barked.

Lisa pouted. "She can be tired now. Who you to say she can't?"

"Girls!" Grace shouted. "I'll explain it all. Give her some space."

Grace explained the whole situation to Tsula and Lisa. Though they were saddened by the council's opinion, it brought them great joy that Annabelle was now free. The women continued to work until it was time to close the supply store. As they went home, Tsula walked next to Grace as Annabelle and Lisa talked to each other.

"How do you plan to tell my papa what you did?" Tsula asked.

"I'm going to tell him before we have supper," Grace replied.

Tsula cocked her head back as her mouth curved downward. "Why would you pick supper time to tell him? His temper will ruin the food. You could wait until we finish our supper."

Grace grunted. "I want Annabelle to join us for supper. I don't want her eating alone anymore. It will help her heal being around all of us."

Tsula rolled her eyes. "You have a gift for making storms, Grace, but I guess that's what we need. Papa will be mad once he hears what you've done. Don't say anything until we finish cooking all the food."

"Why is that?"

"So the rest of us can sit down and eat while he yells at you. It'll be the fun of the night." Tsula laughed while Grace struggled to hold back a smile.

"What's so funny?" Lisa asked.

"Nothing, I was making fun of Grace," Tsula said.

The women arrived at home, greeted by David. He ran to the young women while Lizzie watched with her arms crossed.

"Well, I'll wait for the lightning of this storm to hit," Lizzie said.

"What do you mean by that?" Grace asked when she approached Lizzie.

"The look of joy on the Negro's face as y'all walked to the house tells me all I need to know. You kept your word, and now she's free. Allow me to applaud your rebellion, sister." Lizzie clapped her hands sarcastically as Tsula, Annabelle, Grace, and Lisa watched.

"Look here, Lizzie. Don't start more trouble than we need," Grace snarled.

Lizzie shrugged and grinned. "I have no real fight in this.

I could care less about the choice you made. All of this was started by John anyway. Soon she'll find out she could never be one of us," Lizzie said in Cherokee."

"You take your anger somewhere else," Lisa replied in the Cherokee language, "if you're going to stay that way. You've done nothing but be mean. She's lost everything like we did."

Lizzie responded in their native tongue. "I doubt she's suffered as much. We owe her nothing, and I want nothing to do with her. You're forcing her into our family."

Still speaking Cherokee, Tsula said, "She has lost a child. She must understand what real pain feels like. Even if she didn't, how can we call ourselves Cherokee by not helping her? Drop your guard and go inside. It's time for us to cook supper."

Lizzie stomped her foot, grunted while she turned around, and entered the log cabin. Grace smacked her lips and pouted as she watched Lizzie go inside the house.

"Don't worry about her, Annabelle," Lisa said. "She has some anger to let go, but no worry."

"Alright, that mess is over, and the men are still working, so let's cook supper," Grace said.

Tsula playfully picked up David and entered the house with Lisa. Annabelle and Grace followed while Grace reassuringly patted Annabelle on her shoulder. The women cooked supper as Lizzie aggressively stirred the chicken stew. Grace hummed a tune to weaken the tension.

The men arrived from the fields, exhausted and hungry. The smell of the food lightened their mood. They sat down at the large wooden table.

"That supper smells good, girls," George said.

"Thank you, Papa!" Lisa yelled.

Samuel entered the kitchen, watching the women arrange the food while Lizzie watched the chicken stew on the old stove. "So, did you continue with the plan, Grace?" Samuel asked.

Grace replied, "I did, and she is now a free woman."

"That's why you have Lizzie making chicken stew? You know my papa is going to be so mad." Samuel picked up a spoon as he approached the stove. "Let me get some first before you tell him what you did."

As he anxiously lifted up the spoon, Lizzie gave him an irritable glare. Grace smacked Samuel's hand, and he pulled his hand back, rubbing the pain away.

"Go take a seat before I make sure you get served last," Grace told him.

Samuel shook his head as he continued to hold his hand. "You're pure evil. How can anyone swing that fast and be mean?"

The other women laughed as Grace smirked. "Little boy, go take a seat before it's my foot that does the swinging next."

Samuel backed out of the kitchen, making sure he faced Grace the entire time.

Later, the women brought out the food. Uncle George, John, Michael, and Samuel were sitting down at the supper table, anxious for the meal. George wore a red cravat that he adjusted anxiously as the food was placed on the table.

"Mmm-mm. Mmm-mm. My favorite meal, chicken stew," George said.

"I'm sure you will enjoy it, Papa," Tsula said.

"I know I will. My girls made it, and this good food is calling my name. Well now, girls, take a seat so we can bless this good food."

Tsula picked up David and tickled him. The toddler giggled.

"Uncle George, before we eat, there is something you need to know," Grace said. "I'm actually excited about it, and I know it will be good for the family."

George replied, "Well, come out and say it, Grace. Me and the boys need to fill our bellies." George cackled.

John and Samuel looked at Grace with big eyes as Uncle George continued to chuckle.

"Okay, Uncle George. Wait a moment, please." Grace quickly walked out of the log cabin and brought Annabelle in behind her.

Annabelle's hands felt clammy to Grace as the woman stared at the men sitting down at the table.

"Why did you bring in the Negro?" George asked as he put his elbow on the table.

The women watched quietly as Grace grinned. "Uncle George, I decided to free Annabelle today. I've written an affidavit acknowledging my release of her from slavery."

George slammed his hand on the table. "What the hell is this, Grace! You couldn't hold a slave for more than two days? I don't think your momma would have done something so crazy."

"We have no laws limiting manumission, and I see it fit to free her."

Uncle George slammed his hand on the old table again. "How dare you make such a selfish decision! You ignore my words and then to add to this disappointment, you free this Negro? Where's she going to go now? What could she possibly do?"

Grace raised her voice, "I have offered her a choice to stay here or go on her own. She has chosen to stay here with us, and she can continue sleeping in the other log cabin with me."

"The nigger can't stay here."

Grace frowned when she stared back at her uncle.

"Take her somewhere into the wilderness and tell her to run and don't come back," the older man continued. "You hear that, nigger? Run away and don't come back here."

"She isn't going anywhere," John boldly said. "Look at her. She is a kind-hearted woman that has gone through enough. How can we send her away with nothing? That makes us no better than the white men that forced us here to suffer."

Samuel replied, "Papa, I agree with John, and I think momma would've—"

"Shut up, Samuel," George yelled. "I cannot believe what I'm hearing in our home. Tsula, Lisa, are you also a part of this foolishness?"

"Me and Lisa agree with Grace, Papa," Tsula said.

"Lizzie!" George screamed. "I guess you agree with this too."

Lizzie stared back at her uncle and said nothing. Michael sat down quietly, trying to avoid eye contact with his father.

"She isn't welcomed here," George said. "No, not in my home. She isn't welcomed here."

Grace replied, "You treat Annabelle like she's done evil against you, Uncle. Your vision is blind, and you're showing the problem with our people. We're fools to hold ourselves higher when we couldn't even fight to keep our original home. This is our home too. We helped build it up from the ground as children. Annabelle will eat alone no more."

Uncle George's face turned red. He stood and pushed the pot of chicken stew on the floor. Annabelle jumped seeing the sight, and David cried, forcing Tsula to calm him down.

"Well, I guess none of us is getting our way today," George said.

Grace looked at Lizzie, gesturing to her. Lizzie stood up, went into the kitchen, and brought out a bigger pot of chicken stew, placing it on the other side of the table.

George's mouth dropped open, and he sat down.

Grace escorted Annabelle around the supper table while George angrily watched. She had Annabelle sit on the opposite side of the table adjacent to George. Lisa served plates as Grace and Lizzie cleaned up the spilled stew. The silence at the table was only ended by the happiness of David while Tsula played with him.

Grace sat down next to Annabelle, and Lizzie sat across the table.

"I will bless the food this evening if that's okay, Uncle George," John said.

George grunted, giving approval.

John blessed the food, and the family ate their supper. The tension was still present as George kept scraping his bowl to get the stew. Tsula fed David as Lisa's cheerful spirit seemed to nullify the tense atmosphere. The women spoke to each other and laughed about their day.

Annabelle kept her head down at her plate and ate silently. She looked up and noticed John looking at her. John smiled and nodded at Annabelle, and she smiled back. As the family continued to eat, Uncle George abruptly stood up and marched to the bedrooms. The family watched silently to avoid any more drama for the rest of the night. Later, Annabelle and Grace said good night to everyone and walked to the smaller house. Annabelle entered the house behind Grace, emotionally exhausted.

The women sat down in the old rocking chairs, too exhausted to celebrate Annabelle's freedom.

"I never imagined how bad your people were treated by white men," Annabelle said. "I always thought it was my people. I'm sorry for being so blind."

"There's no reason for you to apologize," Grace said. "We were children when it happened. There was no way you would've known. These white people have done this for centuries. They keep us from talking with each other, and they lie to us saying one is better than the other."

"Elder Joyce is 123 years old? She looks like an old woman that's, like, sixty."

Grace laughed when she sat back in the old rocking chair. "She took care of my great-great-grandma when she was a child. When I was a child, it was hard to believe, but the older I got and hearing the stories she'd tell of how we used to be, it's scary how much a people can change in just one hundred years."

"What was that like leaving your home?" Annabelle asked.

Grace huffed. "It was scary. We didn't get a chance to get most of our family valuables. My mother begged a soldier to let her go to our home and get our things. We had two oxen and three horses. They placed us children in the wagon. We were forced to eat salt pork for so many days, we became sick of it. We were never big on pork. It would sometimes hurt our stomachs, so it was rare for my family to eat it. My papa got lucky a few times hunting while we traveled and brought back some turkey.

"The coughing sickness was common in the children. A lot of us died. I was twelve years old when I lost my cousin, William. He was my cousins' older brother. Lisa was ten, Tsula and Samuel were eight, and Michael was five. I remember when the coughing began. It was different than any cough I heard before. Sometimes, he would vomit after coughing so hard. He later died in my Auntie Shay's arms when we were in the wagon one day. John was close to William, and he never did take the death well. The truth is that John was never the same after.

"William was an older brother to us. I still remember his laugh. John grew a lot of hate for white people, and our mother's death added to it. I was once that way too, but I listened to my momma, who tried hard to heal our hearts while she was sick. We would have to sit with cloth over our face to protect us from the sickness, and this is where she passed. My father wanted to burn this place to the ground. He almost did one day when he was drunk."

Annabelle sat back in the rocking chair, now understanding the trauma the family had experienced. The flashbacks of comforting John when he continuously came to Mr. Boston's store ran through Annabelle's mind.

She thought, *So much death to have gone through at such young ages. How did they turn out to be so kind?*

Grace could see the sadness in Annabelle's eyes. "You were right when you said it isn't fair. But when I look at what the Father has left me with, I have to be grateful. I still have my family, even if losing my mother was the worst feeling. It prepared me to deal with my Auntie Shay's passing and Camille's."

Annabelle gave Grace a worrisome look. "I hope I never go through pain like this again."

Grace scratched her neck. "So do I, but if you do, will you stay mad at the Creator or look for the blessings to make up for the unfairness of this world? I think we both have had enough drama today to fill us for the month."

"I agree."

The women stood up, walked to the bedrooms, and said good night to each other before going into their separate rooms.

Annabelle lay down in the bed and cried uncontrollably. "I'm free. Thank you, Jesus, I'm free." Annabelle continued to cry as she held herself. "God, please show me what to do here. There must be some reason why I'm here."

CHAPTER 6
Bitterness

T HE NEXT MORNING, ANNABELLE AND Grace arrived at the supply store to open it. Lisa entered the store with a big grin on her face, and Annabelle's eyes widened when she saw an agitated Lizzie following her.

Lizzie wore her signature white bonnet, and Lisa's hair was styled into twin buns. Lizzie had styled her hair into a single long braid.

"Well, isn't this a great morning," Lizzie said, her voice dripping with sarcasm.

"There will be none of that today," Grace replied. "Tsula is at home watching David for a good reason, and you won't mess this up."

Lizzie glared at Grace with her narrowed almond-shaped eyes as she approached the counter.

Annabelle avoided eye contact with Lizzie.

"I go with Annabelle today and help her in the fields," Lisa said.

"Good, go with the Negro. Save me the pain of having to look at her," Lizzie bickered.

Grace slapped Lizzie, and Annabelle's eyes widened while she let out a weak gasp. Lizzie held her cheek as she locked eyes with her sister. She took a deep breath while Grace watched, then pulled out money from a small sack to count it.

Lisa tugged Annabelle's hand to follow her to the chicken coops, and they went outside to release the chickens.

"Lizzie would stab me if she had the chance," Annabelle said.

"Don't say that," Lisa replied. "Lizzie better now, so no worries."

Annabelle didn't feel reassured, but she could tell Lisa meant what she said. The two young women fed the chickens and searched the small soybean field. The day continued with the young women getting eggs for customers, and in a few cases, butchering chickens. Later on, an exhausted Annabelle and Lisa walked back into the store carrying two sacks of soybeans.

"Good, it looks we are having a great harvest this year," Grace said.

"Chickens in chicken coops for the rest of the day," Lisa said.

"Well," Lizzie said, "that was the easy work compared to what we've been doing in here. We had to deal with Mrs. Hayes today because she can never make up her mind. She's stubborn and refuses to learn how to count money."

Annabelle chuckled, and Lizzie's keen eyes locked on her. Grace noticed the slight disapproval Lizzie expressed, so she tapped Lizzie on her shoulder and placed a broom in front of her.

⸺⸺◆⸺⸺

"You will sweep the store today when we close," Grace said.

Lizzie scowled. "I don't want to sweep the store today."

Grace walked to the storage room, and Lizzie followed her.

"Why are you giving me that pain in the butt job?" Lizzie asked.

Grace turned around to respond, but an old woman with long gray hair entered the store. The peanut butter skin-toned smiling woman held a wooden cane, and the sun outlined her old body.

"Hello, young ladies," the old woman said in Cherokee.

Grace replied in the same language, "Mrs. Armstrong, how are you doing? I see you're wearing your green and yellow dress today."

"Yes, I'm wearing my favorite dress. I feel good today. I need three bags of flour put on the wagon. If you strong young women can do that for me, I would be so grateful."

"That's no problem. Annabelle, Lisa, and Lizzie can put the bags into your wagon."

"I know your whole family. Who is Annabelle?"

"The Negro," Lizzie uttered.

The old woman looked to her left and noticed Annabelle standing slightly behind Lisa. "She is a cute young thing."

Lizzie rolled her eyes when the old woman pointed her finger at Annabelle. "When did she start working here? I know I'm old, but my memory is strong."

"She started a few days ago. She is a free Negro," Lisa said, still speaking Cherokee. "She has been doing a good job here."

"Hello, Annabelle," Mrs. Armstrong said in Cherokee.

Annabelle seemed stunned by the cheerful nature of the old woman because her eyes widened, but she remained silent.

"Are you shy?" Mrs. Armstrong asked. "I know I'm not as good-looking as my younger self."

Grace replied in Cherokee, "Oh no, she isn't, Mrs. Armstrong. She doesn't speak Cherokee." "Today is actually her first day to start learning. She'll be going to Elder Joyce later today."

"Tell this beautiful young lady I look forward to her being able to speak our language."

Grace turned to Annabelle, beaming. "Mrs. Armstrong can only speak Cherokee, but wanted me to tell you she thinks you're a beautiful young lady and excited for you to learn Cherokee."

Annabelle smiled, replying, "Tell her I said thank you."

Grace spoke in Cherokee, "She said, 'Thank you.' "

Mrs. Armstrong replied, "Good, now I will pay for the flour." She strutted to the counter.

"Go put three bags of flour on her wagon. Each of you grab a bag," Grace said.

<hr>

Annabelle and Lisa walked toward the flour bags. Lizzie rolled her eyes and followed. Lisa and Annabelle went out of the store carrying the heavy bags, and Lizzie trailed behind them. Lisa could barely put the flour bag on the wagon, and Annabelle struggled with her flour bag, so Lisa helped her.

Lizzie moved forward to put the flour bag on the wagon, and out of kindness, Annabelle reached out to help her. Lizzie sighed while Annabelle tried to help, focusing on carrying the bag to the wagon. Being taller than Lizzie, Annabelle tried to adjust her hand on the heavy bag. Annabelle could feel her arms start to struggle and pressed harder on the brown bag. Her thumb abruptly tore into the bag. Annabelle's eyes enlarged as she heard the tear, and her thumb rapidly slid through the bag. Flour puffed onto Lizzie's face.

Lizzie choked on the fine powder, and Lisa laughed. Annabelle felt a chill go down her spine as she tried to stop the flour from coming out. Lizzie growled as she coughed out the flour and wiped it off her face and dress.

Lizzie shouted something in Cherokee that Annabelle didn't understand.

"She's not clumsy. Calm down. It was an accident," Lisa said, continuing to laugh. "You can't get mad about that. How could she have known?"

Annabelle backed slowly to the supply store's door.

Grace stepped outside. "What's going on?" she asked.

Grace turned to Lizzie, whose face was full of agitation as she cleaned flour off her dress and out of her hair. Lisa covered her mouth, struggling to control her laughter.

"It was my fault," Annabelle said. "My thumb went into the bag, and the flour spilled on Lizzie."

Grace could see her sister's hands slowly turning into fists. "It's okay. Go to Elder Joyce's home and come home in an hour. We'll fix this small problem."

"Okay, I'm leaving right now." Annabelle quickly left.

Lizzie stopped brushing off the flour and watched the other woman leave, her eyes burning with rage. Shrieking, she stomped. "Are you serious!"

Annabelle moved faster, realizing her fear was legit. She arrived at Joyce's house and was welcomed inside by the old woman. Annabelle tried to explain the accident to Joyce, but Joyce laughed at the situation. Joyce's laughter lightened Annabelle's spirit, though she still took Lizzie seriously.

"Well now, child, that has to be the funniest thing I have heard in a while," Joyce said. "I would've paid a hundred dollars to see that. Poor child. Lizzie has always been a fighter, but I will talk with her soon about her attitude. Grace told me ever since that young man hurt her, that anger grew."

"She definitely has no fear. It's confusing because she almost has a playful voice like Tsula, but it's higher pitched."

"Child, don't let her voice fool you."

"I won't. Why would she be angry with me? I don't understand."

"I'm not sure, but Lizzie has always had a strong presence. As a baby, I've never heard a child with such a strong voice. Girl could've broken glass if given the chance. Take her seriously, but don't worry about it too much. Wildcat has always got into little fights with the boys, especially after the children walked home from seminary. A lot of the girls were terrified of her when she got angry, but it didn't happen too much. Sarah used to beat that behind when she needed it. I couldn't imagine what Lizzie could've turned into if she'd never been disciplined."

Annabelle scoffed. "Lizzie sounds a little like someone I know."

"Well then, good. You should know how to stay away from her when she starts to lose control of that temper."

Annabelle nodded in agreement.

"Well, that story was so funny, I almost forgot you're here to learn to speak Cherokee, so let us begin."

Joyce worked with Annabelle for an hour, making it easy as she laughed at Annabelle's mispronunciations. Joyce's demeanor made her feel welcomed and almost made her forget about Lizzie. After she finished her lesson, she stood up to leave.

"Try going over the words with Grace to help you."

"I will. I'll see you tomorrow."

"Take care, sweet girl," Joyce said.

While Annabelle walked home, she felt the warmth coming off the sun. When she arrived at the house, Tsula and David were playing outside, and the toddler squealed with excitement. His excitement made Annabelle wonder if her own daughter would've sounded like that.

"Annabelle, how was your time with Elder Joyce?" Tsula asked.

Annabelle answered, "It was a good time. She is patient with me."

"Well, come inside. We need to make supper for the boys." Tsula picked up David, and Annabelle followed them into the house.

Grace, Lisa, and Lizzie were already busy getting supper ready when Tsula playfully pranced inside the house. "The most beautiful has arrived."

Grace smirked when Lisa and Lizzie each lifted an eyebrow and stared Tsula down with pressed lips.

"Oh, please," Lizzie said.

Lisa chuckled.

Grace immediately handed Annabelle a basket full of corn.

Tsula replied, "So jealous, Flour Face."

Lizzie scowled and continued to aggressively skin a chicken.

"All of these need to be shucked, so get started," Grace said.

"Well, okay. Where do you want me to do this?" Annabelle asked.

"Get it done on the supper table so there is enough room," Grace replied. "Lizzie, go help Annabelle."

Lizzie grunted as she put down the chicken.

Annabelle shucked the corn, but Lizzie viciously ripped off the husk. Annabelle could feel her throat tighten, but she was determined not to be intimidated. Tsula kept watch on David as Grace and Lisa finished other cooking tasks. David suddenly threw a ball, and it hit Annabelle. Annabelle stopped shucking the corn and giggled. She picked up the brown ball when an excited David ran to Annabelle.

"Well now, here is your ball, you beautiful little boy," Annabelle said.

Tsula watched, liking David's response to Annabelle. "Don't they look cute together," Tsula murmured.

Annabelle gave David the ball back, and David gave Annabelle a hug.

"Aw, you're a lovely little angel," Annabelle said.

David smiled and ran back to Tsula.

"Look here, Negro," Lizzie uttered. "It's bad enough I'm stuck here shucking this corn with you. Don't touch my nephew with your dirty hands."

Annabelle fixed her bold eyes onto Lizzie's fierce expression. "Look here, your sister, your brother, and your cousins welcome me! I don't need your liking. I've done nothing wrong to you, but you treat me almost as bad as the white people. I'd say the man that said no to you was smart not to want you." Annabelle put down the last corn cob. She glanced at Lizzie, whose eyes had dilated. "Here, you can shuck this last one since I have dirty hands." Annabelle then thought, *I don't know why her voice bothers me so much when she's mean. It's like being told what to do by a teenager.*

Annabelle stormed out of the house, taking a deep breath just as Lizzie followed behind her.

"Don't you ever speak to me like that!" the other woman yelled. "You don't know anything! This is the last time I tell you! Don't touch my nephew!"

Annabelle's defiance rose the moment her blazing eyes dilated, and they locked on Lizzie as the other girl continued to approach her. "If that sweet little boy wants a hug from me, I will gladly give it to him. He clearly knows how to treat people better than you."

Lizzie growled, ripped off her white bonnet, and stomped on it with her moccasin. Abruptly, she sprinted toward Annabelle. Her speed caught Annabelle off guard. Lizzie tackled Annabelle to the ground and slapped her.

"You smart-mouthed nigger. I'll break you!" Lizzie screamed.

Annabelle's dilated eyes widened when she felt Lizzie's strength. She kneed Lizzie in her stomach. Lizzie fell on her side. She jumped on top of Lizzie and smacked her as hard she could.

"Those white people see you as nothing but a savage, a grass nigger, a prairie nigger, but you call me a nigger!" Annabelle said, slapping Lizzie again. "You're the real slave!"

Lizzie slapped Annabelle off of her. Annabelle struggled to gather herself as Lizzie punched Annabelle in her right cheek. Annabelle collapsed. Lizzie quickly jumped on top of Annabelle and punched her again.

"You're nothing but a worthless, nappy-headed Jezebel! How about that!" Lizzie punched Annabelle again.

The force of Lizzie's punches dazed Annabelle. The second Lizzie was about to punch Annabelle again, Lisa appeared behind her and grabbed Lizzie's arm to push her off Annabelle.

"What is going on out here!" Grace yelled.

Annabelle's face began to swell as Lisa stood between Annabelle and Lizzie. She quickly helped up a dazed Annabelle.

"Look what you did to her," Grace said. "That's it. You tell the truth where all this anger is coming from." She placed her hands on Lizzie's cheeks. "What evil has taken over you?"

Lizzie stepped back and shrugged, saying, "I don't know. I'm so angry. I can't get Jacob out of my head and...then those two idiots bring her, endangering us!"

"That's not a good reason to give Annabelle such a hard

time. Are you jealous? Worried Annabelle is a threat?" Grace asked.

Lizzie huffed. "Jealous? Of what? She isn't the threat!" She punched the air. "The white folks that'll come looking for her are the threat! Why do you care so much?"

Grace sighed. "We should care, and I know you care. That's why you're trying so hard to get her to dislike you."

Lizzie shook her head. "I'm going to lose it if she brings us trouble."

Grace narrowed her eyes. "Look what you did to her, and now we have to hide her wounds. Hmm, she left a nice mark on your face too. Apologize to her."

Lizzie took a deep breath and looked at a now-scruffy Annabelle. "I'm sorry for not doing right by you," she mumbled.

Grace smacked the back of her head.

Lizzie glared at her sister and scoffed. "I'm sorry for not being fair to you. I'm a Christian woman. I should act more like it." She then grinned. "You have a nice swing, but you're not better than me. Remember that." Spitting on the ground, Lizzie stormed off as she wiped the dust off her. She picked up her white bonnet while an agitated Grace watched her arrogant sister enter the house.

"This won't happen again," Grace said. "Let's clean you up for supper."

Annabelle spat blood on the ground as she rubbed her cheek. "The inside of my mouth is bleeding," Annabelle said.

Grace grimaced when she looked inside Annabelle's mouth. "Well, it's not that bad. Let's get you cleaned up before supper."

Annabelle and Grace went to the house. Lisa followed and looked to her left.

"Flowers dead. Y'all killed my flowers," Lisa whined.

Grace looked back at a frustrated Lisa and giggled while she comforted Annabelle. "It'll be okay. The flowers will grow back," Grace said.

The women kept silent about the fight as Annabelle sat down at the supper table with her left cheek facing the men.

Annabelle and Lizzie continued to give each other dirty looks. While they ate their food, a grumpy Uncle George refused to acknowledge Annabelle. John noticed Lizzie staring down Annabelle at the table. After dinner, Annabelle and Grace soon left for the smaller house while the other women were about to get ready for bed.

Later in the evening, John knocked on his sisters' bedroom door and said, "Lizzie, come out for a little while."

Lizzie walked out in her white nightgown and put her hands on her hips. "What do you want? I'm tired."

"I saw how you looked at Annabelle today at supper. Please show her some kindness. You never had problems with Negroes. Why start now?"

"Don't worry about it. We've worked out our problems. I felt Grace gave her too much."

"She has nothing. We are it."

Lizzie took her hands off her hips and folded her arms. "I'll try to be nicer," she murmured, speaking in Cherokee. "Is that all, brother?"

John gave Lizzie a hug. "Yes, that's all," he responded in their native tongue.

John left, and Lizzie returned to her room, lit by a brightly burning lamp on a wooden desk. Tsula and Lisa looked at her.

"You know you're wrong for that," Lisa said, speaking Cherokee.

"Her dress was already dirty and then you made it worse," Tsula replied. "We were barely able to clean off her dress in time for supper. What would we have said to papa?"

Lizzie replied in Cherokee, "What's done is done. I have no more reason to fight her."

"Well, she gave you a nice hit to the face." Lizzie gave Tsula a skewed frown. "What if Jacob ends up liking her? Are you going to ruin their happiness with your rage?"

"Why would you bring him up? If he wants Annabelle, he

can have her. It's his loss if he wants her. It shows that some of these half-bloods don't have any loyalty to us Cherokee."

Lisa stared at her troubled cousin and sighed. "You know you're beautiful, don't you?"

"Yes, I know," Lizzie grumbled. "It's not that. I always thought it was going to be me and him, even though I know Uncle George would get angry. At least he's not a white man. We have enough of that going on."

"Well then, that's that. No more fighting," Tsula said in Cherokee. "Goodnight, ladies."

"Good night," Lisa and Lizzie said.

Lisa pulled up her wool blanket and smiled as she went to sleep next to Lizzie. Lizzie stared at the dark ceiling.

As Tsula and Lisa slept, Lizzie wept silently. "Jesus, please heal my heart so I can show that pain in my side Negro some kindness," Lizzie whispered. "Please heal my spirit. I hate the angry woman I am."

Lizzie soon fell asleep as the wolves howled into the night.

CHAPTER 7
Introductions to Wisdom

THE NEXT MORNING ARRIVED WITH clouds outlining the sun. Annabelle and Grace were about to go to the supply store when Annabelle saw a tall man with a light brown complexion wearing a white long-sleeved cotton shirt, brown trousers, and black shoes walking toward her and Grace.

"Good morning, Grace," the man said in Cherokee.

"Good morning, Jacob," Grace returned in the same language.

Jacob stopped in front of the women. Annabelle gazed at the smiling and handsome man with short wavy hair, a fit body, and brown almond-shaped eyes.

"I'm here to continue helping with the horses and your fields today, as agreed with my father. Who is this beautiful young lady?" he asked.

Grace playfully hit Jacob on the chest. "Behave yourself. She doesn't speak Cherokee, fool. It's a good thing too. I'm sure she'd give you a good smack on the face."

"No need to be aggressive. I get enough of that from Lizzie." Jacob turned to Annabelle. He looked into her eyes and said, "Good morning, Annabelle. I'm Jacob."

Annabelle was speechless while she gazed at Jacob. "Oh, yes, I'm Annabelle. It is nice to meet you. I have heard much about you."

Jacob laughed. "I hope only good things."

Annabelle smiled. "Yeah."

"So, who are you owned by?"

Grace slapped Jacob upside his head.

He grunted.

"She's free. Don't forget it," she snarled, crinkling her nose.

"Who are you owned by?" Annabelle asked as she folded her arms.

"I was never really a slave," Jacob answered. "My papa wrote papers to give me and my brother and sisters our freedom as a birthday gift when we turned three years old." When I was ten years old, he freed my momma for good, and we been a strong family from then on."

Annabelle's eyebrows slightly rose. "Who is your father?"

"Mr. Tate is my papa. We live—"

Annabelle's eyes bulged. "What! I met your father a few days ago when I was in the fields with Tsula. He's a nice man."

"Where are you from?"

Grace smacked Jacob upside his head again. "You ask too many questions when you're supposed to be working. Go on. I'm sure Lisa has most likely forgotten that she is supposed to help you this morning," Grace barked.

Jacob rubbed his head, and he walked toward the large log cabin. "You got too much strength for a woman. You and Lizzie," Jacob whined.

Graced noticed Annabelle wince and watched as her tongue ran over the inside of her busted right cheek.

◆

Annabelle and Grace strolled to the store, and Jacob knocked on the front door. Lizzie opened it, and Jacob and Lizzie's eyes met. Jacob couldn't take his eyes off her.

Lizzie scoffed, saying, "Mm-hmm. You're a brave man to show your face at my front door."

Jacob replied in Cherokee, "Lizzie, please stop making this

difficult. We've been friends our entire lives. I wouldn't change any of it."

Lizzie sighed and replied, "Lisa, come here so Jacob can work with these horses."

Lisa came to the door, smiling. "Good morning, Jacob!" she said, also speaking Cherokee. "Let's go get the horses ready. Papa said Big Boy was acting bad again."

"I think you're the only person those horses like all the time," he responded. "I need to pay more attention to you."

Lisa giggled as she left the house and moved toward the large green barn. Jacob's eyes followed her.

Lizzie smacked Jacob upside the back of his head. "I see you, Jacob Tate," she grumbled.

Jacob rubbed his head while Lizzie closed the door, and she gave Jacob an agitated look before she went away.

"Between Grace and Lizzie, I might lose my memory," Jacob murmured.

He went to the large green barn as Lisa waited for him patiently. Jacob and Lisa entered the barn. The horses neighed and nickered once they saw Lisa.

Lisa picked up a bucket filled with hay as she skipped toward Big Boy. "Now today, you'll behave, won't you," Lisa said in Cherokee.

The horse made a soft neighing sound as Jacob watched with a big smile.

"You amaze me with how you work with these great animals," Jacob said in Cherokee.

Lisa grinned. She fixed her eyes on Jacob and scratched the horse's mane. "All they want is to be loved and treated good, something we all want, I think."

"Yeah, I think you're right." Jacob slowly approached the large horse and petted him as he ate his hay.

Lisa and Jacob continued to work with the horses in preparation for the horses to work the field harder due to the harvest season.

George and John entered the barn from the fields. "Ah,

Jacob, it is always good to see you, my friend," John said, speaking in Cherokee.

Jacob and John shook hands. "It is good to see you too," Jacob replied.

"Well now, that's enough of that," George said in Cherokee. "The two of you act like you haven't seen each other in a year. It has only been two weeks, and I expect us to do this harvest quickly with all of us working the fields. Your father is a man of his word. I see he has managed to pass that down to you, Jacob. Don't lose that, boy. I promise life will be much harder if you do."

Jacob replied, "Yes, sir, Mr. Strongman. I won't."

***

Jacob and John directed the horses out to the farming equipment while Michael and Samuel waited.

As Jacob and John walked the horses to the fields, George walked toward his daughter. "You continue to keep your eyes on the half-blood," George said in Cherokee. "He has always been too comfortable around us."

"Papa, you need to be nicer to Jacob. He's been around us his whole life," Lisa said in Cherokee.

"That's the problem. I can't tell who is more to blame. Your auntie or your momma, God bless their spirits."

Lisa frowned, and she crossed her arms. "They loved Jacob and his family as they needed to be. Did you forget they momma died on the way here?"

George sneered at his daughter and walked away.

Lisa exited the barn and watched Jacob interact with her brothers and John. Seeing the young men interact with each other brought joy to her spirit. After comforting the horses some more, Lisa walked off to the supply store to join the others.

***

Annabelle continued her lessons that day with Joyce. She told

Joyce about the fight between her and Lizzie, showing Joyce the damage the other woman had done.

"My word, child. Well, telling you not to wake the sleeping bear is no good when the bear is waiting for you," Joyce said. "I'm glad you can take a hit. You need to be strong in this world, and you left her a mark too. Good, she wins too much. At least she'll show you some form of respect for fighting back. People like her have a low liking for cowards."

"I'm still a little scared of her," Annabelle said. "To be honest, I've never been hit that hard by a woman before. I guess I'm a coward in some way."

"Being afraid does not make you a coward. Not standing up for what you believe is what would make you a coward. You could've stayed in that dirt and took a beating. Instead, you fought back. Remember that the Father hath not given us the spirit of fear; but of power, and of love, and of a sound mind."

Annabelle grinned. "Thank you, Elder Joyce."

"Anytime. I think you'll fit in good here in Cherokee land. We need more fighters around here."

"Elder Joyce, why don't I see any of your family when I come over?"

Joyce chuckled. "Because I'm not a babysitter. I raised my children as my momma raised me. I expect them to do the same. They do come by every morning and bring the younger ones around. You know it helps keep my mind sharp having to know all those names, but I love it."

Annabelle giggled. "Thank you again. I'll see you tomorrow." She stood up and stretched while she went to the door.

"Before I forget, Annabelle, tell that angry wildcat to come see me in two days. She better not make me walk all the way over to y'all's home."

"You mean Lizzie?"

"Yes, the one that thinks with her fists instead of her smart mind. Don't let that anger of hers fool you. She was always a strong thinker at school and against other people. Does she still shuck corn like she's going to kill that too?"

"Yes, I've never seen someone shuck corn like Lizzie. Is it okay if I tell her tomorrow?" Annabelle asked with a hesitant tone.

"That's fine, Annabelle. I'll see you tomorrow."

Annabelle left the house and took a deep breath while she walked home. She thought, *I think Elder Joyce expects too much of me. She could get me killed.*

The day continued on as the ladies later prepared the supper, and Annabelle ate with them. George ignored her again when they ate.

———◆———

Two days passed, and Annabelle instead asked Lisa to tell Lizzie that Joyce wanted to speak with her. Lizzie reluctantly went to Joyce's log cabin. Arriving at the house, she stared at the old wooden door. She sighed while shaking her head and knocked on the door.

I'm too old for this. I'm grown. She can't demand for me to be here, she thought.

Lizzie grabbed her braid and started to redo the bottom of it as she waited.

The door creaked open, and Joyce looked down at Lizzie. "Child, remove the anger off that beautiful face right now," Joyce commanded in Cherokee.

Lizzie's mouth straightened out, she gulped, and her eyes widened as she looked up at Joyce. "I'm sorry, Elder Joyce," Lizzie replied in their language.

"I'm sure you are, Wildcat. Come on in here."

Lizzie walked inside the pine-scented house, forcing herself to keep a straight face as she let go of her long braid. "Did you want me to sit in one of the rocking chairs?"

"Yes, that's fine."

Lizzie sat down on an old brown rocking chair, and Joyce sat down in the other one.

"You have a lot to work on, Lizzie Lightning. I've seen the

damage you've caused Annabelle. Do you have anything to say?"

Lizzie took a deep breath, and her eyes fixed on the wooden floor. "I'm not proud of myself. She…didn't deserve it."

"Well, the ability to speak the truth is step one. What's going on with you, child? I know this isn't over spilled flour."

Lizzie shrugged. "I'm angry. I can't focus. I'm even having a hard time teaching David."

"I feel there's a deep root here. Are you having nightmares about your father again?"

Lizzie's grip tightened on the armrest of the rocking chair. "No." She curled her lip into her mouth while her head slowly shook. "The day I fought Annabelle, I cried when I tried to sleep. I hate crying."

"You're holding onto pain too strongly. It's poisoning you. It's not giving you strength."

"I'm trying to be positive, but I feel so…disappointed in Jacob. He can't even give me a real answer for why he won't try with me. I can feel it. There's something he's hiding, and then John brings Annabelle from Mercy."

"What's your problem with her?"

Lizzie's voice rose. "Nothing! It's not her. It's what will follow her!"

"Calm yourself."

"We have a stupid US Embassy here, and some of our people are slave owners. They're the embarrassment of our people's entire history. We're endangering ourselves."

"You don't know what's to come. Your brother and Samuel weren't followed here. Ever since your mother walked on, you've had a hard time connecting with others."

Water started to well up in Lizzie's eyes. "I don't want to talk about her."

"You care, and that makes it hard on you. The fear causes you to push Annabelle away, and the anger makes it worse. You must go against your feelings to be free."

The two women talked for another hour, and Joyce prayed

with Lizzie. After Joyce finished counseling her, Lizzie walked to the front door. Joyce slowly followed her. Lizzie opened the front door, and the sunlight outlined her body.

"Wildcat, don't you touch that girl."

Lizzie froze in place. "I won't. She—"

"I mean with those eyes and that face. Don't you put fear into her. Enough is enough."

"Yes, ma'am. I'll see you tomorrow."

Joyce smiled. "Yes, you will."

———◆———

One late September day, Lizzie returned to Joyce for more guidance.

"Lizzie, I see a younger version of your mother in you as I do Grace, but you still have so much anger," Joyce said in Cherokee. "You're a beautiful and gifted young woman. Don't feed that anger anymore. Let it all go, Wildcat."

"It's hard for me," Lizzie replied. "I feel alone in my feelings."

"I understand, and I see you have placed Jacob too high in your life. You must keep Jesus first so you can see clearly. Now, I don't know if you and Jacob are meant to be. I have seen things like this go both ways. But I can tell you this: A bitter person quickly becomes ugly."

"I will do my best to clean my spirit. I don't know why it hurts me more to think Jacob will end up with a Negro. I'm ashamed my mind follows that path."

"We talked deeply about this for two days not long ago, and I failed to ask. Do you think you're better than them?"

Lizzie sat back in an old rocking chair. "In some ways, I do think we're better. I think our blood is stronger, and I think the white men fear us more. We are not the children of slaves like they are."

Joyce sat back in her chair and nodded. "There's some truth that we have different blood than the Negroes, but neither is stronger than the other. We all have the same responsibility to take care of and respect the life that binds us. The Creator loves us no different than them, and He even went so far as to send Jesus to us when none of us deserved such mercy. When I was your age, we feared the white man's slavery. They saw no difference between us and the other tribes. Even now, some white men see no difference. Don't look down on the Negroes when our people once took in runaway slaves without question.

"If you go back far enough, our blood is the same. We're all children of Adam and Eve. This new generation of Negroes knows little to nothing of where their ancestors came from. It weakens them. If we were more careful in the old days, we could have taken in more of the Negroes like we should have and created better alliances with the other tribes. An alliance like that would have made the white people think twice about their evil ways."

Listening to the old woman's wisdom, Lizzie's gaze went downward. She pouted, gripping the rocking chair's armrest tighter.

"I'll try harder to think about my words before I speak."

"Good. Your words are powerful, but action is greater."

"I'll keep an eye out for her."

"Your biggest fight will be letting go of control and trusting in Jesus."

"Yes, ma'am."

"You'll always be your own greatest enemy, but trusting Jesus and understanding yourself will help you win."

The two women finished their conversation with Lizzie promising to return if she continued to have serious problems accepting Annabelle.

CHAPTER 8
Welcomed

TWO WEEKS PASSED WHILE ANNABELLE and Lizzie worked to keep peace in the household. John also noticed the calmness between the two women, giving him hope he had been able to give Annabelle what she deserved: freedom.

One day, when the women returned home from the supply store, Grace and Lisa whispered among themselves. Annabelle noticed as she walked alongside Lizzie. The whispering between the cousins intrigued Annabelle so much that she ignored the warm October breeze. Suddenly, a crow flew over the women while they approached their home.

Annabelle was surprised by the bird's anxious nature and thought, *It must've found a corncob left behind.*

Annabelle noticed the cousins were going to the smaller log cabin instead of the larger one. Lizzie followed as Annabelle slowed her pace.

"Come, Annabelle, you must see this!" Lisa said.

Annabelle followed the women inside the house when her eyes fixed on Tsula standing in front of the old fireplace and holding a red cotton dress.

"What is this?" Annabelle asked.

A smiling Lisa bolted toward Annabelle and grabbed her hand, pulling Annabelle toward Tsula. "Your dress!" Lisa squealed. "Our gift for you so you welcomed here."

Tsula grinned, and the corners of Annabelle's mouth lifted into a big smile.

"It's why I started to watch over David more," Tsula said. "We figured I would get this done faster being home and watching him instead of trying to do it all at night after work. Do you like? It is a little thicker than normal to prepare you for the winter."

Annabelle felt the thick cloth dress, her eyes widening. The kindness of Tsula reminded Annabelle of Marilyn. It made Annabelle slightly saddened as she struggled not to cry.

"Thank you so much, Tsula," Annabelle said. "I don't know what I could even do to show how thankful I am."

Tsula gave Annabelle a hug and handed Annabelle the dress. Lizzie looked away as tears built in her eyes.

The day went on as Annabelle beamed while eating supper with the others. George still mocked the acceptance the others showed Annabelle and ignored her. Annabelle saw Tsula regarding her father and his noticeably continuous efforts at avoiding conversation with Annabelle. Tsula opened her mouth to speak, but Grace signaled her to keep silent. Tsula bit her lip and did as requested.

The family finished their supper as George stood up and went to his chair to read the Cherokee Phoenix newspaper. Annabelle, Lisa, and Grace brought dishes to the kitchen. Tsula and Lizzie followed.

"You go home. Enjoy the dress," Lisa said.

"It's okay, Annabelle. There isn't much here," Tsula said. "Go try on the dress and let me know if anything needs to be changed."

"I don't know how to thank you, Tsula," Annabelle said. "It means so much to me that I don't have to wear this dress every day."

"No worries. Your happiness is a gift for me. Soon, I will be nineteen years old, and Samuel will follow me down that road."

Annabelle raised an eyebrow. "I don't mean to sound inappropriate."

All the young women abruptly fixed their eyes on Annabelle.

"But your parents must've been busy when they were younger," Annabelle continued.

The young women fell out laughing. The women were laughing so loud, John and Samuel couldn't help but go over and stare into the kitchen.

"You have a funny spirit, Annabelle. Samuel is my twin brother," Tsula said.

Grace gave Annabelle a hug, trying to control her laughter. "They should've told you. I think that's a signal for me and Annabelle to go," she said.

"I'm so sorry," Annabelle replied.

"Don't be sorry. I know it is hard to believe someone so childish is my twin," Samuel said. "I know you must've thought I was the older one."

Abruptly, Tsula grabbed a wooden spoon sitting on a table and marched toward her brother. Samuel backed out of the kitchen doorway and ran toward the front door. Tsula pushed John out of the way. Tsula watched her brother run toward the large green barn as she stood in the front doorway. Tsula marched back to the kitchen and placed the wooden spoon back on the table.

"Yeah, he still knows his place," Tsula said.

Grace and Lizzie snickered while Tsula continued to clean the dishes.

"I would've thought one of them would say something about being a twin earlier," Grace said.

"Well, I'm not one to brag about being a twin...being the better half," Tsula said.

Grace sighed. "Well, I believe that's enough. Goodnight, ladies."

Grace moved past John, and Annabelle followed, but before they walked to the front door, Annabelle glanced at John.

"Goodnight, Annabelle. I'm glad things are working good for you," John said.

Annabelle smirked and shrugged. "I have you and Samuel to thank."

John smiled as Annabelle went toward the front door while Grace held it, and the two young women strolled toward the small house. John watched them converse and laugh. It was the first time John had heard Annabelle laugh in Indian Territory. John continued smiling as he went toward his bedroom.

CHAPTER 9
Revealed Shame

As October of 1847 passed, Annabelle continued to adjust to living with the Cherokee. In late October, the grasses had lost their color, and wildflower petals littered the landscape. Annabelle's relationship grew stronger with Grace and Lisa. Tsula's sense of humor cheered Annabelle, and she adored David. However, Annabelle dreamed about her family and friends, causing her to hate her dreams.

White settlers in the area occasionally came to the supply store. Annabelle's fear of the men was moderate, so she remained silent around them. A few Cherokee ignored Annabelle, but she accepted their disapproval. Through Joyce, Annabelle learned that the view of race was not strong among the tribe until the influence of the British. Annabelle's ongoing battle was the passive aggressiveness Lizzie sporadically showed. Annabelle preferred that over the possibility of another fight, and Lizzie slowly began to show more kindness to Annabelle.

To Annabelle's amusement over the past few weeks, a man named Buck Scott—born to a Scottish man and Cherokee woman—showed obvious interest in Grace, to her annoyance. He didn't think highly of Annabelle, but his continuous failed attempts were enough for Annabelle to maintain her kindness toward him.

One day, the supply door opened with the cool November breeze flowing into the store. Buck Scott stood in the doorway, holding a black cane and a self-assured smirk on his light olive-toned face. Buck wore a black frock coat with a high-collared white shirt, a fancy green vest holding a gold pocket watch, black trousers, and an extravagantly tied blue cravat. He anchored his hazel eyes on Grace as she stood at the counter, playing with her unbraided hair.

"The shining of the stars and a full moon couldn't light my night like you could," Buck said. "How about you allow me to walk you home today?"

Annabelle and Tsula chuckled but stopped when Buck glared at the two young women.

"What can we help you with, Buck?" Grace asked.

Buck walked toward the counter in a proud manner. "I think maybe the ignorant giggling of the Negro and Tsula erased my grand entrance. Allow me to escort you home today. I know you will be closing the store soon."

"I'm sorry, but I lock down every door, and the others usually wait for me to leave. It's a time of bonding for us while we walk home."

"I think you should reconsider. Surely, Lisa or Tsula can be responsible enough to make sure all the doors are locked. I understand why you don't trust the Negro. She is bound to make some mistakes."

"Once again, her name is Annabelle. How can you expect me to give you time when you won't respect someone I consider family? What runs through that thick Scottish head of yours?"

"I think he's too busy thinking about kissing you," Tsula said in Cherokee.

The women giggled, and Buck gnashed his teeth while exhaling.

"Now, all I ask is that you not speak that in front of me," Buck said. "You know I don't understand it."

Grace replied, "You don't want to learn. Tell me, how do you treat your slaves? I know how your father treats them."

"I treat them like they're meant to be treated. I expect them to work and do as I say. If they don't, they pay the price for being disobedient."

The corner of Grace's mouth pinched. "It's sad you think so low of them when they serve you."

Buck put one hand in his pocket. "Grace, don't act like this is new. If it wasn't for us learning how to manage our land properly, the Cherokee would be in worse shape than we are now."

Grace's voice slightly rose as she said, "If we hadn't trusted the white men like we did, we'd still have our land back in the South. Don't justify what our people have accepted. Slavery has done nothing but weaken us as a people."

"I think you fail to see the fruitfulness coming from the way we do things now. I also think you should show more appreciation for the attention I give you. You're a beautiful woman, but you're not getting any younger."

Grace fixed her brown eyes on Buck while he stood prideful in front of Grace. "I see what you've learned from your father. That Scottish blood must be something else to believe you determine who can be treated better than others. I don't have time for fools, especially fools that are so full of pride."

Buck scoffed. "I see the Indian is strong in your veins. The fact that you let a Negro live with your family and work in your family's store tells me you don't know your value. I'll make it a point to see you again. I believe I have overstayed my welcome."

Grace leered at Buck. "Maybe if you really knew the history of our people, your stay may have been welcomed more."

Buck clenched his teeth. He pressed his lips together and left the store, slamming the door.

"He really is more like the white man, isn't he, Grace?" Lisa said in Cherokee. "So arrogant to believe all that we do is right."

Grace exhaled when she picked up a sack of soybeans. "How about we end this day early, ladies?" Grace asked. "Besides, today is your birthday, Lisa. At the harvest festival, we can celebrate a little longer if we leave now."

"That sounds like fun to me," Lisa replied.

The women finished cleaning up the store and went home, Annabelle splitting from the group to visit Joyce. Joyce continued to work with Annabelle, teaching her the Cherokee language. Annabelle had now reached the level of not being allowed to greet Joyce with English, and Joyce's wisdom and sense of humor helped Annabelle stay encouraged to keep trying.

Joyce pulled a turkey out of her iron stove. "Now, this bird will last me for a week," she said in her native tongue.

"It smells so good," Annabelle said in Cherokee.

"Sit down, child. I'll cut you some meat."

Annabelle shook her head. "Oh, I couldn't."

"Nonsense, sit down." Joyce cut two slices off the bird and placed them on a wood plate. She gave it to Annabelle as she sat down.

"Thank you, Elder Joyce."

Joyce smiled and nodded.

Annabelle took a bite of the turkey. *This is the best turkey I've ever tasted in my life,* she thought.

"Are you having any more nightmares?"

"No, I think the prayers have been helping."

"Good. Still, give it time. There is no shame in missing your friends, especially Judy Mays."

Annabelle put down the turkey slice, her mouth curving downward. "I'm worried I'll never see her again."

"Don't worry about what you can't control. If you have to wait for her father to die, so be it."

"What if she's angry at me? She *must* be angry at me."

"If she's angry, understand where it comes from. You felt unable to tell her the truth, and you ran. Tell her the truth while seeing things from her eyes too. The truth will hurt her.

She may even call you a liar because of how much pain she'll feel."

"I wish I'd stayed in her room the whole night."

"Focus on the now, so you're prepared for what's to come. Go on and eat up. I have to hurry up and finishing cutting this bird up before my grandbabies come in here like hungry dogs."

The two women giggled.

Annabelle finished eating and returned to the log cabin to help make supper with the others.

———◆———

As the family ate their food and enjoyed each other's company and conversations, Uncle George continued to ignore Annabelle. George's attitude seemed to be testing Grace, but Annabelle assumed that Grace tolerated it over him treating Annabelle wrongfully with his words. Lizzie also kept Annabelle at a distance, though it seemed her anger had diminished. Annabelle reached for a corn cob when Lizzie gave a prideful leer to an unaware Annabelle.

"Maybe you should rethink how much you're eating, or you might get fat one day," Lizzie insolently said.

"I guess I should learn how to eat like you, Lizzie. I can get stronger, but I'll keep my happier spirit," Annabelle replied in Cherokee.

A smile arose on Tsula's face as she looked across the table at Lizzie, and the others at the supper table remained silent. Grace and Tsula abruptly cackled as Samuel and John looked at each other with big eyes while they processed Annabelle's speech. Even Michael, with his shy nature, smiled at Annabelle's response.

"Careful, Annabelle, I don't think anyone can keep up with Lizzie's eating. It's amazing she looks as good as she does," Tsula said in a lighthearted tone.

Lizzie chuckled, and everyone else laughed but George.

"You're learning well, Annabelle," Lizzie cheerfully said. "Maybe you can keep up a little."

"I think she'll keep up. Now, I'm going to tell a truth," Tsula said in Cherokee. "When Lizzie was born, she had the voice of a warrior, and she kicked John the moment she saw him."

Everyone except George laughed.

"Deadly from day one, Lizzie never has liked the word no. She used to beat up all the boys after school. It was a good day for them if she left school happy."

Tsula continued to make everyone laugh so hard that Lizzie forgot to continue challenging Annabelle with her Cherokee. For the first time, Annabelle looked more at peace, as though she felt truly accepted at supper.

Grace noticed George continuing to eat while staring at his plate.

The evening continued as the women cleaned the dishes and joked among themselves. John and Samuel walked outside to look at the stars before going to the harvest festival. Michael played with David.

"Annabelle, I'll follow you shortly to the festival," Grace said in Cherokee. "I have to speak with my uncle."

Annabelle smiled at Grace, excited to practice speaking more Cherokee, and replied, "We will see each other again. I feel good today."

Grace went outside.

Annabelle began to go to the festival when Lizzie walked out behind her.

"Wait for me, Annabelle. I can't let you walk to the festival alone," Lizzie said in Cherokee. "If you come back with a black eye, I will be blamed for it."

Annabelle lowered her eyebrows, unsure if she was supposed to be offended or not, but she waited for Lizzie to lead the way. "Where are Tsula and Lisa? They should be ready to go already."

Tsula rushed out of the house. "Good, the two of you didn't leave already."

"Where is Lisa? Is she coming?" Lizzie asked, also speaking Cherokee.

"She said she doesn't feel like going this year, but we have Annabelle with us! This is going to be a fun time. Where's Grace?"

"She said she wanted to talk to George before she came," Annabelle replied. "She said she would meet us there."

Tsula grinned at Annabelle as she heard her speaking in the Cherokee tongue. Lizzie rolled her eyes and walked toward the harvest festival. Annabelle and Tsula followed her.

<hr>

Grace sat down in a rocking chair next to her uncle while he read a newspaper. "I'm worried about you, Uncle George. You've been quiet at supper for a long time now," Grace said.

George put down the newspaper and looked at his niece. "Are you asking me what's wrong or trying to cheer me up?" George asked.

Grace shrugged. "I guess I'm trying to do both."

"I worry so much about all of you. You use your momma's strategies to get your way for a Negro you owe nothing to. The family has grown to like her a lot, and she's only been here for two months."

"Uncle George, is it so hard for you to get to know Annabelle? Your only stance against her is she is a Negro and nothing else."

George raised his voice as he said, "Nothing else! The only reason she came into our world is because you bought her from that white man. It was a mistake no matter how desperate that man was."

Grace pouted. "I tried life a different way, but I really saw the darkness in it. It scared me a lot, and I'm happy with what I did for Annabelle."

George ran his hand through his hair. "You are your mother's child. She and your auntie never did look at the Negroes differently. I never understood it, and I still don't."

Grace frowned while she rocked the chair. "That's because

you never wanted to try. Does it bother you that they're not lesser than us? Is it so hard for you?"

George scowled. "You forced this woman on our family, Grace. You dishonored me by even turning my own children against me. I can tell Lizzie has a problem with that girl living here with us."

"I'm not surprised by Lizzie's attitude. She still needs to grow up, and she's trying to be nicer. Her attitude isn't the same as your bad view of Annabelle. How are you being a Christian man when you can't show kindness to a woman that needs it? How are you being a good example to David? I won't allow my nephew to be raised to hate Negroes. The mistakes of my father died with him. I refuse to let them continue to the next generation."

George leaned forward. "Your father was a good man that loved you!"

Tears shimmered in Grace's eyes. "He did love us, but he gave that rum more time than me or the family. I can't let David learn hate. I want to see him grow into a man better than my father and better than you. Will you help us raise him that way, or will you poison his mind like these white people have poisoned yours?"

George sat back in the rocking chair. "I'll try what you're asking of me, but respect my position in this family. You have a lot of wisdom for your age, but you use some brutal ways to get your way."

"I will try to listen more as you asked me before. I will give John more opportunity to lead."

Grace gave her uncle a kiss on the cheek and went to the festival with the moonlight guiding her way.

✦

George rocked in the rocking chair. He huffed and frowned a little before he stood. Looking around to see if anyone else was awake, he quickly walked outside. On the side of the log cabin was a wooden shed. George entered it, constantly looking back.

Inside the shed was an old desk with a broken leg. George opened a lower drawer, pulled out a bottle of rum, and drank.

George slowly got drunk while he sat down in front of the cabin door, but eventually, the door opened. George dropped the bottle and tried to roll it away from him when he stood up.

"Papa, are you okay?" Lisa asked.

George answered in Cherokee, "Yes, yes, I'm fine. I was enjoying the stars. How strong they bright shine and—"

"Papa, are you drunk?" Lisa asked.

"Why, no. No, I had just one drink. You know, Grace can really test my patience and challenge my mind at the same time. She is a gifted child."

Lisa sulked as she looked at her father who attempted to stand upright. "I can smell it on you. I don't want to lose you like we lose Uncle Cliff. He was a good man, but he couldn't let go of that rum. If Grace saw you now, it would break her heart like mine is breaking now."

"Don't you start with me too," George slurred. "I need this between Grace always in some way rebelling and now having a nigger at our supper table that's now speaking our language. I never thought I would see a day like this, and who taught her? We need to keep things balanced. It's the only reason why these white folks have any respect for us," George yelled. "Where is Grace? She needs to answer more of my questions."

George tried to kick the rum bottle but suddenly stumbled and fell over, prompting Lisa to run to her father. Lisa put her father's arm around her shoulders and helped George stand. George vomited, and some of it got on Lisa's nightgown. Lisa gagged and held her breath as she held her father up and trudged to his room without waking David or Michael.

"Go on, Papa. Lie down."

George plopped on his bed, and Lisa helped him take his shoes and vest off.

"You give me high hopes, Lisa," George slurred. "Every time I look at you and your sister, I can't help but feel blessed and sad at the same time. Your momma blessed me, giving me beautiful two girls that look so much like her."

George quickly passed out, and Lisa left his room to clean off her nightgown.

"Lisa," Michael said, rubbing his eyes. "Is Papa alright?"

Lisa smiled at her little brother reassuringly. "He's fine. Just tired. Go back to bed, okay? I'm sure the others will be back soon."

Michael came up to Lisa, not noticing the puke on her nightgown, and gave her a hug,

"Good night." Lisa kissed Michael on the forehead, and he went back into the bedroom.

Lisa quickly entered the kitchen to get a bucket and a cloth. She walked out of the back door, got water from a well, and cleaned her nightgown. As Lisa cleaned the vomit, she became overwhelmed with sadness and cried.

Lisa stared at the stars with her flooded eyes and said in Cherokee, "Jesus, you clean us of our sins and heal us of our pain. Please help us stop my papa from drinking before he destroys himself like my uncle. Thank you for helping us heal when momma walked into heaven, but papa has given up hope."

Lisa went back into the house and went to sleep.

In the meantime, Annabelle and the others were enjoying the harvest festival. Having the freedom to walk where she wanted was new to her. Though some Cherokee ignored her, others acknowledged her and were interested in her because of Grace. The festival also gave Annabelle more opportunities to practice her Cherokee.

Grace and Tsula introduced her to friends who only spoke Cherokee, and they seemed excited she'd learned so much already. The most surprising element of the festival for Annabelle was the few drunken men. Grace and Lizzie grimaced anytime they saw them. Lizzie scoffed at them, and Tsula frowned as she watched some of her people behave in such a way.

Annabelle was afraid to ask them why they showed such obvious displeasure. While the women walked together through Tahlequah, Annabelle noticed Jacob. Jacob smiled at her, and she waved back, trying to remain uninterested.

Lizzie noticed the connection and stopped walking, anchoring her intimidating almond-shaped brown eyes onto Jacob before he noticed her stare. Jacob gulped and waved at Lizzie, who smirked and rolled her eyes at Jacob before walking away to follow the others.

Later, Annabelle was introduced to Clyde Walton, a Choctaw man and a close friend of George. Clyde was a bronze-complexioned man with short, dark brown hair, and barely taller than Grace. Annabelle felt comfortable around Clyde. He seemed to welcome Annabelle.

The festival ended as John and Samuel joined the young women on the walk home.

"Grace, come inside with me. I want to show you this other dress I've been sewing," Tsula said.

"Okay, but we need to do this quickly," Grace replied. "I'm tired. Annabelle, go on. I will be there shortly."

Annabelle nodded and approached the small log cabin, and she noticed John had followed her.

"Hello, Annabelle," John said in Cherokee.

Annabelle turned around, flattered by John's greeting. "Hello, John," she replied, also speaking in Cherokee. "Are you enjoying the night?"

John smiled. "I am, and I'm surprised how fast you learn."

Annabelle tried not to smile at John, and she gave a nervous sigh. "I have a great teacher. I know you know that."

"A good teacher does help, but being a strong learner helps too. We will see each other again."

Annabelle nodded, grinning. "We will see each other again, John."

John went to the big house. Annabelle's confidence grew, and she felt the pain of her past weaken. Annabelle entered the small house for the first time, feeling content living in Indian Territory. During the night, Annabelle kept tossing in her bed with a smile on her face. For Annabelle, it seemed God was answering her prayers.

<hr>

A brutal winter arrived in Oklahoma. Much of the activity in Tahlequah drastically decreased. During this time, the white men living in a small town outside of Tahlequah rarely appeared. The unforgiving cold wind trickled into poorly made houses, and firewood was a highly valued treasure. The heavy snow made traveling into the business area of Tahlequah difficult. Those who didn't own a horse were at a disadvantage and forced to rely on neighbors who did own a horse. The beginning of this cruel winter also prevented children from going to school. The smallest families already struggled with farming during the summer, and winter amplified their struggle.

The supply store had now become a major food supply for many in the area. A large amount of the corn and soybeans grown by the family was given to the people for little money or sometimes for free to the poorest. Some of the cattle ranchers even donated meat to some families. The other women continued to teach Annabelle the culture, and she learned alcohol was illegal in Cherokee territory, explaining further why the women were angry when they saw a few drunken men. It was clear to Annabelle the tribe was still recovering from the Trail of Tears even after years of being forced into Indian Territory. She hadn't met a single person who hadn't lost a loved one because of the forced removal. Though the Cherokee were able to have a society, in her eyes, they shared a commonality of struggle with the Negros.

As more time went on, Annabelle noticed the lack of children in Tahlequah. When she asked Grace about it, Grace explained that sickness had become the biggest threat to the children, along with poverty. The last two years had been the first time that the number of children hadn't increased. Annabelle was shocked the tribe had continued to lose so many children after being forced into Indian Territory, though it was no surprise to see the people still in mourning for the loss of their children and their land.

During the winter of 1847, Annabelle spent more time with Tsula and Lisa while they waited for customers. Grace encouraged Annabelle to start reading her Bible again, and Annabelle used this time to help Lisa improve her English. Simultaneously Annabelle progressed in speaking Cherokee with Joyce, and Joyce's place in Annabelle's life grew. Joyce encouraged Annabelle to read her Bible more and ask Jesus for guidance.

Grace also sometimes visited with Annabelle to help and spend more time with Joyce. Annabelle had now started attending the local Pentecostal church with the Lightning-Strongman family, giving Annabelle more foundation. Annabelle was one of the six free Negroes attending the church service. Annabelle was welcomed by Pastor Bluebird, and the old man's cheerful manner reminded Annabelle of Mr. Boston. It gave Annabelle comfort but also made her miss the cheerful man and his spoiled cat.

CHAPTER 10
Shadows of Trauma

DECEMBER 22, 1847, USHERED IN Grace's twenty-second birthday. Grace was excited but seemed almost indifferent to the special day. Annabelle noticed Grace's fake demeanor but decided to ignore her worry, believing Grace would say if there was a problem.

The winter weakened, bringing in 1848. Annabelle had become well-liked around the neighbors of the Lightning-Strongman family. Mr. Tate became quite fond of Annabelle and introduced his other children to Annabelle. She had already met Jacob Tate, but she was pleased to meet his quiet teen-age brother, Wren. He had Jacob's build but was smaller than Jacob. Jacob's loud older sister, Piper, was good friends with Tsula. She had long curly hair but kept it in two long braids, hiding her curls. Florence was Mr. Tate's youngest daughter, though older than Wren. Her soft-spoken voice almost made Annabelle forget she'd survived the Trail of Tears. The talkative young woman was Lizzie's height, but she was almost the complete opposite in nature. Jacob was the only child of Mr. Tate that spoke English well.

Annabelle learned the Tate family had actively avoided past Indian agents to keep the peace. Mr. Tate had lost all of his father's family, and their family home in Georgia was burned to the ground. The family bible was lost in the fire, along with all the names of his ancestors. This transgression made Mr. Tate short-tempered with white men. Annabelle was saddened when she learned about the Tate family's trauma.

She also met the Thompson family, neighbors who lived closer than the Tate family. The Thompson family were slave owners with two children, Thomas and Samantha, but they were polite to Annabelle. Annabelle first met the family as she and Grace strolled to their house bringing supplies, and she could barely tell the difference between the slaves and the owners. The Thompsons had two large brown barns with one large house that held the family. Several small slave houses were placed behind the two barns. The family farmed corn and raised cattle.

The slaves Annabelle met seemed happy, but one slave stood out to Annabelle. Doll Thompson was older than Annabelle and well-mannered. A nice-looking young woman, she was shorter than Annabelle with short hair brushed down and a soft, welcoming voice.

Doll seemed surprised to learn Annabelle was a free woman. However, Doll didn't envy Annabelle. She was content with being a slave. None of the slaves on the Thompson farms seemed unhappy, which was shocking for Annabelle. Annabelle was convinced the Thompson family had treated their slaves so well, their slaves truly believed their place belonged under a Cherokee master.

March of 1848 came with a strong hope for Annabelle, who was moving slowly forward after losing Benjamin and her daughter. Joyce continued to mentor Annabelle, explaining to her there was nothing wrong with remembering them. However, Annabelle needed to move on so she could live a happy life.

Mrs. Armstrong also became a pleasant presence to Annabelle. She always had something nice to say to Annabelle and showed great approval with Annabelle learning the Cherokee language.

One day, Mrs. Armstrong arrived to buy more flour. She stood in the doorway with her wooden cane, smiling. "I'm happy to see how much you beautiful young ladies helped our people over this winter," Mrs. Armstrong said in Cherokee. "You honor God and our ancestors with your unselfish acts."

Grace and Lisa smiled at the old woman while they stood behind the counter. "It means a lot for you to say such a thing, Mrs. Armstrong," Grace said in Cherokee.

"Your mothers smile at you all," the older woman said. "I only wish they could have stayed a little longer so they could fully see the wonderful young women they raised."

Annabelle watched from the side and smiled as she sewed a sack when Mrs. Armstrong turned toward her.

"Annabelle, I'm also pleased with you," she said. "You've taken the time to learn a lot here, and such discipline is the sign of someone who wants to be something special. Keep that attitude."

Annabelle replied in Cherokee, "Thank you, Mrs. Armstrong. That means a lot to hear you speak highly of me."

Mrs. Armstrong grinned as both of her hands rested on her wooden cane. "Where are Tsula and Lizzie? I need this flour put on the wagon. You know, I look good for my age, but my strength isn't what it used to be."

She patted one of her hair buns and giggled, and the other women snickered.

Grace replied in Cherokee, "Tsula should be back shortly, but Lizzie is home watching over David."

"You should've had them switch, Grace. As strong as Lizzie is, I think your mother didn't nurse her long enough. She's always had a mean streak." Mrs. Armstrong chuckled. "You know, Lizzie gave my nephew a black eye when they got out of school one day. He ran screaming home to my niece that he had been beaten by a girl, and Lizzie was so mad. I know your momma gave Lizzie some good smacks on her backside for that one."

The women laughed while Mrs. Armstrong smiled, reminiscing.

Mrs. Armstrong's smile quickly curved downward slightly. "My, how I miss Georgia. Well now, ladies, I need my supplies."

Annabelle, Grace, and Lisa put the bags of flour on Mrs. Armstrong's old rusty wagon. The women said their goodbyes to Mrs. Armstrong, and she rode off. The young women continued the day, excited with the arrival of spring.

"Annabelle, are you excited your birthday will arrive soon?" Lisa said.

Annabelle calmly replied, "I am. I'll be a woman in my twenties, and it really is a blessing I've made it this far."

"You need to choose a date, Annabelle, so we can always have one day to celebrate your life," Grace said.

Annabelle thought deeply about a date and replied, "The others never pushed me to pick a day, but I'll have to think about what Rebecca told me. I have it...March twenty-fourth. I think that's the best date. A little before April with only a few days left in March."

Grace replied, "Sounds good to me."

The old wooden front door opened, and a beautiful young raven-haired woman entered, wearing a dark brown floral dress. The olive-toned woman was as tall as Lizzie, making her shorter than Annabelle, and had ringlet-styled hair. The woman exhaled and fixed her round dark brown eyes on Grace and Lisa.

"Good evening, ladies. I was looking for cornmeal and flour. Do you have them in your supply?" the woman asked with a Spanish accent.

"Why, yes. We do have those things here," Grace replied. "We had a good harvest this past year, so we had a lot to store up for the people."

"Good, I will take two sacks of each of them."

Lisa grinned as she fixed her eyes on the young woman standing with a snobbish and proud manner. "What is your name?"

"My name is Maria Santos. What are your names?"

"My name is Grace Lightning."

"Hi, my name is Lisa Strongman."

"I'm Annabelle Mays."

Maria replied, "Such pretty names. It is nice to meet you ladies. Now can I receive the supplies I need for today?"

"The sacks are right there. We will put them on your wagon for you," Grace said.

"You don't have any men here to do that?" Maria asked.

"Well, the sacks have some weight on them, but we have been doing this for so long that they're not heavy to us anymore, Grace replied. "You're one of the Mexicans, aren't you?"

Maria looked at Grace nervously. "Yes, I was born in Mexico City and lived there until I was fifteen years old. I now live in a town three miles north of here."

"It's a terrible feeling losing out to white people, isn't it? I heard that war went bad for your people."

Maria frowned, and her gaze shifted downward. "I did lose some of my family in the war, but what has happened has happened. We have to keep moving forward and pray for the ones we lost. I guess this type of pain is something that's hard for your people to understand."

Lisa replied, "This was never our original home. We were forced from our homes with guns to our heads. We were children when it happened."

Maria replied, "So, you do understand the feeling of being cheated. At least I have my freedom. Are you a free woman, Annabelle?"

Annabelle replied, "Yes, at least here, it feels like it, but if I was to leave, it would feel very different. I've tried already. It isn't the same as living here."

Maria's gaze dropped then returned to Annabelle as she tightened her lips. "Well, I guess I'll pay for those supplies now and be on my way. It was nice to meet you all. At least I've come to a supply store that knows how to treat a lady."

"You're welcome here anytime," Grace said as the woman paid for her corn and flour. "We will put these sacks on the wagon for you."

"Thank you," Maria said.

Samuel walked inside carrying a sack. "We forgot this bag of soybeans, but they're still good," he said, stopping when he saw Maria and staring into her round, dark brown eyes before his lips drifted into a smile.

Maria grinned at Samuel.

"Samuel," Lisa barked.

Samuel jolted and looked at his aggravated sister.

"Show some manners," Lisa chastised. "Why are you staring at her like that for?"

"I think you better listen to your wife," Maria encouragingly said.

"Wife!" Lisa said. "He's my younger brother. Please forgive his rudeness."

"Rude behavior," Samuel said. "You're the one acting badly. I was surprised by her beauty. Is that a crime?"

Maria giggled, saying, "You're a funny man. What was your name again?"

"My name is Samuel Strongman. What is your name?"

"My name is Maria Santos. I was leaving. They were about to give me some supplies and put them on my wagon."

"That's your wagon outside? Well, I can put your supplies in the wagon for you. A woman with such a beautiful voice should be treated properly."

Maria smirked as Grace and Lisa rolled their eyes.

"Fool, what you mean to say is you like her Spanish accent," Grace said in a mocking tone.

Maria giggled when Samuel shifted his glance around the room, shook his head, and walked to the counter. "What did she need put in the wagon?" he asked.

Lisa replied, "Two bags of cornmeal and two bags of flour."

Samuel went to the left of the store to pick up one of the bags from an aisle and strutted past Maria, grinning as he walked toward the wagon.

Samuel put one of the bags in the wagon and went back to the store, smiling at Maria.

"What are you smiling at her for? It's not like you have a chance," Tsula said in Cherokee with the back door closing behind her.

Samuel turned red in the face while Annabelle, Grace, and Lisa laughed hysterically.

"What was so funny?' Maria asked.

"One of the Mexicans," Tsula said. "You look beautiful in that dress."

"Thank you. I like yours too," Maria kindly replied.

"Why, thank you. Please excuse what I said. I was teasing my brother," Tsula said. "It's so easy to do, especially because I'm the older, smarter one."

Samuel quickly grabbed another bag next to Tsula as he tried to avoid eye contact with her.

"Hmph, when did you get an eye for Mexican women?" Tsula whispered.

Samuel glared at Tsula as she giggled at her brother.

Maria couldn't hear what Tsula said and watched. Samuel marched to the wagon as Tsula giggled.

"He must be the youngest out of all of you. You seem to get a lot of pleasure from teasing him," Maria commented.

Tsula tilted her head. "Well, I must. I'm only twenty minutes older than him. If he had stayed in a little bit longer, we could have had our own separate birthdays, but no. He had to be selfish."

Maria gasped. "Wow, he is your twin! What an interesting way to grow up. I have never met twins before, but I can see the resemblance. How old are you?"

"I'm eighteen, and I will be nineteen on April third. It's the greatest time of the year, I think."

"Okay, so you're a year older than me. I will turn eighteen on March twenty-ninth."

"That's interesting. Annabelle's birthday is on March twenty-fourth," Grace said.

"Really!" Maria replied. "I guess we have a lot of spring people here."

"It is the greatest season. Far better than winter," Tsula said with a smirk.

Grace and Lisa conceitedly glared at Tsula, prompting her to stick out her tongue at them.

Maria giggled, and the ladies continued to talk while Samuel worked putting the sacks onto the wagon. Standing by Grace and Lisa, Annabelle stayed quiet, observing the interactions between Tsula, Grace, and Lisa. Annabelle admired their relationship. It made her wonder about her little brother. Even though the young women connected with Annabelle, she was still healing and worked to discipline herself not to fall into self-pity. Maria later left the store with Samuel watching as her wagon rode off.

"She was an interesting person. I've never met a Mexican before," Annabelle said. "She almost looks like y'all."

"Normally this past summer, there would've been more Mexicans coming into town to get supplies," Grace said. "It was odd. They suddenly stopped coming, but I guess you should expect that when people are always on the move."

Annabelle's eyebrow rose. "What war were you talking about?"

"There was a crazy war going on between the Mexicans and the US Army," Grace informed her. "It's not surprising you didn't know about it, but long story short, the war ended about a month ago. I was told the Mexicans lost so much land, your eyes can't see it all."

Annabelle's eyes bulged as she tried to imagine it. The women continued their day, and that night, for the first time, Annabelle was able to continue reading *The Three Musketeers*. The old burnt book no longer gave Annabelle pain, but it inspired her to never forget the great memories she had with Benjamin. Cuddling with Benjamin while she'd read the book and taught him words had been a favorite activity for Annabelle.

✦

On March twenty-fourth, Grace prepared eggs with grits for Annabelle to celebrate her birthday. Annabelle felt welcomed by the surprise. Tsula and Lisa warmed Annabelle's heart by telling every customer it was her birthday. Later in the day, the young women closed the store and separated as Annabelle traveled to Joyce's home.

"Well, it seems that you're growing," Joyce said in Cherokee. "You even decided to choose a birthday. I'm proud of you."

"Thank you. That means a lot," Annabelle said in Cherokee.

"This is the second time you've visited me, and I've seen you smile for real. Have things between you and Lizzie improved, or is she still giving you a hard time?"

"Things have been better. You see, I don't have any bruises on my face." Annabelle giggled. "Lizzie did say happy birthday to me in her own way."

"How did she wish you well?"

"I saw her this morning when I walked to the store, and she said that she heard today I was celebrating my birthday. She was kind enough to ask me why I care about celebrating it when it would mean I'm getting old. Then she went back into the house and closed the door."

Joyce chuckled. "Jesus, that child. Well, I guess that's better than her taking hits at you. At least she does like you in some way. How are other things going, dear? Are you still having nightmares?"

"No, I haven't had any nightmares this whole month. It's been a good and weird feeling sleeping through the whole night without waking up in tears. Grace heard me in my sleep. Sometimes, she would sit in the bed with me to help me sleep. I'm sorry I didn't tell you earlier. I didn't want you to worry more than you needed to."

"Don't hide things. If you remain silent, it makes it harder for me to help you. That's almost as bad not praying to the Creator for guidance."

Annabelle sighed. "I won't do it again."

Joyce folded her hands. "Do you understand it isn't normal

to love your enemies? Nor natural to have unforgiveness? In order to love your enemies and keep unforgiveness out of your heart, you have to put effort into it. The Father helps you grow like a corn stalk. He puts the change in us. That's why it is important for you to always pray to the Father and read the gospels. That's something I can't do for you.

"I'll continue to take time to read and grow stronger the best I can."

Joyce rocked in her chair. "I believe you will. You know, following Jesus is an interruption from the life you wanted to live because he cleans out the poisons in your life. Living in the flesh leads to death. Don't forget, Jesus made peace between us and the Father. Holding to truth is your foundation of faith. Well, I think that's enough of the serious talk. Have you met anyone interesting? I know you're ready to try since our last talk."

Annabelle beamed, trying not to blush as she sat in the old wooden rocking chair. "I've tried not to really think about it so much. Honestly, there's still a part of me that doesn't feel ready, and a part feels guilty for even thinking about finding someone new."

"If Benjamin loved you, then he would not want you to live the rest of your life alone in that part of your life. It's okay to keep your eyes open for someone in town."

"There is someone who does interest me. He is a very charming and handsome man. I wish I had more time to talk to him when he and his father come to the store."

Joyce's eyes somewhat widened. "Who are you talking about?"

"Jacob Tate. I know that's asking for trouble, but I can't help how I feel about it."

Joyce shook her head. "Yes, it is asking for trouble. I think you need to take a lot more time in making a decision like that. I want to make sure you realize the man you end up with isn't meant to complete you. You need to be complete without him. A spouse is meant to compliment you and be your partner to help the kingdom of heaven in whatever way the two of you are meant to. Don't base your happiness on finding someone new. In fact, he should be the one to find you."

"I never really thought about it that way. Is it okay for me to signal I would like to spend more time with him?"

"That's fine, but don't allow yourself to make him the most important thing you're focused on. The gospels speak of being planted by the rivers of water and producing your fruit for your season. Your leaf shall not wither, and whatever you do, you will prosper. Focus on you, Annabelle. Don't let your wants cause you to forget the grace the Creator has given you. So for now, I advise you to wait a little longer before you do anything with that young man. There may be something else you haven't seen."

"Thank you. I do want to walk in what God wants me to do. I guess I'm excited to move on finally."

Joyce smiled at Annabelle and stood up from her rocking chair. "Be anxious for nothing and take time to be quiet and listen." Giving Annabelle a hug, the older woman walked into the kitchen to figure out what to cook for supper. "Think of it this way, if the wildflowers were so quick to bloom, they would never be as beautiful as they're meant to be."

Annabelle beamed as she thought about Joyce's metaphor. Annabelle went home, had supper with the Lightning-Strongman family, and strolled to the small log cabin with Grace. Annabelle slept that night, encouraged as Joyce's words still echoed in her head.

The next day, Tsula woke up violently ill, forcing Lisa to stay behind to help her and watch David despite Lizzie's demand to watch David. Lizzie's anger was obvious the moment she stormed off to the supply store, Annabelle and Grace following. Grace ignored her sister's anger while Annabelle kept quiet to avoid Lizzie's anger. Grace worked the counter as Annabelle fed the chickens outside. Lizzie bitterly moved around sacks of different supplies while serving customers. The day continued when Grace heard a thud in the storage room.

"Great, some of the bags must've fallen," Grace said.

Annabelle walked inside after finishing cleaning up a chicken for a customer.

"Oh, good, you're done with that chicken. Please go help Lizzie stack the bags. They fell down in the storage room."

"Okay, is she back there already?" Annabelle asked.

Grace's mouth slanted the moment her cheek pinched. "She is."

Annabelle entered the large storage room lined with glass jars and sacks as Grace served another customer who entered the store.

"Well, what are you standing there for? Pick up a bag and stack it," Lizzie barked in Cherokee.

Annabelle quickly picked up a small sack and stacked it with the others. She could feel the heat emanating from Lizzie's irritated spirit. She then grabbed a larger sack and could barely lift it. Lizzie walked toward her and grabbed the other side, helping Annabelle stack it. Annabelle felt more exhausted when she saw two other large sacks needing to be stacked.

Annabelle was about to help Lizzie pick up the sacks when Lizzie grabbed the sack by herself before lifting and stacking it. Annabelle's eyes widened as she watched Lizzie do it with ease, and as she was about to pick up the last sack, Lizzie lifted it and left Annabelle speechless. Lizzie's eyes focused on how everything was arranged while Annabelle processed what she saw. It was the first time Annabelle had seen Lizzie work alone. Normally, two women would have lifted up a sack.

Lizzie turned to look at Annabelle and said, "Thanks."

Lizzie left the storage room, and Annabelle quickly approached the sacks and poked them. The sacks Lizzie lifted were full.

Annabelle thought, *I would've never spilled flour on Lizzie if I had known how strong she is.*

She patted her dress and left the storage room, scratching her forehead. After the young women finished their day in the store, they went home, and Lizzie appeared joyful. Annabelle couldn't figure out if she was joyful because they were going home or if Lizzie was thinking about something.

Annabelle wanted to thank Lizzie for helping her, but she was nervous about changing Lizzie's mood. During supper, the feeling to thank Lizzie continued to bother Annabelle, but she tried to suppress the urge. After dinner, Annabelle walked to the small log cabin. She turned around, ignoring her fear, and returned to the main home.

Annabelle nervously approached Lizzie's bedroom and stared at the old wooden door. Annabelle exhaled and knocked.

The door abruptly opened, and Lizzie stood in the doorway. She held a comb and stood in her short-sleeved nightgown with Tsula and Lisa already asleep.

While looking up at Annabelle, Lizzie asked in Cherokee, "What do you want? Shouldn't you be getting ready for bed?"

"I wanted to come by and say—"

"Say what?" Lizzie walked toward the lamp in the room and put down the comb on the wooden lampstand.

Annabelle suddenly noticed the light from the lamp shined partially through Lizzie's nightgown. Annabelle's eyes widened and she gulped, looking at Lizzie's strong hourglass figure, especially Lizzie's calf muscles. When Lizzie turned around, Annabelle could also see the muscle in Lizzie's quads, shoulders, and stomach, something she'd never seen on a woman before.

She blinked and refocused on Lizzie. "I wanted to say thank you for helping me. I couldn't have done it on my own. God has gifted you with wanting to help others."

Lizzie scoffed and folded her arms, revealing her biceps. "You're welcome, Annabelle. You tried hard. That's better than giving up and crying about it."

Annabelle suddenly caught a familiar smell. "Do I smell lilac?"

Lizzie's eyebrow lifted. "Yes, it's my favorite type of perfume. John would get me a bottle from your white friend, Marilyn, you spoke so highly of once in a while."

Annabelle was surprised Lizzie considered it her favorite,

but she decided not to say it was also her favorite fragrance. "It is a great smell. Well, I guess I need to go to bed now. Good night." Annabelle walked out the door.

"Good night. Sleep well."

Annabelle turned around, half-smiling at Lizzie while taking a quick glance at the outline of Lizzie's muscles the second she closed the door.

Lizzie turned off the lamp. With the moonlight guiding her, she lay down in bed next to Lisa, who was secretly awake and smiling with her back turned to Lizzie.

Annabelle entered her room and sat on her bed, somewhat inspired by Lizzie. She thought, *No wonder she was able to give me those hard hits. I don't think Master Brown ever came close to hitting me that hard.* Annabelle picked up her Bible later, falling asleep as she read it.

CHAPTER 11
A Glimpse of the South

TWO WEEKS PASSED INTO APRIL, and planting season had already begun for the Lightning-Strongman family. George, John, Michael, and Samuel, with the help of Jacob, had taken the horses out to help them plow the fields. Annabelle would walk to the farming fields to watch them work. Sometimes, Lisa would join her to spoil the horses with food.

Annabelle had developed a love for watching the bison herds from afar as the magnificent animals grazed. She had never seen the animals until one day, she noticed the herd pass the farming fields in February. Watching the carefree animals gave Annabelle peace as she sat on a hill next to an old eastern redbud tree decorated with its pink-purplish flowers.

On April 17, 1848, Grace told everyone to go home early while she closed the store. Grace later walked home, anxious to spend time with her family.

"Grace. Grace, wait a moment," Mr. Gross said.

Grace was halfway home, walking past a two-story, brown-bricked building with a few other townspeople, when she turned around and saw Mr. Gross approach with his black cane. "Mr. Gross, it's a pleasure to see you today," she said.

"I'm glad I saw you. I have been meaning to come by the

store and visit you." Mr. Gross pulled out his gold pocket watch and placed it back into his brown vest. "I'll tell you this quickly because I'm having a meeting soon. There have been kidnappings going on recently."

Grace's brow lowered while her mouth turned downward slightly. "What kind of kidnappings?"

"Mostly free Negroes at first, but we made the mistake of not taking it seriously enough because it was a few Negroes. However, both the Choctaw and Creek have reported the kidnappings of mixed-blood Negroes. The Choctaw had experienced these troubling events in the past, but we never thought this would follow to Indian Territory."

Grace put a hand on her hip. "Who is doing the kidnappings?"

Mr. Gross let out a harsh breath. "White men, mostly southerners. They're claiming many of the free Negroes and mixed-bloods are really runaway slaves with no rights. We don't know how many have been taken, but we're certain at least fifty-four have been taken from the Choctaw, twelve from the Natchez, and thirty from the Creek. All of the kidnappings have occurred at night, and many have happened in towns home to mixed-bloods and tribal members."

"That's awful. Those poor families. What is the council doing to stop this?"

"That's where I'm walking to now. It has been getting worse every year. The worst part is that there have been several kidnappings of young children from the Choctaw and Natchez. We had decided to quietly keep our eyes open for white settlers we felt were dangerous, but we can no longer remain quiet on the issue."

Grace placed her hand over her heart. "They're selling the children as slaves, aren't they?"

Mr. Gross looked at Grace, and his eyes shifted from her.

"Have they taken any Cherokee children?" Grace's voice rose. "Have you done us an injustice by not telling us our children are being taken as slaves like their Negroes?"

"Calm down. We have no reports of missing children, but we also don't want to risk such a thing happening. Me and some of the other council members joined John Ross on a visit to the Choctaw land, and it was sad. Letters have been sent to the American government requesting they look into these disappearances immediately. The Choctaw still have family in the South to keep their own eyes open."

"What about the others? Are the other tribes really going to leave their own kin in chains because they also have Negro blood?"

Mr. Gross sighed. "They are divided in what they should and—"

"And nothing. I hope in my heart our people will never have to argue about if we should save our kin who were wrongfully taken away from their own homes. What is wrong with us? What kind of evil has entered these councils' minds that they're divided on saving their own?"

Mr. Gross stuck his hand out. "All I can say is keep an eye on Annabelle."

"And what about my nephew? Do I have to fear these white men entering into our towns now? Do I have to fear they see no difference between David and a Negro child? May the Creator have mercy on us. We're led by cowards who won't tell the United States what we won't tolerate."

"We have to be careful with what we say. We can't afford to upset them. It could cause a war."

"Maybe a war would've been a better solution. Uniting with all the tribes and standing our ground instead of losing everything and being forced here. Thank you for having the heart to warn me of these tragedies."

Grace walked away.

Mr. Gross threw his hands in the air and grimaced.

Grace arrived at her family's home, looking for Annabelle. David ran up to Grace to give her a hug, and she picked up David as he hugged her, giving him a kiss on his cheek. Tsula watched while she sewed a patch on Michael's shirt.

"How is my Big Bear," Grace said in a playful tone.

David laughed and excitedly said, "Auntie Grace, I got to touch Big Boy today."

Grace playfully let her mouth drop. "You did? I know that was fun, wasn't it?"

David smiled and nodded at his aunt.

"Is Daddy still outside?" she asked.

"Daddy went outside with Uncle George."

"Okay." Grace put David down and walked toward Tsula. "Where's Annabelle? I needed to see her."

"She is outside sitting on the hill by the old tree," Tsula replied. "Is there something on your mind? You don't look happy."

Grace responded in Cherokee, "Nothing is wrong. I wanted to see what she was doing. Is Lisa outside too?"

"Yes, Lisa is outside with Jacob working with the horses. Lizzie is somewhere. She's been gone for some time now."

"Lizzie is most likely going through town. That's not weird for her to go explore when she can. I'm going outside to see Annabelle."

"Okay, smile more, Grace. You do seem bothered today."

"I will. I promise." Grace smiled at Tsula and left the house in search of Annabelle. She eventually found the other woman sitting by an old redbud tree. "Amazing animals, aren't they?"

"Yeah, I think they are," Annabelle said. "I'm jealous of them, I guess. They seem like they don't have a worry in the world."

Grace sarcastically replied, "Put a pack of wolves out there or a cougar. I promise your belief in that would change."

Annabelle chuckled. "Besides that, I think they have a pretty good life."

Grace looked at Annabelle and could see the joy in her. "Come walk with me. I want to practice my shooting again."

Annabelle followed Grace. "It's impressive with how good you're shooting arrows. I haven't seen you miss once."

While Annabelle walked with Grace, Lisa prepared the horses' food as the men worked them in the fields.

Jacob went back with Big Boy. The large horse with his white coat and small brown patches on his hindquarters moved faster when he saw Lisa. Jacob tried to steer the horse into his pen, and the horse lightly grunted and pulled forward to the woman. Jacob reluctantly agreed, not wanting to upset the horse, and walked Big Boy to her. Lisa laughed when she approached the horse and petted him.

"I'll put him up, Jacob. He's being a big baby today," Lisa said in Cherokee.

As she put the horse in his pen and gave him grains, Jacob said, "You have a strong connection with the horses."

Lisa smiled and moved toward him. "I know how to work with them. I'm sure he works well with you in the fields."

Jacob folded his arms and smiled at Lisa. "What makes you think that?"

"He let you walk him back to the barn instead of running away from you. Big Boy must sense something good in you."

Jacob chuckled. "I think the horse has better judgment than me. I think I might have more to learn from the horse."

Lisa cocked her head. "What do you mean?"

"Big Boy trusts you. There must be a good reason for it. Maybe he can feel your good spirit better than me."

Lisa smiled as she walked toward the barn door. "The Creator has blessed the animals in that way, being able to feel good and bad in people. Be careful not to let your eyes fool you, Jacob Tate."

Jacob smirked. "I think it might be too late for me. Real beauty comes from the spirit, and it's hard not to see it."

Flattered, Lisa turned around. "It's like that sometimes, isn't it?" She went back to the house while Jacob watched.

"Jacob, we're ready for the next field," Samuel said.

"Okay, let's finish the job," Jacob replied, turning around.

The next day, Annabelle went to church. After the sermon, she walked back with the others, enjoying their company. John had stayed home. Annabelle stood outside the family house, talking with Tsula, when she saw a white woman approaching. The woman wore a white and yellow Victorian dress with a yellow bonnet.

"Good afternoon, Tsula. I'm here to see John. Is he here right now?" the woman asked.

"Nancy Hicks, is that you?" Tsula asked.

The brunette continued to approach the house. "You know it's me."

"John is around. John, come here!" Tsula shouted, then leered.

Nancy stood in front of Tsula and Annabelle. As tall as Annabelle, the woman seemed to have a self-centered presence.

Nancy's blue eyes studied Annabelle. "Who is this?"

"My name is Anna—"

Nancy sneered. "I didn't ask you, Negro. I asked Tsula. Or is her name Tsula too? How about that, Tsula? You have the same name as a Negro. How cute."

"Her name is Annabelle," Tsula replied. "Don't be walking up here being rude. This isn't your home, my lady. It's our home, and it's in your best interest you show respect here."

"Still quick with your mouth, I see," Nancy said with a belligerent tone. "What is taking your cousin so long? I'm officially here for good in this uncivilized land."

"That's a great way to talk about your own people, but I guess I can't expect more since you're so little of us."

Nancy's eyes narrowed as she clutched her white reticule. "I'm a far better breed of Cherokee than you could ever be. If more were like me, we would have far more than the other tribes. Instead, we still refuse to live beneficially, and because of it, the US government looks at us like we are brutes. Speaking of brutes, where is she? I don't need her ruining my hair again."

Tsula laughed, causing Annabelle to chuckle as well. Nancy

scowled, and her eyes narrowed again. Annabelle couldn't help but stare at Nancy, noticing her eyes were a little almond-shaped, and she had high cheekbones.

"Wow, she is Cherokee. I see it," Annabelle blurted out.

Nancy anchored her eyes on Annabelle. "How dare you try to determine who I am. You're nothing but a nigger."

Tsula stepped in front of Nancy. "You're to never say that word on this property, you white-washed Cherokee. You embarrass us using that word. White people have used it against us, you forgetful grass nigger."

Nancy's eyes widened, and she gasped. "It seems you've established yourself well here, Annabelle," she said.

"There are a lot of good people here," Annabelle replied. "I'm thankful to be a free Negro here. This is our home."

Nancy scoffed. "What did you mean by our home, Tsula?"

"Annabelle lives here," Tsula replied. "Grace and Annabelle sleep in the small house."

"Wow, I guess you really have established yourself," Nancy said with a snobbish tone.

Annabelle suddenly noticed Lizzie come off a trail to the house. Lizzie's keen brown eyes fixed on Nancy as she unbraided her hair. Nancy suddenly noticed Lizzie coming toward her, and she appeared unimpressed. Lizzie shook her head to help loosen up her wavy hair and leered at the taller Nancy.

"Hi, ugly," Lizzie said.

"I guess it would kill you to behave like a lady," Nancy snarled.

"Says the white woman with Cherokee cheeks. Whatever, I don't have time for this white Indian," Lizzie said in Cherokee with her Southern, high-pitched tone deepening with each word.

"You know I don't speak it well," Nancy yelled. "You arrogant—"

"Nancy?" John said.

Nancy beamed and slanted her head welcomingly. "John!" she said. "What took you so long. I miss you so much."

"I'm sorry. I was with David. Grace is watching him now."

"How is that beautiful little boy?"

John grinned. "He's doing good and growing strong."

Nancy smiled and shifted her weight. "That's good to hear. I'm sure Grace is doing well too. May we take a walk? I would like to know how you have been doing these past months. I'm sure you want to know how I've been doing."

"Sure, I have some time."

Nancy's grin grew bigger the moment John exited the doorway. Tsula and Lizzie watched with their noses slowly scrunching and their lips forming into a pout. Nancy leered at the two women.

John walked toward Nancy as she turned toward a trail with her eyes on him.

Nancy sighed. "I was beginning to think I should have sent one of my slaves over instead of coming here personally first. I almost thought I made a mistake and came to the wrong home with that Negro standing there."

Tsula tightened her hand into a fist. "If you really want to know about mistakes, you should ask your parents," Tsula bellowed. "It only takes one time."

Annabelle and Lizzie laughed hysterically.

Nancy turned and stepped forward, eyes round and red-faced. "How does she do it?" Nancy growled before shrieking, "We're leaving! I'm not standing here while she continues to insult me."

Nancy marched off, and John followed her, attempting to calm her down.

"Nancy, you better watch your hair. You know I don't like the ringlets," Lizzie said.

Nancy turned her head and stomped her feet on the dusty trail as she walked.

"Careful, Nancy. We know you need a slave to put on your shoes," Tsula yelled. "I would hate to see you going home with one shoe in your hand because you don't know how to put it on."

Annabelle and Lizzie laughed again.

Nancy furiously turned her head and continued to walk away with John following her.

"That was fun. She actually got some color in her face," Lizzie said, walking into the log cabin as Annabelle and Tsula stayed outside.

"What is her story? She looks almost all white." Annabelle said.

Tsula answered, "Her momma is half Cherokee and white, but her daddy is a rich white man. Her family actually has a lot of slaves. I think they have about twenty."

Annabelle's eyebrows lowered while her mouth twisted. "So, why do y'all not like her so much? Is it because she has a lot of white blood?"

"Honestly, no. It has nothing to do with her being part white. Since we were children, she's always acted like she is better. Always had the best clothes, always said her daddy was better than all of ours... She was always a pain. The most annoying part is when Camille died. Within a week of her passing, Nancy started flirting with John. She's like those white women who have no sense of honor. Their worth is placed on what man they get."

"I haven't been talked to like that since Mr. Hildebrand," Annabelle said. "She reminds me of the South. It was a little scary. She really sees me like the white people do."

"Yeah, be careful around her. She has a temper on her. She's not strong like Lizzie, but still, be careful around her," Tsula said.

Annabelle had already experienced rejection from some of the Cherokee, but this was the first time she'd come across someone in Cherokee land that made her feel like she had truly returned to the South.

CHAPTER 12
Doll

A FEW DAYS PASSED, AND ANNABELLE became even more comfortable exploring Tahlequah. It bothered her when she saw the slaves working the fields, though she didn't witness any brutality. She decided on her small breaks that if Grace decided not to walk with her, she would give water to the slaves.

One April day, while on a break, Annabelle traveled to the Tates' farm carrying a bucket of water with a small cup.

Mr. Tate watched, impressed by Annabelle's kindheartedness.

Mr. Tate's daughter, Florence, sat next to her father, also impressed by Annabelle's actions. "Papa, do you want her doing that?" Florence asked.

"Let her be. She is a good woman," Mr. Tate said. "I think more Negroes need to see more of this good behavior. It will bring them more happiness."

Florence smiled at her father and continued to watch Annabelle give their slaves water.

Annabelle continued to the Thompson's farm. She walked out to the cornfields, where she saw a few slaves and gave them water. Mr. and Mrs. Thompson watched, surprised by

Annabelle's actions. The Thompsons were both olive skin-toned people of middle age.

"Well, I thought I'd seen everything until today," Mrs. Thompson said. "What would cause her to come out here?"

Mr. Thompson, sitting in his chair, smiled as he smoked his black pipe. "I think she can't help herself," Mr. Thompson said. "Annabelle has such a good heart. I think even the thought of other Negroes not doing well bothers her. She has a kindness like Doll."

Mrs. Thomas somewhat frowned. "She concerns me. I like the girl, but I think she has overstepped her bounds. She's a free Negro woman, but there are still rules for her to follow."

Mrs. Thompson glared at Mr. Thompson, and he took a deep breath.

He walked out into the fields and adjusted his brown trousers. Scratching his face, he took his gold pocket watch out of his green vest when he approached Annabelle. She had greeted Doll and was about to give her water when she noticed Mr. Thompson walking toward her.

"Good afternoon, Mr. Thompson. I wanted to give Doll some water if it is okay with you," Annabelle said.

Mr. Thompson stood in front of Annabelle and Doll with a blank face.

Mrs. Thompson watched them as she stood on the porch.

"My, all this effort just to give a slave some water," Mr. Thompson said, putting his gold pocket watch back into his green vest. "May I have a drink?"

Annabelle's eyes widened at hearing Mr. Thompson's request. "Why, yes, sir. I'd be happy to give you some water."

Annabelle smiled and handed a cup full of water to Mr. Thompson. He drank while Annabelle and Doll watched.

"My, now that's good water, very good water. I appreciate your kindness, Annabelle, but I must ask that you come no later than this time of day. I don't want the slaves' work slowed down too much. Your presence is welcomed. You even impressed Mrs. Thompson. Next time, please come earlier in the day if you would like to give water to the slaves."

"Yes, sir, Mr. Thompson. I can do that."

"Well, good. I'm going inside now to rest. Doll, please go talk to Mrs. Thompson so you know what she wants cooked for supper today, and make sure you drink some water."

Doll replied, "Yes, sir. I'll go right now."

Annabelle gave Doll water, and Doll went to the main house as Mr. Thompson watched.

"Have a good day, Annabelle," Mr. Thompson said.

Annabelle replied, "You as well, Mr. Thompson."

———◆———

Annabelle traveled back to the supply store carrying the bucket. That night, she read her Bible and couldn't help but feel surprised by Mr. Thompson's demeanor. Mr. Thompson's confidence made Annabelle believe the Thompson family slaves would forever stay there.

Maybe with these slaves, it is better for them to stay there. They're living much better than I did as a slave, Annabelle thought.

Annabelle continued her passion for giving water to the slaves of those two families, much to Grace's dislike. Annabelle agreed with Grace to only give water to the slaves twice a week.

A week passed, and Annabelle decided to visit the Thompson farm first to respect Mr. Thompson's rules. As Annabelle strolled through Tahlequah, she passed Nancy. Nancy turned her blue eyes to Annabelle, but Annabelle chose to keep walking and avoid her. Nancy scoffed and continued on her way. When Annabelle approached the Thompson farm, she saw Mrs. Thompson riding in a carriage.

Mrs. Thompson sat back in the carriage in a blue and white Victorian dress, and she wore a white bonnet.

"Slow down, Tyler. I'd like to speak with Annabelle," Mrs. Thompson said.

The carriage stopped in front of Annabelle.

"Ah, Annabelle, it's good to see you this afternoon."

"Mrs. Thompson, it is a pleasure to see you as well," Annabelle said, adoring the beautiful dress Mrs. Thompson wore.

Mrs. Thompson smiled at Annabelle. "I was a bit concerned with your imposing actions, but it seems it has helped boost the work efforts of our slaves. What a kind Negro woman you are. I'm off to meet with some friends for a moment, but Mr. Thompson is still home, so you're welcomed to give water to the slaves."

"Thank you, Mrs. Thompson. That means a lot."

Mrs. Thompson cheerfully nodded at Annabelle, and the carriage continued forward. Annabelle moved once again toward the Thompson farm. On the way, she felt conflicted. Her anger rose at seeing that Mrs. Thompson saw no problem with having slaves, but she was pleased to lessen the slaves' burden. Many of the Cherokee didn't care about Annabelle's race but her social status. The complexity of the social system tested Annabelle because she understood that the mention of freeing slaves would destroy her reputation.

Annabelle arrived at the Thompson farm looking for Doll as she met with the other slaves. Annabelle was impressed every time she came to the Thompson farm, looking at the cattle herds and the growing cornfields. Annabelle felt in her heart this was something God had put on her heart to do. Annabelle finished giving water to the slaves who tended the cattle and cornfields, and she was greatly confused when she didn't find Doll or a slave named Nathan.

Annabelle decided to take a different route around the farmland, and to her disappointment, she still didn't see Doll or Nathan. Annabelle figured Doll was in the main house, and she went on the side of the large house to knock on the front door when she heard moaning as she moved beneath a window. Annabelle stopped and stood under the window, trying to listen when she heard more moaning. She covered her mouth.

They must've gone crazy to be doing that in their master's house. I need to talk to Doll. No master would allow such a thing in their house, Annabelle thought.

Annabelle paced as she carried the water bucket and kept glancing at the barns, expecting Mr. Thompson to walk out eventually. Suddenly, Annabelle saw one of the large barn doors open, and her heart dropped, waiting for Mr. Thompson to walk out. However, it was Nathan taking one of the black horses to one of the cornfields.

"Ah, Miss Annabelle, do you have some water left?" Nathan asked in Cherokee.

Annabelle's mouth dropped, and she nearly dropped the bucket. "Oh! Why, yes, Nathan," Annabelle replied in the same language. Annabelle frantically put on a smile for Nathan. "I have more than enough for you."

Annabelle quickly approached Nathan, and he drank the water while she petted the black horse. "Thank you, Miss Annabelle. It helps."

"Anytime, Nathan. You have a good day."

Annabelle's mind raced as she nervously waited to see if it was really Doll inside the house. A couple of minutes passed when the front door opened, and Doll walked out of the house, adjusting her yellow cotton dress.

"Annabelle!" Doll said in Cherokee. "How are you doing?"

"I'm doing well. I brought water for you and the others."

Doll moved closer, and Annabelle gave her some water.

"Thank you. I needed this," Doll said, grabbing a sack off the ground. She sighed. "I need to get some cornmeal from one of the barns. You can come with me."

"Sure, I'll walk with you."

The women went to the barn. Annabelle carried the water bucket and couldn't help but stare at Doll. Annabelle was confused because Doll seemed happy, and she even hummed as they walked.

The women went around to the back of the large building, and Doll opened a large barrel to scoop out some cornmeal.

Annabelle continued to stare at Doll, lightly tapping her finger on the bucket handle. "I heard you with Mr. Thompson."

Doll stopped scooping up the cornmeal, and her face went blank. She stared into the barrel. "What did you hear?"

"I heard the two of you together when I walked under the window."

Doll's eyebrows creased as she stared at Annabelle. "It's best if you not tell anyone about this."

Annabelle shook her head. "I understand what you're going through. I've been raped by a man before."

"I have heard of women being raped by men, but it isn't that way between me and Henry. I love him."

Annabelle blinked several times. "What? I've never heard of a slave falling in love with a master. I mean, how does that happen? Does Mrs. Thompson know?"

"When I was bought by Henry and his father, I was seven years old and already separated from my other family. Henry was sixteen years old, never treated me badly, and his white daddy never treated me badly. I guess since I was twelve, I began to have feelings for him. When he married Mrs. Thompson, I was sad but grateful she didn't treat me badly. I still loved him and his kindness, even though they were married.

"When his daddy died, Henry didn't take it well. I would cook with Mrs. Thompson to make his favorite foods, but that still didn't do enough. Mrs. Thompson went to bed early as he sat in that rocking chair on the porch. I stayed behind later than the other slaves and saw him. He cried while he sat in that chair, and it hurt my heart to see him sad. I walked over and wiped a tear from his face. Told him I will stay there with him and watch the sunrise if that helped him heal. He held my hand with so much love."

Doll sighed deeply. "I sat in his lap, watched the stars with him, and reminded him of the good memories of his father. It was the first time I'd seen him smile. The first time in two weeks. I brushed his hair and held him as he rocked the chair. Over time, our feelings grew. Sometimes, I felt bad for Mrs.

Thompson, and other times, I thought I deserved to love some-one too. I knew him longer than her. I realize it's not so right, but he has my heart."

Annabelle remained silent as she listened. It was the first and only time Annabelle had met a slave woman in love with her master. Annabelle could see Doll couldn't help but smile telling her about her love affair.

"I do wonder how God will judge me, loving a married man," Doll continued. "Maybe I should have told him sooner, but I was still growing into a woman. I looked very different than I do now."

"How long has this been going on?" Annabelle asked.

"I was eighteen when the love between us started, nineteen when I gave myself to him, so this has been going on for ten years now. Time really can go by quickly."

"What about his children? How do you keep it a secret so well?"

"I was eighteen years when Thomas was born and twenty when Samantha was born. I've always felt like, in many ways, they were also my children. Megan, the four-year-old girl that's always in the house, is my daughter. I suppose when she is older, I will ask Henry when he wants the others to know she is their sister. I don't want them to become separated. Those children adore their sister. I guess that's my only regret, not being able to tell Megan right now who her daddy is. For now, she is happy with papa Thompson."

Annabelle slightly shook her head. "I never would've guessed she was your daughter. I mean, she looks like a young Negro girl but different. When I think about it, she does look a little like him. What does Mrs. Thompson think of her?"

Doll bit her lip. "She thinks I was approached by a mixed-blood man and taken advantage of."

"You mean raped?"

"No, that a man cornered me, and to avoid being raped, I let him have me. It's a very real thing being afraid to say no, but looking at Megan, I think I can live with that lie. I think she has a beautiful brown color, but her hair... I couldn't hide that. If she'd gotten my hair, it would've been easier for me to say it was a Negro man." Doll beamed. "She has Henry's smile and laugh too. She is so different than I was when I was a child."

Tears flooded Doll's eyes, but she fanned her face. "Henry takes good care of her. I see the way he looks at Megan, and it's no different than how he looks at Thomas or Samantha. He loves his daughter, even though it's a secret. She is loved here. Few Negro women can say that. I know that's true. I know not every master is the same, but I'm happy not being a slave to the white men.

"The truth is, I understand English, but I've spoken Cherokee so much I can barely speak English now. I know I sound crazy, but I have forgotten words. My baby girl doesn't know English at all. Henry is friends with some of the Choctaw, and because of that, Megan can speak some of their language. The scariest thing to me is if she would become a slave to the white people who would think she should know how to speak their language. Megan is already a beautiful girl. When she grows up, her beauty will grow with her. I know how those white men would look at her."

Doll grinned. "Meeting Negroes here that could only speak Cherokee was probably the biggest surprise for me. The slaves here are different than other slaves in the South. There are laws here that say what you can or cannot do, but I have never met proud slaves. I hope Henry will give Megan her freedom so she can have a life better than me. Sometimes I wonder what is going through his mind. I see that he loves her, but I hope much that he can let her go."

A confused glare formed on Annabelle's face. "Why wouldn't he? She is his daughter."

"I don't believe he would keep her status a slave to lower her value, but so he can always have his eyes on her. He once gave Thomas a little smack on his rear when he knocked her down a year ago. Mrs. Thompson wasn't around to see it, and he has no idea I saw it. Henry is a kindhearted man and made

Thomas apologize to his sister. So I thought out of love, he will give her freedom, or to my pain, keep her close. I guess it takes a mother's eyes to see things like that. I think when you have children, especially a daughter, you will understand the over-protective nature fathers can have."

Annabelle tried not to frown when memories of Benita flowed through her mind. "I had a daughter some time ago, but I lost her as a baby."

Doll dropped the sack of cornmeal. "I'm so sorry. I didn't mean to insult you."

"No, you're right. It is difficult for me to understand. Even though I loved my daughter, I never had the chance to see what you have." Annabelle smiled at Doll reassuringly. "But maybe someday, I will be blessed enough to see that."

Doll picked up the sack of cornmeal and went toward Annabelle. "I think you will. You're a young, smart, and beautiful woman. Don't accept a man your heart hasn't accepted."

"Yeah, I have no reason to not trust God with giving me someone new in my life. Love can be simple and complicated at the same time."

The women were exiting the barn when Doll placed her hand on Annabelle's shoulder. "Please remember not to tell anyone about me and Henry. The other slaves don't even know about us."

"After seeing the love you have for him, there is no way I would want to see you lose that. You have my word that nothing will be said of it."

Annabelle walked to the Tates' land to give the slaves water while they worked. She ignored the beautiful scenery of tall grass and wildflowers as she walked to the other farm.

I never thought I'd see love grow this way, Annabelle thought. *What a difficult choice she made. God, please protect Doll and Megan as you have all these years.*

Annabelle strangely felt motivated to speak with Jacob once she saw him. She gave water to the slaves on the Tate farm but didn't see Jacob.

Jacob must be home helping John and the others today.

After Annabelle left the Tate farm, she arrived at the supply store in deep thought but in a good mood.

"You're quiet," Lisa said. "What has your thoughts?"

"Nothing important, I guess," Annabelle responded. "I was surprised by someone's kindness today."

"Who surprised you?" Lisa asked.

Annabelle replied with a hesitant tone, "Well, Mr. Thompson. I watched how he treated a slave child. It was actually really cute."

Lisa smiled while the two women continued to talk to each other and work with the chickens. When night came, Annabelle lay in her bed staring at the stars and thinking of how to approach Jacob. Annabelle said her prayers, asking for guidance, and fell asleep to the background of the wolves howling.

CHAPTER 13
Learning Acceptance

THE NEXT DAY ARRIVED WITH Annabelle anxious to see Jacob. Annabelle put on her red plaid dress and walked out of the small log cabin when Grace followed her.

"Annabelle, where are you going right now?" she asked in Cherokee.

"I was going to take a quick walk to the Tate farm," Annabelle replied.

A crease appeared between Grace's brows, and Annabelle saw suspicion in her friend's expression. "Okay, well, you should come back soon to practice using the bow with me."

Annabelle cocked her head. "I don't think I could ever shoot an arrow like you."

"If you never try, then you can never improve."

Annabelle smiled even though she felt a little guilt-tripped. "Okay, I will be back soon."

Annabelle walked to the Tate farm, but on her way, she saw Jacob coming toward her. Jacob wore his brown trousers and a matching brown vest that covered his high-collared white shirt.

Oh, this must be God, Annabelle thought.

"Annabelle, good morning," Jacob said in Cherokee.

"Jacob!" she replied.

"How are you?" he asked.

"I'm doing well. I was taking a walk. What are you doing over here?" Annabelle asked.

"I was actually looking for you or Grace. I'm glad I found you."

Annabelle tried not to blush the moment Jacob smiled. "Well, we can go over by the old redbud and sit on the hill together."

"Sounds good to me. It would be nice to spend some time with you."

Annabelle and Jacob went to the old redbud tree and sat under it.

"What did you want to talk to me about?" Annabelle asked, smiling.

"I'm not sure where to start, but I'm interested in someone," Jacob said, his voice nervous. "I'm sure a beautiful woman like you has caught the attention of a man before. How can I make it clearer I like her?"

Annabelle forced herself to continue smiling. "Well, most women like a good conversation. We like men that smile, and I think it helps when a man purposely asks to spend more time with her alone. I think probably one of the most important signals is how you look at her with your eyes. I think those are things letting her know you're looking for more than friendship."

Jacob leaned back against the old tree. "So, the eyes tell you something?"

Annabelle chuckled. "Yeah, I think so. I don't know why, but I do know the eyes help," Annabelle said in Cherokee. She continued to look out into the field, avoiding eye contact with Jacob.

"You impress me. You came here not knowing any Cherokee, but you're now speaking to me like this is natural to you."

Annabelle blushed but continued looking at the fields.

"Thank you for the help. It means a lot. Now I know how to let her know how I feel."

The grin dropped from her face as she looked at Jacob. "Sure, you're a good man."

Looking away at the fields, Annabelle attempted to brush away her feelings. The bison herd returned, and the appearance of the bison helped lift Annabelle's spirits.

"Wow," she said, "look at them so happy. I always enjoy watching those animals."

"I remember watching them as a child. The herds used to be bigger, but over time, they just keep getting smaller and smaller."

Annabelle frowned. "Do you know why?"

"No, we're not sure what is causing less of them to return. Maybe a new water pool has appeared further out."

<hr>

Annabelle and Jacob continued to watch the bison herd together and talk about other things as Lizzie walked out of the large house with a bow and some arrows, and Lizzie saw Annabelle sitting next to Jacob. One of her braids swayed in the wind. She tapped her foot and scoffed. Lizzie aligned an arrow with the bow, and her brown eyes fixed on Jacob. She took a deep breath with the bowstring pulled back, then Lizzie grudgingly relaxed and lowered the bow.

"Lizzie," Grace shouted. "Come on. We don't have all day." She stood by the small log cabin with a bow and arrows of her own. "Have you seen Annabelle?"

"I see her," Lizzie replied.

"Tell her to come so she can try to shoot the arrows."

Lizzie stomped her foot and walked off to get Annabelle, murmuring to herself as she approached Annabelle and Jacob. The two friends continued talking and watching the herd.

During the conversation, Annabelle giggled, saying, "Tell me the truth. Why did Lizzie get so mad because you said you'll remain friends with her?"

Jacob picked up a blade of grass and broke it apart. "When Lizzie first told me, she kissed me, and I kissed her back. I liked it, but later I felt bad because I think I hurt her more. I do think Lizzie is beautiful, but my feelings for her are as a friend. Sometimes, I think I'm foolish for saying no to her, but I think I care too much for Lizzie to play with her heart."

Lizzie heard the end of the conversation and purposely stepped on a fallen branch. "Annabelle, it is time to go," Lizzie said in Cherokee. "Grace is looking for you."

Annabelle turned her head. Her eyes widened when she saw Lizzie armed and stood up immediately. "Okay, I'm ready to follow you," Annabelle said in Cherokee.

"Good afternoon, Lizzie," Jacob said.

Lizzie rubbed the bow with her fingers. "Jacob, you look nice today," Lizzie replied. "At least today, you don't smell like the animals."

Jacob slowly stood up, wiping grass off his trousers. "Looks like Grace is going to give you a hard time again. Smiling might loosen up those muscles."

Lizzie gave Jacob a smirk. "I think today will be a good day. I'll give my sister a stronger challenge now that I have some stronger motivation. It's time to go, Annabelle."

Lizzie left as Annabelle waved at Jacob. Jacob waved back, smiling. Lizzie slightly turned her head back a little. She gave Jacob a small smile but snobbishly turned her head away.

"There are some of my favorite ladies. It's time to have fun," Grace said as Annabelle and Lizzie approached.

<hr>

The women enjoyed each other's company, though Lizzie still belittled Annabelle. Grace worked with Annabelle, teaching her how to use the bow and arrow. Annabelle's first attempts were terrible, and Lizzie made fun of her. Grace rebelled slightly, shoving her sister every time Lizzie mocked Annabelle's failure. Noticing the accuracy of Lizzie's shots motivated Annabelle.

"Lizzie, you're shooting strong today," Grace observed.

"I have some strong reasons to do so," Lizzie said in Cherokee.

"Hmph. Annabelle, you're doing so well now. If you keep practicing with us, I'm sure you will do better," Grace said before picking up her bow to shoot her arrows.

Grace's accuracy always left Annabelle speechless. Annabelle's attempt made her realize how difficult archery was. The women ended their time together using Samuel's rifle to shoot rocks, enjoying the challenge.

As the women strolled back home, Lizzie reached into her quiver and pulled out a small tomahawk before ruthlessly throwing it at a large redbud tree. The action startled Annabelle, and she watched Lizzie retrieve the tomahawk.

"You're good," Annabelle said, speaking in Cherokee.

Lizzie smirked. "Lisa is actually better than me. We used to practice as children, even though the white people saw it as savage."

The experience was surprising for Annabelle, learning that Lisa and Lizzie would actually practice throwing tomahawks at trees.

What happened to little girls playing with dolls and running around? Annabelle thought. *Well, Ruthanne used to cut the hair off her dolls. I guess I shouldn't be shocked that some little girls would practice throwing sharp objects.*

The day continued, and late evening found Annabelle sitting up in her bed, continuing to read *The Three Musketeers*. She fell asleep while reading.

"Annabelle, pray for John," a soft voice whispered, waking Annabelle from her sleep.

Spooked, Annabelle looked around her room. She walked to the door and opened it slowly, but she didn't see or hear anything. She turned back to her bed and crawled into it, feeling in her spirit that it wasn't a dream. She prayed for John and went to sleep.

CHAPTER 14
The Unheard Warning

A MONTH PASSED AS THE LIGHTNING-STRONGMAN family celebrated David's birthday. Annabelle adored the toddler. She allowed herself to welcome David, believing it would help heal her from her past. Annabelle had also grown fond of watching John interact with the boy.

Nancy noticed the attention Annabelle constantly gave David and John. Each day, it became seemingly more aggravating to Nancy. Annabelle noticed Nancy's strong dislike for her, and she felt more of Nancy's aggression at the church. Annabelle couldn't decide if it was Nancy's refusal to greet Annabelle or the specific glare of disgust Nancy gave her every day.

One Sunday, the women attended church, and David sat on Annabelle's lap. Nancy's expression seemed envious as she watched the two of them interact.

After the sermon ended, as the women left the church, Nancy approached Grace. "Grace, good afternoon, dear. How are you?" she asked.

Grace replied, "I'm well. How are you doing?"

"That's good to hear. Grace, I was wondering if John would be comfortable with the Negro taking care of young David. Surely, at least Lisa could have sat David on her lap instead."

Annabelle overheard the conversation as she walked by

with David. Her eyes locked with those of Nancy, but Annabelle chose to keep moving.

<hr>

"Annabelle has been around David for a while, and she's done a good job with him." Grace put her hand on her hip. "You're a bold one to say something like that."

Nancy shrugged a shoulder and leered. "What can I say? I think she has too much freedom around David. She's already a free Negro. What else would she feel comfortable doing? She belongs out in the fields."

Grace stepped forward, and Nancy took a step back.

"Nancy, don't make me drag you out of this church and beat you," Grace snarled. "There's obviously something else bothering you besides her being Negro."

Nancy pouted. "How dare you try to tell me what I'm thinking! Why can't you two be more civilized like John? You're here with your little nigger pet and practicing things like a savage, which shows you aren't a true woman like me."

At that time, most of the congregation had left the church. Grace grabbed Nancy's dark green Victorian dress and forced Nancy outside of the church.

"Tell me, you weak woman, when I roll you around on this dirt road, how much of lady will you look like after that?"

"Get your hands off me!" Nancy shouted.

Pastor Bluebird, a peanut butter skin-toned man with an average build, had been standing by the pulpit and about to grab his Bible from the pulpit when the confrontation escalated. He rushed over to the two women and placed his hand on Grace's hand. "Grace let her go," he said. "The two of you haven't even walked away from the church grounds and you're already fighting."

"I'm sorry. I guess I have to continue to work on my temper like Lizzie," Grace said. "I struggle to tolerate such a prideful blue-eyed woman.

Nancy growled. "And you care too much about the Negroes.

They can do nothing for you, but you keep trying to treat them like they're one of us. Why don't you go practice shooting your stupid bow like the savage you are?"

"Keep talking like that, and my aim might miss a tree for once and hit you."

Pastor Bluebird replied, "Ladies, enough. Grace, go home."

Grace's eyes met Nancy's before she walked away.

"Nancy, you were wrong," the pastor said. "We're to love each other as Jesus has loved us all. You didn't like it when Grace talked about your blue eyes. How is that different than you treating the Negroes badly? Don't allow your father's teachings to define you."

"My father is a far better man than most of the men in this town," Nancy snarled. "He earned his living."

"But what has he done for our people? He holds onto his profits and gives nothing. Rarely does he come to listen to the gospels, and I've seen how he treats the slaves. All of these are signs of a weak Christian man, selfish and unwilling to change as he needs to."

"The slaves are treated as they need to be," Nancy said with a snobbish tone. "They're slaves, after all." Nancy stormed away from the church, clutching her reticule tightly.

Annabelle and the others arrived home shortly after. The carriage had been set up, and John had hooked Big Boy to it alongside Ray.

"You're ready to leave already?" Lizzie asked.

"We do better when we begin the ride in the daytime," John replied. "Samuel, are you ready now?"

"I would like to eat something first," Samuel said. "Give me ten minutes."

"Alright, please don't take too long."

David held Annabelle's hand as she walked toward John. "Where are you guys going?" she asked.

John smiled. "We're going to Mercy to get supplies. We can't take you with us, but if you want to write a letter for us to give to Ruthanne, we can do that."

"Yeah, I want to do that." Annabelle left David with John and rushed into the small house.

"How long are you going to be gone this time?" Lisa asked.

"The usual four days, maybe even three," John said.

Lizzie approached John and gave him some money. "Bring me back some more lilac perfume. Don't forget this time."

John replied, "I'll remember. Last time was eventful."

Lizzie picked up David and left with him. "Yeah, don't bring back any more strangers."

"You need to let the boy walk," John said. "He's four years old now, and you have some nerve to tell me not to bring back any strangers."

Lizzie turned her head with her brown eyes narrowed in a stubborn glare. "I can still carry him, and I'm not asking. We don't need anybody new around here. It will be another mouth to feed."

John murmured, "Yeah, you're difficult enough on your own. We don't need any more drama."

Lizzie put her hand to her ear. "What did you say?"

"I said you need to go play with David since you won't let him grow up."

"Pff, say goodbye to your daddy, David."

David smiled at his father. "Bye, Daddy. I love you," he said.

"I love you, my little warrior," John said.

Lizzie entered the house carrying David while Lisa followed. Tsula stayed back and gave John a hug.

"Be safe. The two of you are idiots," Tsula said. "And I agree with Lizzie. You already have a crazy white woman, so don't bring back something else."

John glared at his cousin as Tsula cackled and walked to the house.

"That wasn't funny, Tsula," John said.

Tsula continued to laugh. "Oh, but it was."

"Keep on stepping, Tsula. It's what you're good for."

"I'm sorry. Did I hurt Honey Bear's feelings?" Tsula glanced to her right to see Grace coming home, Nancy not far behind her. "Well, look. Here comes Sweet Corn right now."

"You need to stay in your own business, Tsula Strongman," John barked.

"Oh my, is that anger or embarrassment, Honey Bear?" Tsula joked.

Tsula walked away laughing, and John stood by the horses clenching the reigns.

"Hey, Flour Face, hold the door open. I'm coming inside," Tsula said.

Lizzie looked back at Tsula the moment she entered the log cabin, and she closed the door in Tsula's face.

"Real cute. Jesus is watching you," Tsula said.

Grace approached John as he finished getting the horses ready to leave. "Are you and Samuel ready to leave?" she asked.

"Yeah, I'm waiting on Samuel right now," John answered.

"The two of you be safe. Did you tell Annabelle where you were going?"

"I told her a few minutes ago. She went inside to write a quick letter."

Grace heard Nancy approach and huffed when the woman pranced closer to John. "I don't like her," Grace said, her tone irritated. "She's a real princess with a messed-up heart."

John scowled. "Don't say that about her. Nancy has been around since we were children."

Grace folded her arms. "So what? The moment Camille passed, she went after you. That should bother you. And the way she treats Annabelle is no different than the white people. She has a lot to learn, and I don't just mean the Cherokee stuff."

"Please stop mocking her, especially about her having blue eyes. That really hurts her feelings," John said. "So she doesn't know the language well, and she acts a little different. I still like her."

"You need to open your eyes," Grace barked. "Honestly, I don't care that she's blue-eyed. It's the fact that she represents the very people that put us out here. She sees anything that represents the old ways as uncivilized. She has no pride in who she is, and she has no interest in developing it. Even in the church, she is a handful."

"All I'm asking is for you to continue to give her a chance," John replied.

"She's been given chances, but you need to ask yourself this: Are you interested in how Nancy looks and how she gives you attention or who she really is?"

Grace heard Nancy come even closer and walked toward the log cabin.

Nancy approached John as Grace left. "Hey, Honey Bear," Nancy said. "You look like you're ready to leave town."

John replied, "Yes, it's always a good trip visiting Mercy."

"You look so handsome, like a real man. How long are you going to be gone?"

"We'll be gone for three or four days. We have a few things to do while we're in town."

Annabelle exited the small house and walked toward John with two letters in her hand. "John, would you please make sure you give this to Ruthanne or Rebecca Keys? If one of them gets the letters, I will know all that I need to know," she said.

John replied, "Sure, I would be happy to do that for you. It would be good to see Ruthanne. She reminds me of Lizzie in some ways."

Annabelle began to hand John one of the letters when Nancy suddenly snatched it from her. "You need to deliver the letter yourself," Nancy snarled. "I'm sure you being gone for some time would do the family some good."

John suddenly snatched the letter from Nancy. "The trip would be too much for her to do alone, and they're friends of mine. I'm excited to see them soon, and don't speak to Annabelle like that. She's done nothing wrong to you."

"Why are you defending her?" Nancy sneered. "She has no value. The reason the family allows her to even stay here is confusing to me. She isn't one of us."

In a harsh tone, he replied, "She's been valuable since the first day she asked to work for us. She treats all of us fairly, she took the time to learn our language, and David loves her. Never speak such a lie ever about her again."

Nancy directed her icy blue eyes on Annabelle and gripped the back of her skirt tightly. "I'd recommend you not let your son take a liking to a nigger. Otherwise, he may grow up not understanding they're beneath us and always will be beneath us. You'll be raising him wrong if you do."

John's nose scrunched as his eyebrows furrowed. "Don't try to tell me how to raise my son. My son has all the love this world can give him, and more. And don't call Annabelle a nigger. I don't want my son learning that word."

Nancy suddenly pointed her finger at Annabelle and shouted, "She is nothing, and I can call her whatever I want! I guess there is part of Camille that did stay with you after all. Have a safe ride, prairie nigger. Maybe the John I knew will return this time." Red in the face, she stormed away.

As Nancy stormed off, John noticed Grace standing in the front door of the large house, unsure if she had seen the entire incident. A chill went down John's spine as he clasped Annabelle's letter. "Annabelle, they will get this letter. That's something I can promise you."

Annabelle grinned at John, gazing at him with trusting eyes. "Thank you. It means so much to me," Annabelle said. "Also, this letter is for Mr. Boston."

Annabelle gave John Mr. Boston's letter, and John nodded at her. Annabelle placed her hand on John's shoulder and went to the large log cabin.

Samuel rushed out of the large house eating a piece of cornbread, and he bumped into Grace, who stood in the doorway. Grace fell down, and Samuel dropped the rest of his cornbread.

"Oh no, my cornbread," Samuel said.

"You knock me down and complain about some stupid cornbread!" Grace shrieked in Cherokee. "I'm going to kill you, Samuel!" The rage in her face was obvious as she stood.

Samuel ran past Annabelle and to the carriage. "Bye, Annabelle!" Samuel yelled, waving. "Slow her down if you can!"

Annabelle looked at Grace, and her eyes widened at the pure anger on the other woman's face as she ran toward the carriage. "I'm sorry, Samuel. I think you'll have to make it to the carriage first," Annabelle said.

"John, get in the carriage now! I'm too fat from eating. I can't move that well," Samuel yelled.

John got in the carriage and grabbed the reins as Samuel approached.

"John!" Grace yelled. "Don't you dare ride off with that little boy!

Samuel held his stomach while he reached the carriage. "Oh, my stomach. It's going to die," he yelled.

Samuel struggled to ignore the pain as he tried to get on the carriage, but Grace pulled him off and smacked him three times on his head.

"That will be the last time you see a piece of cornbread as more important than my wellbeing," Grace said, speaking in Cherokee. She was reddish-brown in the face as she took deep breaths before saying, "I love you, boys. Please, be safe out there."

Grace walked away, and Annabelle watched as Samuel slowly stood up, cleaning his trousers.

"At least it wasn't Lizzie," Samuel said.

"I think she went easy on you," John said.

Samuel sat down next to John, breathing heavily. "What makes you say that?"

"She ignored the tree branch on the ground."

Samuel looked down, saw the branch on the dirt road, and sighed. "Let's leave before she comes back."

John laughed, and the two rode toward Mercy.

CHAPTER 15
Consequences

Two days passed before John and Samuel arrived. Their first stop in Mercy was to Mr. Boston's supply store. The two young men entered Mr. Boston's store, surprising an elderly white woman who stared at the men.

"Well, there are two faces I haven't seen in quite some time," Mr. Boston said. "Mrs. Abbot, here are your grains. I hope to see you again soon."

"Yes, I'm sure you will," Mrs. Abbot replied before she walked past the men uncomfortably.

Mr. Boston rubbed his white hair as the cousins moved closer to the counter.

"It is good to see you, Mr. Boston," John said.

"Yes, indeed," Mr. Boston replied. "I owe the two of you a great deal for saving Annabelle. How is she doing out there?"

John smiled. "She is doing well. I think the change was hard for her, but she is doing good in Cherokee land."

"She has even learned how to speak our language quite well," Samuel said. "My sisters love her."

Mr. Boston seemed overjoyed with the news. His face brightened, and he smiled. "I can't express how much joy I really feel for her right now. Well, let me give you your supplies."

The men loaded the supplies onto the carriage and went back into Mr. Boston's store.

"It is always a pleasure seeing you, Mr. Boston. I will be sure to tell Annabelle you're doing well," John said.

"Tell her I said hi, and maybe in the future, I will come to visit," the older man replied.

"We have this for you, Mr. Boston. It's from Annabelle," Samuel said, reaching into his brown vest to give him Annabelle's letter.

Mr. Boston opened the letter and read it out loud.

"Mr. Boston, I hope you and Mr. Fluffs are doing well. I'm doing well now. I took a lot of time to heal, and I had help from John's sister, Grace. She took me to see their elder, Joyce, and without her, I don't know if I would've been able to get my happiness back. The Indians are interesting and loving people. Most of them have treated me good, but a few have treated me badly. It's sad that I've met slaves here. I feel comfortable visiting the slaves of two different families. I never thought I would meet masters that are nice and care about their slaves. It gives me different feelings, but at least here, I feel safe and even loved. Take care of yourself, Mr. Boston. Annabelle."

Mr. Boston struggled to hold back his tears. "That Annabelle, always finding a new adventure, I see. Thank you, boys. It means a lot. It warms my heart."

"It was our pleasure, Mr. Boston. Annabelle has always spoken well of you," John said. "Do you know where I can find Miss Ruthanne or Mrs. Keys?"

Mr. Boston slightly frowned and explained where the men needed to go. "Before you leave, someone needs to say hi."

The older man reached into his vest and pulled out a bell, ringing it. Suddenly, the spoiled, green-eyed Mr. Fluffs came trotting down the back hallway and jumped on the counter. John and Samuel laughed, petting the blotchy gray and white cat before leaving the supply store.

As the men walked to the Keyses' home, John gave Samuel some money. "Go to the Potses' store and get Lizzie's perfume, or she'll be really angry if we forget again," John said.

Samuel gave John a smirk and replied, "You mean if you forget again."

"Shut up and go to the store. I'll come to the store once I give Mrs. Keys Annabelle's letter."

Samuel rode away in the carriage, laughing to himself. John traveled through the town of Mercy and noticed the town had become more active with people. Going through Mercy made John jealous, seeing how the people were not struggling like his own.

John saw the Keyses' brown bricked home, described by Annabelle, and he saw Rebecca on the porch with Elisha and Esther.

Rebecca looked up while she cleaned Esther's gown. "Is that you, John Lightning?" she asked.

"Yes, it is me, Mrs. Keys," John replied. "I came here to give you or Miss Ruthanne a letter from Annabelle."

Rebecca's mouth curved into a smile as John approached her with the letter in his hand.

"God certainly knows how to answer prayers at the right time," she said.

John handed Rebecca the letter, and the woman anxiously opened it with Esther in her lap.

Rebecca read the letter.

"Dear Ruthanne or Rebecca, I hope all of you are doing well. I miss all of you so much. Ruthanne, Elizabeth, Rebecca, and Marilyn, y'all my four sisters God gave me. My heart breaks knowing it will be a long time before I can see any of you again, but I know God is faithful. Most Indians treat me good here. The amount of love I'm given here makes that hate seem like nothing. The Indians have an elder that's a strong Christian woman. She's done a lot to help me heal and move on. John's older sister, Grace, has also been a big help.

"I have great news. In the Cherokee land, I'm written down in their records as a free woman, Annabelle Mays. It is a long story, but because of John's sister, I have a new life. Rebecca, I could never repay you or Allen for giving me and the girls a home. I cry writing this letter because it brings back so many great memories. I feel now I can once again trust God. Jesus is my rock and my salvation and all I need. I learned that from you, and if this is the only letter I get to write you, I love you, my sister.

"Marilyn, I miss you greatly. It isn't the same having such a cheerful person in my life. I have met someone who makes dresses like you, and maybe one day, you will meet her. Elizabeth, you have such a good heart. I hope your cooking can match that one day. Ruthanne, John's sisters remind me of you. I hope God brings us back together again one day."

A tear flowed down Rebecca's cheek, and she took a deep breath. "It does seem that the best choice in hiding Annabelle was made. Your sisters made quite a good impression on Annabelle." She wiped the tears from her eyes.

"Mrs. Keys, please make sure Ruthanne receives the letter," John said. "I was surprised I didn't see her at Mr. Boston's store."

Rebecca took a deep breath, sadness dulling her brown eyes. "John, there's a lot you need to know, but I think it is best I write Annabelle a letter as well. And one other thing, please call me Rebecca in private conversations. You're welcomed to come in while I write the letter."

John followed Rebecca into the house while she carried the twins. Rebecca finished the letter and gave it to John. Rebecca wished John a safe trip and asked him to tell Marilyn to come to her home when he met with Samuel at Marilyn's store.

John arrived at Pots's Garments and saw Marilyn talking with Samuel. "Good afternoon, Miss Marilyn," John said.

Marilyn replied with a smile, "Hello, John. It's good to see you. Samuel here tells me Annabelle gave two letters to you."

"Yes, she did, and Miss Rebecca would like you to come to her home to talk. She didn't tell me too much, but she wanted you to come as soon as you could," John responded.

"Are the two of you going back to the Indian territory now?" she asked.

John nodded. "Yes, we are. It's best for us to start with the sun high."

Marilyn reached into the reticule she held and pulled out a perfume bottle of lilac. "I know you came here to buy some for a relative, but Annabelle is also fond of lilac as well. Please make sure she receives this gift." She closed the store's door and handed John the perfume.

"I'll make sure she gets it."

"Thank you, John. Tell Annabelle I said she has always looked wonderful in my dresses. Have a safe ride. The two of you are good men."

"Thank you, Miss Marilyn," Samuel replied.

Marilyn walked away to meet with Rebecca as John and Samuel got into the carriage and rode off.

"It looks like we did a good job this time," Samuel said happily.

John looked at Samuel with a little frown. "Ruthanne isn't doing well," he said. "A lot has happened since we rescued Annabelle, and a lot of it is in the letter Rebecca wrote."

Samuel sighed and ate an apple as they rode back to Tahlequah.

———◆———

As John and Samuel headed back to Tahlequah, their family went on as normal. Annabelle, Lizzie, and Grace worked the supply store as Lisa stayed home to help direct the horses. George, Michael, and Jacob did the other field work. While Tsula watched over David and taught him Cherokee and English, Grace worked at the counter with Cherokee customers and white men.

Grace spoke with one of the white men as Nancy entered the supply store. While waiting her turn, she acted in a snobbish manner and played with her curled hair.

Seemingly annoyed with Nancy's obvious impatience, Grace said, "One moment, sir. Nancy, what do you need?"

Her tone irritable, Nancy replied, "I need six chicken eggs.

These stupid niggers can't seem to be able to count half the time."

Grace forced a smile at the woman as she called, "Annabelle, please bring in six eggs." She then turned back to Nancy. "You will have your eggs soon. Please wait while I finish talking with him."

Nancy pressed her lips together at Grace's response, and Grace escorted the white man outside, giggling while he talked to her. Annabelle left and came back inside with a small basket, holding the six eggs. Annabelle saw Nancy and noticed she was agitated.

"The eggs are for me," Nancy barked. "I hope you can count, unlike your incompetent cousins."

Annabelle gave a fake smile and approached Nancy to hand her the eggs. "Just as Grace told me to get, here are your six eggs," Annabelle said.

Nancy shook her head and leered. "Did I say six eggs? No, I said eight eggs clearly. Grace doesn't listen well. Please hurry it up. I don't have all day."

Annabelle walked back outside and returned with eight eggs.

"Well, that's eight eggs," Nancy said. "But no, I think four eggs will be enough."

Annabelle left, murmuring to herself, and she returned to Nancy with four eggs.

Nancy glanced at the eggs with the corner of her mouth pulling back. "Go and get me six eggs. I guess Grace was right."

Annabelle bit her lip and went back outside to the chicken coops. She returned with six eggs.

"Here are your six eggs," Annabelle said, her smile covering a slightly irritated tone.

"I guess you do know how to serve," Nancy replied. "Give them here to me."

Annabelle kindly handed Nancy the basket when Nancy purposely let the handle slip out of her hand. The basket fell to the floor, and most of the eggs cracked.

"Look at what you did, you clumsy nigger," Nancy said.

Annabelle's eyes narrowed. "You did that on purpose!"

Nancy raised her voice, "How dare you accuse me of such a thing, blaming your clumsiness on me instead of admitting your fault. I guess you're not so different than your cousins in chains."

Annabelle's rage flared as she fixed her brown eyes on Nancy.

Abruptly, Annabelle felt the Holy Spirit speak to her, saying, "Forgive her, Annabelle. She is a prideful and hurt woman. She only knows how to express anger, so show her love. Annabelle, show her love. Don't repay evil with evil."

Annabelle took a deep breath and picked up the cracked eggs. "I will clean this and get you another set of eggs so you can go home," she said.

"That's right, nigger. Clean this mess up. I told Grace it was a terrible idea to have a nigger doing any form of business for her," Nancy bickered.

Annabelle responded in Cherokee, "It's sad you're so different than your people. You can barely speak Cherokee. It must be embarrassing."

Nancy's jaw dropped. "What did you say, nigger? What's embarrassing? Don't you ever try to speak that to me! You have no right to be speaking it! You're not one of my people, and you never will be!"

Annabelle replied in Cherokee, "I've become more of a Cherokee than you, and I have only been here for two seasons."

Nancy growled as she spoke in Cherokee. "I understood that! Every breath you take insults me." Nancy then continued in English, "I would be more than pleased to put a whip to your back and teach you your place in this world! You wouldn't be the first nigger for me to let my anger out on."

Annabelle felt the tension rise the second Nancy's furious blue eyes fixed on her. "And you call yourself a Christian woman. What would Jesus say about you if he was standing right here?"

Nancy smacked her, and Annabelle nearly lost her balance. Annabelle looked up at Nancy, who had turned red in the face.

"It's time for you to go home," Lizzie said.

"She's a clumsy nigger that dropped my eggs," Nancy replied. "You don't even like her."

"I like Annabelle's question. What would Jesus say about you right now? I see why the Creator has so much mercy for us. Now, leave before I get mad. You can come back tomorrow to get some eggs if you want them that badly, or send one of your slaves to get them."

"I'm telling my father about this. You can't be a bully forever. Eventually, people get tired of getting pushed around."

Grace suddenly walked in and noticed the tension between the women. "What's going on in here?" she asked.

Lizzie walked toward Annabelle. "Nothing. Nancy was leaving. She'll probably be back tomorrow."

Nancy brushed past Grace and reached for the front door.

"Nancy," Lizzie said, "please remember how much I like how you have your hair put in ringlets."

Nancy rolled her eyes and opened the door.

"Nancy!" Lizzie called.

Nancy turned around, and an egg suddenly smacked her on the forehead. She squealed as some of the egg white went into her hair, and the egg yolk slid down her face.

Annabelle gasped, and Lizzie wiped her hand on her own dress. Nancy ran off, squealing. Lizzie immediately told Grace what happened, and after the women finished working, they went home to prepare supper.

Later, the family ate supper together and joked around as normal. George had become more welcoming to Annabelle, but he took his time to acknowledge her.

"Lizzie, David has become a much better speaker, but you need to make sure you're spending more time on his English," Tsula said. "If we don't, he'll speak more like Lisa. You know how long it took for her to start speaking like white people."

Lizzie arrogantly replied, "Lisa speaks fine. You wish you could speak like her."

Tsula's eyes widened as she replied, "Speak like Lisa? Please. I'm happy with my better speech. It sounds sexier."

Lisa put down her fork and stared at her sister.

Tsula imitated Lisa, "Hi, my name is Lisa. What is your name? Now, see how I sound better. My name is Tsula. What do you want?"

Tsula gave a seductive smirk, and the women chuckled as George grinned at his daughter's sense of humor.

"You wish you sound better than me," Lisa said in a playful tone. "At least I know I cook better than you, and I can throw the tomahawk better than you."

"You can throw it better than me, but if a war happened, the men would be too seduced by my beauty to attack me. That's when I'll be able to take my shots." Tsula shaped her hand into a revolver and made fake gunshot sounds.

The women laughed, and the family continued to eat when there was a knock at the door.

Grace stood up to open the door, and her eyebrows shot up when she saw Mr. Hicks.

"May I come in? Grace, I wanted to speak with your uncle for a moment," Mr. Hicks asked.

"We're in the middle of supper, Mr. Hicks, but I will ask him," Grace replied.

Annabelle turned around in her seat, and seeing Mr. Hicks, she turned back around and lightly tapped the table.

"Uncle George, Mr. Hicks is here to speak with you," Grace said.

Mr. Hicks scratched his grayish-brown hair as George stood up and shook hands with Mr. Hicks. He was a white man with blue eyes.

"What's going on, Walter?" George asked.

Mr. Hicks replied, "I'm sorry to bother you at this time, but that nigger there attacked my little girl at your store. Now, you have her removed from working there again, or some kind of arrangement needs to be made. I'm not going to tolerate a nigger insulting my little girl." Mr. Hicks folded his arms across his green vest with his brown cane in his hands.

"I understand what you mean. The Negro is new here. I'm sure this will never happen again," George replied. "We haven't had problems with her before in the past, but I know this will never happen again. Annabelle, come here."

"No, Annabelle, stay," Grace said. She moved toward the white man, her eyes fierce and bold. "Your little girl came to my family's supply store acting disrespectful. She made fun of Annabelle and cost us five good eggs. Annabelle didn't start the problem. Your little girl did."

"Then explain to me why Nancy is still cleaning egg out of her hair right now," the man replied, his tone furious.

George folded his arms and stared at Grace angrily.

"It was me," Lizzie said with food in her mouth. Lizzie stood as she stuffed her face with more cornbread. "I didn't like the way she was messing up the store, so the spoiled queen got egg in her pretty face and in her ugly hair."

Mr. Hicks tugged his white high-collared shirt with his right hand. "That's inexcusable. You're no longer children," he said. "I think you need to learn how to show more respect."

Lizzie grinned as she finished her cornbread and unapologetically replied, "So does your innocent daughter. It was a sad loss of a good egg." Lizzie continued to go toward the kitchen while the rest of the family at the supper table remained silent.

"I'm sure this won't happen again," George said.

Mr. Hicks sighed and put his hand into his pocket. "I must apologize. I clearly didn't know the entire story," Mr. Hicks said. He then pointed at Annabelle. "I can tell she is a bit different than the others, but she needs to remember her place here."

"If she needs to know her place, then Nancy needs to know hers as well!" Grace said. "And it ain't to make Annabelle's day miserable because she is having a bad day!"

Mr. Hicks nodded. "Fair enough, Grace. I will talk with

Nancy so we can keep the peace. Thank you for y'alls time. I apologize for interrupting your supper."

"It is alright," George replied. "Have a good night, Walter."

Mr. Hicks got on his horse and rode away.

"I see a lot happened today," George commented. "Why didn't you say something to me earlier about this?"

"Because there was nothing more to say about it," Grace said. "It happened as we said it did. There was no blood spilled, just some pride hurt. She's a spoiled little girl anyway." Grace walked to the supper table and grabbed her plate, taking it into the kitchen.

George sat down and watched Grace enter the kitchen as he placed his hand on his temple.

———◆———

The next day, the arrangements stayed the same, and Lisa stayed behind to help with the farming. The warm weather of spring dwindled, and summer winds took over. Carrying horse supplies made Lisa sweat heavily, and she noticed Jacob watching her while she walked back into the barn.

"I guess we can take a lunch break right now," George said. "The two of you meet me back here in thirty minutes."

George sat down on a haystack and took a deep breath. Michael went to the large house, and Jacob went toward the barn.

"It looks like the horses are enjoying their time to rest," Jacob said in Cherokee.

Lisa walked toward Jacob, wiping the sweat off her neck with a rag. "Well, even the horses need time to recover," she said, speaking Cherokee. "What are you doing in here? Why didn't you follow Michael to the house?"

"I wanted to talk to you. I believe I might be jealous of Cari and Queen. They get all the attention."

Giggling, Lisa shyly said, "I said hi to you. It's not like we don't see each other at all. You shouldn't be jealous of them. They're my babies."

"I see how hard you work, and I see how much you care not just for the horses but your family. I think that makes you strong, and it makes it hard for me not to think about you."

Lisa tilted her head when she smirked. "Maybe you need to practice more on keeping your mind on other things."

"I do try, but I hear your voice in the wind, and when I see you smile, I can't help but smile." Jacob came closer to Lisa.

"That sounds more like you can't have enough of me," Lisa said. "I hope you don't feel that way when we are in church."

Jacob blushed, and his mouth quirked, looking like he attempted not to smile. "I'm able to focus in church, but seeing you smile and hearing you laugh holds my attention. I'm hoping you would like to spend some more time with me and talk about some other important things. I know your daddy would not approve of me right now, but maybe later, he'll accept me if you're willing to accept me."

Lisa's heart raced as Jacob stared into her brown eyes. Lisa rubbed her hands the moment she felt herself being drawn toward Jacob. "What about Lizzie?"

"I'll always care about Lizzie, but I don't see her as I see you. Lizzie is a beautiful, smart woman, but I think since we were children, my feelings for you grew differently. I don't know how to deny myself in speaking the truth from my heart."

"Sometimes, I can't imagine a life without you, Jacob Tate, but for now, I have much to think about. I like your courage. Don't lose that." Lisa beamed and went to the horses, rubbing her hands while her heart raced.

Jacob had been sweating the entire time he spoke with Lisa, and he wiped the sweat from his forehead. "I think that was a yes," Jacob said, smiling as he left the barn.

CHAPTER 16
Friends

URING THE EVENING, JOHN AND Samuel arrived back in
Tahlequah. The Lightning-Strongman family was excited to see them return. The family took the supplies,
dividing them up into supplies they would use for themselves
and the supply store.

John approached Annabelle as Samuel took a sack into the
barn. "We were able to give both letters to Mr. Boston and Rebecca," John said. "It seemed to strengthen their hearts reading what you wrote to them. Rebecca wrote you a note, and I
didn't read it."

John handed Annabelle the letter while she reached for it
anxiously. Annabelle gave John a hug.

"Thank you, John," Annabelle said. "It means so much to
me. I don't know if I could repay you."

"There's no debt to be paid, Annabelle." John picked up a
sack and walked to the barn.

Annabelle could feel the palms of her hands starting to
sweat as she stared at the letter as Grace stood next to her.

"Go on, Annabelle. Open it," Grace said.

Annabelle took a deep breath, broke the seal, and read the
letter.

Annabelle, my heart is warmed by your efforts to let us know how you're doing. I'm grateful to God you're safe. So much has happened these past few months. The twins are growing quickly. Both of them are fast learners and showing their different likes. I attempted to once have them sleep in separate beds, but they refused to sleep alone. I hope in my heart you love again and become a mother.

Daniel has become a close friend of Allen's, even though Allen is secretive about it because of his political ties. I see the joy Allen has when Daniel is around. Daniel seems to have been doing well since Benjamin's murder. Marilyn and I have been spending a lot of time together, along with Elizabeth. She has recovered well from losing her father. Elizabeth has returned to Mississippi for a few months to see Robin.

There is no easy way to tell you, but Ruthanne has not been doing well. In December, Ruthanne was arrested by Sheriff Shepard for breaking the law and aiding a runaway slave. She's been sentenced to six months in prison, and I've been visiting her when I can. A month ago, one of the sheriff's deputies attempted to rape her, and Ruthanne fought back. The man received serious injuries and said Ruthanne seduced him. She's been given another month because of this, but we're appealing these lies. Ruthanne fought hard to keep you safe. The best way to honor that is to live a happy life. We love you, Annabelle. Keep smiling, and God bless. Love, Rebecca.

Annabelle's heart dropped thinking about Ruthanne, and she sobbed.

"Annabelle, what is wrong?" Grace asked.

"Ruthanne has been put into the prison at Mercy. It's my fault. She sacrificed everything for me, and now she's suffering for it."

Grace took the letter from Annabelle and read it. Grace gave Annabelle a hug, and Annabelle continued to cry.

"I agree with this woman, Rebecca. The best way you can honor Ruthanne is by living this life to the best of your ability. Calm down and pray for peace in this. At least she is only in this terrible place for a part of a year. It could be worse."

"You're right. I think I need a little time alone. I'm going to go sit by the old tree."

"Alright, I'll come looking for you soon."

❖

Annabelle walked toward the old redbud tree, and Grace went to the family home. Grace entered the house and saw John sitting at the supper table.

"John, did you know Ruthanne was taken into the prison?" Grace asked.

"Rebecca told me after she wrote the letter and gave it to me, John replied. "It seems like the fighting between the white people is getting worse. I'm surprised, honestly. I thought they would come up with a solution to make all of them happy. How is Annabelle dealing with this?"

Grace looked at John, her eyes filled with concern. "She doesn't look like she's taking it too well. I think her greatest challenge right now is realizing Ruthanne's situation isn't her fault. Most of the news was good, though."

John sat back in the chair. "Where's Annabelle?"

"She's by the old tree on the hill. I think she wanted to be alone for a little while."

"I'm going out there to talk to her." John walked outside to the redbud tree and immediately noticed how troubled Annabelle seemed. "Do you care if I join you?" he asked.

Annabelle looked at John, and with a watery smile, she said, "Sure."

"I can see how sad you are through your smile," John said. "Ruthanne is a fighter, and so are you. Don't allow what these white people did to her to kill your spirit."

186

"I'm trying not to. It's not easy. Those people are so evil. I'm tired of them."

"You grew up being told you were nothing but a slave. Somehow, you created a way to love people anyway. How did you do it?"

Annabelle huffed. "I guess all it took was the love of my parents and Judy Mays. I was connected to the other slaves, but I don't think it was through love. I think it was because we all wanted to live in the hope that we might become free one day. It's scary to think the only ones that might have cried if I was sold away would have been my parents, Judy Mays and her sisters, and maybe Ruth."

John gave a half-smile. "I think they did a good job with you. Maybe the Creator saw that was all you needed. I see how you treat my son, and it warms my heart. Knowing the pain you went through losing your daughter makes me sad. When you're with David, I see love in you. He has his mother's laugh, and I used to hate hearing it because it reminded me she is only with us in spirit."

"It's a good laugh. It's the kind of laugh that makes you want to join in."

"Yeah, it is," John agreed, "and when I watch you play with him, it makes me happy to at least have him to remind me of Camille. I guess we're supposed to be like the stars."

Annabelle's eyebrow rose. "What do you mean?"

"The purpose of the stars is to shine their light on us. They keep doing what they're meant to do no matter if the days are good or bad. You told me a long time ago that God gives us all a purpose. I believe that. I believe that also means we're wrong to stop being who we're meant to be because our heart is hurting."

"You're right, John Lightning."

Annabelle and John sat down together for the rest of the evening. They watched the stars and talked about past memories. During this time, Annabelle felt loved by John.

CHAPTER 17
Relationships

THE NEXT DAY, NANCY CAME by and left with John. Annabelle watched John leave with her and decided to go play with David. Later in the day, she traveled with Grace and Lizzie to their practice ground. It was at a lower elevation with a hill overseeing it, and a field stood to the back of it. Wooden targets hung from several large old trees, and two large boulders outlined the four trees. As the women headed to the practice fields, Annabelle noticed Lisa there and felt excited.

"Lisa, what are you doing here?" Lizzie asked, speaking in Cherokee.

"Why ask me such a question?" the woman replied. "As if I never come out here to have fun, and I can tell you've been trying to get better than me."

Lizzie scoffed. "I haven't been throwing that much. Maybe you should pick up a bow."

Lisa threw a tomahawk she had been aiming at an old tree with absolute precision. "I can use the bow fine. You know that." Lisa moved toward the old tree and pulled out the tomahawk. She smiled at the women. "But tomahawk feels a little more personal if I ever had to use it."

"That was impressive, Lisa," Annabelle said in Cherokee. "Watching you is like watching Grace shoot an arrow."

Lizzie rolled her eyes and stepped toward Lisa. "I'm still better than you at the bow."

Lisa chuckled as she moved toward Annabelle and Grace. "Have fun, ladies. I'm going to take a walk. I will be back in time to help make supper."

"Okay, be safe and pay attention to where you're walking," Grace said.

"Like she needs to be told that. She's always fooling people with her smile," Lizzie said in Cherokee.

Lisa went away as the others practiced and enjoyed each other's company. Unknown to the others, Lisa was making a personal trip to Mr. Tate's farm. With her tomahawk in her right hand, she quickly walked to the farm while constantly looking behind her. She grinned the moment she saw the Tate farm, its residence not as large as her home but had two fields of corn and squash. The north side of the farm had a large wooden pen filled with cattle. One large wooden brown house belonged to the Tate family, and three other smaller brown structures housed the slaves. The slave houses sat in front of a brown barn. Lisa walked over to a water well located behind the Tate house.

"I was beginning to think you wouldn't come," Jacob spoke in Cherokee.

Lisa held back her smile. "I had a lot to think about."

"Lizzie?"

"We're cousins, but she's my sister."

"I never meant to hurt her."

"I know you, Jacob Tate. I know that's not who you are."

"You want to take a walk?"

"I'm sure your family will notice you're not around."

Jacob smirked. "I'm a grown man. They're okay with me disappearing for a little bit. What about you? A woman walking around in the wilderness... I'd rather us take a little walk before Lizzie starts searching for you."

Lisa lifted up her tomahawk and leered. "I'm a grown Cherokee woman."

Jacob rubbed his mouth, attempting to cover up his smile. "Well, excuse me."

Lisa pointed to a small hill a few hundred feet away. "How about we go sit on that little hill. Chances are low anyone will see us."

Jacob looked at the grass-covered hill. "Okay, I'll take all the attention I can get."

Lisa's eyes shifted down to the grass while her lips curled up slightly. She followed Jacob closely to the hill, her unbraided, long, thick, wavy hair swaying with each step. The two friends sat down and continued to talk. Lisa found herself laughing and smiling throughout the conversation. She nearly lost track of time but promised to arrange another meeting with Jacob soon.

The evening arrived as Lisa returned home and saw John returning with Nancy. Lisa tried to go a different way, but the young couple saw her. Lisa grunted but waved to John and Nancy as she reluctantly approached them.

"What a lovely day today, isn't it, Lisa?" Nancy said.

"Yes, it's beautiful day," Lisa replied. "What a nice dress you're wearing. I have always liked the color green."

"Oh, thank you. I see you have good taste. Too bad your sister doesn't, considering her reputable sewing skills."

Lisa forced a grin and opened the front door. "I have to help prepare supper. Please excuse me."

Lisa walked into the house, John and Nancy a few steps behind.

"I can't stand that witch," Lisa murmured.

⸺⬥⸺

John and Nancy went inside and sat down at the table, where George sat in his rocking chair.

"Mr. Strongman, it is good to see you," Nancy said.

"Hi, Nancy. I'm surprised to see you here," George said.

"Well, yes, I wanted to spend some time with the family and apologize for my daddy's rudeness. I had no idea he had left our plantation in such a rush after he'd heard what happened. It was a terrible misunderstanding."

George sat up in the rocking chair. "Apology accepted. It will be nice having a guest around for supper."

George later sat down at the supper table next to John, and the two talked.

Lizzie suddenly came out of the kitchen, and her mouth dropped a little as she saw Nancy sitting at the table. "I'll be right back. Annabelle didn't grab enough cornmeal," Lizzie said.

"I didn't know you allowed the Negro to help you cook," Nancy said.

Lizzie replied with a leer, "Well, you have to work with the gifts God gives them. I'll make sure I bring some more eggs inside too."

Nancy struggled to hold her smile while she glared at Lizzie, who giggled on her way outside. "She has always been quite the character," she said in an agitated tone.

John replied, "Don't allow her to bother you, or she'll keep coming after you."

Nancy scoffed. "That's easy for you to say, John. She's your sister. If she had the chance, she would cut all my hair off."

Lizzie soon returned with cornmeal and a few eggs, then stared at Nancy. "You know it wouldn't kill you to help cook since you're going to eat supper here," Lizzie said in a manipulative manner. "Then again, it probably would kill you."

Nancy's temper flared as her and Lizzie's eyes locked. "It would be my pleasure," Nancy sarcastically replied.

"You don't have to go in there," John said.

Nancy replied, "Oh no, it's quite fine, John. This won't be my first time to cook something."

Nancy followed Lizzie into the kitchen, and the others were stunned to see Nancy walk in behind her. "I hope you didn't come here to tell us what to cook. We're not your slaves," Tsula said

Nancy inhaled, pursing her lips. "I decided to help make the food because I'm joining all of you for supper."

Tsula smirked, and her eyes widened a little. "Wow, I'd never thought I'd see this day. Do you know how to boil water?"

The women giggled as Grace nudged Tsula to stop teasing Nancy.

"Come here, Nancy. You can help cut up this beef," Grace said.

Nancy walked over and glanced at Annabelle.

"Here's the cornmeal, Annabelle, and hurry up it up this time," Lizzie barked.

"Hush, like you don't take your time with the chicken," Grace said in a mocking tone.

"Hmph. Well, here are some more eggs too, Annabelle," Lizzie said, placing a basket next to Annabelle.

"Thank you," Annabelle said.

"Annabelle doesn't need all those eggs, but I know where they can go," Tsula said.

Lisa and Lizzie chuckled as Grace stared at the women. The women calmed down and continued to cook.

Nancy watched Annabelle make the cornbread batter.

"That batter looks good, Annabelle. You always do a good job," Tsula said.

Annabelle replied, "Thank you, Tsula. I do try."

Annabelle placed the cornbread on the stove and helped the others take food out to the table as Nancy stayed back. The moment the women left the kitchen, Nancy poured salt and water into the cornbread batter as it cooked. Nancy laughed to herself, but suddenly Lizzie entered the kitchen.

"What is so funny?" Lizzie asked.

Nancy replied, "Nothing. I was enjoying the moment."

Lizzie looked at Nancy, distrust written over her face. "You can go take a seat while the cornbread finishes."

"Why, thank you." Nancy walked out of the kitchen and sat down next to John.

The family sat down, and George blessed the food. While the

family ate and talked among themselves, Annabelle and Nancy ignored each other.

Grace went to into the kitchen and placed the cornbread on the table. Nancy smirked as the family cut up the bread and took the pieces they wanted. Lizzie took a bite of the cornbread and reluctantly swallowed it.

"Annabelle, what did you do to the cornbread?" Lizzie complained. "It tastes bad, and it's soggy."

Tsula curiously took a bite and spat the cornbread out on a napkin. "That does taste bad," she said. "Well, don't worry about it, Annabelle. We all have made a mistake at least once in the kitchen. Have you ever wondered why Lizzie skins chickens the way that she does?"

Lisa, Samuel, and Michael giggled at Tsula's remark. Lizzie poked at the cornbread while staring at Tsula. Grace patted Annabelle on her shoulder.

"Don't worry about it, Annabelle. We know you can cook," Grace said. "Next time, I know you'll do fine." Grace noticed her uncle was unamused as he picked at his chicken.

Annabelle decided to take a bite of the cornbread and spat it out in a napkin. "That was terrible. I don't understand how this could happen," she said.

Nancy chuckled while she ate her soybeans. "Looks like the Negro is lacking in basic skills after all," she said. "Maybe you didn't measure something correctly. You should pay attention to what you're doing more often."

"Nancy, please stop. She always tries to do her best," John murmured.

"Hmph, like I care if she always tries her best," Nancy replied. "She shows she's nothing too special." Nancy took another bite of her soybeans, smiling at Annabelle. "Nothing too special at all, like the rest of them."

Uncle George exhaled and continued to eat. Grace narrowed her eyes as the grip on her fork tightened.

Lizzie noticed everyone else but Nancy had cornbread and

said, "I find it funny you're the only one that didn't get corn-bread."

Nancy put her fork down and gave Lizzie a conceited glare. "I didn't want a piece of it," Nancy snarled. "Is that an offense I didn't know about?"

Lizzie scoffed. "Please, your fake kindness makes me vomit."

"Please, calm down," Grace said.

Lizzie snarled, "Nancy was the last one in the kitchen, and I've watched Annabelle make cornbread many times. Your game is up, you ugly coyote." Lizzie reached into the cornbread pan, grabbing a section of the ruined cornbread, and plopped it on Nancy's plate.

"That was unnecessary," George bellowed.

"If she said she didn't do it, then she didn't do it," John defensively said. "Is it so hard for you to be nice to her for an hour?"

Lizzie looked at John, an unremorseful expression on her face, and scowled. "I'm sorry, I do have a hard time tolerating a trickster," Lizzie sarcastically said. "At least the Negro is real. I don't have to think twice about her ways." She tossed her fork onto her plate and walked to her room.

Grace and Lisa stared at Nancy.

"I'll go calm my sister down," Grace said. "Please, excuse me, Uncle George."

George nodded, accepting Grace's remark.

"If this keeps up, we might run out of eggs," Tsula said.

Tsula and Lisa laughed while Nancy's irritated eyes narrowed on the sisters.

John leaned toward Nancy. "What is so funny about eggs?"

Nancy looked away from John as she took a deep breath.

———◆———

Grace went into the women's bedroom and sat down on a bed next to Lizzie, who was lying down. "I'm proud of you," she said.

Lizzie replied in Cherokee, "Why is that?"

"You didn't allow your anger to rule you when you could

have. You also stood up for Annabelle when you didn't need to."

Lizzie scoffed. "I was speaking the truth. Annabelle is a better woman than Nancy, and I liked putting it in her face. Maybe we will get lucky and she'll get lost in the wilderness, and coyotes will maul her to death."

Grace giggled. "That's not nice at all. We're supposed to pray for our enemies and show them kindness. Showing Nancy kindness will do more to her than you being...well, yourself."

"I did show her kindness. She doesn't have a black eye. I think that's a great way of loving like Jesus. I spoke some of my mind, and I walked away so I wouldn't mess up that pretty face of hers."

"You've been listening to Elder Joyce to deal with your temper better, haven't you?"

Lizzie sat up in the bed, looking at Grace, and dropped back in the bed. "I've been working on my prayers. So yes, I have been listening to what she's been telling me. I ask Jesus every day to help me where I'm blind."

"You have a good heart, but you've been hiding it a lot more ever since Jacob told you how he really felt about you."

"I'm whole without Jacob. Now I understand I have to keep my heart guarded like the scriptures say. I feel stronger and happier understanding that now. Isn't that what you wanted?"

"Yeah, I wanted you happier. Is that what you wanted?"

Lizzie smiled while lying back in the bed. "Yes, it is."

❖

The rest of the family finished supper with Nancy. As Nancy was leaving, she gave an antagonistic smirk to Annabelle. Annabelle sat at the table, scowling.

A week passed as the animosity between Annabelle and Nancy continued. Nancy took every chance she could to mock Annabelle, and her persistence became a great annoyance to Annabelle, especially when she was on her way to give water to the slaves. One day, Nancy arrived at the supply store with her slave, Paul, who was a sturdy, young, well-mannered, brown-skinned man normally sent by the Hicks family to get supplies. Nancy entered the store with Paul behind her, and she handed Grace a list.

"These are the supplies I need, and Paul can help put them on the wagon," Nancy said.

As Annabelle and Lizzie put some of the supplies on the new wagon, Paul helped them. "Miss Annabelle and Miss Lizzie, it's always good to see the two of you," Paul said.

"It's good to see you too, Paul," Annabelle said.

"My, Miss Lizzie, you so strong, it always surprises me," Paul said, grinning.

Lizzie scoffed. "I didn't ask to be spoken to, but thank you."

Nancy went outside hearing Paul talk to the women. "I see you've found yourself a husband, Annabelle," she said, her tone mocking. "I tell you what. You can have him for one thousand dollars."

"You need to watch your mouth, Nancy Hicks," Lizzie growled.

Nancy slowly approached Lizzie with a leer and wide eyes. "Paul is my mulatto slave, and I can say or do as I please with my slave. I think it's best you remember the law is more powerful than you." Nancy strutted up to Paul and caressed his chin. "Look at him in prime condition. He has all of his teeth and good posture." Nancy caressed his short curly hair. "Come now, Annabelle, surely a nigger wants another nigger. It's only natural. But he's a much higher grade, being mulatto."

Annabelle balled her hand into a fist as the women's eyes locked. Abruptly, Lizzie pushed Nancy to the ground. "Take a seat, you snake in the grass."

Some people noticed Nancy fall but kept walking, thinking nothing of it. Nancy screamed, and when she stood up, Annabelle heard a sticky resistance. Nancy looked at her left hand, covered in horse dung, and squealed. She quickly stood up and realized she had also fallen in horse dung. She attempted to look at the back of her dress as she twisted around. While

Nancy turned, Annabelle, Lizzie, and Paul realized the horse dung had completely covered the back of her dress.

Annabelle gasped, but Lizzie laughed. Nancy cried, unable to see how much of the horse dung was on her dress.

"Lizzie Lightning, you hideous animal!" Nancy shouted. "I hate you! Paul, take me home right now!"

Grace hurried out of the store after hearing the commotion. "Nancy, why are you crying and making a scene!" she yelled.

"Your sister...that evil brute! Look what she did to my dress!"

Grace saw the horse dung on her dress and glanced at Lizzie, scowling.

"I swear it was an accident," Lizzie said. "If I wanted to do it on purpose, I would have made sure her face went in it first."

"It was an accident," Annabelle said.

"Calm down, Nancy. Paul, take her home so she can get cleaned up," Grace said, helping Nancy get on the wagon as Lizzie watched, unsympathetic to Nancy's whining. "I know it's a disgusting feeling."

Nancy sat down on the smelly dress and stared at Lizzie furiously. "Lizzie Lightning, I'll make sure you get what's coming to you," Nancy screamed. "You and that nappy-headed nigger. I swear it! Take me home, Paul."

Paul signaled the horses and escorted Nancy home.

"Bye, Paul. It was good seeing you," Lizzie said as she winked at him.

Paul looked back and waved.

Nancy smacked Paul's hand down furiously. "Don't you dare wave to her!" she screamed.

"Yes, Miss Nancy. I'm sorry I upset you," Paul said.

Lizzie watched with a leer while Grace stepped next to her. "I think Paul is a fun mulatto," she said.

Grace sighed as Lizzie went back into the store.

"Let's finish up the day in a nice way, Annabelle," Grace said. "Are you seeing Elder Joyce today?"

Annabelle replied, "Yes, I'll visit her after we close the store."

"I think I'll join you today."

Annabelle walked inside as Grace looked into the sky and sighed again. "I want one year with no drama. Is that too much to ask for?"

CHAPTER 18
The Arrival of the Beast

THE MONTH OF APRIL PASSED. On the second day of May, when the women were cleaning up the store, a tall white man walked into the store wearing a black frock coat and black trousers. The man examined the supply store and strolled toward Grace, who was standing behind the counter. A shorter man wearing similar clothing entered the store and followed the other man.

"Good evening, ma'am. I was told the Indians in this supply store can speak English," the tall white man said.

Grace replied, "Yes, all of us in here can speak English. How can I help you?"

"The name is Brock Jackson," he said. "This gentleman here is Hunter Sawyer. We are the new Indian agents that will be coming in to make sure your people are cooperating with the United States government, to keep peace in the area, and make sure you are respecting our US citizens."

Grace gave a fake smile. "Well, welcome to Tahlequah."

"Why, thank you. I was told this is a family store, so I reckon all of you are related. You might see me often. I hear you give good service," Brock said.

Annabelle felt uncomfortable around the men and tried to go out to the chicken coops when the back door creaked.

"I was never told your family was slaveholders too," the tall man continued.

Grace shook her head. "She is no slave."

Brock cleared his throat. "There seems to be a lot of that going on in these areas. A lot of lying runaway slaves up north, and I'm sure a couple of them have found their way out here." Brock walked toward Annabelle as he adjusted his green vest when Lisa slightly moved in front of Annabelle. "A bit protective, I see."

"I'm not protecting anyone. I thought it was rude for you to not ask us our names," Lisa said.

Brock laughed while he looked back at Hunter, who chuckled. "I've never heard an Indian accuse me of being rude," Brock stated. "You must be something else. Yeah, I can see it in those eyes of yours. Well, what is your name, my dear?"

Lisa's lips constricted while the corner of her mouth pinched. "My name is Lisa, and this is Annabelle."

"My name is Grace," Grace said.

Brock replied, "Nice names for some Indians, and an even nicer name for a Negro. Do you speak English, or have you been around the Indians so much you can't speak a proper language?"

Annabelle stood next to Lisa and shifted her gaze away from Brock's face. "Yes, I can speak both," Annabelle said.

Brock nodded his head and looked back at Hunter. "Well, I guess you do belong here if you can speak both. From the looks of it, you fit in here too. Well, we have to go meet the other landowners out here. We want a good head count on how many of you are here."

"When will y'all be done updating your records?" Grace asked.

Brock replied, "In about a month's time. Right now, they're dealing with the Choctaw and Creek. I'm sure you know how long a month is. You seem like some smart Indians. I will see all of you again soon."

Brock exited the store with Hunter following him.

"Well now, I think we can clean up and go home," Grace said. "Annabelle, are you alright?"

Annabelle answered, "Yes, I'm fine. So, they send Indian agents out here?"

"Yeah, it can be very annoying when they arrive. When you first came here, you missed the last one that worked with our tribal council. They're usually not nice to us, and he doesn't seem that much different."

"I don't like the way he looked at me," Lisa said.

Grace replied, "Well, we're stuck with them until the United States sends out someone new." "Let's finish up here and go home."

The women cleaned up the supply store and went home. Their playful walk home was ended as they saw Brock and Hunter off of their horses and talking to Lizzie, her arms folded.

"Great, of all people for those men to be questioning," Grace griped. She picked up her pace as Annabelle and Lisa followed.

Hunter nudged Brock the moment Grace and the others came toward them. Brock looked over at the women with a leer, and his hands held onto his vest. "Hunter and I were about to leave. We gather that Izzie," Brock said, "is a relative of yours, Miss Lightning?"

"The name is Lizzie, not Izzie," Lizzie barked.

"Yes, Mr. Jackson, she is my younger sister," Grace said in a kind tone.

"I can see she's a strong-willed woman as well," Brock replied. "It must run in the family, even though I think manners escaped this one."

Grace approached Lizzie and calmly placed her arms on her sister's shoulders, turning her to the trail leading to their home. "My sister can be quite blunt, Mr. Jackson, but she is a kind woman. We must continue our day and start to prepare supper."

"Ah, good. Such strong character had me and Mr. Sawyer concerned the women didn't know how to be women around here. The next unnatural thing we were guessing we would see were your men cooking for you."

The men laughed as Grace forced a smile.

"Good day, gentlemen," Grace said delicately, escorting Lizzie to the trail.

Annabelle and Lisa followed closely.

"Well-spoken for a savage, wouldn't you say, Hunter?" Brock asked, his voice mocking.

Lizzie shook off her sister while Brock and Hunter laughed. "Watch who are you calling a savage!" Lizzie yelled.

Brock replied, "My dear, you're showing me right now how much of lady you're not."

"I think it is a safe wager to say she isn't married either," Hunter said.

The two men continued to laugh.

Lizzie scowled and said, "I see nothing but little white boys too weak-minded to understand people different than themselves. I think you need to watch your mouth."

"So, you're a fighter after all," Brock said. "I assure you in time, I'll make sure you and your people know their place. I think it's best you know when to be silent, or my hand will help you learn."

Lizzie charged Brock when Grace grabbed Lizzie and pulled her back.

"I think it's time for you men to leave," Lisa said.

"Just when things were getting interesting," Hunter said.

"Indeed, it is time for us to leave," Brock said.

The men got on their horses and rode away to inspect the other families in the area. Grace released Lizzie. Lizzie stormed off to the house as the men continued down the dirt road talking to each other.

———◆———

"As I said earlier, Hunter, these Indian women are different than our more elegant white women," Brock said. "And I think I've made a new friend. Did you see the look in her eyes?"

"Oh yes, I have no doubt she'd have taken a swing at you for certain," Hunter said. "What do you think of the Negro?"

Brock shrugged. "I think that Negro has a complicated history. The way she spoke and held herself. Certainly not a field slave. Either she was born among these savages, or she was once a house slave and taken by the Indians. It will be difficult to accurately track her past, but I noticed in her...defiance. The lack of respect sickens me."

Hunter scoffed. "I think we will be able to enforce some respect from them. The Choctaw have seemed to continue to cooperate, and I think they will too."

"True, but also remember they're a different people. I have no doubt in my mind that Izzie woman would've happily taken my head if she had some savage weapon on her. These prairie niggers have been too free out here. I think a battalion should have been stationed out here permanently, making it clear who's in control."

"I think that certainly would have started another war, Brock."

Brock sighed. "A war that may have proven a little costly but certainly would've brought their extinction, if not near it. Letting their blood stain this prairie land and lynching them from trees probably would have been a better move instead of giving them land we'll eventually want anyway."

"You're a cold man. I think it's best the Indians didn't hear you say that."

Brock looked at Hunter as they continued down the dirt road and laughed diabolically. "A savage is a savage, no matter how much we try to teach them. I've never seen so many slaves look almost as good as their masters. It disgusts me."

The men continued their day in Cherokee land and made their presence well known.

———◆———

Two weeks passed as Brock and Hunter maintained a campaign that harassed the women, politicians, and landowners. Growing tired of their demeaning verbal assaults, Grace convinced George to allow Samuel to continuously come to the supply store to check on them. Samuel agreed, hoping to see more of Maria.

One day, Samuel was talking to Lisa when Brock and Hunter walked into the supply store.

"Good evening, folks. We are making our runs today," Brock said.

"Good afternoon, Mr. Jackson," Samuel said. "What can we help you with?"

"We're here to make it known that some of your white traders have some complaints. Now, I don't know how to make this any clearer for you Indians, but it greatly displeases me to see a fellow American feel mistreated."

"Nothing like that has ever happened here," Samuel bellowed. "I think these white people are lying on us as they always have."

Brock replied, "How dare you accuse such well-mannered men of being liars. I haven't met an honest Indian yet."

"I've never met an honest white man signing anything. As I said before, no white man that has come here has been treated unfairly."

Annabelle could feel the tension building and slowly moved to stand behind Lisa, trying not to attract any attention.

Brock continued, "I differ in such experience, Mr. Strongman. I have watched your people and these other tribes just like my forefathers did. I see little difference between any of the tribes that are important. In fact, I see in all of you a savage nature. A group of savages that still don't know how to use the land given to them—a group of thieves, drunkards, nigger lovers, and anarchists. Even your women refuse to take the role of a woman."

Samuel folded his arms. "My people are civilized. I find white men like you funny. You come here and tell us how to live, but call yourselves Christian when you can't even show love to us or respect. You can leave now, Mr. Jackson."

"Don't ever question my faith, boy. Maybe the day you prairie niggers can show us you can be civilized, better arrangements can be made." Brock eyed Lisa and smirked. "Let's go, Mr. Sawyer."

Annabelle watched the men leave the supply store while Samuel slowly followed them.

"Good job, Samuel," Grace said.

Samuel replied, "When we first talked to them, they seemed to respect us, but I see now they're no different than the other Indian agents. We have to be careful around those men."

Samuel stayed the rest of the day and walked home with the others. The news of how the men treated the women enraged George, but there was little he could do. George decided Samuel was to go to the supply store at various times since he was still needed to work in the fields.

CHAPTER 19
Snake in the Grass

TWO DAYS AFTER THEIR VISIT with Brock and Hunter, Annabelle was helping Lisa with the horses. Annabelle had now become stronger, but she still struggled with carrying the hay bales. Lisa left for an outhouse, and Annabelle told Lisa she would finish moving the last hay bales. Annabelle became exhausted and could no longer carry them. Sweat glazed her face as she waited for Lisa to return.

John and Nancy were taking their walk when John noticed how exhausted Annabelle looked.

"Nancy, I'll meet you at your home. I need to help Annabelle," John said.

Nancy scoffed and put her hand on her hip. "The Negro is fine. Let's continue on, John."

"Nancy, Annabelle needs my help. Can't you see how tired she is? What if she was to faint out here?"

"I doubt she'd die. None of my niggers have died in the field before."

John glared at Nancy, growing seemingly frustrated with the woman. "What is wrong with you? You never used to say things about Negroes like that."

Nancy shook her head. "Nothing is wrong with me. What is wrong with you? Why would you leave me to help a Negro? I don't understand it. Your sisters can help her."

"I'm going to help her."

Nancy grabbed John's arm and caressed it as she gave a seductive smile. "John, please don't go. We can spend a little more special time together, or have you forgotten how good the past two evenings have been? I'm willing to have some more fun right now if you leave with me."

"I love my time with you, but I can't treat Annabelle wrong."

Nancy's seductive smirk quickly disappeared the moment her eyes narrowed. "I can't stand how you treat her. Annabelle is nothing. She's a symbol of weakness for the Cherokee. How can you treat her like she is our equal!"

"That's enough, Nancy. Go home," John said, his voice raised.

"Don't come looking for me tonight." Nancy stormed off.

As Nancy walked away, she looked back at John as he went toward Annabelle, and rage filled her mind. She growled and continued down the dirt road.

<hr>

"I can get the rest of those," John said.

"I thought you were with Nancy. Where is she?" Annabelle asked.

John smiled at Annabelle and picked up a hay bale, placing it on his shoulders. "Don't worry about it. You getting help is more important right now than me spending time with Nancy."

Annabelle's heart was touched as she watched John carry the last remaining hay bales to the barn.

Lisa walked up to Annabelle with John carrying the last hay bale into the barn. "I'm sorry, Annabelle. Jacob slowed me down," Lisa said. "He was walking to the farm from the other road and saw me as I was leaving the outhouse."

"Why did that slow you down?" Annabelle asked. "He should've come to help us here."

Lisa rubbed her hands together. "Well, he needed to go back to help his dad on their fields, so it's not a problem."

"Alright, I see this heat is getting to you too."

Lisa's eyes widened. "Why do you say that?"

"Because I can see the sweat on your forehead. Can't you feel sweat on you?"

Lisa wiped her forehead. "Well, yes, I can. I'm used to it happening. How about we eat a little, then put away these tools in the small shed."

Annabelle agreed and walked toward the large house. "John, come eat with us."

John followed Annabelle and Lisa into the house and ate lunch with them.

<hr>

Meanwhile, a furious Nancy arrived at her ranch. When she was about to go inside her home, she noticed Paul and two other slaves were gathered around in one of the cornfields. Nancy aggressively approached the men, and as she approached, she heard a rattling sound.

"What are you niggers doing?" Nancy bellowed.

Paul backed up and looked at Nancy. "Miss Nancy, we trying to get this mean rattlesnake to move away. I sorry, but one of the cattle might die because the snake bit it."

The aggravated snake continued to rattle its tail, waiting for one of the slaves to get too close.

"Hmph, a snake in the grass," Nancy murmured. "I'll show her a snake in the grass. I want the snake captured and unharmed. Grab a basket the snake can't bite through. Quickly, place the basket over the snake. Use a stick to force it inside and place a covering over it."

"Miss Nancy, are you sure you don't want us to move it like we always do?" Paul asked.

Nancy pointed at Paul. "Don't question me!"

The men gathered around the aggressive diamondback snake who still rattled its tail. The men forced it into the basket using a stick. One of the slaves turned the basket over to put a covering on it when the snake bit his hand. Paul quickly grabbed a covering to keep the snake from lunging out again as the slave wailed in agony. Paul and the other slave quickly helped him get to one of the slave's houses as an older slave woman tried to tend to his wound.

Nancy sent another slave to see if they captured the snake. The slave returned to Nancy, reporting the rattlesnake had been captured but a slave had been bitten. Nancy returned and vigorously searched for Paul and the others, agitated the slave hadn't brought her the snake.

"Ah, there you are," she said upon finding them.

"Miss Nancy, Joe isn't doing good," Paul said, his voice nervous.

Nancy entered the slave house and looked at the ailing slave. "Well now, how foolish of you to get bitten. Look at you, barely able to breathe, but I guess I shouldn't have expected more from a Negro. Your stupidity may have cost you your life."

Paul pleaded, "Miss Nancy, it happened so fast. It not his fault."

Nancy rolled her eyes. "If he dies, he dies. Where is the snake, Paul?"

"The snake is out here, Miss Nancy."

"Good. Go get the carriage. I'm taking it somewhere."

"Yes, ma'am." Paul retrieved the carriage as Nancy had another slave put the basket in the front with Paul.

He drove Nancy more than three-fourths of the way to the Lightning-Strongman family home when she had him stop the carriage and got out.

"Paul, you're to stay here until I return. Are we clear?" she asked.

"Yes, ma'am. I won't go from this spot right here."

"Good, now give me the basket carefully."

Paul gulped, handing Nancy the basket, and she traveled through the woods. As she walked, she felt the aggravated rattlesnake moving in the basket. A grin spread across her face the instant she got closer to the Lightning-Strongman family home.

Nancy watched the family while George, John, and Samuel

went out to the fields. She saw Lisa and Annabelle moving tools to the barn and shed. Circling the main cabin and trying to avoid being seen, she managed to sit along the side of the main cabin, watching Annabelle and Lisa.

———◆———

"I can put the rest of these in the shed, Lisa, and meet you in the barn," Annabelle said in Cherokee.

"Okay," Lisa replied. "We can get this done quickly and watch the bison herd. They should be returning soon." She walked toward the barn as Annabelle picked up some tools to put them in the shed.

At that time, Nancy moved closer and stood on the side of the shed.

Annabelle came out of the shed as Nancy watched her. The snap of a branch caused Annabelle to turn around, only to see a branch come across her forehead. Nancy hit Annabelle with such force it knocked Annabelle off her feet. Annabelle saw Nancy slowly step up to her before blacking out.

Nancy put the branch to Annabelle's chin. "Now, nigger, I get to make sure you're no longer an issue," she said in a malicious whisper.

Several minutes later, Annabelle woke up with a terrible headache. Annabelle slowly lifted her head and realized she was in the shed. Sunlight pierced through small window. She heard a familiar rattling and looked to her left, seeing the large rattlesnake blocking the doorway. The snake struck at Annabelle, biting the hem of her dress.

Annabelle screamed, "Help, Lisa! Help me!"

The snake attacked Annabelle again, and she tried her best to stay at the back of the shed. She noticed all of the tools she and Lisa had put in the shed were taken out.

"Lisa! Tsula! God, please don't let me die like this."

The aggressiveness of the snake continued as tears of fear streamed down Annabelle's face. f

"Please go away! Go away, you stupid snake! Lisa! Lisa, please help me!"

The snake continued to rattle its tail.

"Just when Lizzie leaves with Grace to have fun shooting arrows, this happens. Lisa, can you hear me?" Annabelle screamed.

The shed door opened, and Lisa stood in the doorway. The snake quickly turned toward her and curled next to the broken desk, shaking its rattle.

"Have you been bitten, Annabelle?" Lisa asked.

"No, I haven't been bitten. I *almost* got bitten," Annabelle said, her voice shaking.

"Where's the blood coming from on your head?"

Sweat trailed down Annabelle's forehead. "It was Nancy. She did this to me."

"Okay, let's see if you can walk around the snake. The snake is scared too."

Annabelle looked at Lisa with wide eyes. "I think I'm more scared than the snake."

"Try to see if you can walk slowly away. Stay close to the wall and walk away slowly."

Annabelle slowly edged toward the doorway. The snake continued to rattle, and as she slowly moved past it, it took another lunge at her, barely missing. She screeched, slowly backing up again. She shook uncontrollably and sobbed.

"Annabelle, calm down. It will be okay."

Annabelle looked at Lisa with tears running down her face. "I can't. I can't. It's not like it's one of the field snakes."

"Stay there." Lisa grabbed a hoe and tossed it to Annabelle. "Try to push him out."

Annabelle tried pushing the snake out, but the snake uncoiled and seemed to slither closer to her.

"Oh no!" Annabelle panicked. "It's getting closer to me. I don't know what to do."

"Okay, don't try to push it anymore unless it tries to get closer," Lisa said. "I'll be right back."

The snake slithered toward the doorway, and Annabelle tried to follow it slowly. The snake abruptly turned around and rattled again, then took another lunge. Annabelle lost her balance and fell. Annabelle hit the snake with the hoe, but it only agitated the snake even more. The snake recoiled in front of the door, and while it stared at Annabelle, a flying tomahawk cut off the snake's head, dropping it to the ground as some blood squirted on Annabelle.

Annabelle felt as though her heart caught in her throat as she wiped the snake's blood off her cheek. She looked up, seeing Lisa in the doorway with Tsula standing behind her. She slowly walked toward Lisa and gave her a hug while crying.

"It's over now," Lisa said.

Tsula approached Annabelle and rubbed her back while Annabelle continued to cry.

"We have a problem. Another snake still needs to be taken care of," Tsula said.

"We can wait for Grace and Lizzie to return. For now, we need to let John know what happened," Lisa said. "Go tell John to come here, Tsula, so I can calm Annabelle down."

Tsula marched to the fields while Lisa took Annabelle inside the family home to sit down. Tsula returned with John, and Lisa explained what happened. John held Annabelle's hands. He knelt down, looking into her bloodshot eyes.

"I'm so sorry about this," John said. "This is inexcusable. You could have been seriously hurt or even killed. No more. Nothing like this will happen again." John stood and opened the front door.

"Where are you going, John?" Tsula asked.

"I'm going to Nancy's ranch. I need answers for this. I'll be back in time for supper."

<hr>

Soon after, Grace and Lizzie arrived back from practicing their archery when Lizzie noticed the dead snake in the shed.

"Why is there a dead rattlesnake in the shed," Lizzie said in Cherokee.

Grace looked inside the shed, and the two women quickly walked into the family house. As they entered, Annabelle saw them while Lisa was cleaning up her wound.

"What happened, Lisa?" Grace asked.

Lisa explained what occurred, and Grace became furious.

"I think we need to see Nancy ourselves. I doubt John will be harsh to her," Tsula said.

"I agree," Grace said.

Tsula, Grace, and Lizzie marched to Nancy's ranch with Lizzie holding the dead snake in her hand. The women arrived at Nancy's ranch and saw John talking to Nancy calmly. Nancy, with her arms folded, looked over and saw the furious women approaching. She exhaled deeply.

"Grace, go home," John said.

"Don't tell me to go home when she almost killed Annabelle using that snake!" Grace yelled in Cherokee. Grace's face turned reddish-brown. "Nancy Hicks, you want to start a war? Well, we're here now!"

"I have already explained myself to John!" Nancy replied. "I don't need to say anything to any of you."

"Snake in the Grass, we have your dead brother. Lisa killed him," Lizzie said in Cherokee, tossing the dead snake at Nancy's feet.

"Don't call me that!" Nancy snarled.

Lizzie smacked her lips. "We know you did it."

"She said she didn't put the snake in the shed with Annabelle," John said.

"Can't you see she's lying!" Grace yelled.

"I have no proof of this, and you don't have proof."

"Nancy, you think you're so smart, but I already know you're lying," Tsula mockingly said. "Explain why all of the tools were taken out of the shed. Lisa said she and Annabelle had put most of the tools away. When she walked away to the barn, that's when you attacked Annabelle, and you tried to make sure she didn't have a way to fight the snake. So you put all the tools on the side of the shed and closed the door."

"Nancy, is this true?" John asked.

Nancy gulped. Her eyes shifted downward.

"You're an embarrassment to the Cherokee people, Nancy Hicks," Grace growled. "You and your family are an embarrassment as far as I'm concerned."

"How dare you say such a thing," Nancy said, her voice hitching. "My family is one of the richest and most respected families in the entire tribe."

"Your family gained wealth on the backs of slaves. Our ancestors would cry if they could see how much you have accepted the evil the white people have brought on our land. You're either too blind or too stupid to see they see us no different than the Negroes. Maybe because you can pass as a white woman, you're too blind to see your people are suffering."

A tear went down Nancy's face while she clutched her fist. "My family grew wise, and we adopted the best way of living while yours refuses to see the hierarchy in place here. Don't tell me that I can't see how the people are suffering. It is their own fault."

"Nancy, did you put that rattlesnake in the shed with Annabelle?' John asked.

Nancy looked at John, wiping another tear from her face. "I can't deal with this right now. I can't."

He shook his head. "The thought of it being true, that you think so little of Annabelle..."

John walked back home as Nancy watched and held back her remaining tears.

"For the rest of the year, don't come on our property unless you're welcomed," Grace said. "As a Christian woman, I do you a favor by walking away before I'm tempted to put some color in your face. You should pray for the Father to open your heart so you can see how messed up your heart is."

Grace turned around and began to walk away.

Nancy took a step forward, her eyes blazing with fury.

"Don't you try to tell me how wrong I am! Like you or your kin live the perfect lives of a Christian. Your own brother refuses to believe, so you can leave my land and take that dead snake with you!" Nancy kicked the dead snake, and it hit Lizzie in her mouth. Nancy's eyes bulged, and she backed up slowly, feeling her body tremble.

Lizzie grabbed the dead snake off the ground and quickly walked toward Nancy, putting it up to Nancy's face when Nancy slapped Lizzie. Nancy stepped back again, seeing Lizzie's eyes dilate as she held her cheek. Tsula and Grace rushed to grab Lizzie, but Lizzie abruptly grabbed Nancy's ringlet-styled hair and stuffed the dead snake in Nancy's white chemise.

Nancy screamed the instant Lizzie gripped her hair. Tsula and Grace grabbed Lizzie, trying to break Lizzie's powerful hold on Nancy.

"Let her go, Lizzie. That's enough," Tsula yelled.

"Let her go, now!" Grace yelled.

Lizzie let go of a crying Nancy, who fell to the ground and quickly pulled the dead snake out of her chemise. She took deep breaths as she wiped the snake's blood off her cheek and chin.

"You always act like you're better than us," Lizzie snarled in Cherokee. "I should give you a black eye for kicking that dead snake at me. I'm ready to go home."

Lizzie stormed off, and Tsula followed her, holding onto Lizzie's shoulders and attempting to calm her. Grace came up to Nancy and reached for her hand. Nancy accepted Grace's hand and slowly stood up. Nancy tried to wipe the snake's blood off her chest as she sniffed.

"You can be a greater person, Nancy," Grace calmly said. "When we were children, you always had a good spirit, but now I can tell your father's teachings have ruined a good woman. Sorry about the snake."

Grace went away.

———————✦———————

Nancy watched Grace walk away and wiped a tear from her face.

"Nancy, what are you doing out here?" a teenage girl asked.

"Abigail? Oh, nothing. Thinking about what will be for supper."

The teenage girl, who looked like a younger version of Nancy, came out of the front door and stood next to her sister. "Oh, it's Grace. Is that what all that yelling was about?"

"There was no such thing going on. You're hearing things, Abigail."

Abigail clamped her lips tight and lowered her brow. "I don't believe you. I know when you're yelling, you liar."

Nancy sighed and went inside their home.

———◆———

Later in the day, the Lightning-Strongman family enjoyed supper together, grateful Annabelle was safe. George even took a brief moment to admit he was glad Annabelle was well. As the family continued to eat their supper and socialize, John walked outside. John stood next to the shed and stared at the inside of it.

"John, what is on your mind?" Samuel asked in Cherokee.

John replied, "I spoke with Lisa before we ate, and now I can't make the images of Annabelle screaming for her life leave my mind. Nancy really set up Annabelle to be hurt, maybe even killed."

"Be careful not to blame yourself. How could you have known Nancy would do something so insane?" Samuel noticed Nancy slowly riding a horse to their home. "Well, look who's come back. Do you want me to stay?"

"No, I need to talk to her alone. Having you around would only make it harder," John said.

Samuel went inside as Nancy approached John on her horse.

"Why have you come here, Nancy?" he asked.

Nancy got off the horse and approached John. "I wanted to

apologize for not telling you the whole truth. I don't know how to apologize for what I did, but to say I'm sorry."

John stood before Nancy, and the sunset outlined their bodies. "How can your heart be so empty? Even if you didn't want Annabelle to die, your actions show nothing but hate for her. What did she ever do to you that was so bad?"

Nancy's eyes shifted downward. "I..."

John shook his head. "You can't even give me an answer. I could blame the white side of you, but I've met white people with good hearts. How much would it surprise you if I told you that because of Annabelle, I met white people who didn't see us as savages."

Nancy's eyes widened as she listened to John.

"Mr. Boston was the first white man I'd met that didn't hate us and treat us badly," John continued.

Nancy stared at John, her eyebrows lifted. "You mean that store clerk in Mercy, Missouri?"

"Yeah, he was one of the few white people giving us supplies on our way here. I remember the look on his face when he saw us in the cold. He was actually sad and pitied us. He gave us a lot of supplies to help us along the way."

"Why are you just now telling me?"

"I didn't feel the need to. I wanted to forget about it," John explained. "When we first came here, you and your family stayed with your white family. The rest of us suffered. I can see it now. You don't understand how it felt to watch people you know die in front of you. To have that feeling as a child, feeling hopeless. I don't think you could ever understand that."

A stream of tears flowed down Nancy's face. "How can you say I don't understand suffering? I'm here now."

"Your family came here during the fall after part of Tahlequah was already built. When did you ever see one of us die?"

Nancy took off her white bonnet, trying not to sob. "Do I have to see our people die to understand the pain? We came this way to make room for more white people. To watch my father sell the land I grew up on was painful. You know this. I told you.”

John's nose flared while his eyebrows lowered. “Besides land, what did you lose?”

Nancy held her hands and raised them to her mouth. “I don't know. Some furniture? Why does it matter how much I lost?”

“It doesn't matter what type of stuff you lose. What matters is you can't see how much of yourself you lose. You've become hateful and molded by the white people. How can you see the pain of our people if your heart is filled with hate and selfishness? I see the way you look at Annabelle now.”

Nancy's breath hitched as she replied, “I can't stand how you treat that nigger. She isn't nothing special, but you treat her like she is special. They're beneath us.”

“My father used to teach me that hate, and my mother tried to protect me from it. When I first met Annabelle, I had my father's beliefs. It was the first time I met a Negro that spoke their mind...that stood their ground against me. But when Camille died and I couldn't stay here, Annabelle helped me heal.”

Nancy's brow furrowed. “Is that why you treat her so kindly? Because you feel you owe this woman?”

“No, it is because that's how I want to be treated. I want David to grow up to be a good man. How can he turn into a good man if he never sees me doing the right thing? I won't make my father's mistakes and continue the hate.”

Nancy placed her hand on her chest. “I don't hate Annabelle, but I feel she doesn't belong here. She belongs with her own people, not with us. Why can't you see that?”

“If all the people she had left were slaves, does that mean you think she should also be a slave?”

Nancy hesitantly replied, “Is that such an evil thing? Serving is what these people are built for. They have no self-guidance. I know if my father or the overseers didn't watch the slaves, they would accomplish nothing. It's their place in our world, and the moment we start seeing them as equals, the white men will forever see us like them."

"Annabelle has no family left to go to. I'd tell you the whole story, but I can see that would be a waste of time. Did you know our people were made slaves by the white people far before we were born?"

Nancy stepped closer to John. "That can't be true. We were never slaves. I know our people had a few battles against them long ago, but that time is over. Who told you that lie?"

"It's not a lie. Elder Joyce told me some time ago. I think at the time, she was trying to remove the hate in my own heart," he explained. "She grew up fearing the possibility a white man could kidnap her and sell her as a slave. The white men saw no difference between Indian and Negro, and she said many of the slaves were women."

Nancy shook her head. "I can't believe that. How could you believe that? It doesn't make any sense. We are not like Negroes. Why would they treat us like them?"

"It was because they saw us as savages, like today. It's easy to forget the bad parts of the past, and that's what we've done. Elder Joyce said we never did get back many of our enslaved people."

Nancy continued to shake her head and pouted. "That does not make me the same as a Negro, and it never will. I know we're better than them. I see it every day, and every day of my life, I have watched them. One Negro that's different doesn't make their race as good as our own."

John shook his head while he listened to Nancy. "I sometimes hate this Christianity that these white men have pushed into our minds, but I've watched the rest of the family. It confuses me because when it matters, I see nothing but love in their hearts. Even as strong-willed as Lizzie is, she puts others before herself. She is a lover, but she guards her heart strongly. I see it when she is with David. I sometimes think that maybe there really is something strong about this Christian way. When our people practice it, I see love. The healer, Jesus, they talk so much about and the stories I have heard of him... I know he always spoke about loving each other. But why do I rarely see that love in you?"

Nancy raised her voice. "I don't understand. John, I do love you. I've even given my body to you! How can you say I don't love you?"

"You show me affection, but what about others? If you're a Christian like my sisters, why is it hard for you to show kindness to people who can give you nothing?"

Nancy balled her hands into fists. "Lizzie never shows *me* kindness. She is a brute! So how can you judge me on how kind I am?"

"Lizzie doesn't trust you. Since we were children, you teased her and treated her unfairly. She at least tries to be kind, as rough as it comes off."

"Lizzie needs to grow up and learn how to be a lady."

"Lizzie isn't perfect, but haven't you noticed how she's changed over time?" John asked. "Lizzie will always have a tough side to her, but she has a good heart. She's been that way since our mother died, but she's still willing to sacrifice. I've never seen you sacrifice anything for anyone. I was hoping that would change."

"Lizzie hates me, as much as you want to defend her. You only say that because she is your sister," Nancy said.

"The real reason Lizzie treats you the way she does is because it hurts her seeing how much you have sided with white people—the thing our momma stood against, and the life I followed for too long. Believe it or not, I've heard Lizzie pray for you more than once," John replied.

Nancy shrugged and huffed. "I guess there is a part of me that needs to change. Please forgive me, John, so we can move on."

"I've already decided. Nancy, there is nothing left to continue. I've been thinking about this the entire day. It hurts me so much. I need someone different in my life to help me raise

David. Right now, you're not that person. I'm sorry, Nancy. You need to go home."

Nancy put her hands to her chest. "It was an accident. Please don't push me away over an accident."

"It was more than an accident, and that's the problem," John said. "If I was to ask you to apologize to Annabelle, would you do that?"

Nancy sobbed, struggling to give an answer. "Please don't make me do that."

"I once tried reading the Bible because Grace tried so hard to raise my spirit when our mom died. I never forgot one of the things she read to me. 'And as ye would that men should do to you, do ye also to them likewise.' I believe that really means the Creator wants us to treat each other well."

Nancy clutched her bonnet as she cried. "I'm sorry I was angry. Please don't end this. I'm begging you, please, John." Nancy gave John a hug and continued to cry. "Please, John. I'm sorry. I swear I'll do better. Please trust me to do better."

John removed Nancy's arms from around his neck and held her hands. "I will always care about you, but keeping you so close to my heart hurts me. Maybe sometime later, we will work it out, but for now, I can't see that." He turned and walked away.

Watching him go with her arms wrapped tight across her chest, Nancy cried, "John! John, please!" When he didn't respond, she got on her horse and slowly rode off.

During the night, John sat outside the family house watching the stars. "I know that was a hard choice for you," Grace said. "We're here for you when you need us."

John replied, "Thank you, Grace. It means a lot. I never wanted to admit you were right about her. Can you believe she asked me not to make her apologize to Annabelle?"

Grace sat down next to her brother. "Wow, even for her, that's something else. Make sure you keep this from Annabelle."

"I know. The thing worrying me is if Nancy will continue to treat Annabelle badly."

"Don't worry about it. We will treat her well and keep pushing to keep the peace. I'll also speak to Lizzie since she still struggles with her temper. It's best she continues to progress with her struggles. She's become a lot stronger than me."

"Lizzie?"

"Yeah, her short, short-tempered self."

"I think I'm going to bed now." John gave Grace a hug and stepped inside the house.

———◆———

Grace went to the small house and sat down in her bed. "Jesus, I pray for protection over us, especially John. I feel there's a storm coming."

CHAPTER 20
Seeking Truth

TWO WEEKS PASSED AS NANCY remained absent. During this time, John spent more time with Jacob, Michael, and Samuel. It was uplifting for John to spend time with the young men he loved, and he even allowed Jacob and Samuel to pray for him. Samuel continued to come to the store randomly to see Maria and guard against Brock Jackson.

In June of 1848, Maria came by the supply store and welcomed Samuel's cheerful flirting. The other women thought it was funny watching Samuel trying to persuade Maria to spend more time with him.

Florence entered the store. "Good afternoon," she said, speaking Cherokee.

"Florence, how are you doing?" Grace responded in the same language.

"I'm good. This is a beautiful day." Florence noticed Samuel standing next to Maria, and she admired Maria's blue Victorian dress. "Hi, my name is Florence Tate. What is your name?"

Maria raised her eyebrows but could tell Florence spoke well of her.

Grace laughed. "Florence, she does not speak Cherokee, but she can speak English good."

"Oh, hi, I'm Florence Tate. What is your name?" Florence asked with an accent.

Maria smiled. "My name is Maria. It is nice to meet you."

"My English is bad. I think you're nice. Grace, please tell her for me I think she looks beautiful in the dress," Florence requested in Cherokee.

"Maria, Florence wants you to know she thinks you look beautiful in the dress," Grace said.

"Thank you, Florence," Maria replied. "Well, I have to leave. I need to stay on schedule today. It's always a pleasure, ladies, and nice to meet you, Florence."

"I can carry that sack of soybeans for you, Maria," Samuel said.

Maria giggled. "I'm sure you could, but I did come here with the wagon."

"Well, I can put the sack on the wagon for you." Samuel quickly took the sack out of Maria's arms and walked outside.

Maria playfully tossed her hands up and followed Samuel outside as Grace and Lisa chuckled.

"What can we do for you, Florence?" Grace asked in Cherokee.

Florence ran her hand through her shoulder-length wavy hair and said, "We need some flour. I need one bag to carry back home."

"Okay, I'll get the sack for you." Grace went into the storage room to get a sack.

Florence smiled and stepped toward Lisa. "Is there something between you and Jacob?"

Lisa replied in Cherokee, "No, what would make you think that?"

Florence's smiled disappeared. "I can see the way he smiles at you. He likes you. I was hoping you felt the same, but he probably still doesn't know what he wants."

Lisa cocked her head a little. "Why would you say that?"

"I'm not supposed to say this, but I haven't told anyone else. Last year, Jacob kissed Lizzie, and ever since, she's seemed a little angry. I think she's finally become a little nicer like she used to be."

"How do you know that happened? Did Jacob tell you himself?" Lisa asked.

"No, I saw it. I saw Lizzie smile after it happened and then she went home. I guess he did something wrong, and she stayed mad at him. It would be nice having a new sister, whether it was you or Lizzie. I would've been happy."

Lisa forced herself to smile at seeing the innocence in Florence's face. Grace walked out of the storeroom and placed the small sack of flour on the counter. "Here you go, Florence, and don't worry about paying. Your daddy left an earlier payment a week ago," Grace said. "I guess he already knew he would have to send you here soon."

"Thank you, Grace," Florence said. "Is Annabelle here?"

"Annabelle is outside checking our soybean field."

"Oh, well, I will see her later when she brings water. Thank you again." Florence then left the store as Lisa watched, lightly tapping her foot.

"I'll be right back. I wanted to get something from home," Lisa said.

"What are you going to get?" Grace asked.

"Don't worry about it. I'll return soon."

Lisa quickly walked out of the store and went home. She marched to the farm, mumbling to herself, and walked into the large barn. Her keen vision scanned the fields through the large back doors and located Jacob. Lisa saw the other men were further out, so she tried calling to Jacob in a low tone so the others wouldn't hear her.

Jacob didn't hear her while he worked, so Lisa picked up a rock and threw it, hitting Jacob in his leg. He groaned in agony and looked over to see Lisa signaling him to come to the barn. He looked at the others to see if they noticed. Jacob came into the barn and left the back door cracked open. He strolled toward Lisa, smiling.

"I didn't think I was going to see you until later," Jacob said in Cherokee.

Jacob leaned toward Lisa to kiss her, but she quickly slapped Jacob.

"You have a lot to explain to me," Lisa replied, her tone furious. "I know what happened between you and Lizzie. When were you going to tell me everything?"

"I didn't think it mattered. It was a long time ago."

Lisa stomped her foot. "You kissed her! No wonder she was so angry at you. All you told me was she kissed you. Is there anything else I should know?"

"I'm sorry I didn't tell you. Don't be angry. I'm not hiding anything else. Nothing else happened between us."

Jacob tried to hug her, and Lisa pushed him away.

Lisa folded her arms and regarded him keenly. "You better not have, Jacob Tate. She is a sister to me. It's hard enough keeping our relationship quiet. No more secrets."

"I know it is. I promise, no more secrets." Jacob slowly walked up to Lisa, but Lisa tried to avoid eye contact with him. "Hey, look at me. Come on, beautiful, I know I can't play no games with you." Jacob slowly tried to give Lisa another hug, but she kept her arms folded as Jacob held her. "Don't be like this. Please show me that beautiful smile. Seeing you smile makes my world better."

Lisa blushed and beamed. "You're a good man. Don't lie to me, even if you make mistakes." Lisa kissed Jacob while he held her. "I have to leave before Grace gets worried."

"I thought you said you haven't told any of them."

"I haven't, but she thinks I came here for something. I need to leave now. Wait for me here. I don't want Florence to see us together too much. She has a good heart, but she's too curious."

"I'll be here when you leave the supply store," he said.

Jacob gave Lisa a kiss, and Lisa returned to the supply store.

❖

After the women closed the store, Annabelle and Grace traveled to Joyce's home while Lisa went home to spend a little time with Jacob. The women arrived at Joyce's home to update her on the most recent events.

Annabelle looked forward to every visit with Joyce.

"So, Nancy has continued to remain in the shadows," Joyce said in Cherokee. "I imagine she has a lot going through her mind. Is John doing better?"

"He's been doing a lot better," Grace replied. "I think he has chosen to be happy. I can't be more proud of him."

"Good, but continue to pray for your brother. Even a smile can hide the deepest feelings of the spirit. Making the right choices and being uncomfortable making those choices are the true tests that build character. I warn both of you to be self-controlled, but you should also love, regardless of how you feel. The Father works with us on our different problems in different ways."

"Elder Joyce, I need help with treating Nancy kindly," Annabelle said in Cherokee. "I've been lying to myself that I would be able to forget what she did to me. I still want her to experience what I did."

"Then you need to pray on this problem," Joyce advised. "It's okay to be angry, but don't allow your emotions to lead you into sinning against Nancy. She needs to be shown love, as much as it may hurt you. I've also been praying for John. He has not accepted the truth of Jesus, putting his spirit and soul in danger."

"I have tried so many times," Grace said. "I feel discouraged every Sunday not seeing him there. For Uncle George to come to church but not John, it hurts my soul. John has continued to allow what the white people did to us to rule him."

"Continue to pray for your brother. Don't ignore the power of prayer. On my walks, I have seen you shooting your arrows. I believe it's best for you to give silent prayers as you shoot the arrows. The Father will hear you."

Grace nodded. "I'll try my best."

"We're meant to become more and more like Jesus," Joyce told them. "It takes time to change, but the Holy Spirit is with you…to help you. I expect you to pray for John also, Annabelle. Remember that love overpowers the evil of this world. When we keep loving people like Jesus, in the end, we win what really matters."

"I wanted to ask you the last time we were here… What do you think about these new Indian agents?" Grace asked.

Joyce answered, "They seem just as prideful as the ones that came before them, but there's something different about them, Grace. It's a darkness surrounding them, especially Mr. Jackson. Be careful around them."

Grace rubbed her hands together. "That's what I was feeling too. Well, I think it's time for us to go prepare supper."

"Alright, I'll be looking for the two of you very soon," Joyce said. "Also, make sure you tell Lizzie to come see me. I'm proud of her for not knocking out some of Nancy's teeth. That's a good step forward for her."

"I will." Annabelle and Grace left the home when Grace suddenly walked back to Joyce as she stood in the doorway. "Do you know about the kidnappings?"

"Yes, in the other nations, there have been random kidnappings of Negroes and children. You didn't tell Annabelle, did you?" Joyce asked.

"No, I think she still needs to focus on other things instead of having another issue to worry about put into her mind."

Joyce whispered, "I agree. We will continue this later."

"Yes, ma'am." Grace ran to Annabelle, who was waiting.

"What was that about?" Annabelle asked in Cherokee.

Grace replied, "It was nothing. I needed to double-check with Elder Joyce."

———✦———

The day continued while the family enjoyed the evening with each other. During the night, Annabelle prayed for John. The thought of praying for John reminded her of *The Three Mus-*

keteers quote: "All for one and one for all." Annabelle felt it strange how her joy increased when she prayed for John.

This may be my purpose here, to help John choose Jesus for himself and not to please the people he loves, she thought.

229

CHAPTER 21
Unspoken Words

A WEEK LATER, NANCY REAPPEARED INTO the supply store with Paul. Grace welcomed them, and Nancy calmly told Grace what she needed. Nancy kept her eyes low as Grace and Lisa watched her. Nancy attempted to instruct Paul politely.

"I don't know what to think of it," Lisa whispered in Cherokee. "Is she still sad about John ending the relationship, or is she actually being nice."

"It's hard to say," Grace replied, "but I think it's best we continue to treat her nicely."

Annabelle entered from the back door carrying some eggs. She noticed Nancy and placed the basket full of eggs on the counter. "What's going on? She's not yelling at Paul," Annabelle whispered in Cherokee.

Lisa replied, also whispering, "We're not sure. She has been polite the entire time she's been here."

The women watched with great interest as Paul loaded the last of their supplies on a wagon. Nancy got into the wagon and went home as the women watched.

"I guess time will tell what all of that was about," Grace said.

Later in the day, George, Jacob, John, Michael, and Samuel took a break from working the corn, squash, and soybean fields.

"This year, it looks like we will have a good crop this time again," George said in Cherokee. "I'm grateful having all of you out here working hard. Jacob, you bring a lot of honor to your family."

Jacob replied, "Thank you, Mr. Strongman."

"I think I'm going to get an apple before we finish up," Samuel said.

Samuel walked to the family house when Michael followed him. "I want to get an apple too," he said.

George chuckled as he watched his sons. "One day, you'll have children, Jacob, like John here," he said. "Protecting the future generations is our biggest priority. We've lost so much over the years, but it seems we are finally rebuilding ourselves."

Jacob replied, "I agree, Mr. Strongman."

"I have watched you and your kin since y'all was children. I didn't know what to really think about you mixed-bloods with Negro blood. But over these years, I see more of you as Cherokee. I can see you and your family care about the tribe. That says a whole lot. I'm sure you will find yourself a good mixed-blood girl. I don't think badly of the Negroes like I used to, but don't choose a Negro wife. It will do nothing but make it harder for your children."

"I'll take your advice," Jacob said. "I do sometimes think about a wife. I honestly would like a good Cherokee woman. It would make me a hypocrite not to see beauty in other mixed-bloods, but I feel like it's better if my wife is full Cherokee, so my children feel more accepted than I did as a child."

George chuckled a little. "I understand why you feel that way. You're a hardworking man with a good heart. I don't think it is impossible. I would've even thought of suggesting Annabelle to you. I do struggle a little showing her kindness, but there's something different about her. She took the time to learn our language and speaks very well. She respects my household better than my daughters and my nieces, but I think I'll never win that war."

George, Jacob, and John laughed.

"I think the Father has gifted Annabelle," Jacob replied. "I enjoy Annabelle's presence, but yes, I think a Cherokee woman will better fit me. Maybe if I had a son and he met someone like Annabelle, I could welcome it."

George shrugged. "I never thought I would feel this way about a Negro, but Annabelle could make a good wife for an Indian man. Annabelle is rare. I understand now why my daughters like her so much. Well, let's finish checking the crops. We can call it early today."

Jacob looked at George, showing agreement. Samuel and Michael returned to help with the fields as the strong heat from the sun bathed the fields. Jacob and John went back to the barn with Queen and Cari. While they were putting the horses back into their stalls, Jacob was thinking deeply.

"What is going through your mind?" John asked.

Jacob replied, "Nothing. I'm a little tired from the heat. It feels like the weather has warmed up faster this year."

"Does my uncle have you thinking about what woman you want, or do you have someone on your mind already?"

Jacob raised an eyebrow. "Why would you think it is that?"

"You seemed sure of what kind of woman you want. I think it is a good thing."

Jacob sighed. "I think sometimes I fear that someone I'll fall in love with will have a father that won't like me because I'm a mixed-blood. I hate that being the only reason her father wouldn't want me to marry her."

John sighed. "I understand. That can be painful. I already told you why I ended things with Nancy."

"Yeah, that wasn't easy for you, but I'm proud of you. It takes a lot to uphold something you believe. I think that's a gift Jesus has given to all of us, and we have to choose to use it."

"That was wise, Jacob. I guess church stuff is good for you," John said.

The two men laughed as they stood by the back doors of the barn.

"Marriage is a good thing, even though me and Camille would fight over the Christian stuff," John said. "She must be some woman for you to take the chance, even if her father might not like you."

"Yeah, she is. Her smile is—"

John grinned. "I knew it. Who is she?"

Jacob pouted. "I can't believe I fell for that trick, you good-for-nothing coyote."

John laughed while Jacob went to the fields. "Don't be that way. What is her name? How long are you going to hide this? I'll keep asking."

"I promised I wouldn't tell. If I did, I'm sure she'd probably kill me. I'll tell you at the right time. I don't want to lose my life."

"Is it Lizzie? If it's Lizzie, I'm fine with the two of you. It would explain why she's been so good with her temper lately."

"It's not Lizzie. Your sister is a great woman, she really is, but someone else has my attention," Jacob said.

"Okay, I'll respect that," John replied. "But know the option is there for you. My uncle may have a little anger about it, but me and Samuel could keep him calm. You're one of us."

Jacob grinned. "Thank you. It means a lot to me, my friend."

"On your way home?" John asked.

Jacob scratched his neck. "Yeah, it's that time."

"I'll see you tomorrow."

"Yes, you will." Jacob walked home smiling.

CHAPTER 22
Humbled

IN THE MONTH OF JUNE, Annabelle experienced continuous harassment from Brock Jackson and Hunter Sawyer. The abrupt nature of the short-tempered men tested Annabelle, but she held her pride to avoid many questions.

Annabelle was able to overlook those dark moments. She had been documented as a free Negro, making her grateful.

July arrived, bringing in more heat. During the mornings, the women didn't open the supply store. They would braid each other's hair. Annabelle watched over David while the others braided and enjoyed watching how the women bonded. Long hair was the one thing Annabelle was envious of. Seeing the women bond like that increased her envy.

One day, Annabelle was staring at the women while they braided each other's hair and saw that Tsula noticed.

"Annabelle, would you like your hair braided?" Tsula asked, speaking Cherokee.

Annabelle blushed. "Oh no, I don't want to slow you down," Annabelle replied.

Tsula scoffed, saying, "You wouldn't slow us down."

"How can you say she won't slow us down," Lizzie bickered. "Adding another person will take more time."

The other three women argued with Lizzie.

"Come, Annabelle, you can finish braiding Lisa's hair,"

Tsula said. "We won't waste time with asking you to braid Lizzie's hair since she's whining."

Lizzie looked back at Tsula with her eyes narrowed, and Grace smacked the back of her head.

"Mind your own business or the braiding will look bad," Grace snapped.

Annabelle stood up from the supper table and walked to the others. She sat down behind Lisa on the living room floor.

"I need two braids, Annabelle," Lisa said.

"Okay, I can do that," Annabelle replied.

Tsula hummed as she sat down behind Annabelle and worked on her hair. It brought joy to her heart.

"You'll like what I do with your hair, Annabelle," Tsula said.

The others watched and talked to each other as Tsula braided, and their smiles excited Annabelle.

"Your hair is so rough, but I finished it for you," Tsula said. "It looks good on you."

"That's a good look," Lisa said enthusiastically.

"I need to get a mirror so you can see it." Grace went toward the women's bedroom.

Annabelle felt her braided hair.

"Well, it looks fine," Lizzie snobbishly said.

Lisa slightly shoved Lizzie.

"What? I didn't say it looks bad. Let her decide for herself."

"You always have something to say, Flour Face," Tsula said.

Lizzie stuck her tongue out at Tsula, and she smirked and rolled her eyes at Lizzie.

"I love you too, bully," Tsula said.

Grace strolled into the living room with a small mirror and handed it to Annabelle. When Annabelle looked at it, she saw that Tsula had braided her hair into four tight braids.

"I really like it. Thank you, Tsula."

"You're welcome."

✦

George and John later returned from town as the others enjoyed the day.

"Hi, everyone," John said. "Where is the little warrior?"

"David is with Annabelle by the old tree," Tsula replied.

"I'm surprised Lizzie isn't watching him."

"Grace braided her hair and then she left to shoot some arrows. She seemed like she was in a good mood."

"That's good," John said. "I think I'll go get David and give Annabelle some time alone."

Tsula snapped her finger. "Make sure to compliment her. I braided her hair today. It's a nice look for her."

John walked outside to the old redbud tree and saw Annabelle reading while David sat in her lap. When John approached them, he noticed David had fallen asleep. John's heart was touched as he watched Annabelle cradle his son and caress his head while she read a book.

"What book is that?" John whispered.

Annabelle looked to her left and smiled at John. "It's called *The Three Musketeers*. I began reading it again."

"What is that about?"

"It is an old story about three good men standing up for what they believe. It's interesting."

John sat down next to Annabelle and looked at David. "You're good with him. Don't let Lizzie see this too much. She might get jealous."

Annabelle and John quietly giggled.

"He is a good child. That makes it easy, I think," Annabelle said.

"Did you bring David out here so you could read outside?" John asked.

"I was hoping the bison herd would be out there around this time, and he could watch them with me. But he comes out here with me and falls asleep, so reading the book was the best idea I could think of doing before helping cook supper."

John's eyebrows lifted. "I think that's a good idea. I like what Tsula did with your hair. Do you like it?"

Annabelle smiled at John. "Thank you. Yes, I do like it."

Annabelle and John sat together, continuing their conversation while David slept.

While Annabelle and John spoke, Lizzie was returning home with two dead rabbits and her bow in hand when she heard a horse riding up behind her. To her surprise, Brock approached her on his horse.

"Is there something you want, Mr. Jackson?" Lizzie asked.

Brock replied, "At this moment, I'm not sure if there's anything I want from you...Izzie, was it? I see you have talent with those weapons."

Lizzie gave a fake smile. "Mr. Jackson, my name is Lizzie, not Izzie. I do have a gift with weapons."

"Hmph, is it so hard to be civilized and get meat from the cattle or poultry your people have raised? Hunting is an activity better suited for a man anyway."

"I do quite well on my own, Mr. Jackson. I'm not bound by the ways of white people. To be honest, I find the weak-minded ways of white women to be disturbing. I have no interest in ever following such a miserable life."

"I'm sure you haven't met the right man to tame you. To refuse to follow a better way will mean you'll live a lesser life. Surely, you want a better life."

Lizzie smirked. "I'm sure a God-fearing man would have a good enough heart to show some form of love to those less fortunate."

"I'm not exactly the God-fearing type, Miss Lightning. However, it is savages like you making this world more interesting. After all these years, your people still struggle to be civilized. You're a wild woman that will eventually know her place."

Lizzie's smirk dropped from her face. "And how do you know a woman like me will learn her place?"

Brock glared at Lizzie with his merciless blue eyes. "I'm here to maintain the peace and protect citizens of the United States.

I think you have an idea of what will happen if more severe policies are made, but I'm sure you'll be one of the last ones standing. You're a woman with a strong spirit that'll break like the ones before you. I'll enjoy watching it."

Lizzie scoffed. "You're nothing but a coward afraid of someone you can't control. I used to give black eyes to the boys who used to tease me as a child. When I got them alone, I bent them like the wind bends the grass."

"I assure you, Miss Lightning, I'm not the grass. Have you been with a man? I find it's not uncommon for your kind to give yourself to the first man that catches your attention."

"I have never known a man. Only my husband will have the privilege of having my body. I guess you're not much of a gentleman to ask a lady such a rude question."

Brock cackled a little. "Yes, it would be quite rude of me if I was asking a lady. By you holding onto your two precious kills, you demonstrate the inability to be a lady."

Lizzie maliciously chuckled. "Would you like to know how I got them?" Lizzie lifted up one of the rabbits, smirking. "This rabbit here... I think his story fits you. I got him because his mind was so focused on one thing—a girl rabbit. I saw him in the bush with a girl rabbit, and because he was so focused on her, he ended up with an arrow in his heart."

"Are you suggesting you're going to put an arrow in my heart? You know, threatening the life of a US official is dangerous. Maybe you could ask God to show me how to give you mercy?"

"I hope the thought of me shooting you with an arrow doesn't scare you. Or is the thought of getting killed by a woman too much for you?"

"A glorious death is something to be proud of, but a prairie nigger deserves no such death," he said. "I'm sure putting you in chains would be an improvement."

"I'm sure I would be a terrible slave. I'd end up using the whip on the one that tries to hold me. I believe this conversation is over for now, Mr. Jackson. I'll be sure to pray for you tonight."

Lizzie walked down the dirt trail surrounded by tall grass when she heard Brock reach for his revolver, and she quickly turned around with her bow drawn.

Brock froze with his hand on his revolver. "Impressive, Miss Lizzie Lightning. I have never seen a woman react so well. I think it's best you think about what you're going to do next."

Lizzie's keen eyes were focused on Brock's chest. "What were you thinking, reaching for your gun? Did I insult you by wanting to end a talk with you?"

"I noticed you were holding an arrow with your bow. I guess my curiosity is what caused my decision. I was never going to take hold of my revolver completely. I only wanted to make enough noise by cocking my revolver to see if you knew any better."

"I have a hard time believing you. I have met many men who have called themselves Christian but have shown no form of it to me or my people. All of them showed nothing but hate and fear, and you seem no different." Lizzie then thought, *I see something darker in this man. I better keep my guard up.*

"What makes you believe you can release that arrow before I can make a shot. Are you so sure I won't be able to move out of the path of an arrow?"

"I think it's wiser to decide how accurate my aim really is," Lizzie replied. "What makes you believe arrows are the only weapons I have on me? All I wanted to do was go home, but here you are, preventing me from being with my family."

Brock looked down at the dead rabbits, noticing both animals had arrow punctures through their hearts. He gazed back at Lizzie with sweat going down the back of his neck. Brock slowly took his hand off his revolver and put both hands in the air. "I apologize for obviously scaring you. May we end this uncomfortable confrontation?"

"Fine, I would like to go home anyway." Lizzie slightly decreased her draw and slowly lowered the bow.

"Go on home, now. It is clear to me you want to be home with your family. I have a few more things to take care of myself before the sun goes down."

A smirk rose on Lizzie's face. "That sounds good to me. Please go ahead of me. I'm sure doing your job for the US government is more important than watching me go home for supper."

Brock's eyes widened when he heard Lizzie's answer, and he gave her a small sarcastic smile. "I see you don't trust me. What a shame I'll have to try harder next time. I will respect your request. We will certainly have to meet again under less aggressive conditions."

"I'm sure we will see each other again."

———◆———

Brock adjusted his vest and slowly rode the horse past Lizzie as she watched with her bow slightly drawn. A subtle warm wind picked up. Lizzie's twin braids blew slowly in the wind.

Lizzie followed Brock while he picked up speed while riding down the dirt trail. Brock kept taking a slight look back while he made the horse pick up speed. Brock looked back again, and Lizzie was gone.

Brock turned the horse around, scanning the land for Lizzie. "What a clever woman. We'll certainly meet again, Miss Lightning. Peace must be maintained in these savage lands."

———◆———

Lizzie moved through the tall grass, singing to herself, "All I need is Jesus. Through Jesus, I'm free."

She arrived home, continuing to sing as she walked through the back door.

The other women were already in the kitchen getting ready to cook.

"There you are. We were beginning to worry," Grace said.

"Actually, she was the only one worried. What did you kill this time?" Tsula jested.

Lizzie rolled her eyes as she plopped the two dead rabbits on a table. "Did you kill the chicken already?" she asked.

Grace replied, "No, I'm guessing you want to make rabbit stew."

"Yes, I'm a little tired of chicken." Lizzie picked up the clever and looked at the other four women. "Does anyone disagree?"

Tsula replied, "Well, you're holding the clever and smiling. I'd hate to stop your fun."

Lizzie scoffed.

Lisa giggled. "Annabelle, you can help me with the soybeans," she said.

When the women prepared the food, Lizzie cut up the rabbits as Tsula and Grace led the conversation.

Every sound of the clever cutting up the rabbits felt like it was meant for someone.

***

The rising moon found Annabelle and Grace in the small living room. They were talking with each other when Lizzie abruptly entered the house.

"What brings you out here?" Grace asked in Cherokee.

"I only came to say I feel Mr. Jackson is different than the other Indian agents that have come here before," Lizzie replied. "I feel he is a lot more dangerous. He began to follow me on my way home. I don't know what would've happened if I didn't have my bow with me."

Grace frowned. "Why didn't you say something earlier?"

"I didn't want to worry the others, but I think it is necessary to keep up with having Samuel go to the store. That man preys on the weak. I can see it in his eyes."

Grace sighed. "Are you okay?"

"I'm fine. To be honest, I guess maybe there was a part of me hoping he would give me a reason to fight."

"You're supposed to be focusing on breaking free of that

temper of yours. Please focus on prayer so you're not tempted so easily. We have to be careful with this man."

Lizzie's voice rose, "I'm trying! I could have killed him easily, but I didn't." Lizzie walked out of the house and slammed the door.

Grace closed her Bible and looked at Annabelle. "I'll have to apologize to her," Grace said, standing. "I will see you in the morning."

Annabelle replied, "Okay, I will go to bed then."

Grace left to speak to Lizzie as Annabelle went into her room. Annabelle undressed and sat on her bed with the lamp lit.

Annabelle touched one of the scars on her back with her right hand and exhaled. "I hope Lizzie was wrong. God, please keep me away from any of this evil. I've had enough."

CHAPTER 23
Free Will

A WEEK PASSED AS TENSION BETWEEN the Cherokee family and Brock seemed to suddenly die. Annabelle still felt nervous about the idea of being found alone. She walked from the Thompsons' farm after talking with Doll and giving water to the slaves. She felt tired carrying the bucket. As Annabelle walked to the Lightning-Strongman farm, she saw Lizzie going toward the family house.

"Lizzie, do you mind taking this bucket and putting it by the others in the house?" she asked. "I'm tired today."

Lizzie stopped, glanced at Annabelle, and bickered, "You can do it yourself. I'm not your slave." She continued moving toward the large house, her braided hair blowing in the wind.

Annabelle grunted, watching Lizzie go away. Annabelle was about to say something but sighed instead. "I'm too tired to fight with her today." Annabelle continued to walk to the house, trying to maintain a positive spirit. "Well, at least she hasn't called me a nigger in a long time. I can see the change in her, Lord, but please let the rest of it come in like a flood."

Annabelle entered the house, placed the bucket with the others, and drank some water. The house was mostly empty. Grace and the other women had left to spend some time with others in town. The moment Annabelle walked out of the kitchen, she saw Lizzie playing with David in the living room.

"I'm going outside to read," she told the woman and child.

"You know, if you're going to be a free woman, you need to act more like a free woman. Like I care that you're going to read by that old tree."

Annabelle bit her lip as Lizzie glared at her. "You're right. I should learn how to be free like you. I imagine being rude is a learned skill of a person that's been free her whole life."

Annabelle walked away while Lizzie watched with a smirk. She sat by the tree and prayed for John. She then opened her Bible and read it as a pronghorn herd passed by on the frontier. Annabelle enjoyed watching the antelope. Their tan coloration contrasted with brilliant white patches. They were beautiful to her, though the bison were still her favorite.

When she heard someone walking behind her, she quickly turned around and saw John coming toward her. "Do you have some free time for me to spend with you?" John asked in Cherokee.

Annabelle smiled at John and slightly moved over. "Sure, I was thinking about you."

John pointed his thumb to his chest. "You were thinking about me?"

Annabelle blushed. "I mean, I was praying for you, that's all. Everyone needs prayer."

"I agree. It's easy to not pay attention to things that have value," John said. "I think it's a weakness in all people."

"I think you're right, and I also think that's something beautiful to work toward."

"And what is it that you're working toward?"

"Becoming a wiser, more patient, and loving person," Annabelle replied. "Being more focused on the Father and Jesus. I think that's the best path for me to walk on."

"I pray to the Creator. Ask for help at times. I do see something different in you, my sisters, and my cousins. I even see the changes in their spirits that have happened over time. Have you always been this way, or have you changed?"

Annabelle closed her Bible. "I wasn't always the person I am today. I'm happy for that, being able to look at the past and see that I've changed. I thank the Creator every day for each step forward."

"But this is something you did yourself, isn't it? You can choose what paths you want to take like me. I think one day, you wanted a change, and it happened."

"Yes, I did have a choice in many ways, but there is something deeper that happens when Jesus does the change in your heart. It's like being awakened. When you become tired of making certain choices or living a certain way, you can choose to go down a different path. When a person tries to change in that way, they still walk blindly."

John gave a skewed frown, and his mouth etched into a small downward curve with his lips flattened. "Why do you think that?"

"Most people still have no remorse of how they lived because they believe it is their life, and no one has the right to tell them they're wrong. I think that comes from people not wanting to admit they're wrong. They are their god, and their pride controls them. They learn through their own reasoning, but they stay blind because they can't see the spiritual side of why the change was needed."

"So, my beliefs that help me change are meaningless because I can't see the spiritual side to why I needed to change. How did you learn that?"

"Elder Joyce is a wise woman," Annabelle said. "I wouldn't say they're meaningless, but changing just because it benefits you is different than changing because you understand why doing things a certain way is a sin. Why continue to poison yourself and say you're well?"

"I understand what you mean. I want to understand why you choose to follow the white man's beliefs instead of following the Creator? Is it because that's all you were shown?"

"It wasn't the only beliefs I was shown. There was a woman on the same plantation that spoke of spiritual ways from the motherland, she called it. I believe the motherland was where my ancestors came from. A few of the slaves followed her, but many rejected it. She would do witchcraft and try ritual healings. Even though those were good things, I always felt there was something darker about it. It's like asking for help from something that was teaching us things the wrong way."

"So you chose this Christianity because of it?"

"No, I believed in the spirit world, but it wasn't until I started to pray with Judy Mays that things changed. I was confused with how the white people treated us when they would preach about Jesus. Judy Mays then taught me how to read, and so I started reading on my own to learn. The first time I felt the Father speak to me, it was so loving and different than my inner thoughts. I was asked to trust him and follow the path of righteousness. I cried because I realized the Creator really is there. I then accepted Jesus as the Father's son after a lot of prayers and letting go of what I was afraid of."

John's eyes fixed on Annabelle's eyes. "What were you afraid of?"

"I was afraid I was wrong. I was afraid being a good person by my standards didn't matter. There was something in me needing to change."

"Years ago, I would've said you don't need to change," John said, "but seeing my own family change over time, I see that would be a lie."

"What are you afraid of, John? Why don't you accept Jesus?"

John looked away from Annabelle and into the herd of pronghorn. "You speak like it is so easy, like the Creator is going to speak to me."

"He will. All you have to do is be still and listen. The Creator's voice is different than our inner thoughts, helping us make choices on our own understanding and wants. His voice awakens us, and it even gives us wisdom beyond what we have."

"You sound like Grace a little," John said. "I don't want to do things like the white people have. If the Creator wants to speak to me, he can do so more boldly. Walking the same path with these white people bothers me. These men gave us a sickness we never had, murdered my people, and then gave us this book to follow their ways."

Annabelle lifted her Bible and held it to her heart. "What is written in this book was never started by white men, but written by men who were instructed by the Father. I always pray for understanding, and sometimes I get an answer. It strengthens my faith knowing the words written here are not rules created by men. I can't lie to you. I have seen many evil things done by men claiming to follow Jesus, but I'm asking you not to let their actions blind you."

John scoffed. "I guess I do admire your faith a little more than my sisters'. Grace used to read the Bible to me after our mother died, but I'm not sure what to think about Jesus. I remember some of the great things, but I don't share your faith. For me to believe he is the Creator's son would take a lot."

Annabelle frowned. "You've never taken the time to pray, have you?"

"I never believed there was an answer. I see the old ways as more noble than what the white people showed my people."

"No tribe of people has ever done everything right. I think that's what the Creator shows us again and again. I learned there isn't nothing wrong with loving your culture, but culture should never take priority over the truth."

"And whose truth would that be? Take a look at both our people. It can't be our truth."

"There's one truth. There has always been one truth. No matter the opinions people have, that can never change what is. There is never something between a lie and the truth. Are you ready to ask for yourself?"

"I'm not accepting their truth, Annabelle. I can't. After all the white men did to us, I can't accept believing what they believe. What does that make me? I've asked Grace and Lizzie, but they seem so willing to believe it, I gave up questioning them."

"We all have the same truth," Annabelle emotionally said.

"Sadly, white people decided to use it to hurt us instead of loving us. That doesn't change the truth. It should push us to learn it to correct their ways. I promise you the Creator loves you. You're a great man. I want to see you become greater."

Annabelle looked at John, expressing love.

John sighed. "I can become a greater man without this. I think you would've become the person you are now without Jesus."

"John, that isn't true. Please listen to me when I say there's more to this world than you're willing to accept."

"Christianity didn't save my mother, and it didn't save my people when we were forced here."

"God cried when he saw how wronged your people were. To see his children treat their brothers and sisters so badly, as if they didn't have a heart. I know God cried."

John frowned. "What makes you so sure?"

"Because when Elder Joyce told me the truth, I felt the pain in my spirit. My inner self felt very sad, but my spirit... I felt my heart break, and I felt God speak to me. Please don't let the hate of one people steal the truth away from you."

"I don't know what to think, but thank you for telling me about your beliefs." John brushed off his trousers. He stood up and went away as Annabelle watched.

Annabelle frowned as her gaze went downward, and she clutched her Bible as John left. She could feel her eyes becoming watery.

"God, please show me how to do better. I felt like I was saying the right things to him."

Annabelle sat under the old tree while she prayed, attempting to calm herself.

"Love him and pray for him," a soft voice said.

Annabelle heard the welcoming voice so strongly, she turned around. She could feel a deep, welcoming presence.

"Love him and pray for him. You cannot force him to believe."

Annabelle's eyes widened, realizing it was the Holy Spirt.

She looked for Constance, the angel she'd met years ago. "I'm trying not to force him to believe. I—I don't want to lose him," Annabelle said. "I'm scared he'll die before he realizes the truth. Please give me more wisdom to do better."

Annabelle waited for almost an hour, hoping to hear what she needed to do, but nothing happened. Annabelle decided to try to have faith in what she couldn't control, and she walked to the house to help cook.

As the women cooked, Annabelle remained in deep thought. "Annabelle, you look worried. Is something wrong?" Grace asked in Cherokee.

Annabelle replied, "Nothing is wrong. I was thinking."

Lizzie recognized Annabelle's blank stare and huffed as she continued to prepare the food. The family supper was normal, though Annabelle was quieter as she listened to the others talk and joke around. As Annabelle and Grace went to the small house, John followed them.

"Annabelle, can I speak to you for a moment?" John asked in Cherokee.

Annabelle turned around. "Yes, I have some time."

"Why did you wait to ask her now when all of the bugs are out?" Grace agitatedly asked as she killed a bug. "Whatever, I'm going inside. I'll see you inside, Annabelle."

"Okay. What do you want?" Annabelle asked.

"I wanted to say I'm sorry if I hurt your feelings today," John replied. "I'm still trying to think about all that you said."

Annabelle smiled. "You're a good man. I like that you're willing to explore what I believe, and I'm still learning too."

"I think that's one of the many purposes in life—growing."

Annabelle was about to say something when she felt the Holy Spirit encourage her to say something different. "When I was a child, I spake as a child, I understood as a child, I thought as a child. But when I became a man, I put away childish things."

John's eyes widened. "How... Why would you say that? I can't believe that I heard what you said."

Annabelle slightly frowned. "I'm sorry, I didn't mean to say anything mean."

"It wasn't mean, I...I've heard that before. It must be a coincidence."

"Well, I'm sure you've heard it before. Grace must've said it to you," Annabelle said.

"No, she's never said something like that to me. If she did, it would be when I made her angry. I had a dream not long ago, and that was spoken to me. Where have you heard that saying before?"

"It's not a saying, John. It is actually a scripture in the Bible. That's why I know it."

John scratched the back of his head. "Well, that was weird, but I'm happy I didn't hurt you. I need to go to sleep and think about today. Goodnight, Annabelle."

"Goodnight, John." Annabelle watched John leave, wanting to say more.

A grin appeared on Annabelle's face as she walked back to the small cabin.

Holy Spirit, she thought, *thank you for guiding me. I know that wasn't an accident.*

Annabelle entered the small house and saw Grace sitting at the table and reading her Bible. "What was that about?" Grace asked in Cherokee.

Annabelle replied, "Nothing, he wanted to know how I was doing. He thought I was sad for some reason."

"There was something important on your mind. Did you want to talk about it?"

"Well, no, not really." Annabelle began to go to her room, but she saw Grace's worrisome face. "John asked me about my faith, and we talked for a while. It was nothing bad. I've been thinking about it all day."

Grace's eyes widened a little. "How did it go?"

"I think it went good. He said he had much to think about."

Grace sat back in her chair. "Keep praying for him and

speaking the truth to him. Don't make my mistake and try to force him to listen. It fails."

"I'll do that for him. Goodnight."

Grace stretched her arms. "Goodnight. I'm also going to sleep too."

<hr>

The women walked into their rooms, both with a new hope.

Annabelle said her prayers for John and fell asleep looking at the stars.

Grace lay in her bed holding her mother's cross. "Your will be done on earth as it is in heaven. Father, I thank you for the changes I know you'll bring forth, and I continue to pray for Annabelle's protection."

Grace fell asleep holding her mother's cross.

<hr>

During the night, John, Michael, and Samuel talked among themselves while David was sleeping. After Michael and Samuel fell asleep, John lay in his bed staring into the darkness. He finally fell asleep and heard the sound of drums. He could see nothing but darkness, but he eventually noticed a fire burning and approached a cobblestone firepit.

When John walked to the firepit, he saw the three tree stumps he once dreamed about. John remembered what the man had told him about what each stump represented.

"Why am I having this dream again?" John nervously asked.

"You're being given the choice to listen," a voice echoed. "Two represent a path that leads to death, and the other leads to life."

John stared at the fire and looked at the tree stumps. "Creator, I feel this is you showing me what I need to see. I want my son to grow into a better man, and I'll throw the bad stumps into this fire."

John approached the rotten tree stump and struggled

to pick it up. The smell of the rotting tree stump was almost overwhelming, but John felt someone help him with it. John couldn't see who it was.

The rotten tree stump was thrown into the fire. The fire grew, engulfing the tree stump. John then went over to the old tree stump, and with help, the stump was picked up. However, as they walked it toward the fire, a growling voice could be heard, and it startled John. As the two moved faster to the fire, something viciously pulled at his arm. The stump fell, and John was dragged and then released.

"No!" a dark figure in a cloak yelled. "You're with me. You follow my needs!"

John's heart pounded faster as the aggressor reached for John with its coal-colored arm. John stood up and pushed the creature back.

"I will never follow you or your needs!" John yelled.

"You can't deny who you are. You're weak without me. Let's control what this world will give us." The creature pushed John back and growled. "Don't be a fool. Don't starve me!"

The creature reached for John again, but it was blown back. The being that John had once been unable to see was now visible, standing tall with his hand outstretched.

"That's enough," the majestic being said in an echoing voice.

The man had a face like lightning, and he wore golden armor with an axe on his back. A gold aura surrounded his body. He walked toward John.

"What kind of dream is this? Who are you?" John asked.

The majestic man replied in Cherokee, "My name is Aranck. I'm an angel who has been given the instruction to show you what you asked and choose for yourself, which you have."

John stood, struggling to stop his body from shaking. "What is that thing over there?"

The creature laughed malevolently and lifted the hood from its head. John gasped and stepped back as he looked at the creature.

The creature smiled when it revealed it had John's face.

"We're the same. I'm you, and you are me, from the beginning of your birth until now."

"How can I believe such a lie? You're nothing like me."

Aranck stood next to John and placed his hand on John's shoulder. "He is the other half of you, the darker nature of who you really are—your flesh, your instincts. He is strong because you have fed him for years and never controlled him. He doesn't want you to destroy this old tree stump because it will represent your first steps in controlling that part of you."

John became horrified, and he looked at the creature eye to eye as it stood before him in the black cloak. The evil grin of confidence it displayed was disturbing.

"Come. Our way was better, our way is comforting, and our way will make us happy," it said.

"Is there anything good in you? I know I did something right in my life. You shouldn't look this way," John replied.

Aranck replied, "This part of you has been overrun by the evil you have done. It does not take much to corrupt your flesh. It's already prone to living in sin, and it is unable to see that sin itself is killing it."

John looked at the angel with great despair. "Please continue to help me destroy this old tree stump?" John asked.

The angel nodded and helped John pick up the stump. The two quickly walked to the fire, but John's flesh walked faster toward them.

"John, wait!" the creature yelled. "I can change. Trust me to change. Please, stop it!" The creature ran toward John and Aranck, roaring like an animal.

John saw nothing but white light and abruptly woke up. John looked around the room and took a deep breath. John curled up and looked down at his son.

"Creator, I'm sorry," John said as he continued to look at his family as they slept. "Help me have the courage to come to you more."

Two days passed as John continued to process the dream. During the evening, Uncle George left after supper to spend time with other men in the town. The others spent time together in the family house, but he suddenly heard a crash. John and Samuel rushed outside as the others waited to see what caused the noise. The men saw some chicken cages on the side of the house knocked down, and Uncle George lay on his back.

"Papa!" Samuel yelled.

George laughed, struggling to roll onto his side. John and Samuel marched over to help him stand.

Uncle George continued to laugh. "Ah, my boys. My good boys," Uncle George slurred in Cherokee. "I made it home in the moonlight."

Grace and Lisa exited the front door and saw George being guided by the cousins. "Uncle George, are you drunk again?" Grace asked in Cherokee.

George replied, "I'm not drunk. I tired of walking, so the boys are helping me."

John and Samuel continued to help George walk toward the house.

"Papa, you've been out drinking again, haven't you?" Lisa asked in Cherokee.

George defensively responded, "How dare you question me on what I have been doing. I was with the other men and having a good time."

Grace could see the frown on Lisa's face, and she insensitively replied, "No more of this. Uncle George, we won't watch you kill yourself like my father. Boys, bring him inside so he can sleep."

"Sleep? Sleep? I need no such thing right now, Grace. I feeling too great for my bed. I see the stars, and the stars see me."

"Uncle George, the stars are frowning right now because they can see how drunk you are," Grace responded.

"The stars are jealous of me. A good-looking Cherokee man with some bad legs. In the morning, they will be good legs."

Samuel tried not to laugh as he and John helped walk George to the door. Grace and Lisa watched with their hands on their hips while they passed.

"You smell like nothing but rum, papa," Lisa angrily said.

"Don't be mad, my beautiful little flower. I had a good time," George slurred.

"Papa, will you even remember what happened tonight."

"Yes, and I can prove it right now. Lizzie, come here so you can punch your brother. I need to see some excitement." George laughed as John and Samuel moved him further into the house.

Lizzie, sitting on the floor, turned around.

"Ah, there is the rest of my family," George said. "And the negro, Miss Annabelle Mays."

"Uncle George, you're drunk again," Lizzie snarled in Chero kee.

"My other favorite niece, Lizzie Fist." George laughed. "I haven't had any drinks the past few days."

"Keep telling yourself that. I think you need to go to bed."

Tsula watched, sulking with David in her lap while she sat next to Michael. The men tried to help George to his room, but he kept trying to approach Lizzie.

"Lizzie, you...you... Oh, I forgot what I was going to say." George glared at Annabelle. "Oh, the Negro. I was wrong about you. You're a loving person, like me. I love my family. I can see you care for them, and they care for you." George's voice rose, "You're welcomed here in my home! I was wrong. I have been learning many bad things from white men."

"Thank you, Mr. Strongman," Annabelle calmly said.

"Such a mannered Negro, Lizzie. You would learn so much from her," George slurred.

Taking deep breaths, Lizzie stared at her uncle.

"You know, she's a warrior. Very loving, very smart too, but she is warrior," George said as he pumped his fist. "God help the man that marries her."

George laughed, and Lizzie abruptly stood up from the wooden floor.

Immediately, Grace and Lisa pulled Lizzie away while she shrieked, "You drunk old man! Let me go! Let me go! It's over!"

The cousins heavily struggled to hold Lizzie back and barely forced her into her bedroom.

After the bedroom door slammed, Lizzie's rant could be heard through the door as Grace and Lisa struggled to keep her in the room. George continued to laugh. John and Samuel used the moment to help him to his room.

"Annabelle, don't call me Mr. Strongman. You can call me Uncle George." John smiled at Annabelle as he and Samuel marched George into his room.

✦

Annabelle could still hear Lizzie arguing with Grace and Lisa. She thought, *Please, God, don't allow her anger to fall on me.* "I think I'm going to leave, Tsula."

"Is everything okay, Annabelle?" Tsula asked.

"Yes, I'm okay. I just want to sleep now. It has been a long day."

Tsula smiled at Annabelle and put David down. "Alright, sleep well tonight."

"Thank you, Tsula. Goodnight, Michael and little David."

"Goodnight, Annabelle," Michael said.

David went toward Annabelle and hugged her. "Goodnight, Annabelle," he said.

✦

As Annabelle walked to the small house, John and Samuel came out of George's room.

"Where's Annabelle?" John asked.

Tsula replied in Cherokee, "She left to go sleep."

A side of John's mouth curved down a little. "Was she okay?"

"Yeah, I could tell papa didn't scare her away. You're cute, John, being so concerned."

John tilted his head. "It was a question, Tsula."

"Yeah, well, one question can open many doors."

"What does that mean?"

Tsula chuckled as she went toward her bedroom. "I see through that thick head of yours, John. It's actually cute."

John shook his head. "What are you talking about?"

"Nothing. Don't hit your head on any of the logs, or we'll have to replace them."

John pouted while he watched Tsula walk to the bedroom. She continued to chuckle with Lizzie's angry voice in the background.

"What is she laughing about?" Samuel asked.

John cynically replied, "I don't know. She's your twin. Let's end the night soon. There has been enough excitement for the day."

Samuel replied, "I agree."

CHAPTER 24
Beliefs

THE NEXT DAY, ANNABELLE RETURNED home after working at the supply store and sat down to read her Bible under the redbud tree. John saw Annabelle as he and Jacob finished putting the horses in their stalls, then approached her as he brushed off his white cotton shirt.

"Do you mind if I sit down with you?" John asked in Cherokee.

"Hi, John. You can sit with me," Annabelle said.

John sat down next to Annabelle and looked at the frontier. "Are you waiting for one of the herds to show up?"

"I was going to sit here and read for a while. I've learned to appreciate this skill. Seeing the animals would be an extra blessing for me."

"I haven't thought about reading that way. So few of us can read, and I think that needs to change. You have an advantage over a lot of the Cherokee here."

Annabelle smiled and looked away from John. "Is that really true? I have met many Cherokee who can read. Your entire family can read."

John chuckled. "You have to meet a lot more of us and then you will see what I mean. You're a smart woman. I like that in you. I think that's why you did so well in Mercy when you lived there. I also believe it's natural for people to like you… your spirit."

Annabelle felt flattered but kept a blank expression. "I try to treat people how I would like to be treated. Sometimes I do well, and there have been other times I didn't control my anger like I should have."

John chuckled. "You sound like Grace." He plucked a blade of grass and broke it apart. "It's a good thing my sister is wise for her age."

"Are you still thinking about what we talked about?"

"Yeah, for different reasons, I'm thinking about it. More than I like, but that's life."

"I'm sorry, I don't mean to push you, John."

"It's fine, Annabelle. I don't feel pressured by you. I'm trying to listen more to what is the truth instead of what I want to be true."

"Elder Joyce told me something that surprised me. She told me that sometimes, the truth can be ruined by the actions of others. She thought about the Creator, and what if the old traditional ways of your people was the spiritual truth. If the Cherokee had found the white man, and the Creator had given instruction through the old ways on how to live right. What if the Cherokee did the same evil acts men have already done? Would their evil change the truth?"

John laid his back against the redbud tree. "I guess that wouldn't change the truth."

"I know if a corrupt man told me the truth, the truth would not be untrue. If an evil man only told part of the truth and used it to give him power over others, does that make the truth that was written a lie, or the man a liar? Does a hypocrite have the power to change the truth because he teaches it but never follows what he teaches?"

"No, none of them change the truth, but it makes it hard for people to believe anything those men say as true. I never thought of that type of problem before."

"I never used to think that way, but seeing things that way reminds me to seek the Creator and trust him."

"Tell me something else about you other than your beliefs. What is your favorite color?"

Annabelle's eyebrow lifted while she fought a smile. "Well, my favorite color is blue. What is your favorite color?"

John chuckled and thought, *Annabelle and Lizzie have that in common.* "My favorite color is green. It reminds me of the summer, my favorite season."

"Spring is my favorite season. I like watching how the plants regrow and seeing the baby animals if I'm lucky. Okay, my turn. What is your favorite animal?"

John shrugged. "I never thought about having a favorite animal."

Annabelle closed her Bible and turned around to face John fully. "How do you not have a favorite animal? You have to have one that means something to you."

"Now my feelings are hurt. I never thought someone would make me feel bad for not having a favorite animal," John sarcastically said.

Annabelle lightly hit John on his shoulder. "You can't fool me with as much grief as Lizzie gives you."

John laughed. "Lizzie has always had her ways of testing me a lot more than Grace. Well, because you're looking at me like I'm crazy, I guess I can choose an animal—the eagle. I like the eagle. It is sacred, and no other birds fly above it."

"I think that's a good choice." Annabelle looked at the sky. At this time, the clouds passed over the empty terrain. "Looks like none of the herds are coming today, but I see beautiful clouds. I think that one looks like the head of a deer. Do you see anything in the clouds?"

John looked at the clouds passing by and folded his arms. "I think that one looks like a man smiling. Do you see which one I'm talking about?"

Annabelle surveyed the sky. "I see it. You have good eyes."

"I'm glad you think so."

Annabelle and John chuckled. The two friends continued to look at the clouds and discuss what images they could see.

◆

After supper, Annabelle and Grace went home. Grace noticed Annabelle had a happier demeanor while they strolled into the small house.

"What has you in such a good mood?" Grace asked in Cherokee.

"Nothing. I was enjoying the day."

"Are you sure? Even when we were making supper, you looked like something really good happened," Grace said.

"Why can't I have a good day?" Annabelle asked. "I don't know. Maybe it was because Lizzie didn't give me a hard time today. I'm just happy."

"I'm sorry. I guess I'm thinking too hard."

Annabelle smiled. "No worries. I would've probably asked myself that too."

After they entered their home, Grace sat down in one of the old rocking chairs as Annabelle went to her room.

Grace sighed. "What happened to you today, Annabelle? I'm anxious for her to tell me. I'll just have to wait."

CHAPTER 25
The Light and the Dark

A WEEK PASSED AS ANNABELLE AND John continued to have their conversations. Annabelle found herself expecting John to ask her more about herself and tell how the day went on the farm.

One day, Brock Jackson and Hunter Sawyer walked into the supply store.

"Good afternoon. I see you ladies are working hard today," Brock mockingly said.

Hunter lightly cackled while he stood behind Brock.

"Mr. Jackson, how can I help you today?" Grace said.

"Miss Lightning, you Indians and your ways. I was politely informed by one of your white customers—who gives you his hard-earned money—that you served Cherokee customers before him when he arrived first. I have no reasons not to believe this man."

Grace folded her hands as she stood behind the counter and replied, "We treat all of our customers fairly. We work as fast as we can. Some orders take longer than others. We have no control over what customers want."

Brock moved toward the counter, Hunter following him. "Miss Lightning, our job is to keep the peace in this area. To make sure the safety of US citizens in this wild land continues.

I have been through the entirety of this land. Few of you have made an effort to do anything with it."

Grace's brown eyes fixed on Brock. "What about the unfair treatment of my people by white men. You say you and Mr. Sawyer are here to keep the peace, but in every way, you support what the other white men tell you. If you Indian agents are here to help keep the peace, treat us fairly or leave us alone."

"That's the only thing you Indians are good for is excuses. Nothing but excuses," Hunter said.

Lisa came out of the storage room and stood next to Grace. "We're making no excuses," Lisa snarled. "What do you know of us? Your people forced us here, and we do what we can to survive. What good are the supplies the United States gives us when many of our people are still struggling?"

"Your people are slow to accept civilization!" Brock yelled. "I see how many of your people treat your slaves, and it's sickening. You clothe them like yourselves, you allow them to choose what to work on first, they speak freely, and the amount of obvious mixed-bloods should bring shame on your kind."

Annabelle walked through the backdoor and froze. She felt her heart drop the instant she stared at the two men and moved toward Grace. "Good afternoon, Mr. Jackson and Mr. Sawyer," she said.

"The accomplished nigger," Brock snobbishly said. "See here, Hunter. This is a prime example of failure by the Cherokee. A Negro who has learned too much for her own good."

Grace angrily replied, "Mr. Jackson, all we ask for is respect. I don't allow my own people to say 'nigger' in our family supply store. I will ask the same of you and Mr. Sawyer."

"Respect will be given when you and your people know your place." Brock's blue eyes fixed on Lisa while he adjusted his green vest. "There might be some hope for your kind after all. Your family is one of the few showing potential. Don't disappoint us like the others."

Grace put her hand on her hip. "Respect will always go

both ways, Mr. Jackson, and the same goes for peace in these lands."

Brock exhaled and moved his hand across his brown hair as his impenitent eyes anchored on the women. "You're different than your sister, Miss Lightning. You may have an easier time teaching that Negro when to speak than teaching your sister how to be a lady."

The two men left the supply store as the young women watched.

"We're slaves without chains," Grace worrisomely said. "Those men are like the ones before them, and they are here to find more reason to treat us poorly."

"Those men are watching us, aren't they?" Annabelle asked, anxiety coloring her voice.

"They are watching all of us," Lisa said. "I say let us finish organizing things. I won't let those mean men ruin my day."

"I agree. They'll obviously keep coming to us," Grace said. "They have a problem with our success. Annabelle, how did your visit to the slaves go today?"

Annabelle grinned as she replied, "It was good as normal. I saw Jacob on the Tate farm today."

Lisa stopped going toward the supply room and listened to Annabelle.

"He went back home to bring some corn back with him," Annabelle continued.

"That sounds like him, always forgetting his food." Lisa smiled and entered the storage room.

❖

During this time, Brock and Hunter rode together on their horses. "It seems that some of the Cherokee are becoming tired of us observing their actions," Hunter said.

"I believe the success of a few is feeding into our trouble," Brock said. "It's no different than when it was a true fear Indian tribes were going to attack the plantations full force. It's a dangerous threat to our security, to our people."

Hunter pursed his lips. "What are you thinking about? We must be careful with these savages, or we might cause a dangerous revolt."

"The Cherokee are no real nation. We need to make them more dependent—weaken their growth and push them to accept our more civilized ways. It is what's best for the people. God be willing, these Cherokee know their rank in this world. Their status isn't much higher than that of a Negro. We have no obligation to help them."

Hunter nodded. "You seem so sure about this."

"Hunter, my father is a well-respected slaveholder, like his father before him, and his father, and his father," Brock said. "I have heard the old stories of how we worked together to build our country, but now this northern threat. These abolitionists and these rebellious Indians—they're the sickness of our country. Maybe we should have kept the whip on the backs of these Indians, just like the niggers."

"I agree, but could we do such a thing now without creating a revolt among the Indians?" Hunter asked. "They are different than the Negroes and far more capable of revolt. The Seminole are, by far, one of the most dangerous, and they still have some hold in Florida."

Brock scoffed. "My family was quite proficient in the use of Indian slaves. I wouldn't be surprised if some of the slaves that served me as I grew had more Indian blood in them than Negro. A solution may be to set a law that any Indian found breaking the law should be enslaved permanently."

Hunter's mouth shifted to the left while he looked at Brock. "These are troubling times. We need to be careful."

"Be careful. Must I remind you that this Underground Railroad plagues us now? My friend, we're on the brink of war against these abolitionists. The Negroes are happy in their place, whether it's out in the sugar cane fields or making supper for their masters. These abolitionists have polluted their minds, and it is our duty to keep the peace here, even if that means reinstating the slavery of Indians."

"What do you propose we do about these kidnappings the tribes have reported?" Hunter asked. "What if they start looking harder?"

"I have no concern for the recapture of runaway slaves, Hunter. I'm surprised that you do."

Hunter huffed. "I have no concern for those Negroes or half-breeds. You know I believe a man's property is a man's property, but these Indians... Many of them don't see it this way. The apparent taking of Indian children is also catching more attention."

"There's no law here forbidding the enslavement of an Indian child as far as I'm concerned," Brock said. "These Indians have no proof of who is doing the kidnappings. If a white man gets caught in the act, well, we must give back to the Indian, but if no proof is given... Who am I to say that these Indians aren't trying to get a slave for free or reclaim kin that's rightfully the property of a good man? The Indians should be grateful for the rank they were born with."

"I suggest we show compassion for their anger, and reassure them we won't tolerate the raids."

Brock caressed the black mane of his horse and they continued to ride to another town. "I agree but I must also say. It is good having those half-breeds on the plantations they make good leaders, they smarter, hell I'd say even stronger in some cases, but it does concern me. They have this unnatural pride in them."

"We've had nothing but Negroes on our plantation, so I don't understand what you mean," Hunter commented.

"In those eyes I see it, the Indian, no matter how much that whip is cracked on their back. The young woman Lizzie and the one called Lisa, I see it in their eyes, pride. It's...rebellion. I know the ones like that. They're waiting for the chance to take control and come through like a summer storm. Their kind must continue to be controlled, or we may see a war greater than our glorious win over Great Britain."

Hunter's brow furrowed. "How can you say such a thing?

After all these Indians have been through, what strength do they have to fight us?"

"I'm telling you if these Indians were ever able to find their kin in chains and free them, I have no doubt in my mind that the tribes would form an alliance and wage war on us like nothing we have seen. My grandfather, the great man he was, told me he fought in the revolutionary war. In one battle, the Indians came in at full force, and it was the Cherokee helping the British. Almost the entire platoon that fought alongside him was mercilessly wiped out. He killed a few, but this one Indian he took a shot at moved fast enough that the musket ball only grazed the shoulder.

"The Cherokee charged at him in a rage with a tomahawk, and he charged at the Indian. That crazy Indian threw the tomahawk, cutting my grandfather's face. My grandfather tried to conquer the Indian in a hand-to-hand skirmish. The Indian was skilled and knocked him to the ground. The Indian went for the tomahawk. My grandfather was too hurt to attack again and decided to jump in the river, but the Indian saw him and threw the tomahawk, leaving a large scar on his shoulder. The tomahawk never stuck in his shoulder, but the damage was so much, he could never use it the same again."

Hunter's eyes widened. "Your grandfather was spectacular to face such a savage man and live to tell it."

Brock smirked. "The Indian was a woman, one of the tribe's war women. It was hard for me to imagine until my grandfather showed me the large scar. That Lizzie woman represents that savagery."

A drop of sweat went down Hunter's face as he gasped.

❖

As the day continued, Annabelle arrived at home with the others, but instead of going to the small house to get her Bible, she stood by the old redbud tree. Annabelle saw John and Samuel walking away from the barn to the family house.

"Hey, Annabelle, how were things in the store today?" Samuel asked, speaking in Cherokee.

"It was a good day," Annabelle replied.

"Good, is Tsula inside?"

"Yes, she is."

Samuel quickly jogged to the house, looking for his sister.

"I'm surprised that you don't have a book with you right now," John said.

Annabelle giggled. "There are other things that interest me."

John smirked. "What other things?"

"Why are you asking more about my interests now?" Annabelle asked.

John scratched his head and gave a nervous smile. "I guess the most truthful answer is I only asked how you're doing. When Camille died, you encouraged me and lifted my spirit without wanting something in return. I'm still impressed by that today. I want to know more about who you are. I see how you treat David, even though he isn't your son. I believe you're worth my time."

Annabelle's heart raced as she stared at John. "I impress you?" John stepped forward as Annabelle's right hand gripped the tree. "I need—"

"What do you need?"

Annabelle's brown eyes locked onto John's. "I need— I need to go and see if your sisters wanted to start supper already. I don't want to upset Lizzie. It's been a good two weeks of some peace." Annabelle nervously rubbed her hands together and walked away toward the family house.

John gave a slight frown. "Are you okay?"

"Yes, yes, I'm okay. I...I just need to go help your sisters. I will see you inside." Annabelle reached for the front door and entered the house, sighing.

John stood by the redbud tree and folded his arms, walking in a small circle.

Annabelle helped prepare supper with the other women and

couldn't suppress the grin on her face. "Why are you smiling?" Lizzie asked, speaking Cherokee.

"I wasn't smiling," Annabelle answered.

"Liar, you're a bad liar. What has you smiling so much?"

"Leave her alone, Flour Face. She is enjoying the day," Tsula bickered in Cherokee.

Lizzie replied, "Why are you defending her? She is in no danger here. There are no secrets here."

Lisa's eyes widened while she continued to prepare the soybeans. "You're a bad liar, Annabelle. Eventually, you will talk."

"Leave her alone," Grace said, her voice sharp.

Lizzie rapidly stabbed the table. "Why is everyone defending her? Annabelle is a grown woman. She can speak for herself."

"Calm down. It isn't serious," Lisa said.

Lizzie scoffed. "Please, you're defending her too. It was a question. If she had nothing to hide, she could answer without lying."

The others looked inquiringly at Annabelle, and she felt the room had turned against her.

"I...I thought it was nice to see all the flowers have bloomed. It makes a big difference."

Everyone except Lizzie, who was unimpressed, smiled at Annabelle and accepted her answer.

The supper ensued as the family sat down and enjoyed each other's company. Annabelle glanced at John and beamed. John smiled back and continued to eat his food. Lizzie caught Annabelle smiling as she ate her corn.

Annabelle immediately stared down at her plate when she noticed Lizzie staring at her with a smirk.

Lizzie mumbled, "Who were you smiling at?" She looked to her right at John and Samuel before looking back at Annabelle, avoiding eye contact.

Grace nudged Lizzie. "What are you thinking about?"

"Nothing, I'm enjoying the time," Lizzie answered before continuing to eat her food.

The next day, Annabelle visited Joyce after working at the supply store. The smell of pine was always comforting to her. During her visit, Annabelle told Joyce what happened between her and John.

"I'm surprised," Joyce said in Cherokee. "Be careful of your feelings. It's obvious that over time, your feelings have grown for him, and the same goes for him."

"I'm being careful," Annabelle said defensively. "I'm unsure with how I should continue to talk to him. I feel excited, and I haven't felt this excited in a long time."

Joyce rocked back in her rocking chair, hearing the compassion in Annabelle's words. "Don't allow yourself to become more attached to him until he gives his life over to Jesus. 'Be ye not unequally yoked together with unbelievers: for what fellowship hath righteousness with unrighteousness? And what communion hath light with darkness?' "

Annabelle frowned, realizing what Joyce meant.

"John is a good man, but he must be right spiritually first."

"I will end his chase of me. I don't know how he'll react. I'm afraid it will push him away from God if I tell him in the wrong way," Annabelle responded.

"Avoid being with him alone completely. If the others can see him talking to you, it will make it easier for you to guard your heart. I've seen many times where one believes and the other does not," Joyce advised. "It is very painful because when children are brought into it, an internal war is created. You don't want that."

"I will follow your advice. I'm also nervous. Lizzie has been watching us, and she isn't easily fooled."

Joyce chuckled. "Lizzie will always be a watcher. Don't let that scare you. She cares, and because she cares, she has a hard time not watching and seeing things others don't. Behind all her serious nature is a loving person. Don't forget that."

Annabelle left Joyce's home and spent the next few days slightly avoiding John.

John became a bit frustrated with Annabelle refusing to talk to him alone, though Annabelle's willingness to acknowledge John helped him stay confident Annabelle liked him.

The following Sunday, the Lightning-Strongman family went to the church and listened to Pastor Bluebird preach on forgiveness. Annabelle listened to his teachings, but she also couldn't help but watch Nancy's reactions. Nancy sat next to her younger sister, Abigail, who seemed riveted on the sermon. The congregation stood to sing their last hymns.

John entered the church as they sang. Pastor Bluebird smiled as John stepped into an aisle behind his family. Some of the congregation looked back and grinned, but they kept singing, trying not to be distracted by John's sudden appearance. Joyce looked back and smiled at John.

Joyce's reaction intrigued Lizzie, who looked back and whispered, "John, you came!"

Uncle George looked back and nodded at his nephew. Tsula, Michael, and Samuel looked back and smiled at John. Annabelle's and Lisa's curiosity got the better of them, and the two women looked back. Annabelle gasped and immediately looked forward, smiling.

Grace became a little agitated with everyone's obvious distraction. She looked back, and John waved at his sister.

"John, when did you..." Grace beamed at her brother, turned back around to sing, and wept uncontrollably.

Lisa attempted to calm Grace down by holding her, but she was too overwhelmed with joy. Grace's emotions were so raw, Annabelle imagined it must be like seeing someone brought back to life.

After the congregation finished the hymns to end the church service, some people welcomed John before they went home. John's family greeted him, but Grace abruptly embraced him and wept with joy.

"John, it is good to see you here," Pastor Bluebird said. "You're welcomed to return anytime."

"Thank you, Pastor Bluebird," John said.

"What made you come?" Grace asked.

"I had a lot to think about for the past couple of days. I feel in my spirit there are more answers here," John said.

"Let's go home to celebrate. This is the first time the whole family has been here together on this sacred ground," George said.

The family later strolled home with an obviously joyful Grace and Lizzie. Annabelle walked behind John, feeling the long-awaited moment of hope. Annabelle, however, still felt the need to guard her heart. Annabelle didn't want to change John's focus on wanting to learn more about Jesus. His salvation was her most important priority.

CHAPTER 26
Good Intentions

I N AUGUST OF 1848, ANNABELLE continued to limit John's approach, but Lisa and Jacob's relationship grew. Lisa would secretly wait for Jacob when he returned the horses to the barn. When Lisa practiced throwing her tomahawk, she would rehearse what she'd say to her father about Jacob.

As Lisa went to the family's practice ground on one particular day, she seemed joyful but murmured to herself.

"Why are you whispering to yourself?" Lizzie asked.

Lisa was startled and turned around to see Lizzie with her bow and arrows. "How long have you been there?" she asked.

Lizzie smiled while she came alongside her cousin. "Not very long. Why have you been coming here so much on your own? It's dangerous to do anything alone now because of the Indian agents."

Lisa avoided eye contact with Lizzie. "I wanted to come here and say a few prayers alone. I'm done now, so we can practice a little."

Lizzie shot her arrows at the hanging targets off one of the old trees.

Lisa glanced at Lizzie and thought, *You followed me because you were thinking about me. This makes me feel worse about being with Jacob. I thought I knew how to tell the truth, but now*

I don't. As Lizzie hit another target, Lisa smiled. "Your aim has become better."

"Thank you. I think I'll catch up with you soon with the tomahawk," Lizzie said.

Lisa threw her tomahawk, hitting an old tree.

Lizzie chuckled. "Don't do that in front of a man. It might make it harder for you to find someone."

Lisa slightly glanced at Lizzie to make sure she was joking. Lisa forced herself to chuckle, Lizzie smiled, and the cousins teased each other while they practiced their skills.

Lisa thought, *Being better than her with a tomahawk gives me no comfort. Lizzie could rip my arms off. Why does she have to be difficult?*

Later in the day, Lisa traveled to the Tate farm and met with Jacob at their barn. "I was going to tell Lizzie today about us, but she was so happy earlier," Lisa said in Cherokee. "Since John started going to the church, she has been much happier. I don't want to break her heart. I hate seeing that anger in her."

"Lizzie is strong. I'm sure she'll let it go when we tell her at the right time," Jacob replied. "I might have to hide for a few days, but she'll let it go. Lizzie loves you."

"By you saying 'when we tell her,' you're meaning me. We've been through a lot together, but I think we need more time to tell my family. My papa won't take it well. I know he wants me to marry a full-blood, but I think Lizzie will react the worst. We can't hide what is between us forever. I love you, Jacob."

"I love you too, Lisa."

Jacob kissed Lisa as she wrapped her arms around his neck. The two smiled at each other and kissed again.

Later that night, Lisa lay in bed next to Lizzie.

Lizzie turned to Lisa and whispered, "I know you didn't go out there to pray. I was already there before you."

Lisa gulped and whispered, "I'm sorry I lied."

Lizzie sighed. "I hate secrets. Please don't lie to me."

Lisa nodded. "Okay."

The cousins hugged each other and soon fell asleep.

A week later, things remained complicated between Annabelle and John.

Annabelle and Lisa went home for a break and ate lunch together as they watched the men work the fields. Jacob waved at them.

"Annabelle and Lisa must've returned to eat some food," Jacob said in Cherokee.

John, who had sweat running down his arms and back, wiped his forehead with a cloth. "I'll be right back, Jacob. I needed to talk to Annabelle," he said.

"Alright, tell Lisa I said hi."

Annabelle didn't notice John's approach while she ate and talked to Lisa. John walked behind Annabelle as he adjusted his beige cotton shirt.

"Oh, hi, John. It looks like you and Jacob are working hard," Lisa said in Cherokee.

Annabelle's heart dropped, and she turned around. "Hi, John. You look good," she said.

"Hey, um, Lisa, I wanted to ask Annabelle something. Can you give us a moment?"

Lisa's eyes widened. She stood up and went to the house despite Annabelle trying to signal her with expressions not to leave.

"I wanted to know how long you are going to avoid talking to me alone," John said. "Are you mad at me?"

Annabelle tapped her fingers together as she looked at John. "I'm not mad at you, John," she said. "I wanted to have some time to think. I know that's not what you wanted to hear."

"Did I do something wrong? If I did, I'm sorry."

"You did nothing wrong. The truth is, I would rather you focus more on Jesus right now, and then I would be happy to talk with you more."

John smiled and folded his arms. "I can do that. I will talk to you later."

"Yeah, maybe before supper, we'll talk a little more."

John marched back to the fields, and Annabelle watched while she attempted to control her feelings. Annabelle stood as Lisa approached her.

"What was that about?" Lisa asked.

"It was nothing. He wanted to ask me a few things," Annabelle answered.

"What things did he ask you about?"

"It was nothing, Lisa. Why are you asking? We need to get back to the store now," Annabelle said, moving in the direction of the store.

Lisa followed, smiling. "If it was nothing, why were you smiling as John walked away. You like him."

Annabelle moved faster on the dirt road as Lisa followed her.

"He's a good man, that's all," Annabelle replied. "So what that I smiled."

Lisa stepped in front of Annabelle, forcing her to stop. "Lizzie was right. You're a bad liar."

"I didn't come here to find a man. I came here to escape my world. I'm still not accepted in your people's world," Annabelle insisted.

Lisa held Annabelle's hands. "If you have grown feelings for my cousin, I will support it. I saw how he looked at you. You're a good woman, a beautiful woman. John is a good man and a good-looking one. If you want to wait to tell the others, that's okay, but if something special happens between you and John, he won't hide it. You need to be ready for that."

"I think your papa won't be happy. The truth is, I feel if John starts courting me, I will be unwelcomed here. I don't want to ruin what I already have here. I already feel like Lizzie has noticed and won't welcome anything."

"Lizzie will be Lizzie. She might say something that isn't friendly, but she likes you. There is a loving side to her. And don't worry about being unwelcomed by my papa. If John does not correct him, I will correct him. You should tell Grace. She would be excited. You're a far better choice than Nancy." Lisa let go of Annabelle's hands and walked toward the supply store.

Annabelle felt her heart warmed by Lisa's support and followed her to the store.

CHAPTER 27
Evil and Fire

A WEEK PASSED, AND ANNABELLE DEVELOPED the courage to tell the others, but more importantly, she was ready to determine if she was ready for a relationship. Annabelle lay in her bed, looking at the stars after she said her prayers and hoping for more guidance, when she smelled smoke and got up.

"Grace!" she shouted. "Grace, wake up! Do you smell that!"

Grace rushed to her door and opened it in a panic. "Where is it coming from? It's not coming from us!" Grace shouted. "Oh no!"

Grace ran toward the door with Annabelle racing behind her. She looked at her family's house and pressed a hand over her heart. "Thank God, they're well."

However, the two women could see the bright glowing orange light out the side of their vision. Grace looked at Annabelle. Both women ran toward the fields. To their shock, an enormous fire had begun to burn the crops.

"No! Uncle George, John, Samuel, wake up!"

Lizzie was the first to rush out of the family house. Her eyes locked onto the blaze. She rushed toward the back of the house.

George came out of the house with John and Samuel behind him. "No, the crops, Grace! What happened?" he yelled.

"I don't know! Annabelle and I were awakened by the smoke."

Lizzie came from around the house in a panic, carrying as many buckets as she could. "We have to hurry. We cannot lose any more of the crops!" she yelled.

Tsula and Lisa came out of the house and gasped when they saw the fire.

"Michael, stay here with David," Tsula yelled. "Don't wake him."

Michael nodded as Tsula and Lisa ran to join the others.

"How did this happen?" Lisa asked.

"We don't know," George replicd. "Everyone, move quickly so we can stop the fire."

The family ran to the well and got as much water as they could. The fire and smoke were intense, and they struggled to prevent any more corn from being lost.

"Keep it up! We can't let it spread!" John yelled.

The fires persisted over two hours before the family suc-ceeded in putting it out. The rising smoke could be seen in the dark. The moonlight and stars outlined the damage that had been done to the fields. The Lightning-Strongman family lost a third of the corn crop. Lisa stepped onto the surged fields and fell to her knees. She clutched the charcoaled corn and cried uncontrollably. Lizzie kneeled down next to Lisa and swayed with her as she cried. Annabelle felt chest pains as tears flowed down her face.

The men stared at the destroyed corn in silent anger. George's brow lowered while he rubbed his chin, walking through the destroyed field as Lizzie helped Lisa calm herself. He stopped on the outer end of the field and picked up the burned remains of a rope as he looked at his distraught family.

"This fire was no accident. Someone used this rope to feed the fire," George said in Cherokee.

"Who would do this? We have no enemies," Samuel said.

"We won't make assumptions on who did this. We will listen and pay attention to learn who would do such an evil act. Everyone, go back to sleep. This has been a day for us to remember." George nodded. "I'm proud of all of you for trying to protect our family."

The family went back to bed silently. Grace hugged Annabelle once they entered the small house.

"You did good, Annabelle," Grace said.

Annabelle felt little comfort in Grace's words. Her anger demanded answers. "Who do you think could have done this?" she asked.

"I'm not sure," Grace whispered. "For now, all we can do is try to get some rest. We will figure it out."

The women went to their rooms and lay in their beds. Annabelle couldn't help but believe Nancy started the fire.

<hr>

Two days passed as the family went on the hunt to discover who had destroyed their crops. Grace alerted Mr. Gross of the incident, asking if they knew anything and requesting that those involved be punished under the law. Tsula and Samuel questioned Nancy, but Nancy denied any involvement. The women worked the store, struggling to maintain kindness for their customers due to their suspicions.

Jacob entered the store and said, "Hi, everyone. I came by to see how the day is going."

Annabelle walked next to Lisa as Jacob approached the counter.

Lisa replied in Cherokee, "Not sure how I feel. Waking up this morning and seeing the fields, I still feel pain in my heart. I don't know if we will discover the truth behind the fire."

"The truth is that we may never find out the truth," Jacob said. "How are you doing, Annabelle?"

Annabelle replied, "I'm doing well. I feel the same way as Lisa. I want to know the truth."

Abruptly, Brock and Hunter strutted into the store wearing their black frock coats. Brock approached with a smirk on his face while he adjusted his vest.

"Good afternoon. I see you ladies have a customer," Brock said.

"Mr. Jackson, welcome," Lisa responded.

"Strange, I don't feel welcomed here." Brock turned toward Jacob. "This Negro looks familiar, doesn't he, Mr. Sawyer?"

Hunter replied, "Why, yes, he was working on the Tate property when we spoke with Mr. Tate. He is quite the specimen, a healthy-looking slave."

Lisa replied, an authoritative tone to her voice, "He is no slave. He is Cherokee. His father is Mr. Tate."

Brock turned toward Lisa with a cocked head. "I guess that explains his features. Do you speak English, boy?" Brock asked.

"I speak English, Mr. Jackson," Jacob responded.

Brock smiled at Hunter, who chuckled.

"I never do get tired of that interesting Southern accent," Brock said with an amused tone. "Do you, Mr. Sawyer?"

Hunter replied, "Not at all, Mr. Jackson."

"Well, know we've come to offer our services and help find the one responsible for the tragic fire we learned about. Miss Strongman, surely your family would like to find the one responsible," Brock said.

"Yes, we would like to know, but we believe it was not one of our own," Lisa said. "Even the one family that would have something against us, we have little belief they did it."

"My dear, it might be because you people don't know the art of questioning," Brock said, his voice seductive. "It takes a strong mind to ask what needs to be asked. I could show you how if you were interested."

Annabelle's eyes somewhat widened at hearing Brock's suggestive tone.

Lisa scoffed and slightly glanced at Jacob. "We need no help, Mr. Jackson. The truth will be learned at the right time."

Brock scoffed as he stood before the counter. "What do you think, Annabelle? An advanced Negro like yourself must have an opinion. I'm sure they encourage it."

Annabelle could feel her heart race as Brock stared her down with his unsympathetic eyes. "Mr. Jackson, I agree with Lisa. Your offer is appreciated, though."

Brock laughed as he moved toward Hunter. "You have what you need? It looked like a large portion of your crops were destroyed, but somehow you don't need help." Brock glared at Jacob with a crooked smirk. "I guess you plan on using this half-blood nigger to help you."

Lisa's eyes narrowed when she heard Brock's insult.

Grace walked through the back door and looked at the two Indian agents with a forced smile. "Mr. Jackson and Mr. Sawyer, how can we be of help to you?"

"I believe there isn't nothing here we need," Brock said, his voice snobbish. "What do you think, Mr. Sawyer?"

Hunter replied, "I agree. There isn't nothing here for us. It is a waste of time if we stay here any longer."

"We were just listening to the ignorance of your cousin," Brock said. "This nigger here agrees with her, and this half-breed nigger plans on being a tool for her. Maybe he should become your slave now, sweetie."

"I'm no nigger!" Annabelle snarled. "You were asked not long ago not to use that word here in this store. I'm a free woman here, and this land belongs to this family."

Lisa smirked as Brock turned toward Hunter with his mouth agape and scoffed. "We have seen your records, Miss Annabelle Mays. Your former master didn't do his job. Georgia would be ashamed of how you were raised, so please don't test my patience." Brock sarcastically chuckled. "I must admit I haven't met a Negro like you."

The tension rose while the two men stood before the women and Jacob. "I think it is time for you to go, Mr. Jackson," Grace said in an authoritative tone. "If you're not here to buy anything, please leave."

"I guess we shouldn't be surprised. You people have always been determined to do things your way," Brock responded. "Such a prideful people...too blind to see better ways."

"I think it is time for you to go, Mr. Jackson," Jacob said.

"So, the mixed-blood has spoken," Brock mocked. "Well, I guess our welcome is over, Mr. Sawyer."

"Indeed, Mr. Jackson," Hunter said.

Brock adjusted his black frock coat, and the men left the store. Standing in the doorway, Brock looked back at Grace and said, "I suggest y'all learn what's best, or you might find another piece of rope set on fire in your fields."

The men went away and got on their horses.

Grace abruptly rushed out of the door. "How did you know a rope was used to help start the fire!" Grace yelled.

The men rode away, ignoring Grace.

"How did you know about the rope when we didn't tell any of our people about it? Get off your horse and answer me, you coward!"

Brock halted his horse and turned around a little. "Miss Lightning, I will always know about things with or without your help. Good day."

The men continued to ride off while Grace watched, clutching her right hand. She kicked the dust on the road and stormed back into the store as the mild wind blew her long hair. "It was them. They started the fire!" she yelled.

Lisa quickly moved toward Grace and placed a hand on her shoulder. "Are you sure, Grace?"

"Mr. Jackson knew about the rope," Grace responded, her voice low. "Think about it. Who have we told about the rope in the field?"

"We haven't told anyone about the rope," Annabelle said. "Even the twins made sure not to mention the burned rope in the field when they questioned Nancy."

"I told Jacob, but you didn't tell anyone else, did you?" Lisa asked.

"I haven't spoken of it to anyone," Jacob said. "Not even my father."

"How are we going to prove it was them?" Lisa asked.

Grace answered, "We will tell the others and bring it to the

Cherokee court's attention, but I'm afraid little to nothing will be done about it. These men will be protected by their government because an Indian's words are not equal to a white man's."

"Grace, I'm worried Mr. Jackson knew too much about me," Annabelle said. "How did he know so much?"

"Through the records in the courthouse, they could have learned that," Grace explained. "If they were after you, they would've taken you away already or attempted to. He said that to scare you."

Later in the day, Grace explained the incident to George and the others. George became furious and went out into the fields to stomp on the ruined crops.

"Jesus, I stand here asking for my family to be covered in your protection," George said. "You instruct us not to repay evil with evil. All I ask is that my family be avenged. I know I haven't been the best example for my family. For them, please make sure we have what we need for winter." His eyes started to become watery. He took a deep breath and left the scorched field.

The only conversation the family discussed was a solution to stop Brock from destroying the crops again. The night was hard as George got drunk. The women prayed together while John and Samuel controlled a drunken George.

The next day, Annabelle and Grace went to Joyce and explained the situation. "All of you must be careful of Mr. Jackson," Joyce said in Cherokee. "He, like the many men before him, see us as lesser. He believes his ways are the right way, and I have no doubt both of those Indian agents wouldn't hesitate to control things here."

"I want them to suffer," Grace replied.

"Don't go after them with revenge, Grace. You let our Father in Heaven give them the beating they deserve for their evil ways. Show kindness to them. Don't let your anger control your actions. Lizzie's response to what these men did needs to be watched. Though she's grown, she may let her feelings take control of her if tempted enough. Guard her the best you can."

"I will. Thank you for your guidance."

The women exited the house when Joyce gently grabbed Annabelle's arm. "Grace, keep walking. Annabelle will follow you soon."

Grace left as Annabelle stood before Joyce.

"There's something you wanted to ask me, but you didn't ask it," Joyce said.

"I didn't want Grace to know John wants to court me," Annabelle said. "I feel confused because my heart wants him to grow closer to God, but I want to let him become closer to me."

Joyce smiled at Annabelle. "Give it a little more time. John has a lot to learn spiritually, and you still have much to learn too. At least wait a month to make sure he is following Christ like he needs to be. I do believe he came to the church on his own will, but give it time. Be patient."

Annabelle huffed. "Thank you. I'll be patient."

Annabelle left to follow Grace, and Joyce went back into her house.

"Father in Heaven, I pray a prayer of protection over Annabelle and Grace," Joyce whispered. "I also pray a prayer of wisdom over Lizzie. I feel those three are the main targets of that family. Please guide me and show me more if it be your will."

There was a sudden soft knock at Joyce's door. Joyce opened the door, and before her stood a smiling little girl with a single long braid.

"I'm here for my lessons, Grandma Joyce," the girl said.

Joyce chuckled. "Come inside, baby. I like your hair. It reminds me of someone."

Smiling, the little girl walked inside.

"Remember, we speak only Cherokee in this house for the first hour, Lea."

"Yes, Grandma Joyce," Lea said in Cherokee.

A month passed, and tension between the tribe and the Indian agents increased. Annabelle put effort into avoiding the two men. The fear of them taking her away consumed her mind and gave her nightmares.

Annabelle's release was her visits to the Thompson farm, and Mrs. Thompson often walked with Annabelle while she gave slaves water. Mrs. Thompson seemed to look forward to Annabelle coming to the farm.

One day in September, Annabelle visited Mr. Thompson's farm and gave water to all the slaves. She spent a short time with Doll before she walked with her to visit Mrs. Thompson. As the two young women traveled to the Thompson house, Annabelle heard a horse snort and turned around.

Annabelle felt her heart plummet when her eyes locked on Brock Jackson's smirk and Hunter Sawyer behind him.

"Well, look who we have here? Miss Annabelle Mays," Brock said. "This is one of Mr. Thompson's slaves. What is your name, Negro?"

"Doll my name."

The two men chuckled while they sat on their horses.

"She certainly sounds like a slave," Brock said. "Come here and let me take a look at you. I think I need to have a little talk with Mr. Thompson. You're looking a little too nice there."

Doll stared at the men with a raised eyebrow and blank stare.

"I said come here, little woman."

Doll stood behind Annabelle as Brock's frustration grew.

"So, either you a dumb Negro, or you want to test my patience."

"She doesn't understand English well or speak it good," Annabelle snapped. "She only understands Cherokee."

The two men looked at each other and looked at Annabelle with pressed lips.

"I guess that makes you her interpreter, my dear Annabelle," Brock said. "Mr. Sawyer, take a look at this. The future is what I see here. A naïve slave speaking no English and a free Negro with unheard-of freedom. I do believe we are seeing a dark future before us."

Hunter replied, "Indeed, this is quite troubling."

Annabelle wrapped her arm around Doll's and escorted her to the Thompson's main house when Brock abruptly blocked their path with his horse.

"Annabelle, how rude of you," Brock said. "You were not given permission to leave without saying goodbye."

"I'm no slave. Don't expect me to ask you for permission like a slave. We will be on our way, gentlemen," Annabelle responded.

"You're a bold one, Miss Mays, but even out here in these Cherokee lands, you will know your place," Brock smirked. "There would be a nice price on you. Young, healthy, and pretty for a Negro, I'm sure you would go for an above-average price."

Annabelle looked back and saw Hunter on his horse right behind her and Doll. "I'm sure some slave masters would pay a high price for me, but promise I would die before serving another white man. That includes you, Mr. Sawyer, or any of these white men that come onto Cherokee land."

Brock chuckled. "Indeed, you are a different nigger. You've learned a lot from the Indians, but remember, it's a reason they're out here now. I see they even did two braids in your hair. It must be their way of claiming you."

Brock and Hunter chuckled as Annabelle stood her ground.

"I can let you pass, and Doll too," Brock said, "but you need to clean some of the mud off my boots. Come on, now. I'm sure it's not the first time you've cleaned someone's shoes."

"Can I help you fine men?" Mr. Thompson said, approaching Brock.

"Mr. Thompson, it seems you're doing quite well with your land," Brock observed. "You set a great example for your people. We were having a conversation with Annabelle here."

Mr. Thompson nodded. "She is a rare Negro woman. Much

like my Doll here, she works hard and has always been respectable."

"Mr. Thompson, Mr. Sawyer and I were concerned with how well you're treating your slaves. Does it not concern you they would turn on you because of your casual ways? It would not be the first time an Indian master was revolted against because of the lack of authority."

"I appreciate your concern, Mr. Jackson, but I have never had serious problems because of how well I do treat my slaves. I learned from my father. His ways have done well for me and the family." Mr. Thompson turned to Doll. "Doll, you may go to the house. There is no reason for your presence here around these white men," Mr. Thompson said, speaking in Cherokee.

"Yes, Master. We will see each other again, Annabelle," Doll replied, also speaking Cherokee before smiling at Annabelle and nodding at Mr. Thompson.

"What an interesting moment," Hunter said. "What did she say to you, Annabelle?"

"She told me goodbye."

"Mr. Thompson, it seems you do have a system here similar to the other slave masters, but I strongly suggest making some changes," Brock said, his voice persuasive. "She should have asked for your permission to say bye to Annabelle."

"And what for?" Mr. Thomson asked, sarcasm in his tone. "Doll has always done what she is supposed to do, and sometimes more. Is there anything else you gentlemen want? I was on my way to check on my cattle."

"There was nothing more, Mr. Thompson. I believe it is our time to go, Mr. Sawyer."

"Good day, Mr. Thompson," Hunter said.

"See you men around," Mr. Thompson replied.

The two Indian agents rode off as Annabelle and Mr. Thompson watched.

"Do you have to leave?" Mr. Thompson asked. "I know those men slowed you down."

"Yes, I do have to leave. Grace and the others will be expecting me back at the store soon."

"Well, alright, you know you're welcomed on my land," he said. "We will see each other again."

"We will see each other again, Mr. Thompson."

Annabelle walked to the supply store, later telling Grace and Lisa about the incident, which enraged the women. The women went home on the dusty dirt road surrounded by the prairie filled with wildflowers, all wearing their blue plaid dresses. Annabelle went into the small house and picked up her Bible, determined to keep her joy, and walked to the old redbud tree to watch a small pronghorn herd.

To Annabelle's surprise, Tsula was sitting under the tree.

"Don't look so surprised, Annabelle. You're not the only one that likes watching the animals," Tsula said in Cherokee.

Annabelle sat down next to Tsula and opened her Bible. "When did you start sitting under the tree?" she asked.

"I've always sat under the tree while you were away. I love the warm air in September. It's a nice spot to think and be peaceful. You can sit closer. The tree has enough room for us. We're blessed women. We don't smell bad, and we're not fat, so we can both sit under the tree."

Annabelle and Tsula laughed.

"That's true. We are blessed," Annabelle responded. "Would you like to read with me? I was going to read Psalms."

Tsula grinned and scooted closer to Annabelle. "Yes, I would like that. The other reason I sit here is because I often think about what the other parts of the world look like. I wish I could run away sometimes, but I see all of you, and I change my mind."

"I understand what you mean. The truth is that I never thought it would be so hard to be away from my parents or my little brother," Annabelle said. "I miss Judy Mays, but I know I can't go back. I think so much time has gone by, they would probably kill me if they caught me."

"If they ever catch you, smile in their face and ask your

former master how badly he wanted to sleep with you. Jesus is watching them. Maybe you will get lucky, and he'll get hit with lightning."

"That wasn't a Christian thing to say, Tsula."

"I know, but it's funny. Jesus knows my heart," Tsula said, imitating Pastor Bluebird.

Annabelle laughed uncontrollably while Tsula chuckled. The women read some verses in Psalms and made jokes during their conversations before helping prepare supper.

CHAPTER 28
Imperfect Timing

A WEEK PASSED AS ANNABELLE PAID attention to John's spiritual growth, but she allowed her feelings to feed her impatience. Annabelle understood John may not be her next husband but struggled to ignore him.

Toward the end of the week, John and Samuel harvested crops together as George, Jacob, and Michael worked the other parts of the fields.

"Samuel, what do you think of Annabelle?" John asked.

"I think she's good," Samuel said. "I'm glad we met her back in Mercy. I was wrong to tell you that we should ignore Mr. Boston's request to take her with us. David has grown to like her a lot."

John smiled and replied, "Yeah, I noticed. He has a lot of Camille in him."

"Yeah, the boy does. It's a good thing. Why did you ask me about Annabelle?"

John shrugged. "I was just asking. Annabelle has been here for a while. I was curious about how you thought about her now."

Samuel looked at John as the other man continued to pick the corn. "Do you like her?"

John looked up at Samuel sternly. "No, I was asking because I wanted to. I swear, between you and Tsula."

"What does that mean?"

"Nothing. It's obvious the two of you are twins," John said. "You and Tsula are always asking questions just to start trouble."

Samuel scoffed. "You like her. Did you end things with Nancy for her?"

"No, I never planned to end it with Nancy. You know that. I'm a little tired of hiding my curiosity with her, and she is good with David. David is happy around Annabelle."

"Give it a try. She is a good woman," Samuel encouraged.

"I have, but then she stopped me and asked me to wait. That wasn't too long ago."

"If she wants you to wait and you want her, I would wait. I think that's how the Creator works on our patience as men. He shows us the right woman but has us wait for her permission," Samuel said.

John's eyebrows lowered. "Who did you learn that from?"

Samuel arrogantly beamed. "I'm a wise man, brother. You never realized it."

"Hmph, you learned from Grace when you asked about Maria, didn't you?"

Samuel remained silent and picked corn as John stared him down.

"Yeah, I thought so, brother."

"Well, at least we can have fun harvesting the fields, sweating, hurting, and getting smellier as the days go on." John chuckled as the two young men continued to work the fields.

━━━◆━━━

During the last week of October, Annabelle caught John's eye as she walked to the redbud tree. While Annabelle took her time reading *The Three Musketeers,* John approached her.

"Are you trying to enjoy the outside before it becomes colder?" John asked in Cherokee.

Annabelle replied, "I guess I am. Most of the plants have changed colors, and the last of the harvesting was done this week. So now, I'll have to wait for the next few months to see something beautiful again."

John grinned. "I think you see something beautiful every day when you look in the mirror. I also know there is beauty inside a person's heart."

As John stepped forward, he tripped over one of the tree's roots. He reached to grab the tree but lost his grip. Annabelle dropped her book as she tried to stop John from falling, but she fell with him. The two laughed as they sat in the grass with Annabelle's hands still on John's chest. Annabelle's eyes locked onto John's. He continued to laugh and abruptly stopped. With her heart racing, Annabelle lightly kissed him.

John smiled as he placed his hand on Annabelle's hand. "What was that?"

Annabelle took a deep breath. "I...I don't know. I'm sorry. I don't know what I was thinking."

"Don't be sorry. I wanted to make sure you wanted to do that." John glanced over to his left and saw Tsula staring at them, grinning.

Annabelle looked over and saw Tsula, who chuckled and quickly entered the family house.

She panicked as she stood. "What are we going to do? Tsula will tell what she saw!"

Annabelle began to rush toward the family house when John gently grabbed her arm. "Is this what you want? Do you want me?"

Annabelle's eyes widened while she looked into John's eyes, then looked away from him. "I don't know." She looked toward the house again before looking back at John. "Yes, I do want you. Now you know."

John smiled at Annabelle and hugged her. "At the right time, we'll tell them, or we'll try to keep Tsula from telling everyone."

"I want to tell Grace myself," she said. "Lisa has known how I feel for some time now, and I think I'll let you tell the others.

It's almost time to make supper, and I think I better go find Tsula. She has probably told everyone by now."

"Alright, I'm glad we decided on something."

Annabelle smiled and rushed to the family house, hoping Tsula had kept quiet. She walked inside and saw Michael playing with David.

"Hi, Michael, where are your sisters?" she asked.

Abruptly, Lizzie came out of the kitchen. "There you are. Come, we need to start making supper now," she said in Cherokee.

Annabelle followed Lizzie into the kitchen, helping to prepare the food as Tsula hummed and smiled at Annabelle. The women remained silent, but Annabelle was nervous, unsure of what Tsula was thinking.

Tsula giggled as she prepared the soybeans.

"What is so funny?" Lizzie asked in Cherokee.

"None of your business," Tsula said, her voice blunt.

Lizzie squinted. "You watch your mouth and focus on preparing the food."

Tsula waved her wooden spoon in the air. "Don't tell me what to do, Flour Face. I'm enjoying myself. And if you wanted to know what was so funny, your face is what's funny to me."

Lisa chuckled.

Lizzie put down her knife. "Keep on talking, wearing your hair like the white women with your stupid twin buns. I'll hit you so hard, your hair would straighten."

Lisa chuckled while the two women stared each other down.

"That's enough," Grace grumbled. "The both of you behave and finish cooking."

"I want to know what was so funny," Lizzie bickered.

"None of your business," Tsula yelled. "Is it so hard not to know, bully?"

"I'm not a bully, you smart-mouthed—"

"Can the two of you go one day without arguing!" Grace yelled.

Annabelle felt her throat tighten as tension in the kitchen increased.

Lizzie replied, "She needs to watch what she says. Am I wrong for asking? I was curious."

"Okay, Miss I-want-to-know. I saw someone kiss someone else," Tsula said, her voice childish.

"Who?" Grace and Lizzie asked.

Annabelle noticed Lisa's eyes widen, and she stopped shucking the corn, shaking uncontrollably.

"It was me and John," Annabelle said, anxiety filling her voice. She caressed her hands as she stared at the women.

Lisa dropped the corn cob she was holding as Grace and Lizzie stared at Annabelle with big eyes.

"It happened today. I didn't mean for it to happen. It just happened."

Grace and Lisa shrieked with excitement, but Lizzie remained speechless. Grace gave her a hug as Lisa asked Annabelle questions.

Tsula stood next to Lizzie, smiling. "Now you know, sister," Tsula said mischievously.

Lizzie's eyes narrowed at Tsula in irritation, and Tsula leered at her cousin.

"How long has this been going on?" Lizzie sharply asked.

Annabelle replied, "It happened today, but he has shown interest in me before."

"Hmph, well fine," Lizzie said. "Whatever, let's finishing cooking. I'm hungry."

Annabelle accepted Lizzie's response, believing that was the most approval Lizzie would give her.

Grace smiled, accepting her sister's unenthusiastic response. "I agree. We can finish cooking and celebrate this a little later," she said.

The women finished supper while Annabelle explained what John wanted to tell the others. Though Grace was pleased with the news, she voiced her concern regarding how her uncle would react, and there was a general feeling of mentally preparing themselves for a civil war. During supper, the family enjoyed each other's company, though Grace seemed much more joyful than usual.

———◆———

Two days passed as John and Annabelle now felt comfortable expressing their relationship around the others. During this time, John and George went into town to drop off two sacks of soybeans at the supply store. When the men traveled, John became nervous as he glanced at his uncle.

John said a prayer in his mind and exhaled. "I have wanted to tell you something important about these last two days," he said.

"What is it?" George asked.

"I have decided to spend time Annabelle, and she's accepted me. I've been thinking about this for a long time," John responded. "I know you may disagree with my choice, but I'm not going to hide my feelings for her."

George's expression was blank as he continued to walk with his nephew. "There really are moments I see your momma and your auntie in you. It's a good thing. You were with me when Jacob talked with me about women. Do you really want to do this, John?"

"I do. There's a good difference about her, and I see the way she treats David. David also enjoys being with Annabelle. I never thought I would grow feelings for her like this."

"Would it be so hard to find another Cherokee woman like Annabelle?" George saw the look of disappointment on his nephew's face and sighed. "The Father works in mysterious ways. I myself said she would make a good wife for an Indian man. I spoke the truth when I said that. You must prepare for hardships you'll go through. The children she gives you won't be seen as Cherokee, and they will be seen by many as lesser."

"As long as the family sees my children as Cherokee, I don't care about the thoughts of others. My children will belong to the Wolf Clan, regardless of the old ways. If she gives me children, I will love them, protect them, and always remind them who they are as you have done for me."

George patted John's shoulder. "Good luck when Nancy finds out. That woman has a lot of anger. Maybe we should keep Lizzie by Annabelle for a while."

John chuckled. "I think I might have to ask Lizzie for the favor. Nancy is like a war party, but Lizzie is like one of the great storms clearing the land."

George laughed, and the two men strolled home after they dropped off the soybean bags.

CHAPTER 29
Desire and Innocence

THE HARVEST FESTIVAL ARRIVED ON Friday. The family was excited with this being the first time David would attend. Annabelle appeared overjoyed as she walked next to John. The sound of laughter and good times carried through the town of Tahlequah.

People moved around, eating corn cobs and bread, and several dishes had been offered by the Cherokee government. Grace and the other women showed great resentment as they watched the Cherokee men who were obviously drunk and had found themselves the entertainment of onlookers.

As the family strolled through the festival, Jacob approached the family wearing a high-collared brown shirt and a blue cravat, which was covered by a brown frock coat with matching brown trousers.

"Hello, everyone," Jacob said in Cherokee.

"Hello, Jacob," everyone responded.

"That's a good look for you, Jacob," George commented.

"Thank you, sir. My father surprised me with the shirt and cravat today. I was about to go and get one of the hot corn cobs and watch people show off their older foals."

"I'll come with you," Lisa abruptly said. "Does anyone else want to come?"

"No, we see enough of you," Tsula replied, her tone sarcastic.

Lisa smirked. "Okay, stay here with Lizzie then, smart mouth."

"What does that mean?" Lizzie grunted.

Lisa smirked at Lizzie and walked away with Jacob. The rest of the family enjoyed the other parts of the festival as George met with his friend, Clyde Walton.

"I'm surprised the others didn't come with us," Jacob said to Lisa.

"It was probably the talk of horses or that they were hungry." Lisa smiled. "At least you can spend time with me without hiding."

Jacob blushed, and the two watched owners show off the colorations of their foals that were born in the spring. The couple decided to go down the dirt trail while they looked at the stars.

Lisa kissed Jacob on his cheek. "Now we are alone."

Jacob put his arm around Lisa. They moved along the trail with the moon and vast stars shining down on them.

"Why would the Creator give us the stars when he could have given us eyes to see in the dark?" Jacob wondered.

"I think it was because he wanted us to stay in the light. I also think it keeps us humble to have some form of weakness because then, we have to ask for help," Lisa replied.

"You always have a lot of good ideas. I think that's a gift in your family."

"Your family has a lot of thinkers too," Lisa said. "I think you're a good thinker. You thought not to tell me that you kissed Lizzie."

"What more do you want me to do? I said I was sorry, and I shouldn't have done it. I did not mean to hurt Lizzie."

Lisa smiled as she looked at Jacob's frown. "I think your kindness is a gift. My family sometimes says I'm so kind, but then I look at you. I see how you work with the horses. They listen to you."

Jacob chuckled. "I learned from you. The horses would listen to you over anyone else. I think they have good judgment."

Lisa blushed as Jacob leaned over and kissed her.

Abruptly, a cold wind came while the couple walked down the trail. Lisa shook, and Jacob placed his brown frock coat on her.

"I'm still cold. Let's go to your home. It's closer," Lisa said.

The young couple entered the Tates' house, and Jacob lit a fire at the fireplace. Lisa took off her white bonnet and lightly flicked her long hair. Jacob got a thick blanket. Pulling the blanket around Lisa, he wrapped his arms around her. Lisa snuggled against Jacob's chest, smiling. Lisa kissed Jacob. She felt nothing but comfort and love for him.

"My papa accepted John's relationship with Annabelle. That gives me so much hope for us," Lisa murmured.

Jacob held Lisa's hands and caressed them. "I will only say something when you're ready. As long as the Creator blesses what we have, and I have your heart, I'm happy."

Lisa slightly turned her body, placed her arms around Jacob's shoulders, and softly kissed him. "I love you, Jacob Tate. I didn't think life for me could be this good."

"I love you too, Lisa Strongman." Jacob placed his hand on Lisa's cheek as he looked into her loving brown eyes. "I'm a blessed man."

Lisa's breathing became deeper as Jacob kissed her back. As the couple continued to kiss, her heart rate increased as their breathing grew deeper. Lisa caressed Jacob's short, thick, and wavy hair. The thick blanket slid off Lisa as she straddled Jacob, and Jacob moved his lips to her warm neck. Lisa held onto John's back, and she moved his right hand on her breast.

Jacob and Lisa felt their body heat rise, and Jacob slowly rolled on top of Lisa. Lisa grinned at Jacob before she calmly pushed him off her. She took off his cravat and loosened her dress.

"I want you to have all of me," Lisa said, her voice seductive.

The two undressed and stood before each other by the fire. Jacob approached Lisa, his eyes expressing his nervousness as he caressed her face. The two lay down on the thick warm blanket, kissing each other passionately. They made love as they caressed each other's bodies and held hands. A tear of love went down Lisa's face, and she wiped it from her face as the two enjoyed each other.

When they were done, the couple traveled back to the festival, holding hands. Strolling back, they saw other townspeople walking down the dirt road. The couple let go of their hands and greeted everyone.

"There you are," Lizzie said. "I was looking for the both of you. Where did you go?"

Lisa defensively answered, "We didn't go anywhere. We stood here waiting for you and the others. Where are the others?"

Lizzie pointed east. "They're over there waiting for you."

"Okay, let's go." Lisa slightly bit her lip. "We will see each other again."

Jacob smiled at Lisa and replied in Cherokee, "We will see each other again."

"Jacob," Lizzie snobbishly said.

"We will see each other again, Lizzie," Jacob said.

The two women walked to their family, and the family went home together in the cold fall night. As the family walked home, Lisa kept to herself, struggling not to smile.

"How can you smile in the cold, Lisa?" Lizzie asked. "What is on your mind?"

"Oh, nothing. I'm happy to be with the family," Lisa said. "I guess I'm seeing more reasons to be happy. I enjoyed this night. I can see that I'm loved. That sounds weird. I know you love me, but I think I'm more aware of it now."

"You're always smiling, Lisa, but you were really thinking of something good. I can see it in your eyes. I know I have to work on being happier without getting what I want."

The cousins wrapped their arms around each other and marched home behind the rest of the family.

———————◆———————

Lisa's birthday passed on the fifth of November. It had become difficult for her to control her feelings for Jacob, but having him around lessened her frustration. One afternoon, Lisa went to the well to get some water for the horses. While she carried the filled bucket, she saw Annabelle sitting with John and grinned.

Look at those two, she thought. *They do look like a great couple. I wish I was as brave as them. Jesus, why did I have to be born in a time like this? I love Jacob so much, but I feel trapped.* Lisa's mouth curved downward while her face remained blank. *I'm afraid. What if I have to end things?*

She walked to the barn, watching Annabelle and John's boldness, but she felt fear at the thought of her own relationship. She entered the barn and walked toward Big Boy, her mouth still etched into a small frown. Her eyes fixed on the large horse as she petted him.

"All I want is freedom. Is that so much to ask?"

Big Boy nickered.

Lisa smiled. "Oh, you think it's easy. I wish it was."

———————◆———————

The weeks of November passed while the Lightning-Strongman family rationed their food. The family barely had enough and were unable to give away any free food to others in the tribe. Grace left the supply store to take a break and entered her house alone. She sat down in a rocking chair and fiddled with her fingers while looking at the fire crackle in the fireplace. She looked over at an empty brown sack on the table. Her grip tightened on her chair.

She moaned, "I don't know how I can forgive them. I can feel those evil men bringing out the worst in me." A tear hit the armrest of the rocking chair. Grace wiped her eye as her lips quivered. "Please help me forgive them, Jesus. I have to do this for my family...for Lizzie. I'm worried she's not handling this well. I feel devastated. My people are struggling with rations." Her emotions fully released, and she wailed. "Please heal us, Father. This is unbearable, like we've been rejected. Thank you that we do have the crops that we have, and thank you for protecting us." She wiped her face and returned to the store.

◆

The winter storms brought in a heavy snow, preventing the family from going to the store for a week. Rations that were supposed to come from the US government were late, and some of the people were starving.

Annabelle had never witnessed starvation but had grown up only being given rations of food. Seeing the desperation of the people broke her heart. Helping Grace and Lisa made her feel like the Cherokee were her own. As December of 1848 arrived, Annabelle struggled when she saw Grace's demeanor change from anger to sorrow. In the family house, Annabelle approached Grace, who was staring out of the window.

"You seem really sad today," Annabelle said.

Grace exhaled. "I'm trying to figure things out. It's hard knowing your people are struggling."

"You have a giving heart. You're a rare person."

"Thanks, Annabelle. This may be the first day I can forgive those white men."

"Sometimes, I think people can test you more than the devil."

Grace turned her head toward Annabelle. "Ain't that the truth. I'm sorry if I have you worried. I'm doing better. I was struggling to do the right thing."

Annabelle nodded. "Yeah, that can be hard."

"Elder Joyce once told me a sign of maturity is to trust the Father and not seek vengeance. I wish she'd never told me that."

"I'm with your family. I'll keep helping you. I never want to be a burden."

Grace half-smiled. "You've been nothing but help, Anna-belle."

Annabelle smiled.

"Come on. Let's see what we can come up with for supper. I am tired of cornbread."

"Sure."

Grace walked to the kitchen and looked back at Annabelle. "Don't tell Lizzie I said I'm tired of cornbread."

Annabelle grinned while following Grace closely.

The family decided to give more of their rations to help the others, and even Lizzie seemed concerned. The family prayed together each morning, realizing their need for a miracle.

———◆———

On a warmer day, John joined Lizzie on a walk to the practice grounds. While she practiced with her bow, he had planned to cut some firewood. A lone pronghorn was seen, and the two hunted the animal. The siblings slowly moved toward the pronghorn, attempting to stay downwind. While stalking their prey, they also scanned the land for predators. The hunt continued for several minutes. John raised his rifle, but Lizzie calmly signaled for him to lower it. She took aim, pulled back the arrow while taking a deep breath, and released it. A breeze came, causing the arrow to hit the pronghorn in its leg. The pronghorn began limping away, but John took a shot, killing the animal.

John and Lizzie dragged the pronghorn back to the farm. "I think only you and Grace could've made the shot," he said.

Lizzie withheld her smile. "Thank you."

"Relax. We've been blessed."

"I know. I'm thinking."

John let go of the buck, hugged his sister, and gave her a kiss on the cheek.

Holding onto the buck with one hand, she hugged John with the other. "Now we can give several of our chickens to some of our people," Lizzie said.

"Yeah, this was a good hunt," John replied. "I needed you for this."

Lizzie turned her head, hiding her smile while John grabbed the buck's other leg.

John and Lizzie continued dragging the pronghorn home. "Uncle George, we have more meat," he said.

George and Samuel walked out of the house and looked over the healthy buck.

"This is a blessing. Good job, John," George said. "I'm proud of you."

John looked at his sister. "Lizzie took the first shot. If she hadn't injured him, I wouldn't have succeeded."

George looked at his niece and frowned. "I apologize, Lizzie. Well done."

Lizzie smiled at her uncle.

"Alright, well, let's start cutting him up while the sun is still up."

As John and Samuel dragged the dead pronghorn to the barn, Lizzie noticed Annabelle watching.

◆

"Grace, they've killed a pronghorn," Annabelle said in Cherokee.

Grace moved toward the window with a sigh. "There is our blessing, which will last us until January. Their meat tastes good. I was afraid we would eat almost all the chickens."

Annabelle felt nervous that she wouldn't like the meat, and she felt it would also ruin her enjoyment of watching the herds. During supper, Annabelle frowned as she took strips of pronghorn meat. Annabelle ate the meat, and her mouth salivated. The meal gave Annabelle hope God would continue to provide for them.

◆

The weeks passed, along with Grace's twenty-third birthday, then 1849 arrived. As the next two months passed, Annabelle's and John's relationship grew. Annabelle took more of the role as David's mother. Even George became more welcoming of Annabelle.

Her relationship was opposite to Jacob and Lisa's relationship, who would often sneak into the barns of their families to spend time together. Though Jacob's visits became infrequent because of the weather, their relationship remained strong. Lisa took quick looks at Annabelle and John when they were alone. Her mouth curved upward into a big-dimpled grin while she watched them. She felt comfort when David was with Annabelle. Annabelle was becoming a mother figure to David before her eyes. Lisa went with Annabelle to Joyce's home a few times. Through Joyce's instruction, Annabelle was learning how to love people who treated her wrongly. Lisa listened to Joyce, attempting to gain Annabelle's bravery. She had grown tired of hiding her love for Jacob. On the practice ground, she could feel her tomahawk throws become angrier, even though she found joy in Annabelle and John's relationship. The news of Annabelle's relationship with John wasn't welcomed by Nancy. Lisa noticed Nancy's old demeanor seemed to have returned. Though Nancy was a concern, Brock Jackson and Hunter Sawyer remained the major threat to the family. Lisa could tell Annabelle felt the same rage against the men as she did, but she was careful not to show it.

When March of 1849 arrived, Jacob resumed his schedule by coming every day to the Lightning-Strongman farm. Lisa also resumed temporarily helping the men with the horses, much to her pleasure. While the men prepared the fields, Annabelle sometimes enjoyed watching John work them.

CHAPTER 30
The Other Side of the Coin

TWO DAYS BEFORE ANNABELLE'S BIRTHDAY, a heavy thunderstorm abruptly covered the land of Oklahoma. Annabelle ran inside as the strong spring rain poured down. Annabelle was soaked and put wood into the fireplace to help her dry off, but she noticed Grace wasn't inside.

Grace is in the other house. I should have run inside there, she thought. The front door opened, and she said, "Grace."

"Do I look like Grace?" Lizzie asked as she walked inside, scowling.

"I'm sorry. I'll have the fire started soon." Annabelle quickly put the rest of the wood in the fireplace and started the fire.

Lizzie knelt down next to Annabelle as the heavy rain continued to drum on the roof. Annabelle lightly tapped her finger on her thigh, feeling Lizzie's seriousness, and remained silent. Annabelle kept looking at the fire when Lizzie took off her white bonnet. She unbraided her thick wavy hair.

"I hate this cold rain. It brings life, but it can also bring sickness," Lizzie said in Cherokee.

"I agree," Annabelle replied in the same language. "I don't like it. I like the rain in the summer."

"You speak well. Better than some people that were born Cherokee. It is a gift."

"Thank you. Elder Joyce is a good teacher."

Lizzie scoffed. "Yes, she is a good teacher. I've learned a lot from her over the years."

Annabelle felt Lizzie's guard drop and smirked. "She told me that one day, you gave a boy a black eye, and your momma gave you a beating for it."

Annabelle giggled, but Lizzie didn't laugh. Annabelle quickly stopped laughing as Lizzie stared her down.

"Elder Joyce told you that old story. Well, I guess it did happen more than once." Lizzie flicked her wavy hair. "That old woman needs more to do. She must've been bored when she told you that."

Annabelle shrugged. "I guess."

Lizzie took off her moccasins and sat upright. "Now that we're alone, you have no one to protect you."

Annabelle felt her throat tighten, and Lizzie looked at her while squeezing water out of her thick hair.

"What is it between you and John?" Lizzie asked.

Annabelle looked at Lizzie, her brows drawn together. "What do you mean?"

"Did John approach you, or did you let him know about how you feel?"

"He approached me first. I never let him know how I felt until later," Annabelle answered.

"Did he approach you after he came to the church or before?"

"He first came to me before. Why does it matter to you?"

Lizzie huffed. "It matters because he is my brother. He's my brother before he is your man. You're not his wife. My last question is this: Do you think he came to the church to win you, or because he really believes?"

Annabelle looked down as she thought, and she looked back at Lizzie confidently. "I believe he made the choice on his own, not because of me. Haven't you seen the changes in your brother for yourself? Is it hard to believe that he believes now?"

"I wanted to know because his spirit is more important to me than his feelings for you," Lizzie stated. "I have seen the changes in my brother, but I still want to give it time. When you love someone, you want what is best for them, even if it means disagreeing with them."

"I understand, but I feel it in my spirit—his awakening. I'm proud of him."

"So am I," Lizzie admitted.

The two women sat in front of the fire as the thunderstorm continued.

"Nancy will probably come for you," Lizzie stated. "She probably believes John ended things with her to be with you."

"That's not true, but I think you're right. I don't know what I will do about it."

Lizzie scoffed. "Give her one good slap. Nancy is weak. She has no real fight in her, just a pretty face. Don't fear her. She likes to hear herself talk."

"That's easy for you to say. She didn't try to kill you with a rattlesnake."

Lizzie chuckled as she looked at the fire. "That was an interesting day, but I understand your worry. I don't think she is brave enough to take a life, but you're alive, so be grateful for that."

"I'm grateful, but my patience with Nancy is weak. I won't let her make my life miserable."

Lizzie picked up a tiny piece of wood and threw it into the fire. "You're alive for a reason. That's why you didn't die that day. If we didn't have any purpose in this life, there would be no reason to live in this world. It would be better to go to the spirit world than to suffer here anymore."

Annabelle slightly glanced at Lizzie while she stared at the fire. For the first time, Annabelle could see the genuine loving side of Lizzie toward someone besides David. Joyce and Grace were right. Even George's drunken rants about Lizzie became perceptible.

Annabelle continued to watch the fire as the heavy rain continued and thought, *She really keeps love for people in the shadows. Was it just your momma's death that did this to you?*

"In the old days, we would be out in the fields planting corn, beans, and squash. The men would be out hunting," Lizzie reminisced. "It's changed so much over time, but in truth, I think I would've made a better hunter. At least I'm blessed enough to be able to practice with bow and arrow."

"I would pick corn over cotton any day."

Lizzie slightly chuckled as the two women sat before the fire, and Annabelle grinned.

<hr>

A week and a half later, Lisa and Lizzie traded places so Lisa could work with the horses. During the time Annabelle, Grace, and Lizzie worked the store, Nancy came.

"Good afternoon, ladies," Nancy said.

"Good afternoon, Nancy," Grace said. "How can we help you?"

Nancy walked up to the counter and handed Grace a list of supplies. "I'm sure you ladies will be able to take care of this quickly. I don't have all day."

Grace forced a smile. "We'll get this done for you as soon as we can. Annabelle, please bring out a whole chicken—one of the older roosters."

Annabelle nodded and prepared the dead rooster for Nancy. While Annabelle returned from the chicken coops, she moved past Nancy.

Nancy turned her cold eyes on Annabelle the moment Annabelle was about to walk to Nancy's wagon. "I guess it's no surprise you got my list correct on the first try. You can count."

Annabelle stopped and stared at Nancy. "Well, there's more to me than my beauty," she said.

Nancy clenched her teeth, and she tightened her grip on the reticule.

"Go outside, Annabelle," Lizzie said in Cherokee as she approached the door.

Annabelle left, and Lizzie walked past Nancy, staring her down.

Annabelle placed the dead chicken on the wagon, but she noticed Paul seemed to be in pain as he stood by the wagon.

"Paul, what is wrong?" she asked.

"It nothing, Miss Annabelle. I be fine," Paul said, sounding exhausted.

Annabelle noticed a bloodstain on Paul's shoulder. Annabelle gasped and approached him, lifting his beige shirt as Lizzie placed a sack of flour onto the wagon.

"What are you doing to Paul?" Lizzie asked in Cherokee.

Annabelle answered, "He's been beaten, and I think he's still bleeding. Paul, does it feel like you're still bleeding?"

"I don't think so. I feel a little weak, Miss Annabelle."

Lizzie abruptly walked toward Paul, saying, "Take off your shirt and turn around, Paul."

Paul grunted when he took off the shirt and turned around. Lizzie's eyebrows raised, and her mouth dropped the moment she saw seven bleeding wounds. Annabelle also looked worried.

"You're coming inside so we can clean your wounds better," Lizzie commanded.

"Thank you, Miss Lizzie. I don't know if I could repay for your kindness," Paul said.

"What do you think you're doing with my slave, Lizzie Lightning?" Nancy barked.

Lizzie replied, "He is bleeding from his wounds. They weren't cared for like they needed to be."

Nancy sneered. "He is my slave! I say leave him be. He'll live."

Lizzie's eyes dilated when she stepped in front of the taller Nancy. "Do I need to remind you of how much I hate your stupid ringlets? The only two choices I see here are me ripping your hair out for being difficult, or me cleaning his wounds. What did Paul do to deserve this?"

Nancy folded her arms. "That nigger forgot to tie down one of the horses two days ago, and he wandered off. My papa found his carcass yesterday about six or seven miles away from here. The wolves had a great time with him. Only the hooves and some of his bones were left, so he got lashes this morning. He's a mulatto, and he shouldn't be making mistakes like that. It won't be tolerated."

"Careful, Nancy, you're intolerable."

Nancy smacked her lips. "That's a big word for you! I guess you did learn something in school besides fighting."

"Go take a seat in your wagon. I know you're too lazy to take it home yourself. Come, Paul, she won't punish you."

Nancy growled, "Believe what you want."

Lizzie balled her hand into a fist. "Test me! I welcome it! How foolish would you look if he died because of your pride? He's your best slave, and you know it."

Nancy clutched her reticule. "Paul, go with her. She says she can take care of your wounds. We will see."

"Yes, ma'am," Paul said.

Lizzie scoffed at Nancy and entered the supply store, Paul following her. Annabelle followed when Nancy abruptly put her reticule in front of Annabelle's path.

"We have something to discuss," Nancy said.

"I have nothing to say to you," Annabelle replied. "You can move now."

"How long did you think it was going to be before I learned about you and John? You better remember you're not my equal here. You're on the low end of power here, and everywhere you will go, it will be no different."

"I have my freedom. If people judge me without knowing me, that's their loss. I can only pray for them and forgive them for not treating me fairly, just as you're treating me now. I pity you. I've met some interesting women over the years, and to be honest, you're one of the most hateful and the most prideful. I've been around white people enough to feel the difference between hate and pride. It's sad you struggle to connect with your own people. Must be hard."

Nancy gasped, seeming to hold back tears. "You're going to tell me the truth. You owe me at least that much respect. Was there anything between you and John while we were courting?"

"No. At the time, I was focused on my life and healing from my own problems."

"I guess you do have some form of honor for yourself."

"I'm a Christian woman, and I will always try to live my life in a way that makes Jesus proud. Why don't you try to do the same?"

Nancy put her hands on her hips. "I am, but for me to lower myself...I can't. My family worked so hard to gain what we have. What benefit would it be for me...to sacrifice my status in this world? The world isn't fair. We're born without the ability to choose our parents, and we have to live our lives either being lesser or greater. I, too, have spent a lot of time with the white men, and I'll tell you this: They hold the power to make the rules, and the rules are not in the favor of either of us."

"Then why support their ways by having slaves?"

"You don't get it, do you? By keeping you Negroes as slaves, it gives us power. If we let that go, I know they'll create something else to control us. I know this much. I bet if God gave you a choice to be Negro or white, you would pick white."

Annabelle lifted her chin. "I'm proud of who I am."

"A proud Negro," Nancy mocked. "Be proud, but that will never give you full freedom. You wouldn't dare go to the South."

Nancy's words made Annabelle bite her lip. She took a deep breath and said, "I guess, in a way, we're both slaves. I cannot hide who I am, and you're not free to be proud of having Cherokee blood."

Annabelle walked inside the supply store as Nancy looked away.

<hr>

Nancy sat in the wagon, impatiently waiting as she watched the townsfolk go by her. Lizzie came out of the store with Paul walking behind her.

"He's cleaned up. You can go home now," Lizzie said.

"Are you pleased now you helped the mulatto?" Nancy bickered. "It took long enough."

"He's your prized property. Why didn't you? If you acted like a Christian woman, I wouldn't have to help him."

Nancy shrieked, "You're nothing but a brute, and you question my kindness? Go to hell!"

Infuriated, Lizzie grabbed Nancy by her hair, pulled her down from her seat, and slammed her against the wagon. "Who do you think you're talking to! I did what you should have done, you hypocrite!"

Nancy held onto Lizzie's arm and cried, "I'm sorry, Lizzie! Please let me go! Paul, get her off of me!"

Some of the townsfolk stopped what they were doing to watch the commotion.

Paul put his palms up to his chest. "Please let her go. I take her home now," Paul said. "Miss Lizzie, please."

Lizzie released Nancy, and she stumbled back.

"Thank him," Lizzie demanded.

Nancy wiped tears from her face while she stared at Lizzie.

Lizzie took a step forward as Nancy held her ground. "I said to thank him."

Nancy huffed and looked at Paul. "Thank you, Paul. Now take me home."

Paul got into the wagon and helped Nancy get in. A small crowd stood near the wagon.

Grace hurried out of the supply store and rushed over to Lizzie. "What's going on here now?" she asked.

"Nothing, I'm going home, but maybe you should work on teaching Lizzie some more manners," Nancy said arrogantly. "She has the temper of a wild animal."

Lizzie scowled, grabbed her braid, and walked away as she unbraided her hair. She then turned around with a smirk on her face. "Maybe I do need to change, but at least I helped you be humble today because from this day on, you'll always have the memory of getting saved by a slave."

Nancy's face turned red, and her eyes shimmered with tears. "Take me home," Nancy said, her voice breaking.

Paul signaled the horse. "Thank you, Miss Lizzie and Miss Grace," he said.

The wagon went on its way as Grace watched with an eyebrow raised.

Grace entered the store after Lizzie, and Lizzie continued to unbraid her hair.

"What was that about?" Grace asked.

"Nothing, I will talk about it later," Lizzie replied.

Grace pouted and went back to work.

Two days later, Lizzie told the women what had happened when they prepared supper. Grace wasn't pleased, though Tsula was entertained by it. Grace decided not to fully condemn Lizzie's actions, but she told Lizzie that she would pray for her improvement. Everyone hoped the rest of April would be peaceful.

CHAPTER 31
Reopened Hearts

TWO MONTHS PASSED ALONG WITH David's fifth birthday. John and Samuel prepared for another trip into Mercy. During this time, Annabelle had prepared a letter for the women in Mercy and was anxious for their trip. She also tried her best to avoid Nancy, only wanting to focus on her relationship with John. As the men prepared the carriage, Annabelle gave John her letter and noticed Lizzie hadn't said goodbye.

"Where's Lizzie?" Annabelle asked.

Samuel replied, "She wanted to be alone for most of the day. She is around."

Annabelle immediately thought Lizzie had gone to the practice fields.

As Annabelle rushed to get there, she thought, *I must be crazy to be looking for Lizzie.*

Annabelle arrived at the practice fields but stopped once she saw Lizzie. To Annabelle's shock, Lizzie was sitting down with her bow and arrow in her lap, praying. Annabelle quietly backed up and walked back to John and Samuel, feeling inspired by Lizzie's discipline. Annabelle wished the men well, and they rode off to Mercy.

———◆———

The cousins arrived in Mercy after three days passed, pleased to see Mr. Boston, who updated them on things in town.

"It's always good to see you, Mr. Boston," John said.

Mr. Boston grinned. "It's good to see the two of you as well. Give Annabelle my blessings."

"We will," Samuel said. "Take care, Mr. Boston."

Mr. Fluffs gracefully hopped on top of the counter. The men petted the purring gray and white cat and then exited the store. The men double-checked their supplies in the carriage in the active area filled with townspeople.

John stood in front of the carriage and patted his frock coat to feel for Annabelle's letter. "We have what we need. Let's find Rebecca or Ruthanne."

John and Samuel set off in the carriage together, heading deeper into town.

"Well, these are two faces I expected to see sometime soon," Ruthanne said.

John's eyes widened as he turned and watched Ruthanne approach down the brick road with a grin. "Your timing is a blessing," he said. "It's good to see you're free."

"It is good to see the two of you," she replied. "And yes, it is good to *be* free."

"Ruthanne, what happened to your eye?" Samuel asked.

The woman frowned, straightening the scar now under her left eye. "I guess you could say it was a welcome gift from the prison. There's much to talk about. Let us go to the Keyses' home. I'll ride with you."

John opened the carriage door and helped Ruthanne climb in. A few townspeople watched with wide eyes while moving along. Ruthanne rode down the brick road of Mercy with John and Samuel. The three arrived in front of the Keyses' brown-bricked home.

Rebecca was sitting on a hammock with her daughter, Ashley. The brunette looked at her mother. "It's the Cherokee," Ashley said with a joyful tone.

"Go on inside and bring out some plates for our guests," Rebecca said. "I've been expecting them."

Ashley got off the hammock and quickly went inside the brown-bricked home.

John and Samuel got off the carriage and helped Ruthanne out.

"Look at what I found," Ruthanne said.

Rebecca grinned. "You do have a talent, Ruthanne. Welcome back to Mercy, John and Samuel."

"Mrs. Keys," the men said.

"Oh, let's go inside so the both of you aren't forced to call me that." The smiling women entered the house, followed by the men. "Please take a seat at the supper table. If we're lucky, Allen will stop by the house soon."

"This is exciting," Ruthanne said.

The men sat down at the Keyses' supper table with Rebecca and Ruthanne.

"Judging by your happiness, I assume things are going well with Annabelle," Rebecca said.

"Yes, I also have a letter from her," John replied. "She was specific that it had to be one of you to read the letter. I don't know what she's written."

John handed it to Rebecca, who took and stared at it. Smiling at Ruthanne, she held the letter toward her.

"I believe it is only right you be the one to read it," Rebecca said. "I already had to read her first letter before you."

Ruthanne took and opened it anxiously. "Dear Ruthanne or Rebecca," she read. "I was terrified to read what had happened to Ruthanne. Ruthanne, I was heartbroken you suffered on my behalf. I prayed for you every day. Maybe one day, the Lord will bless me in such a way that I can repay you.

"I have learned how to speak the Cherokee language, and I like it more than English. I've become close to John's family, especially his older sister, Grace, and his cousins, Lisa and Tsula. John's younger sister reminds me a lot of you, Ruthanne, but she is crazy.

"The Cherokee elder has continued to help me. I feel mostly healed from the past. I'm falling in love with John. He has given his life to Jesus. It has been a blessing watching him change.

"Rebecca, I miss your love and wisdom. Life isn't the same not seeing you every morning. Tell the children and Allen I miss them. Marilyn, your cheerful spirit is unlike any person I have met, and I hope you stay that way. Elizabeth, when the right time comes, I hope you'll cook me a meal.

"I love all four of you. My only request is for prayers of protection. The two Indian agents out here are evil men. I fear they'll do whatever they can to control the tribe. I guess being free still comes at a price, but at least here, Annabelle Mays has hope. I know God will bring us back together again one day. Annabelle."

Smiling, Ruthanne looked up at John. She handed the letter to Rebecca. "A lot has occurred here this past year that my hidden sister should know," she said.

While Rebecca reread the letter, Ruthanne got a piece of paper and wrote a letter with Rebecca following. As Rebecca and Ruthanne wrote, the women talked with John and Samuel. The time spent listening to the women was joyous for the men. Before the men left, the women prayed over them. John looked at the sealed letters as the men rode back to Tahlequah, and Samuel sat back in the carriage, looking into the sunset as he ate an apple.

"We did good today," John said.

"Yeah, I think we did," Samuel replied. "I still feel bad about that scar by Ruthanne's eye. Those white men beat her for helping Annabelle."

"We can't change the past, but we can only try to make the most of the sacrifices done to help change the future. Ruthanne knew the risks of hiding Annabelle, and at least she is free now."

"Imagine if she was an Indian. She'd be dead or a slave."

John sighed. "Yeah, no real choices for us."

Two days later, the cousins arrived back in Tahlequah as

the sun dipped below the horizon. Their family was excited to see them, and they listened to any new stories the young men had. Annabelle gave John a hug, welcoming his return.

"I have two letters for you. I haven't read them, but I can tell you that they're doing better," John said.

Annabelle kissed John on his cheek and grabbed the letters. "Thank you," she said.

—————◆—————

After supper, Annabelle walked to the small lamplit house with Grace and sat in a rocking chair. Annabelle opened the first letter anxiously, reading, "Dear Annabelle, I miss you, dear. So much has happened that I can't write right now. To be brief, I'm free from the prison and grateful to the Lord for my release. It was hard, but securing your freedom was worth it. Don't worry about me, and don't feel bad about what I went through. I'm a stronger woman from the experience, and I have a scar to prove it. I know Rebecca told you about the guard. He was dealt with. Elizabeth is back in Mississippi, depressed. Her family has denied her access to transportation, but she finds comfort in spending time with Robin. There are many other things occurring, but I will let Rebecca tell you. I'm also a married woman now. I married Peter last month. I couldn't be happier. I'm excited to hear about you and John. May more blessings come your way. I love and miss you, Ruthanne."

Annabelle was touched by the letter and tried not to cry as she opened the second letter anxiously. She read, "Annabelle, your letter brings comfort to my heart. The children are growing, and Allen is doing quite well. Ashley will begin schooling this coming fall. Marilyn has coped quite well with Mr. Pots's passing. She's been visiting her sisters regularly now and spending time with us. However, to my surprise and Ruthanne's, she is pregnant. She's been reluctant on telling us who the father is, though continuously defending him and says she loves him. I have my suspicions as to who the father is, but for now, I'll keep my silence. Now for this next part, and you must destroy it once you have read this. Allen and I have been helping those running the Underground Railroad. We've ushered thirty slaves to the north so far, and we will continue to do so secretly. We've also had the pleasure of meeting a Mr. Fredrick Douglass. He is an interesting man. He is a Negro, intelligent, well-mannered, and supports the railroad. Pastor Avail also aided in the movement of three slaves. Allen and I have joined the American Anti-Slavery Society. I have strong hope for us to see true changes in our lifetime. I love and miss you, Annabelle. Rebecca."

Beaming a wide smile at Grace, Annabelle stood up from the rocking chair and put Rebecca's letter in the fireplace. She went to the kitchen, wiping tears of joy from her face. During the night, she couldn't sleep because she was filled with so much joy, especially thinking about Ruthanne.

June of 1849 brought larger herds of bison and pronghorns, pleasing Annabelle. John would sit with her as they watched the herds, prayed together, and talked about their day. It was a cycle Annabelle enjoyed. Annabelle would read *The Three Musketeers* to John, a book he found interesting.

While Annabelle and John's romance was unhidden, Jacob and Lisa's engagements remained in the shadows. Lisa became more envious of Annabelle's relationship, though she admired it. Jacob and Lisa snuck off to the prairies around their homes to spend time with each other. It became frequent for Lisa to give Jacob a light kiss when he walked into the barn, but in her heart, she wanted the freedom to show her family how much she loved him. The excitement of making love to Jacob had become a bit of a thrill for her. Though the guilt of being intimate with him would run through her mind, Lisa justified her actions by the love she had for him.

<hr>

The next two months passed, and Annabelle still feared the Indian agents, not believing their intimidations were temporary. She frequently found herself watching John work when she went to the Tates' and Thompsons' farms. One day, she returned from the Thompsons' farm and stood by the barn, admiring John's hard work.

"Enjoying the day off?" Tsula asked in Cherokee.

Startled, Annabelle glanced at Tsula. "Well, yes. I just returned from the Thompson farm."

Tsula chuckled. "I see you watching John."

"I was not. I stopped to rest for a moment."

Tsula rolled her eyes. "If you say so. The two of you look so cute when you sit under the tree."

"Do you have anything else to do but watch me and John? And where is Samuel? I only see George and John in the fields."

"Samuel is spending some time with Maria. His begging finally tired her," Tsula explained. "Lisa and Michael left not too long ago to meet with Jacob. They should be returning soon. You must've missed them."

"They must've arrived at the Tates' farm before I walked past it. Is Grace still home?" Annabelle asked.

"No, she went to the store. She said she forgot something, so I'm watching David while she's gone. I need to go back and watch David, unless you want to."

"Oh no, not right now. He probably wants to spend more time with you. He likes your mind games."

Tsula smiled and strolled back into the house.

Annabelle continued to watch George and John work the fields. As John worked, he sighed and wiped the sweat from his brow. He then went to the barn with Queen, giving her grains for her hard work. When John escorted her into her stall, Annabelle approached him.

"You look tired," Annabelle said in Cherokee.

"My shoulders are sore today. That's why I decided to use Queen here. I don't think I have the patience to work with Big Boy today." John chuckled.

Annabelle giggled, looking at John as he wiped the sweat off his face. "Come here."

John moved toward Annabelle, and she kissed him. "Let me rub your shoulders so you feel more relaxed."

John and Annabelle strolled to the small house as they held hands, and he went to Annabelle's room. As he sat on her bed, she kneeled down behind him and massaged his shoulders.

"Wow, your hands are so soft," he said. "You need to do this more often."

Annabelle giggled. "I think you've been working too hard. Your shoulders are so hard. I think you need to relax more."

John looked over his shoulder at her. "But I'm relaxed when I'm with you."

Annabelle blushed and bit her lip, trying not to smile.

"Why are you hiding your smile? I know how to make you smile in another way."

Annabelle cackled and lightly smacked John on his shoulder.

"Stop it." John moaned in pain.

Annabelle quickly rubbed the area she'd just smacked. "See, that's what you get! Loosen your shirt so I can rub the rest for you."

John took off his shirt and tossed it on the floor.

Annabelle stared at his back muscles, then forced herself to stop. "I said to loosen your shirt, not take it off!

"What's the difference? I need care after you hit me."

Annabelle felt her heart race but decided she was fine. "You need to behave yourself, Mr. Lightning. Otherwise, you can go back outside in the heat."

"That would be so mean of you, Miss Annabelle. Sending a tired, sore man back into the fields with no love. You're a mean woman."

Annabelle struggled not to grin, then kissed John on his cheek. "There is your love, John Lightning. That should give you the strength to continue."

"Was that it?"

Annabelle laughed while John smiled at her. John turned around and kissed her. Annabelle kissed him back and chuckled. John wrapped his strong arm around Annabelle, and she slid onto his lap. The couple caressed each other's faces, Annabelle's heart pounding as a million thoughts rushed through her mind. She felt John's heart pounding as he placed his hand on her shoulder and smoothly slid it under her dress.

Annabelle panicked and stood from John's lap. "I think we need to leave."

"Did I do something wrong? Did I scare you?" he asked.

"No...no. I think we need to slow down and think a little."

John stood and grasped her hand. "We can take it slow," he said. "I'm in no rush." He kissed her again.

She fell into her emotions and desire. The two embraced each other, becoming lost in their emotions. John's warm touch soothed Annabelle. They tumbled into the bed, and she kissed his neck, causing him to gasp. She craved the intimacy, and the two fell victim to their desires and made love. Afterward, they dressed and lay in Annabelle's bed, and Annabelle felt guilty for giving in to her feelings.

Annabelle stared at the ceiling before looking at John. "We shouldn't have done that," she said, her tone full of regret.

John caressed her face. "What are you saying? What's wrong?"

"I love you, John, but we're Christians," she explained. "We need to do things the right way. We can't let this happen again."

John's eyebrows lowered. "I love you too, but it's hard ignoring how I feel about you. How can we continue like this? Controlling ourselves in such a hard way?"

"We pray and ask for the strength to continue to do things God's way. Not what our feelings want. We made a big mistake doing this."

"You weren't saying that a while ago," John commented.

Annabelle grunted and rolled over, getting out of the bed.

"Annabelle? Annabelle, I'm sorry. I shouldn't have said that."

She frowned. "We have to be stronger than this. *I* need to be stronger than this. I love you, but I have to follow what is right.

I was wrong to let this continue. I think we can't be around each other alone like this."

"What are you saying?"

"I'm saying that I love you, and if you want me to rub your back again, it is going to be under that old tree where everyone can see us. You tempt me, and I love you too much to not try to do better. We can do this. I can't give in to you again unless you marry me. I'm not pushing you away. I only want to take a step back."

John sighed. "I understand."

"Good, now hurry up and leave. I don't want Grace to learn about this. Your sister welcomed me into her home, and I ruined it by giving in to you."

"Well, I'm going to go do something I have never done before after being with a woman."

"What is that?

"I'm going to go pray." John kissed Annabelle on the cheek.

"There's one thing I want to say," Annabelle replied. "Don't ask me to marry you to be with me like this again. You better honor me."

John winked at Annabelle. "I can do that."

Annabelle beamed as John walked away, heading back outside. She struggled the rest of the day with not being able to tell the others what had happened. Keeping the secret troubled her because she wanted Grace's advice, but she wanted to keep the peace more.

CHAPTER 32
Confrontation

A MONTH PASSED WHILE ANNABELLE AND John avoided being alone with each other. She was pleased with how John handled the change, but the temptation was constant. In her spirit, she still felt the need to ask for prayer. She later went to Joyce and broke down in tears when she told her what had happened.

Joyce embraced Annabelle. "Child, there is still so much you have to learn, and I know you will grow," the older woman said in Cherokee. "Did you already pray for forgiveness?"

Annabelle nodded. "Yes, I did, but I still feel bad."

"Then you have already done your part and must continue beyond your mistake. The evil one is using this against you," Joyce advised. "You're free through Jesus because you were sincere in asking for forgiveness."

"I was foolish," Annabelle admitted. "I haven't felt held like that since Benjamin was alive. Instead of breaking away from my temptation, I ran to it."

"To be honest, I'm surprised and disappointed that you have made a mistake like this, but you have done far better than many other Christians I know," Joyce commented. "This one mistake does not define who you are. I certainly failed in this area of my life. In our culture, it was not unusual for a sixteen-year-old girl to fall in love and be with a boy. However, now the culture has changed for the better."

Annabelle sulked. "I want to do better, but I don't know how to trust myself anymore."

"Remember that we are made aware of sin to protect us from ourselves, not to control us. We've always had free will and will continue to have it. Love is a powerful thing, and it is through love that you'll succeed."

"Thank you. That means so much to me."

Joyce smiled. "Stay strong with your readings and continue to grow closer to Jesus. There will continue to be hard times in life, but with a strong faith, you'll make it through any form of pain. The world was never promised to be fair."

"The world not being fair, I think, is one of the greatest truths," Anabelle said. "I'm grateful Jesus loves us enough to give us a chance to do better."

Joyce folded her hands. "The Father's wisdom sees all and knows all. Trust in that and tell John I want to see him before the next Sunday. That boy better not have me go all the way over there."

Annabelle thanked Joyce and went home. She later told John that Joyce wanted to see him, and he reluctantly agreed to visit the elder.

As the days went by, John remained in the process of growing in his faith. When he wasn't speaking to George or the other men, he prayed while he worked in the fields. He later felt the need to speak with Pastor Bluebird about his mistake.

Pastor Bluebird welcomed John and was pleased he wanted to do better. He directed John to scriptures to help him and encouraged him to keep praying. Pastor Bluebird also prayed for John, giving him the confidence to move past his mistake.

A day later, John stared into the October sun before taking a deep breath and walking to Joyce's home.

"I'm pleased you came to visit me," Joyce said in Cherokee. "You haven't been here since Camille walked on."

"You comforted me, even when I was unwilling to take comfort from anyone," John replied. "Not even my sisters. I've been going to the church and afraid of what you would say."

"John, I have watched you grow from a child to a man, and now to a man following Jesus," Joyce said. "Your mother would be proud of you. I was pleased to see you when you came to the church the first day. It was an answer to very old prayers."

"I talked to Pastor Bluebird about what happened between me and Annabelle," John admitted. "I see now how our relationship has changed because of it. She loves me but guards herself with everything she does around me. I've asked him for guidance to help me deal with this better."

Joyce's eyes were piercing as she stared at John. "I can see your feelings are strong for her, but for the good of you both, you must continue to keep your feelings in control and live in the spirit. There will be easy days and hard days, but don't be discouraged by your mistakes. People have made worse choices. How our people live right now was caused by men who called themselves Christians."

John huffed. "I find myself always forgiving them for what they have done to us. The two Indian agents that destroyed our crops... I wanted to beat them until they bled. Those men will never pay for the pain they caused us."

Joyce shook her head as she scrunched her face. "Don't believe such a lie, John. Those men may not suffer in this life for what they did to your family, but they will be judged by the Father. The Father's judgment will be far greater than what we could do ourselves, so keep forgiving them as much as you need to. It is better for you to forgive and be free than to be a slave to unforgiveness."

"I will keep that in my prayers. I was also surprised with Lizzie. I believed we were going to have to keep her at home for a while," he said.

"Your sister has grown a lot over the years, but she still has to work on that temper. She is trying, and she may always be at war with her pride. She is a gifted young woman but struggles with humility. Her love for you and the others helps her push it away. Her growing love for Jesus helps her acknowledge her problem."

John leaned forward. "I've noticed a change in her. She has been much happier these past two years."

"Love your family, John, and lead like you're meant to. They need you, especially your sisters."

John nodded. "I will work harder to do that, but to be honest, I don't see how Grace, Lizzie, or the others need me that much."

Joyce chuckled. "You have been around strong women your entire life, but even strong people need to be reminded that they're loved. I've seen over the years that sometimes the ones seeming the most prideful have the biggest hearts. Their pride is used to shield their hearts."

"Thank you."

John stood up and gave Joyce a hug.

"Keep doing what's right, baby," the elder said as John walked to the door. She stood and slowly followed him. "And, John, you stay out of that girl's room. If I find out you found yourself back in that bed, I'm going to give you a beating."

John's eyes widened, and his mouth dropped. "I will. There will be no fooling around."

John walked away as Joyce watched.

"Father," Joyce whispered, "I pray a prayer of protection over John's heart and mind. Help him stay from his temptations and be patient in your timing. I see a young man fighting to be more."

CHAPTER 33
A Step of Faith

THE HARVEST SEASON ARRIVED IN November of 1849, and the Lightning-Strongman family remained on guard. George and John took rounds of waking up in the middle of the night to check the fields. Over the months, the family remained concerned for their crops, and unknown to them, they were constantly being watched by Brock and Hunter.

Annabelle continually felt pressure from the men. Her freedom signified their fear. She continued her work in the supply store, enjoying her role. It helped to protect her from white men coming into town and from the Cherokee that disliked her.

Her limited time with John also allowed her to take more time to strengthen her faith. Some nights, Annabelle struggled while she stared at the ceiling, hoping for more guidance. In her heart, she wanted John to ask her to marry him, but she was worried John might ask her out of lust. Annabelle realized her worry was stressing her out, and she remembered the scripture telling her not to worry.

———◆———

As the days went by, the harvest festival fast approached, and Grace saw John going to their practice grounds with his rifle.

She grabbed her bow and arrows and followed her brother. She heard the rifle shots as she drew nearer.

Grace stood behind her brother as he focused. "It looks like you're having a good time," she said, speaking in Cherokee.

"Hey, Grace," John replied. "Yeah, I was taking a moment since David is sleep. Are you here to show your skills?"

"I'm here to practice a little, but I'm also here to spend time with my brother." Grace walked next to John and took aim at a small wooden target hanging from the old tree. She released the arrow, hitting the target right in the middle.

"You would make a lot of men jealous with that shot," John said. "I think that's why father didn't like you coming out here so much when we were children."

The corner of Grace's mouth pinched. "I came out here to escape momma's death and pray. Being forced to help papa with the supply store gave me no time to mourn. I used to hate him for making me work there."

"We would've lost the store if it wasn't for you."

"I know." Grace took another shot with her bow, hitting the target perfectly. "I have been watching you. I've seen the changes in you. You smile at the white men that come into our town, you're happier, and you're seeking the Creator for yourself. My heart fills with joy looking at you."

John sighed. "You never gave up on me. I'm grateful for that—the love you showed me, even though I refused to listen. I was walking blind, but now I feel like I can see. I don't know it all, but now I have a stronger faith in my own path." He smiled at Grace before taking aim and firing at an old glass bottle.

"We're shown things at the right time. I do want to know something that I have been thinking and praying about for some time."

John's face went blank. "What?"

"Did you come to the church because Annabelle was there?"

John's eyebrows shot up when he heard his sister's question, and he laid his rifle down. "Annabelle challenged me in a way I didn't expect. She never tried to force me to believe in any of it. She only asked me to really look to the Creator, and I did, believing I wouldn't find anything. I had two dreams, both trying to show me who I was, and it hurt. I realized there was truth in what she said. I started reading those old words for myself, and in another dream, I felt the Creator speak to me. It was love that I felt, a welcoming love that was trying to wake me up. That's when I decided to go to the church."

Grace's eyes shimmered with tears as she looked at John. She hugged her brother and held him. "Momma's prayers have been answered. I will always love you, little brother. We will always run together like the wolves."

Grace and John spent the rest of their time together taking practice shots and laughing. As they spent time with each other, John realized his sister was right about him. It was a humbling moment for John to realize the changes in his heart.

The harvest festival passed, and December of 1849 arrived. During the first week, John and Samuel went out to gather firewood, and John saw Annabelle and Lisa return from the supply store. After helping Samuel gather firewood, John went into the family house.

"Annabelle, I need to speak with you," John said.

"What do you want?" Annabelle asked.

"I would like you to come with me for a moment. Come with me to the small log cabin."

Annabelle shook her head. "I'm not going there alone with you. I love you too much to allow us to make another mistake."

"Trust me. I will walk in first, and you come in after me with the door open. Please trust me."

Annabelle stared into John's eyes and sighed. "Okay, you lead the way."

As Annabelle walked behind John in the cold, she struggled with her thoughts. John entered the cabin as Annabelle stayed in the door's frame. Annabelle noticed Grace was in the house, and she felt comforted knowing the other woman was there.

"Hello, Annabelle. Why do you look so nervous?" Grace asked.

"I'm not nervous," Annabelle replied. "I didn't know why John insisted on me coming here."

Grace smiled. "Tell her, John!"

"Don't rush me, Grace, or she'll think you're making me do this," he admonished.

"I'm sorry. I will say nothing else," Grace said.

Annabelle raised an eyebrow and looked at John.

"Annabelle," he began, "I have been praying about this for some time and talking to Pastor Bluebird. I'm a blessed man. I could complain about many things, but when I look at what I have now, I'm blessed. When I see you, you warm my heart more than the sun ever has, and I'm asking if you would be my wife. I love you, Annabelle."

Annabelle gasped and breathed heavily. "What did you ask me?"

"Annabelle, will you be my wife? Will you make me a more blessed man?"

Annabelle wiped tears from her eyes. "Yes, I will marry you."

John strolled up to Annabelle and gave her a hug as Grace shrieked with excitement.

"I've been waiting for you, John," Annabelle said. "I'm blessed to have you."

The three marched to the home, and over supper, they announced the engagement to the entire family. The family sounded with excitement, giving John and Annabelle hugs. To Annabelle's surprise, even George approved their union. Lizzie, however, showed no expression and remained in her seat.

"Today is a special day, and from this day, your union will be recognized in this family," George said in Cherokee. "Have you decided if the two of you are going to try to have your marriage recognized by the court?"

"I will try," John replied. "I have no reason to hide Annabelle. She is a free woman. I've already asked Pastor Bluebird to come and support me if Annabelle had agreed to marry me."

George's eyes widened a little. "She already knows the marriage laws?"

"I told Annabelle a long time ago about the marriage laws," Grace said. "I think they'll be fine with or without the court's recognition."

George somewhat frowned and said, "We'll continue our supper and talk about this some more. May Jesus bless the both of you, now let us eat."

The family finished their supper and continued to enjoy the evening. During this time, Lizzie had said nothing since John's intent to marry Annabelle had been announced. When the family got ready for bed, Grace told Annabelle she would follow her shortly to the small house. Annabelle went to the small house while Grace went to the women's bedroom.

Grace entered the bedroom the moment the young women were changing.

"There's no such thing as privacy in this home," Tsula sarcastically said in Cherokee.

Lisa chuckled.

"You have some nerve as many times as you've walked in on me naked," Grace responded.

Tsula stuck her tongue out at Grace.

"Lizzie, what is going through your mind?" Grace asked. "You were quiet."

Tsula and Lisa looked at Lizzie while she stretched her back and put on her nightgown. "I'm waiting. I don't know what to think about John marrying Annabelle."

"Why do you stand against them?" Lisa asked, her anger evident in her tone.

Lizzie rolled her eyes. "I don't stand against them, but I'm not putting my hope into their marriage. The council will most likely deny their union legally. It will be no surprise."

"You could have shown some form of happiness for them," Grace bickered.

Lizzie blurted, "What for? To get Annabelle's hopes up? He loves her. That should be enough for her."

"I'm sure you'll smile with joy if the council recognizes them," Tsula sarcastically said.

Lizzie rolled her eyes at Tsula and said, "I'm in no hurry to see what comes of this."

"I won't ask you to show excitement in their union, but please don't show dislike in it either," Grace said.

Lizzie put her hand on her hip. "What my brother decides isn't as important as other things. I find it strange we were able to grow the crops this season without them being destroyed. Don't any of you think more will come? Those Indian agents always coming to the store to complain and control what we do. Annabelle's involvement with my brother is low in my mind."

"I agree," Grace replied, "but we cannot live in constant worry. We have to keep protecting each other the best we can, not by worrying."

Lizzie scoffed. "Those men will never leave us alone. Whatever, I'm ready to pray and go to sleep."

"Me too. Now, no worries for us tonight. We can pray for peace tonight," Lisa said. "We should be excited Annabelle is becoming a part of our family. I'm excited."

Sitting on her bed, Tsula smirked at Lizzie and giggled as she said, "You should be the most pleased, Lizzie. Jacob didn't go after Annabelle."

Lizzie narrowed her eyes at Tsula and gripped her blanket. Lisa looked at Lizzie, her eyes wide.

"Well, I think it is time we pray and go to sleep," Lizzie repeated.

"Tsula, that's enough," Grace snarled. "You always talking too much. Say your prayers and go to sleep."

Tsula frowned as she sat in her bed.

"We will see each other again. I love all of you." Grace gave them hugs, left the women's room, and returned to her house.

CHAPTER 34
Standing Against the Wind

TWO DAYS PASSED WHILE GRACE and George helped John develop a defense to plea for a marriage license with Annabelle. Sitting at Grace's dinner table, they continued planning.

"I'm sorry, John. We've run out of ideas to persuade the council to give you and Annabelle a marriage license," Grace said. "This will be difficult."

"It's okay," John replied. "If our family and church recognize our union, that's good enough for me."

Grace slammed her hand on the table. "That isn't okay!"

"Calm yourself, Grace," George said. "We cannot control the constitution. I agree that our people have made the mistake of trying to please white men in too many ways. We made foolish laws while never thinking about the future the way we should have. Your mother and your auntie were right. We betrayed ourselves. We create laws to copy the white men, and they forced us from our homes."

"I think having Pastor Bluebird go with you, John, is the most powerful choice we have," Grace said. "It will make the council think. You and Annabelle would not be the first Indian and Negro to have their marriage recognized."

"Okay, I will speak with Pastor Bluebird and see what he says," John said.

Grace sighed. "I'll go with you."

George and John left the small house and walked to the church as Grace sat in her chair with elbows on the table and hands on her temples. She then walked outside and saw Annabelle playing with David. Grace frowned, seeing the genuine love between the two, and went back into the house to pray.

In deep prayer, Grace felt the Holy Spirit speak to her and believed she'd been given a plan.

During this time, Pastor Bluebird spoke with George and John. He seemed pleased with John's spiritual progress and agreed to accompany him to the courthouse and attempt to gain a marriage license. Later, the Lightning-Strongman family ate supper together, deciding not to worry about the next day. The family laughed and told old stories, and even Lizzie's spirit seemed higher.

The next day, Annabelle, John, and Grace marched to the courthouse in the cold winter breeze.

"I'll meet the both of you and Pastor Bluebird at the courthouse. I have to do something first," Grace said in Cherokee.

"Please hurry," John replied. "We will need you there."

Grace nodded and went down another path while Annabelle and John walked to the courthouse. The young couple waited inside for Pastor Bluebird, and he entered the courthouse with a grin.

"Pastor Bluebird, we are glad you came," John said.

Pastor Bluebird replied in Cherokee, "I'm a man of my word. God is with us, no matter what happens this day."

Annabelle felt comforted by Pastor Bluebird's positivity.

"Annabelle, are you alright? You keep rubbing your hands together."

"I'm fine, Pastor Bluebird. I'm nervous," Annabelle replied. "The last time we were here, Grace lost her temper. It was almost as bad as Lizzie's. She can be very strong in her ways."

"That I agree, but don't worry, Annabelle," Pastor Bluebird said, his tone comforting. "Trust that the Father has a plan."

John handed paperwork to the secretary, Jane, and she looked at John with big eyes. Jane walked to the council's room, and several minutes passed.

"John, the council would like to see you," Jane eventually said.

"Thank you, Jane," John replied.

John entered the council's room, Annabelle closely following him and holding his hand. Pastor Bluebird entered the room last.

"Welcome, John Lightning. It is beyond surprising to see you here today," Mr. Gross said.

"Mr. Gross, it is good to see you," John replied.

"Annabelle, I have here a marriage license document, which you have filled out, John. This must be some form of a joke. Normally, it takes only one of us to sign this type of document, but as you can see,

Mr. Smith, Mr. Whitetail, and Mr. Ridge are as confused as I am. Were you not courting Nancy Hicks?" Mr. Gross asked.

"I was, but we went our separate ways," John said. "It has been over a year."

"I'm going to be honest from the beginning here," Mr. Ridge said, adjusting his cravat. "I'm not going to approve a marriage license between you and this Negro woman. Her status of being free changes nothing. We can't ignore the laws put in place to protect our people."

"I have come here begging for my love and for this woman to be recognized by our government. She is a Christian woman, God-fearing, warm-hearted, and I'm a blessed man to have met her. I know what the law says, but I believe the law cheats the people. The laws were made to protect Cherokee women, but at the same time, we cursed our brothers and sisters with Negro blood."

Mr. Whitetail abruptly hit his fist on his desk. "How dare you say such a thing!" he yelled. "We're not equal to any breed of Negro. Those carrying Cherokee blood bring embarrassment to our nation and weaken our power. Negro people are at the bottom of our society, and they will never rise higher. I refuse to agree to this arrangement. A half-breed Cherokee with Negro blood is a Negro not capable of representing our people. To recognize this union would be another thing that poisons our people."

"I must disagree with you, Mr. Whitetail," John argued. "I have learned from my sister that our biggest mistake was to believe the white men would see us as equals. We made laws following their ways and not the ways of our people. I believe now is a dangerous time for the tribe because we have forgotten who we are, and we are more white than Indian."

"We have done what is best for the people! We made our laws so a white man must remove his American citizenship to become recognized in our nation if he wants to marry a Cherokee woman, we developed schools, and yes, we adopted the white man's way of slavery. I would vote again for slavery if we had to."

John's nose crinkled, his eyes narrowed, and his brow furrowed. "Then you're a fool. Slavery hasn't made us equal to white people. It made us as evil as they are. Maybe they're right to call us savages now."

Mr. Ridge abruptly sat up from his chair.

"Sit down, Mr. Ridge!" Mr. Gross yelled.

"I have listened to your arguments. It breaks my heart because our tribe is fallen," Pastor Bluebird said. "How can any of you continue to call yourselves Christian men when we support this evil. I have watched Annabelle for some time now, and she'd be an excellent wife to John. We ruined ourselves by creating these laws lined with hate."

"Those laws are not lined with hate," Mr. Smith replied in a sharp tone. "They're lined with our plan to survive. We have far too many Negroes with Cherokee blood as it is. Say we take away our ways of slavery, then what will the Negroes do?"

Pastor Bluebird shrugged. "If our people did such a noble

thing, there would be praise like no other. Keeping the freed Negroes here would be the right thing. Accepting those into the tribe that marry Cherokee would make us stronger."

Mr. Ridge gave a sarcastic chuckle and said, "We do that, and I promise you those southern white men would come in full force to take whoever they want. We have already had numerous cases of free Negro, mixed or not, being kidnapped. Some of the tribes have even reported kidnapped children, and we're trying our hardest to work with them and this President Taylor."

"You should have spoken of this sooner to the people," Pastor Bluebird stated. "I will speak with Chief Ross myself later about these kidnappings."

"I have to agree with Mr. Ridge, Mr. Smith, and Mr. White-tail," Mr. Gross said. "We have a responsibility to our people, though I think a Negro can be more than a slave. I won't bypass the law because you love this woman, John. Annabelle, I have watched you work in that supply store, and even my daughter has spoken highly of you, but this we cannot grant you."

Annabelle frowned, remaining silent. Grace entered the room, and Joyce walked in behind her.

"I apologize for walking in late," Grace said.

"We were about to end this brief meeting," Mr. Gross said.

Grace looked at her brother and could see the disappointment in his eyes. "I have here the signatures of several Cherokee citizens recognizing Annabelle as a Cherokee woman and not a Negro."

"What did you say!" Mr. Ridge growled.

Cocking her head, a leer appeared on Grace's face. "Mr. Ridge, I'm sure your hearing is well." She approached Mr. Gross and handed him several pages filled with signatures recognizing Annabelle as a Cherokee woman. "Annabelle isn't Cherokee by blood, but she has adopted our culture and speaks our original language. I have signatures from all of my family, the Tate family, the Armstrong family, the Thompson family, the Gross family, and several others."

Mr. Gross looked at the papers in disbelief, seeing his daughter had signed the papers.

"Annabelle's character is by far welcomed here in the Cherokee nation, and she is loved here," Grace continued. "With all of this proof, surely you can recognize Annabelle as adopted into the tribe by my family and others. We do this with white men who want Cherokee women all the time."

"Even your unpredictable sister signed her name on that paper, and what is this? Mr. Gross, did you sign that thing?" Mr. Smith bickered.

Mr. Gross replied, "No, but Lillian did sign her name."

"Impressive, Grace Lightning, but this changes nothing," Mr. Ridge said.

"I have heard enough of this!" Joyce bellowed.

Joyce's outbreak left the entire room silent when she approached the three council members with her cane.

"Three young fools given power is what I'm seeing right now," the elder admonished. "In all my years, I have seen too much prejudice displayed by my own people."

"Elder Joyce," Mr. Ridge replied, "this a courthouse, and this—"

"Quiet, boy," Joyce interrupted. "I cleaned you, your momma, and your grandma, so don't test me. This racial ideology is the real poison here. I look at Annabelle, and I see a young woman that has shown more heart than too many Cherokee. She is, as far as I'm concerned, a Cherokee woman of Negro blood, and she should be allowed to marry the man she loves."

Mr. Smith's eyes widened. "You dare make the claim that she is more Cherokee when she has no blood related to us? This is foolish!"

"Willard Smith, you blue-eyed arrogant hypocrite!" Joyce snarled. "Your father has no blood, no clan, but he was given citizenship to our tribe. How dare you use that against Annabelle."

Mr. Smith pointed at Joyce, "Don't judge my family!"

"Calm yourself, Mr. Smith," Mr. Gross said. "Elder Joyce, if we bypass the law, others will come and demand the same."

"Mr. Gross, who do you think you're fooling? Annabelle and John won't be the first Indian and Negro pairing given a license," Joyce said. "Don't shame our ancestors with this foolishness holding to a law that gives us false hope. It divides us against the Negroes, who were never our enemies. Ask those two Indian agents how different they see us from the Negroes."

"You speak strongly of Annabelle, Elder Joyce, and you have served our people far longer than any of us in the government today," Mr. Ridge said. "However, I don't see any good coming from this. Any children she gives John will be Negro. She can't even go to the South safely on her own."

"You men forget so easily that it was not too long ago our people had to be on guard against the plantations of white men," Joyce advised. "I grew up with that fear, that painful truth, and now, it seems the nightmare is continuing in the shadows. These kidnappings are an obvious disrespect not only to us but to the other tribes. All of you seem to have the same claim that because she has no Cherokee blood, she could never be a Cherokee woman, but she can speak better than the three of you."

Mr. Gross tapped his foot while Annabelle looked at him. "Annabelle, do you understand my words?" Mr. Gross asked in Cherokee. "Do you love John?"

Annabelle replied, also speaking Cherokee, "I understand you well. I love John Lightning with all my heart. Elder Joyce taught me and loved me. She is the grandmother I never had, and I'm grateful to the Father for putting her in my life."

Mr. Gross looked at the other three council members.

Mr. Smith folded his arms. "What did she say?" he asked, his tone jealous.

Mr. Gross replied, "She said she loves John, and she is grateful to Elder Joyce."

"I did understand that much," said Mr. Ridge. "She clearly stated she loves him, but love shouldn't be allowed to bypass the constitution."

"The Father has brought Annabelle here for a reason. I believe it is a lesson many of us Cherokee need to learn," Joyce said. "We're to love those different than us, no matter what color their skin is. We've copied the white man's ideology, and it is killing us. Annabelle has bonded with the Lightning family, and I have spent many days with her. Give John the freedom to marry this woman."

Mr. Gross rubbed his wavy brown hair. "Everyone, please give us a moment."

Mr. Smith frowned when he heard the request.

"Come, everyone, let us give them a moment," Joyce said. "Good afternoon, Pastor Bluebird."

Pastor Bluebird replied in Cherokee, "Good afternoon, Elder Joyce. You truly are gifted."

Joyce walked to the door while everyone followed her, and the men sat with each other and debated as the doors were closed.

Several minutes later, Mr. Gross opened the door. "Please come in, everyone."

Everyone entered as Mr. Gross took his seat.

"I believe this will always be a divisive viewpoint of many Cherokee today," Mr. Gross stated. "It is clear that there is strong support for the union between Annabelle and John. Most of us agree it would be a lie to say our constitution is perfect and represents the beliefs of all the Cherokee. The Cherokee court is a democracy, and we also have laws to abide by. However, after a serious and deep discussion, we've decided to recognize the union of John and Annabelle legally in our court."

John hugged Annabelle while the others watched.

"We're not finished here," Mr. Gross said.

John and Annabelle calmed down the second they looked at Mr. Gross.

"Your marriage will be recognized by the nation, but any children she gives you will be seen as Negro and not recognized as citizens. This was the only agreement we could decide on."

Joyce pursed her lips but remained silent. Annabelle looked at John with a slight frown.

"I'm grateful for your offer," John replied. "I will accept it if Annabelle is willing to accept it."

Annabelle gasped, and John looked back at Annabelle, smiling.

"Mr. Gross, will my children be able to learn?" Annabelle asked.

"If you and John have any children, they will be able to learn, but as previously stated, they won't be recognized as Cherokee citizens," Mr. Gross said.

Annabelle looked back at John and smiled. "Let's get married!"

John smiled at Annabelle and then looked at the council members. "We accept the offer. The love of my family and friends is all that matters to me. I know they'll see my children as members of the tribe and of the Wolf Clan," he said.

"You're a brave man, John Lightning. I hope you remain as loyal to our people as your mother did," Mr. Gross said. "Come and take this signed marriage license before we change our minds, John."

John immediately approached Mr. Gross and was handed the marriage license. "I will always remain loyal to our people, Mr. Gross," he said. "Thank you for this privilege."

The four council members stood as John went back to Annabelle and hugged her.

"We will see each other again," Grace said in Cherokee.

Mr. Gross kindly replied, "We will see each other again."

------◆------

Everyone left the courtroom, and as they exited, Joyce noticed Mr. Smith staring angrily at them. She frowned and continued walking, whispering a prayer of protection over Annabelle and John.

The young couple returned home with the great news. The family celebrated the union at supper, and even Lizzie smiled at hearing the news.

------◆------

The next day, on December 9, 1849, Annabelle and John had a small ceremony. A few of the family's friends stayed, and Pastor Bluebird blessed Annabelle and John's marriage. Annabelle became Annabelle Lightning.

As the new week continued, to Annabelle's surprise, Grace decided to switch rooms with her. Grace felt it was only proper that Annabelle get the larger room.

On that particular night, as Annabelle and John lay curled together, Annabelle watched him sleep. She kissed his forehead and couldn't stop smiling as she snuggled next to her new husband.

As Annabelle caressed John's hair, she prayed to the Father, "I was cheated by an evil man, and I wanted to die. I wanted nothing to do with you after that, but you decided to bless me with another family. Thank you, God." She placed John's hand on her belly and rested her hand on top of his hand, smiling as the sound of howling wolves echoed throughout the night.

———◆———

Albert Brooks looked up at his family, his wrinkled hands still holding onto the letters encased in plastic film. "Annabelle struggled to heal from her past, but Aunt Grace and the others helped her," he said. "Cherokee land had its benefits, but it also had its trials. Nancy Hicks was a shadow of the South for Annabelle, but those racist Indian agents... They were the proof that she couldn't return to Judy Mays. Their evil was pervasive not only for the Cherokee but the other tribes. She never thought she would find love again. John's kindness, encouragement, work ethic, and genuine protectiveness won Annabelle's heart. His own interests in Jesus added to her attraction to him."

"So that's how Annabelle fell in love with John," Liz said with her mouth curving into a big smile. "She was stronger than I gave her credit for."

"Even strong people need love and support. Their world was brutal, no different than our own."

Liz looked at an old photo, smiling. "John was a handsome man. She had good taste."

Albert gave a light chuckle. "Besides that, our family continued to be tested, and Elder Joyce was a force to be reckoned with. She was a pillar for our family."

Liz shrugged. "Well, I mean they lived through the Civil War, Daddy."

Albert shook his head. "Our family went to war way before the civil war." He handed Liz a bundle of letters in plastic.

Liz's eyes widened as she flipped between the letters. "This one says it was written by Lisa, and this one by Lizzie. The rest of these letters are written by the others. Daddy, what happened to them?"

Albert exhaled, looking down at his hands and then back at his daughter. "More than I told you because I believed you were too young to know the truth. I was wrong. I always credited your strong personality to your momma, but I may have exaggerated. It's fair to put the blame on me."

Coney rolled her eyes while she grinned.

"Annabelle's journey isn't complete without telling their side too. They helped shape her into who she was. This is only the beginning." Looking at his family, Albert folded his hands. "It's time for all of you to understand how our family is a reflection of the two wolves. Go on, read it."

Liz looked at the letters, then back at her father. "The two wolves?"

Albert grinned. "I think it's only right my most challenging child learns more about where we came from and how the two wolves impacted our family."

TO BE CONTINUED

I hope this adventure was an enjoyable experience for you and that you will visit your favorite retailer to leave a review because your feedback is priceless!

ABOUT THE AUTHOR

Hi, everyone! I'm Marcus, from the south side suburbs of Chicago. I'm a descendent of two Native American tribes. I have two degrees in zoology, love the Olympic games, and I am into Native American history, especially regarding issues that have divided families. Some of the stories I enjoy creating focus on parts of history rarely talked about and revolve around genealogy and interracial relationships, particularly between African American and Native American communities that cause us to reflect on the choices we make especially in our teenage and young adult years. This focus is to help young adults see the bigger picture earlier in their lives. God's greatest commandment is to love each other. I hope to fascinate your minds, to educate, to make you think about your family, and make you reflect on your own choices in life.